INYO'S RING

N.H. Schwabacher

For Nate, Jules and Milo

Table of Contents

Author's Note

This story is a work of imagination, inspired by a Tudor-era legend that connects the origin of the Irish Claddagh ring to 16th-century Spanish Armada shipwrecks along the Irish coast and the sailors who washed ashore.

I have taken considerable narrative license in depicting life in the 16th century, the Spanish Armada and her crews, as well as the portrayals of Queen Elizabeth I and Irish chieftain Grace O'Malley, including their famous meeting at Greenwich Palace. The historical notes at the end of this book shed more light on the facts that underpin my story and characters.

Hold the course your soul has sworn
Even if the planets flee
Be ye bold when oceans burn
Love, your true north ever be

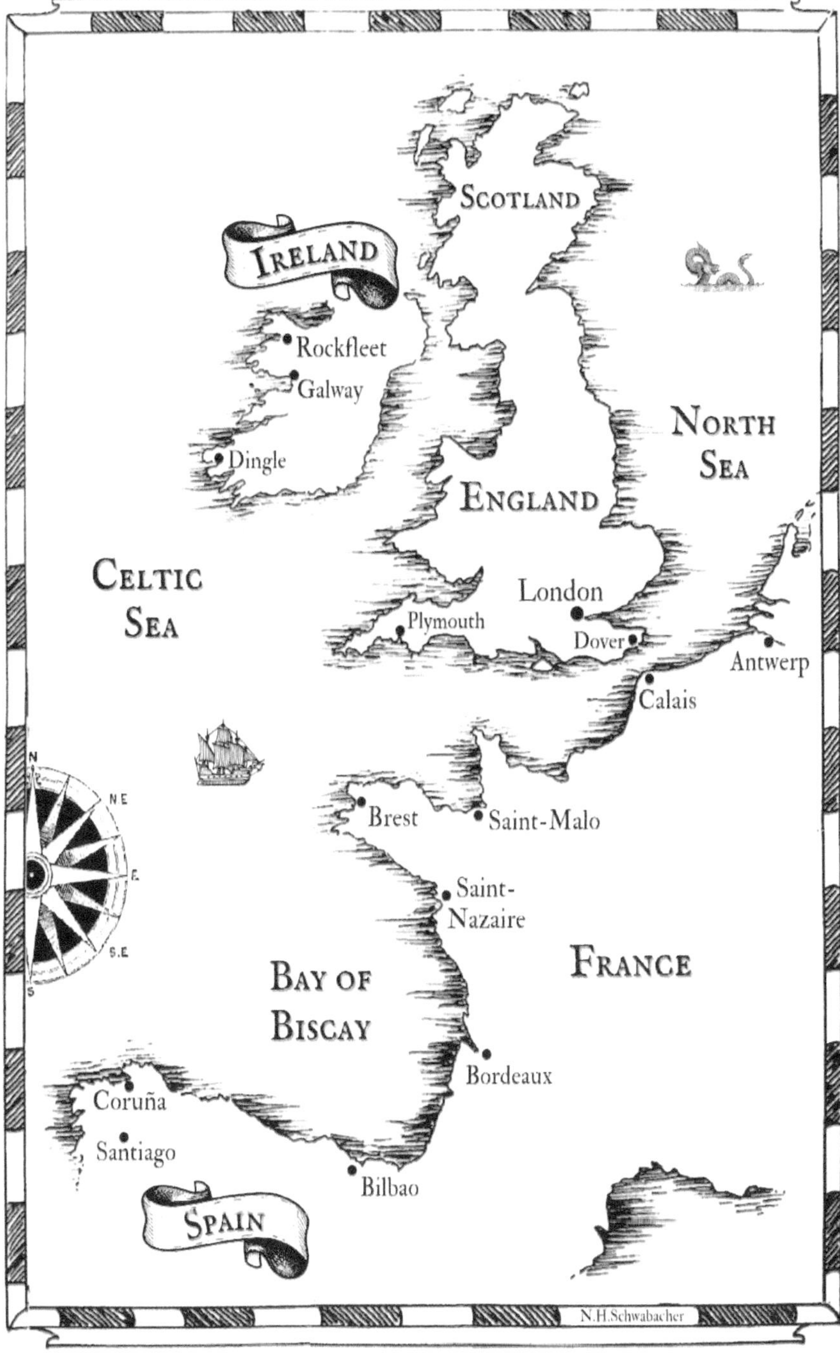

Scotland
Ireland
Rockfleet
Galway
Dingle
North
Sea
England
Celtic
Sea
London
Plymouth
Dover
Antwerp
Calais
Brest
Saint-Malo
Saint-
Nazaire
France
Bay of
Biscay
Bordeaux
Coruña
Santiago
Bilbao
Spain
N
NE
E
SE
S
N.H.Schwabacher

Characters

Inyo

Marina (mother)
Juan (uncle)
Francisca (aunt)

In Coruña:
Bernardo (carpenter)
Clara (baker)
Adrián (printer)
Isabella (mayor's wife)

Finley

Grace O'Malley (grandmother)
Maeve & Brian Morris (parents)
Teagan, Ronin (siblings)
Owen, Tibbot (uncles)

Neighbors:
Fergal MacDermot
Padraig and Ellis

In Galway:
Aldred Bensbury (Engl. governor)
Sarah (his wife)

Ships & Crews

The *Gaviota* – 1583
Juan (captain)
Antonio (first mate)
Crew: Diego, Ansa, Pedro, Inyo

The *Gavilán* – 1585
Owen
Finley and Ellis
Tibbot, Father Whelan
Padraig and Geoffrey

The *Santa Catalina* – 1588
Don Luis de Sandoval (captain)
Don Álvaro de Benavente (guest)
Martínez (sailing master)
Fra Rodrigo (ship's priest)
Miguel Sabado (carpenter)
Inyo (carpenter's mate)

The *Gavilán* – 1588
Grace O'Malley
Finley and Inyo
Sarah, Ellis
Liam and Geoffrey

Wilder Waves

GALWAY BAY, IRELAND 1588

The gale screamed in the rigging, a demon of unknown mythology. It battered and shoved the hull of the *Santa Catalina*, lifted her to the crest of a wave. The ship crashed through the rollers, flinging the sailors about like chaff. With raw fingers grasping at the soggy rigging, they struggled to rise again on the shuddering decks, knowing this night was their last. A sickening *crack* ripped through the darkness. Inyo wiped the rain from his face and ducked as tentacles of shredded ropes whipped past him.

Why, Inyo wondered, had the sea, his first love, become a savage beast today? He thought of the massive fleet when it left his hometown, Coruña, under summer skies two months ago—the magnificent Armada. Invincible, so it was said. Hundreds of billowing sails and thousands of soldiers, sailors, and officers, all standing tall and straight as arrows. Muscles flexed under the gleam of their armor, determination and pride welling up in their faces. It would be an easy campaign, they were promised. And certain victory. Among the many ships, all laden with cannons, ready to invade England in only a matter of days, was the *Santa Catalina*.

But today, the ship was a skeleton of her former self, a shadow, alone at the edge of the world, amid the howl of the winds and the fury of the waves. Land had been spotted to the east that morning—Ireland, the crew had guessed, shocked at how far off course they were. They panicked when fog and rain veiled the faint coast again. They *had* to get to safety, away from the dangers of the coast, but how could they in this gale?

With his stomach growling and nightmares fogging up his mind, Inyo had tied into the safety line and labored alongside his gaunt shipmates, the pitiful remnants of Spain's navy. Despite the roaring dissonance all around him, despite the violent and unpredictable motion of the ship, and despite the icy rain clinging to his disheveled black hair, his eyes closed several times. He found himself slipping into the edge of unconsciousness. Hazy images of his home pulsed in his head. The port of Coruña on a sunny day, the timbers of his uncle's trading vessel, tinged with the scent of dry pitch, his mother's smile, her kitchen, a loaf of fresh-baked bread.

Inyo's grasp on time had nearly dissolved, but then someone's wail nearby snapped his attention back into the present. His eyes shot open. The waves reared higher and higher in the stiffening gusts. Inyo cast a dejected glance at the furled sails and frail masts, useless limbs, trembling in fear. While the dismal afternoon surrendered to twilight, the ship continued her feverish and helpless tarantella in the gloom.

The ocean thundered in anger and swept over the crumbling decks. The hollow face of Martínez, the sailing captain, sinking to his knees next to Inyo, spoke of hopelessness and defeat as the *Catalina* jolted and creaked. Martínez was balled up now, weeping. There was nothing he or anyone else could do. The ship and her crew were entirely at the mercy of the elements. Inyo shielded his eyes from the needle-sharp spray, and an involuntary sob escaped through his clenched teeth.

The shrieking around him intensified, slashed into his thoughts, and tore apart all sense of time. His grip on the ropes tightened as the

Catalina shot up to the summit of another monstrous roller, tilting as she fell into the trough. One after another, the sailors were plucked off their feet again, fell hard, and cowered where they landed. Certain death was awaiting them all. It was only a matter of time. Inyo squeezed his eyes shut, trying in vain to escape the dread that raked over him.

Fears flashed in his mind, scenes of lightning-lit cliffs, of hulls cracking open, of bodies flung into the waves. While timbers screeched under his feet, another spar fractured in the darkness above his head. He whipped forward, landing on a rail, the impact jarring his breath and sending a sharp pain through his ribs. The sudden weight of wet canvas slapped his back.

A final, booming wave barreled into the ship's hull, forcing her to surrender. The churning ocean devoured the decks, engulfed Inyo, squeezed a voiceless scream from his burning throat, swallowed him whole, pulled him under, heedless of his twisting and jerking. Panic had seized him so forcefully that he couldn't edge a single thought past its rage, its frigid mass. He was only half-aware of his fingers fumbling with the rope tied around his waist. The safety rope had become a death trap! In the rush to unravel the knot, a golden ring slipped off his numb hand unnoticed. Its glimmer spiraled and vanished into the murky deep.

Kicking and kicking and kicking his legs against the surge, Inyo broke through the waves with a choking gasp, his arms flailing. He was desperate to free himself from the chaotic tangle of rigging all around him. With a cruel promise of reaching the heavens, the ocean lifted him high like a cork, then snatched away all his hopes and pulled him under.

—

That night, waves of unimaginable height crashed into the rocky headlands of Ireland's west coast, the gale keeping farmers and fishermen cowering under thatched roofs.

In the village of Barna, a mile from where the *Catalina* sank into her watery grave, forlorn flames quivered in the fireplace of a cottage. Rain drummed on the door in a relentless staccato. Window shutters rattled in belligerent protest under the clawing of the wind. "Haven't had a storm like this in a long time," Brian Morris mumbled as he lifted his lantern to inspect the roof. Stubborn and strong, like the land's inhabitants, the hand-hewn timbers of his farmhouse arched above his head, holding out against the elements. "I reckon we'll be alright," he added with an encouraging nod as he made his way past his daughter.

Hunching under a blanket, the girl frowned at the dimming fire, lips pressed together into a hard line. The glow of embers reflected in her pale face, in the furl and frizzle of her rebellious hair. It was impossible to sleep that night. The unusual summer storms and high winds of the previous weeks showed no signs of easing and instead culminated in a sinister crescendo. Never before had Finley heard nature in such fury. Drawing a ragged breath, she reached for a poker and thrust it into the hissing flames, unleashing a scattering of sparks. She added a log to the grate and wrapped the wool blanket tightly around her shoulders again while the storm outside raged on.

What was this gnawing unease? It rose in her chest, like the weak smoke from wet kindling, writhing snakes that insistently wafted into the edges of her thoughts. It felt unmistakably like five years ago, during that awful week when she found out about Falkyn and his drowning.

Falkyn

GALWAY BAY, IRELAND 1583

A dreary spring drizzle had veiled Galway Bay and its surrounding forests for hours. Finley leaned over the side of the boat, reaching and straining. The heavy weight of the full net kept her awkwardly suspended above the sea, and her fingers slowly turned numb.

It was dark early that morning when she'd followed her father and brother past the dripping ferns down to the shore. They readied the nets, clambered into their fishing boat, and launched into the dull waters of the bay under perfect conditions of droopy clouds and rising tide.

"Come on, Fin, pull!" her brother shouted as he reached for the net repeatedly, hauling in the catch with a surprising strength for an eleven-year-old. Finley fought to take a full breath, laboring on the bow in her sopping clothes, unable to keep up with Teagan's pace. She was a few years older than he, but her arms were shorter and skinnier than his. A growl of frustration rumbled deep inside her.

With a chuckle and an encouraging wink, her father moved swiftly to her side. He hauled in the net with ease. Brian's warm eyes peered out from under his cap, a few brown strands of disorderly hair flapping about his handsome face, rain beading up in his beard.

Finley's brother, Teagan, was a young version of him—hardy, cheerful, and full of life.

As they rowed back with their huge catch of fish, Brian and Teagan pierced the fog with their lighthearted banter. Strangely, their cheerfulness didn't have the usual buoyant effect on Finley. Instead, her eyes filled with unexpected moisture, making her vision swim. While the melancholy sea drifted past their hull, she turned her back, sorting through the nets. The oars splashed a rhythm behind her, and her father hummed one of his favorite shanties. Finley's eyebrows remained furrowed, and she stared into the smudgy nothingness of the mist.

The haunting image of an alabaster body drifted through her mind. A man, suspended above the shadowy sea floor, his eyes closed, pale hair undulating in the currents, the bottle in his grip dragging his arm like a useless anchor. Falkyn. She wanted to shove the vision away, but it was as insistent as the tears dripping down her cheek. She wiped her wet sleeve angrily across her face while the voices of her father and Teagan repeated the bouncing chorus of their endless song.

A few days ago, when Teagan was already in bed, her parents pulled her aside with solemn faces and said there was something important she needed to know. They paused to glance at each other and arranged their postures before revealing to Finley that Brian was Teagan's father but not hers. Gently but with apparent unease, her mother had said, "Your *real* father, he, well—his name was Falkyn, but he disappeared right before you were born."

For the length of several heartbeats, Finley sat silently, unable to speak, unaware that her fingers clutched and twisted the fabric of her shift. Why had she never suspected something like this? Why had they never told her before? Why now? "What happened—why did he disappear?" she asked.

"He died at sea," her mother answered, then squeezed Finley's arm. "I'm so sorry, my sweet."

Died at sea. The words crashed into Finley like a rogue wave. Finley was stunned. She stared at her parents with brimming eyes, then bolted into the night, hiding behind the barn for an hour.

Brian had found her, cradled her like an injured lamb, carried her back inside, and kept her wrapped in an embrace while they sat by the fire. With stiff shoulders and stinging eyes, she looked up as her mother slid her chair close and began to tell her about Falkyn. Shreds and shards of information that Finley tried to assemble into an image of him that resembled a mosaic, incomplete and riddled with jagged holes. "Falkyn was a good man," her mother remembered. "One of Rockfleet's best warriors and finest sailors. Helped us fight off Barbary corsairs more than once.

"I know he drank too much. And many people found him stubborn and rash. They said he had quite a temper. But I didn't see that side. Oh, how he made me laugh! Falk and I had made plans to marry. But one night, when he was sailing back from Spain with my brothers, they were all drunk, and Falk must have fallen overboard without anyone noticing. I didn't find out you were on the way until after his death."

Her mother described Falk's sparkling eyes, bright as the sky, and long hair as flaxen as a field of young barley. Finley was acutely aware that she looked nothing like him. She had stopped counting the times she heard how much she resembled her mother and grandmother, and how she had obviously inherited the O'Malley mane: unruly hair, the color of brick. On top of it all, she had shockingly pale skin and way too many freckles, ugly splatters of mud covering her entire face, arms, and shoulders.

For as long as she could remember, Finley had dreamed of having blonde, soft, flowing hair. Like a fairy queen. But instead, her wild and uncooperative curls were a daily reminder that she was destined to be a broom.

After the long day of fishing, Teagan and Finley huddled near the crackling hearth, yawning. Finley's shoulders rose and fell in a long, silent breath. As she watched the steam waft in ribbons from the damp work clothes, her thoughts wrenched themselves out to sea again, to the ghost of Falkyn.

She had seen Galway drunks stumbling about or sleeping by the shore. The townsfolk cast disapproving glances at them and called them good-for-nothing sots. One man was found drowned along the coast once, and all sorts of cold-hearted gossip circulated for days. He got what he deserved, people said. It's no wonder. His father was just like that, yes, just like him, that same fickle sobriety, same life of debauchery. It's hereditary. That's right, this sort of temperament is passed on from parent to child, they said, which worried Finley—no, terrified her. *Are some people destined to become good-for-nothings, like Falkyn?*

With a bitter taste in her throat that slowly turned to fury, she kneaded her sore forearms, mulling over her dismal efforts out on the boat today. Her eyes wandered to her parents and Teagan as they talked. Her father worked the big loom, and her mother sat at the spinning wheel, her green linen dress flowing over a barely protruding belly, a new sibling on the way. Finley found herself observing them all as though from a far-off distance, or in a wayward dream, a mere spectator of the scene, questioning her role and if she should be here at all. Wondering who she was. A puny, mud-splattered bastard, was that who she was? Was that all she was? And was *this* truly where she belonged? A frown had taken over her forehead when she turned her gaze back to the flames in the hearth.

Over the following weeks, the questions churned in her mind. They slithered deep into her heart, sprouting into strange thoughts, into self-doubts whose gnarly tendrils infiltrated her every waking moment. Yes, she sang along with the shanties, pulled in the nets harder than ever, and refused to let a single growl escape her clenched jaw, carried heavy armloads of firewood and stacked them briskly, then hurried to help with the sheep and the cooking, felt her heart bursting with love when she told Teagan stories by the fire and showed him how to carve wood, but despite all her striving, the insecurities remained. Insistent, icy knots in the pit of her stomach.

—

One day, early in the summer, Finley stood at the stern rail of the *Gavilán*, one of the clan's trading vessels, waving at Teagan and her parents in the distance just as the horizon behind them lit up with the early morning sun. Finley was thrilled to be on her way to Rockfleet, her grandma's fortress, but now that she saw Barna's harbor retreat into the distance, the three figures on the dock growing smaller and smaller, a tightness filled her throat. She tried for a look of stoic determination as she took in the ever-growing distance between her home and the *Gavilán*.

Her thoughts were interrupted by the sounds of her uncle Owen's boots reverberating on the deck behind her, confident and brisk. "Alright then, Fin, time to get to work!" he said. Owen O'Malley towered above her, a grin widening his rectangular face, a Herculean torso concealed under a dark leather jerkin, shaggy hair whipping in the breeze.

A steady wind filled the mizzen sail when Owen and Finley trimmed it, setting a course out of Galway Bay. Above them, the sky wheeled with laughing gulls. Finley had sailed to Rockfleet many times before, but this year, she would arrive a few months before her parents to help aboard the various ships belonging to her uncles and her grandmother. While she looped a hemp rope around a belaying pin, her mind sailed over the indigo waves. It drifted south towards Spain, wondering exactly how much ocean stretched between here and there. Was it true what she'd heard about the goddess of the

Celtic Sea, Cleo, who watches over the ships sailing between Ireland and Spain? That she could send dolphins to rescue sailors in need? But that she could also lure unsuspecting men into the deep, turn them into aquatic creatures that could never return to land again?

A sudden movement caught Finley's eye: a glistening shape below the surface of the water. It had flitted away in less than a heartbeat. Finley gasped and leaned out over the rail, a strong wind lashing her face. What had she seen? For a long time, she stared at the patterns of spray that stretched to the horizon. Owen shouted, "There!" and pointed far ahead over the *Gavilán's* bow, where two dolphins repeatedly breached, matching their speed. Finley hurried to her uncle, who slapped the gunnel and laughed out loud, saying, "Look, the dolphins are guiding us, a sure sign of good fortune." Finley had seen plenty of frolicking dolphins before, and Owen's cheerfulness certainly was infectious, but today the sight of them unleashed within her a silent sob, made her choke, and turned her knuckles white as she gripped the gunnel.

Something in her stance or in her face must have given her away, she guessed, because Owen draped his massive arm around her shoulders and became quiet. She couldn't get herself to look into his face and instead melted into his soothing embrace. He cleared his throat. "Maeve mentioned she finally told you about Falkyn a few weeks ago, and . . ." Finley hung her head, sniffling, leaning closer into her uncle, unable to speak. Owen continued, "If he's on your mind, Fin, just know you are not alone. He—he was my *best friend!* And I think about him every day."

Crow

CORUÑA, SPAIN, 1583

Glittering reflections of the morning sun danced in Coruña's harbor between the gently swaying ships. An azure and cloudless sky stretched above Inyo's head as he hurried past the bustling docks. The seagulls' squawks mingled with the flapping of sails, the fishmongers' shouts, and the rattling of carts in the narrow streets. Under the commands of wealthy merchants dressed in velvet and lace ruffs, workers shifted heavy loads off carts and onto ships.

Tambourine and flute music wafted over a group of sailors clustering around a dancer in a colorful shawl. Inyo reached the entrance to the Delfín, one of the harbor taverns, combing a hand through his unruly hair, while he waited for his mother, Marina, and her brother. Where were they? Inyo's eyes darted back and forth over the crowd. His attention was briefly drawn to the dancer's long, black curls as they whipped through the air in a dizzying swirl.

Finally, Inyo saw Marina approaching. Her red dress and white linen sleeves fluttered like banners to the rhythm of her steps. She gripped her brother Juan's arm and waved at Inyo, beaming from ear to ear.

"Inyo!" Juan roared. "How are you? Marina tells me you wanted to see me. I don't have much time, though."

They found a table inside, and their mugs arrived quickly. Inyo squared his shoulders, forced his most winning smile, and took a deep breath. Beneath his bushy brows, Juan narrowed his eyes at him suspiciously and thundered, "Out with it, then!"

Inyo swallowed, blinking furiously. "Uncle Juan, could I—" he stuttered, "I was wondering if I could join you aboard the *Gaviota*. I want to go to sea with you." Inyo kneaded his fingers while his uncle took a sip from his mug, then lowered it with a wary frown.

Inyo cringed at the memories of that autumn day last year when he'd worked aboard the *Gaviota*, a trading vessel that had been Juan's ship for many years. Her aging timbers, masts, sails, and rigging desperately needed repairs, so Marina had sent Inyo down to the docks to help.

He was shown how to replace planks and rails, caulk the weakening seams, and carve a few new pulleys. The work took a long time, but Inyo had found it all interesting. Juan had pulled him aside at the end of the day and slapped his back, making him wince. When the words of praise tumbled out of his uncle's mouth in a trumpet-like fanfare, several of Juan's men stopped their work to crane their heads, looking Inyo up and down with judging eyes. He stared at the plank below his boots, pressing his lips together, sensing an instant heat flooding his face, his hearing strangely muffled, his throat constricting. In that moment, he had wanted nothing more than to morph into a small insect and disappear. Why was he unable to look up? Why did he have to blink again and again? Was it something to do with the many eyes that bored into him?

Finding it too much to bear, Inyo had bolted up and scrambled off the ship, gasping for air, tripping on the gangplank, landing on the hard dock, pain jolting through his hands and knees, and ran home without a goodbye. Since then, he had barely spoken to his uncle, much less looked into his eyes.

"Juan, you know how desperate Inyo is," Marina said. "He's been aching for months to sail with you. And you need the help, that's for sure!"

"*Sí,* Marina." Juan scratched his gray beard. "I know, I know. It's just that, well—"

Inyo was painfully aware that Juan already had his regular crew. All of them seasoned and accomplished men. Gruff, strong giants who never needed any rest, so Inyo thought.

"Inyo, you're a fine carpenter," Juan said. "But my men, well, you've seen 'em; they're gritty. They work hard, they don't complain. And they can take whatever the weather throws at 'em. They wouldn't—ever just run away from nothing. I don't know . . ."

Biting his lower lip, Inyo stared at the crinkles painting doubt into Juan's face, the reluctance to take on anyone so inexperienced, especially someone this nervous, this unreliable. Inyo, realizing he'd forgotten to breathe, forced a ragged inhale that triggered a torrent of coughing and brought Juan's giant paw pounding on his back.

While Inyo cleared his throat and took a swig from his mug, Marina turned to Juan. "Remember when you started with old Lopéz? Weren't *you* also just a little pollywog back then?"

Juan shrugged and nodded. "All right. It's true; I *do* need capable hands. How about a trial period, Inyo, hm? To see how you hold up. In a few days, I'm out on my first Biscay loop of the season."

"Which ports?" Inyo asked.

"Brest, Saint-Nazaire, Bordeaux, San Sebastián, Bilbao, Santander. We'll be back here in ten or twelve days with fair weather. And I wanna be clear; you're coming along just this one time. Can't promise nothing beyond that. Would be best if you start tomorrow when we load."

"I'll be there at first light!" Inyo assured him, while Marina smiled and gave Juan a grateful nod.

They emptied their mugs, and Juan wiped his face. "I best get going. The *Gaviota* is waiting for me."

Marina reminded Juan about supper the following day, to come with a big appetite, and to bring Antonio, Juan's first mate, whom Inyo and Marina had gotten to know well over the years.

"Much obliged!" Juan smiled. "We'll see you tomorrow."

Juan was usually at sea for weeks or months, sailing and trading in the Mediterranean, as well as in the Low Countries, Denmark, and Ireland. But whenever he was in town, Marina loved to dote on him. Despite feeling intimidated by Juan and Antonio, Inyo had always been fascinated by their yarns, their stories of rough seas and faraway ports. Crossing the Bay of Biscay, according to Antonio, was not an easy undertaking.

Inyo walked next to Marina toward the southern end of town, a nagging unease bubbling under his joy and relief. How would he do this time? How long would it take to learn the ropes and adapt to life at sea? They passed a church, several shops, and warehouses, then turned right at the corner, their steps now accompanied by the rhythmic hammering from the blacksmith. They soon arrived at their home: a narrow warehouse with living quarters upstairs.

Marina waved at Clara, a pale figure across the street, standing at the entrance to her bakery. Inyo looked at the girl briefly, at the annoyed way she tried to brush off the flour that covered her from head to toe. "Bernardo and I have to finish that table for the mayor," he said as he continued on the dusty road towards the carpenter's shop.

"Good." Marina nodded. "I'll see you tonight then."

Just before reaching Bernardo's shop, Inyo paused to glance at the gentle hills in the distance, his thoughts drifting forty miles south, to Santiago de Compostela.

When Sister Francisca brought Inyo from the orphanage in Santiago, he was eight years old. He had been quite apprehensive about leaving Santiago, but Coruña was Francisca's hometown, and she told him about her sister, Marina, how desperately Marina had wanted a son and how much Inyo would be able to help her, and wouldn't it be wonderful to have a mother *and* Francisca as an aunt at the same time?

He remembered his arrival day well, how he had stepped into Marina's warehouse, wide-eyed, too scared to say a single word. She showed him how to inventory the crates and bundles and assist the merchants when they delivered or retrieved their wares. Soon, though, the shaded garden behind the building had become Inyo's favorite place. He loved planting and harvesting herbs and vegetables.

A year after he moved in with Marina, he started working for Bernardo, the carpenter, whose shop was a few doors up the road. And now, Inyo already had a reputation for being one of the finest carpenters in town.

—

At sunrise the following day, Inyo strode towards the harbor and the *Gaviota*. This would be the *best* summer of his entire life. He'd learn everything about sailing. He could already picture it clearly in his mind: confidently climbing the rigging, furling sails faster than anyone else. *I can't wait to see the world! In a year or two, I'll command a ship of my own and—*

He had arrived at the *Gaviota*. The men aboard paused their work and stared at Inyo. A cluster of them crossed their bulging arms in front of their chests. One of them spat into the water and huffed, "Oh great, that skinny crow again!" Then he whispered something that brought on laughter from the other hands.

Inyo's heart sank, but he willed himself to jump aboard. He

quickly got to work, taking orders from the crew. Inyo wondered where Juan and Antonio were while he began rolling heavy barrels up a plank and down onto the main deck. Sweat stung in his eyes. Finally, Juan burst out of his cabin, Antonio right behind him.

"Ah, there he is!" Juan cheerfully grabbed Inyo's shoulder. "Men, my nephew Inyo will join us for a few weeks. He wants to learn everything there's to know about the wind and the waves. How to sail! How to trade! And…" Juan paused and lowered his voice, "…how to make the *most* of time in port!"

Roaring laughter exploded around them. While many of the shipmates still grumbled and shook their heads, Antonio smiled and slapped Inyo's back. "Welcome aboard, Inyo!" Antonio, tall and broad-shouldered, towered above the rest of the crew. "I'm glad you're joining us. You'll shadow Juan and me for the first day at sea before we assign you duties."

Meanwhile, Juan growled with mock irritation, "All hands, back to work!" The order reignited the busy loading and stowing of the cargo. Inyo swallowed. Marina had cautioned him to work hard and not to expect special treatment, even though Juan was his uncle. He realized he was neither a full-fledged crew member nor a paying passenger, but he was determined to pull his weight.

Hour after hour, Inyo labored alongside his brawny shipmates, wrangling barrels, bottles, casks, crates, and bundles into the hold. *Careful. Out of my way! Bring it over here. Faster! No, not like that.* Inyo could feel his strength drain away at the end of the day, like an outgoing tide, and couldn't stand the crew's stern gazes and rough shouts anymore.

Finally, he was heading home. With a grumble in his stomach, Inyo strained to keep up with Juan and Antonio as they hurried through Coruña's streets. When they arrived, Marina's smiling voice rang from upstairs. Their boots rumbled on the wooden steps leading up to the kitchen. Marina embraced them all, one by one, amid the golden glow of the setting sun falling into the window like oozing honey. She waved them to the table and poured wine.

Inyo's shoulders relaxed. During the meal, they talked about the upcoming voyage, the merchants in town, the growth of the port, and Marina's latest cartography work. Over the years, she had gained experience as an illustrator and mapmaker and was hoping to one day open a shop of her own. Spread out on a worktable in the corner of the kitchen was the map she was currently working on, along with her illuminations, a piece of parchment with printed Latin text, and several books and scrolls.

Inyo took another sip of wine, leaned back on the bench, and folded his hands behind his head, yawning. Juan turned to him with an encouraging smile. "Excellent work today, Inyo!" he thundered. "Tomorrow, we'll finish the loading and repairs. And then we'll be underway." Juan and Antonio added details about their route, how profitable it all would be, and what they planned to buy and sell in which port, but Inyo's mind had already released itself from their words and drifted towards his bed.

—

A few days later, after a long goodbye hug from Marina, Inyo hurried through the sleepy roads in the small hours of the morning. Curiosity and excitement pulsed through his veins, but he couldn't shake off the weight of doubt and unease. Over the first few days of loading and repair work, the crew, for the most part, had made him feel like an outsider, a kid underfoot. Someone had constantly been watching him with a stern frown, often whispering behind his back. Inyo caught himself sneaking wistful glances at the men. Their camaraderie and their carefree banter scraped and burned against his hot, sweaty skin. He didn't want to give away the slightest sign of weakness, but this morning, with every step he took towards the docks, his confidence floundered and the color in his face faded.

Under a squawking and swooping cloud of seabirds, the *Gaviota's* crew set and trimmed the mizzen and topsails, their geometric shapes stretching and filling with the wind as they rounded out of the harbor. Soon, Juan and Antonio's commands to set the main courses arrowed past Inyo. He watched with wide eyes as the magnificent canvas sails of the foremast and mainmast unfurled and billowed in the breeze, setting them on a north-easterly course towards Brest. Inyo's ears filled with the wind and the mighty breathing of the ocean, along with more of the mysterious language of the sailors. "Wind on the beam," the lookout bellowed, prompting a "One point large" from Antonio and a loud "Aye, aye" from Pedro, who stood at the helm, topped off by Juan's "Keep her full and by!"

There was so much he'd have to learn, Inyo realized. He sighed, his eyes darting back to Coruña as it slowly retreated, to the old, massive Roman lighthouse, and to the craggy shoreline hugged by emerald waters, dappled with shadows from clouds.

The *Gaviota's* bow sliced through the waves, leaning under the press of the wind in her sails. Inyo braced his feet on the deck as it creaked and hummed under a tense synergy between rudder, keel, wind, and sail. He closed his eyes and inhaled the translucent whispers of the sea. His adventure had begun! Already, he was head over heels in love with the ship and in awe at what she was able to do. A few hours later, however, giant waves rolled towards them from the north, violently swaying and heaving the hull. Inyo gasped when the bow reared up, making the timbers underneath him groan in protest. Juan reminded him to grip the safety line that ran from bow to stern. "Wouldn't wanna become shark bait now, would we?"

Inyo had never seen the ocean this way. An outlandish and staggering seascape of endless, towering rollers spread out before him with no land in sight. The entire world had turned into liquefied uncertainty, and the convulsions of the ship beneath him reverberated in a strange knot in the pit of his stomach.

The *Gaviota* lurched through the crest of a swell and tilted into its trough. Spray blasted past the bow, cold and salty, and washed over the decks. "Three points to starboard!" Juan shouted.

Three points—what does that mean? Inyo wondered while suppressing a queasy ache and a flustered awareness of how useless he was. He stared at the sail crew, bewildered by their proficient and fast-paced movements between the maze of rigging.

Juan checked his compass and the trim of the sails, then nodded his approval to Antonio. Inyo suddenly lost his balance, one arm swooping through the air, the other one grasping the safety line as he swayed towards the lee rail. Diego sneered at him and elbowed another shipmate. Juan shook his head with a wry half-grin. "Remember *your* first sailing, Antonio, eh?"

"*¡Madre mía!* Yes, took me three full days to get my sea legs!" Antonio turned his face to Diego and boomed, "And if I remember it right, Diego, didn't *you* liberate your suppers into the sea for an *entire week?*"

As he gripped his midsection with one hand and the rail with the other, Inyo only numbly registered the crew's laughter and Diego's grumbling coming from the main deck.

—

Weak and covered in sweat, Inyo found himself flat on the folded spare sail, the rough texture of canvas chafing at his arms, the light of his lantern flickering against the dark and damp edges of the tightly packed hold. Soon, though, Antonio tumbled down the companionway under the confident drumming of his boots. He settled down next to Inyo.

"Don't worry, everyone gets seasick." Antonio patted Inyo's

shoulder. "Know what helps? If you can, get back up on deck where you can keep your eyes on the horizon."

Inyo slowly sat up and tried to rise on shaky legs. He groaned and plopped back down, grateful for Antonio's company.

By the time Inyo clambered above deck and staggered towards the gunnel, the air held a chill and the sun hung low in the western sky behind him. The sea had calmed, and the Gaviota soared onward with the wind abeam. He inhaled and exhaled in the rhythm of the creaking hull, his eyes glued to the horizon that stretched out before him, a steadfast ribbon of hope. Antonio, getting ready for his watch, turned to him. "Feeling better?"

"A little. But—" Inyo broke off, staring off into the distance, feeling useless and small, still bruised from the pang of the other hands laughing at him. He hung his head.

"Trust me, you'll feel stronger tomorrow," Antonio predicted. "The crew will teach you everything you need to know about the sails and the rigging."

"What—what about lookout duty?" Inyo stammered.

"Right, that's important for us traders. We want to make sure we see any trouble before it sees us. Pirates, African corsairs, and the like. We have at least one set of eyes up in the lookout at all times."

"When will I get to do that?"

Antonio looked up the main mast, cupped his hands around his mouth, and shouted, "Ansa, Inyo is going to keep you company for a few hours." They didn't see Ansa's head but became aware of a stream of inaudible muttering that trickled down from the crow's nest. Antonio smiled at Inyo and tilted his head towards the shrouds. "Up you go. When Ansa's watch is over, come and find me. If we have a clear night sky, I want to show you something."

Inyo began his climb, counting the rungs, *seven, eight, nine.* Antonio's instructions followed him, saying, "The horizontal ratlines are only for the feet. Notice how thin they are? Always keep a firm grip on the vertical ropes, the *shrouds*. They are much thicker and more reliable."

Halfway up to the lookout, the ship pitched abruptly, and Inyo's stomach bottomed out. He hung in place for a moment, calming his erratic breathing, blinking hard against an adamant gust of wind that filled his ears and whipped his raven hair into his eyes. The entire world swayed between sky and sea, compelling his fingers to tighten around the thick ropes that vibrated with the tension under which they held the mast in place. Earlier, when he had watched his shipmates, they had seemed to fly aloft with such ease, making it look like there was nothing to it.

Inyo hesitated, inhaling in timid sips, and continued. When he finally reached the lookout, jittery and out of breath, Ansa rolled his eyes, then turned his gaze back toward the horizon. Inyo gripped the mast with both arms and gasped. The nest's railing was entirely too low!

What would it be like up here in heavy seas? Inyo wondered, imagining a scene of sailors being flung out of the lookout. He shuddered. Unsure what to do or what to ask, he slowly lowered himself to his knees next to Ansa, one arm firmly wrapped around the mast. While the rigging creaked rhythmically below them, the evening sky farewelled the sun in a magnificent celebration of gold and pastel swirls.

Inyo's gaze wandered along the yards and ropes below him. The repairs he'd done on the *Gaviota* last year while she was docked seemed so easy on a sunny day in the mellow waters of a safe harbor. Today, out in the open ocean, he found himself vulnerable and overwhelmed, but the ship had revealed her defiant resilience against the elements. There was a mysterious pride about her.

When night came, the moon's reflection on the seascape of ink painted a white path of hundreds of tiny dancing glimmers. Breath after breath, Inyo willed himself to adapt to the height, giving himself over to the lulling effects of the creaking, the rocking, and the sea's hypnotic whispers.

Ansa remained silent the entire time. Tiny and wiry, with a dark complexion that reminded Inyo of the rare Saracen traders he'd seen in Coruña, Ansa was one of the more solitary figures aboard, and by far the most serious, which oddly contrasted his small stature. Juan only hired fully grown sailors, Inyo knew, but Ansa's huge eyes and skinny frame made him look almost childlike. Inyo risked a timid glance at him, dismayed that a scowl still hardened his face. He was surprised when Ansa cleared his throat. "So, you're Juan's nephew, hm?"

For the length of several heartbeats, Inyo found himself unable to answer, but then he croaked, "Yes, my mother is Juan's sister."

Ansa huffed dismissively, "Your *mother*—" Inyo was taken aback by the poison in Ansa's tone. Shaking his head, Ansa continued, "But you're actually from Santiago, *sí?*"

Inyo's eyebrows lifted. "How—how did you know?"

"I used to live at the convent. Like you."

"At the orphanage? *Convento de Santa Columba?*" Inyo asked, watching Ansa nod absentmindedly, a trace of a frown lingering in his face. "But—I don't remember you." Inyo had many vivid memories of the orphanage and his peers, but none of Ansa.

"Of course you don't remember me. You were still pretty young when I left."

"How long were you at *Santa Columba?*"

Ansa's scowl softened. "My whole life as far as I can remember, 'til I was seven." After a pause, he added, "One of the nuns let it slip once that an old gypsy had dropped me off."

Inyo had seen the mysterious nomads and their humble camps on the outskirts of Coruña and Santiago. He frowned. "Why did you leave Santiago when you were still so young?"

"I don't know. I liked the freedom and earning my own wage."

After an uncomfortable silence, Inyo asked, "Do you miss Santiago?"

Ansa shrugged. "Sometimes. I learned a lot. There were a few really kind sisters. One of them used to call me her little bee."

Inyo's face lit up. Ansa must have been thinking of Sister Francisca, who had nicknames for all the children. "Little bee" was one of her favorite terms of endearment. Inyo turned to Ansa with an exuberant smile, about to reveal how close he was to Francisca, and that she was Juan's sister, but Ansa's face was turned away now, and Inyo hesitated. He didn't know why, but could mentioning his close connection to Francisca and Marina agitate Ansa, embitter him even more? Inyo bit his lip. Best to leave some things unsaid, for now.

Conflicting emotions knotted themselves up inside Inyo. A sense of closeness to Ansa, the joy of finding a fellow bee, but also a strange unease, a vague awareness of some hidden pain. Ansa kept his lithe arms wrapped tightly around his knees, and for a long time, they sat side by side, slowly drifting on currents of memories and stifled emotions while the sea around them sparkled under the moonlight.

—

Later that night, Inyo and Antonio met on the quarterdeck. "I want to show you how to determine our current location, our latitude." Suspended from Antonio's finger hung a circular metal disc, the size of a large hand. "This," Antonio sounded like a padre gushing over a sacred relic, "is an astrolabe." He lifted the instrument until it reflected the glint of the nearby lantern.

Inyo was familiar with the use of a compass but he had never seen an astrolabe. The metal disc featured a rotating pointer and markings on its edges, similar to the complicated mechanical clock he'd seen in the mayor's office.

Antonio asked, "So, why do you think we're out here in the middle of the night for a latitude reading?"

"Juan mentioned the North Star helps him navigate at night," Inyo said as he instinctively glanced up at the constellations above him.

"Precisely. Here, look at the North Star and then lift the astrolabe up to your face, like this, so your eye follows the pointer to the star."

Inyo closed one eye, raised the instrument by its suspension ring, and adjusted the pointer to his line of vision.

"Hold everything in place when you lower it and read the number at the tip of the pointer."

"Forty-six."

"That sounds about right. It's always tricky to get an accurate reading out at sea, on a swaying deck, but indeed, we're currently at about forty-six degrees latitude. See how simple it is?"

Inyo stared at the numerous markings, twirling the pointer with one finger. It didn't seem "simple" to him. "Who invented the astrolabe?" he asked.

"I think the ancient Greeks and Romans already used something like it. I once saw a Saracen trader's astrolabe, a real beauty from Damascus."

"What happens on cloudy days?"

"Ah yes, days without sun or stars. Tomorrow, you'll see how we use the lead for depth soundings and why those are important when we have clouds."

Most of the shipmates were fast asleep when Inyo bumbled around below deck in search of a nook for the night, the trembling sphere of his lantern light pushing against the blackness, casting deep shadows along the hull. Inyo blew out his light and pulled a scratchy blanket up to his chin, mulling over the dismal start to his adventure, how the sails and rigging still mystified him, that he probably looked like a hopeless fool, and how he felt like one, too. He sighed. With queasiness lingering, he drifted off into restless sleep.

—

Ansa shook Inyo awake early. There was much work to be done before breakfast: scrubbing of decks, pumping the bilge, and turning bits of filthy rope into a material called oakum. Inyo's stomach growled by the time he sat down with Ansa, Pedro, and a few other messmates for breakfast, a rather bland experience. He hunched over a wooden bowl and pushed a hard piece of bread into the mysterious stew in his dish. Lifting a spoonful of the murky slop to his lips, Inyo struggled to keep his face expressionless.

While they were finishing their meal, Inyo cast an envious glance at several bantering shipmates playing dice and noticed again that Ansa preferred to keep to himself, with his hat pulled deep down to his eyes.

A few hours after the sun had reached its zenith, a cheerful *"¡Tierra a la vista!"* rang out from the lookout. At the bow, Antonio and Juan watched the details of the coast materialize before their eyes. They studied a few nautical charts in a conspiratorial whisper, then waved Inyo over to examine the maps. Antonio bemusedly handed him a compass and pointed toward land. *"We* know the coast well, but let's see what our young navigator thinks. What's our exact location and which way to Brest?"

Regular sailors rarely got personalized instruction in navigation, Inyo knew. He took a deep breath, aware of Diego's intense glare. Inyo's eyes flitted along the coastline on the wrinkled chart, following the thin lines marking latitude, the names of the islands, and the tiny numbers indicating depth. His home, Coruña, sat at forty-three degrees. Inyo lifted his face and bit his lip while he considered the latitude reading from last night, Antonio's reading two hours ago, and their steady north-easterly heading. *Most likely, we've reached forty-eight degrees.*

He squinted at the shore, at a cape with a lighthouse, west of it a small island. He turned the pale chart, placed the compass on it, and scratched his chin. *Hm, let's see, forty-eight degrees latitude—ah, it's this line here—so maybe that's the Pointe du Raz and the Isle de Sein?*

Inyo placed a timid finger on the map and turned to Juan. "I think we're here."

"*Muy bien*, Inyo." Juan beamed from ear to ear. "That is indeed our location, a league or so south of the *Isle de Sein*."

"What course will help us avoid the reefs?" Antonio pointed to a cluster of depth markings on the parchment. Inyo's glance wandered back and forth over the chart while his finger slowly traced a route.

"Looks like the reefs stretch west for at least two leagues. I think we should head due west until this island lies well aft our starboard quarter, then turn west-northwest until the reefs are passed. And from there, northeast right towards Brest."

Juan smiled and turned to Antonio. "We'll do as our young *comandante* says!" He then slapped Inyo's back and informed him, "Alas, can't let you celebrate tonight. Remember, Pedro and you are on watch."

Inyo nodded. He was to stay aboard, tending to the ship while the rest of the crew had the evening off. Would Pedro also give him a hard time, just like Diego?

A little while later, Inyo watched curiously as Pedro prepared to take a depth sounding with the lead line. The end of the line was tied to Pedro's belt, its length neatly coiled in his left hand while he leaned over the gunnel of the main deck. He wound up the lead weight, threw it out far ahead, and waited until the lead hit the bottom of the seafloor. When the line became taut and perpendicular to the surface of the water, Pedro quickly hauled it up again and shouted, "Nine fathoms!"

Antonio mumbled contentedly, "That's plenty deep."

Inyo rechecked the map, studying the depth markings. The numbers made sense to him now. Juan had mentioned that the *Gaviota's* draft was three and a half fathoms. As long as she sailed in at least five or six fathoms of depth, she'd be safe. "So, we're right about here then?" Inyo asked. Antonio nodded with a genial smile. Pedro gathered the dripping lead line, each fathom marked by colorful ribbons and small wooden sticks knotted into the rope. While stowing away the lead line, a few whispers passed between Pedro and Diego. Their cold eyes briefly darted toward Inyo. Inyo swallowed hard, unable to keep the shriveled remains of courage from plunging into his boots.

They sailed into the mouth of a wide river under cerulean skies, then past an impressive fort, watching the town of Brest and its port come into view. Narrow, half-timbered houses faced the water behind bobbing hulls and a forest of masts. There were bustling markets filled with carts and stalls, locals loudly offering their wares, and merchants hurrying back and forth on the docks while the *Gaviota* found a berth between two other vessels.

With Juan eager to commence their first sale of wares here, the crew unloaded barrels of wine, jugs of olive oil, and iron ingots to shipside as local traders clouded around them.

After the cargo was sold, Juan ordered all hands to tidy up the decks, coil ropes, and see to minor repairs, while he strode away with Diego and Antonio to purchase local goods. "Brest has become well known for its quality hemp canvas and ropes. I always make a profit bringing a load of these back," Juan had explained at Marina's dinner table last week.

Bolts of canvas and the heavy coils of brand-new rope were delivered on handcarts and piled up at the bottom of the gangplank.

"Get to it, men!" Juan shouted, and the crew started loading.

Inyo lifted a large coil of rope that obscured his view. Grunting and breathing hard, he staggered up the wobbly plank, which suddenly bucked, throwing him off balance. With a startled gasp, he fell sideways into the harbor, the rope splashing down next to him.

Inyo came up for air, quickly shaking the water out of his face. High above him, Juan frowned. Diego, Ansa, and Pedro were at the gunnel, shaking with laughter. While Inyo swam back to the dock, frustration stole his voice. Would anyone extend an arm to help him up? Footsteps reverberated on the plank, and his uncle's voice grumbled about everyone needing to be more careful and what a loss of time this all is.

Many hands had to work together to retrieve the rope. The water had doubled its weight, and now it had to be laid out on deck to dry. Avoiding all eye contact, Inyo staggered back aboard, leaving a trail of dripping seawater.

When the wares were all stored away and the decks were finally in order, the crew made for the tavern, from where lively music and singing beckoned. Inyo, however, was relieved to be on watch so he wouldn't have to be in the tavern with the men. He climbed up to the quarterdeck, leaned back against the mizzen mast, and exhaled deeply, glad to finally be alone. Down there on the gangplank was Pedro, lounging with his arms crossed behind his head. Inyo tried to ignore him, his obvious glee, his smirk.

Instead, he lifted his gaze to take in the view over the town while night slowly draped her blanket over the alleys. The warm glow from dozens of windows created a candle-lit, festive atmosphere over the harbor and town.

Taking in the peaceful scene, Inyo mulled over what had happened that day. *Was it an accident? Or did one of them kick the gangplank on purpose?* There was nothing he could do about it now, and so he shoved the thought aside. He wasn't going to be intimidated, no he was not! Clenching his fists in determination, he lifted his face to the first pinpricks of light above his head, two planets silently drifting towards a sliver of moon. Inyo found comfort in the sight of those mysterious gemstones pinned to the darkening sky, icons of steadfastness.

Ansa

The *Gaviota* was underway again at first light, rounding the Pointe du Raz reefs, then setting a south-easterly course along the coast with the endless mirror of glittering ocean drifting along below her hull. Inyo worked the rigging next to Ansa. Soon, the sails billowed and the breeze carried them along at an exhilarating pace.

Antonio motioned Inyo to the quarterdeck and began a lengthy explanation on holding a course relative to the wind. With animated arm and hand motions, he explained the angles of wind direction, the keel, and the sails. It was surprising to find out a ship didn't necessarily need wind directly from astern. Antonio said, "Wind coming from port or starboard quarter, or even from abeam, with the sails angled just right, can generate the fastest speeds."

The *Gaviota* sailed into an estuary, rounding a peninsula to reach the protected bay, where they anchored for the night.

The following day, they arrived in Saint-Nazaire, a busy city at the mouth of the Loire. That evening, after a successful day of trading and after the decks were put in order, Juan turned to Inyo with a smile. "Go and explore the town; this is your first time in a French port, after all. Ansa will go with you. Have fun. Well, not *too* much fun!" Juan winked at Inyo, handing him a few coins.

"Oh—thank you!" Inyo uttered in surprise as he stared at the silver in his palm. Judging from Ansa's ambivalent stance, he wondered if Juan might have ordered or bribed Ansa to accompany him. It was a relief when Ansa led the way, motioning for Inyo to follow. Ansa's expression was empty, but at least not unkind, as they made for a street vendor where they bought a meal.

With the filled pasties warming their hands, and the savory taste painting contentment on their faces, they strolled along the vibrant and teeming harbor streets, past warehouses for grain and salt, taverns, a bakery, a barber, and the busy shops of wheelwrights, carpenters, coopers, and blacksmiths.

"I'm sorry about what happened," Ansa said with unexpected honesty in his voice, causing Inyo to ponder. Maybe Ansa had nothing to do with the gangplank incident after all? He had laughed along with everyone else yesterday, but now, away from the rest of the crew, Ansa was a different person. Inyo shrugged but labored to make his voice sound unstirred when he replied that it wasn't a big deal, and the swim was so refreshing—no really, it was.

Ansa chuckled. They came upon a crowd gathered around an acrobat. The jovial man in a colorful jester costume balanced on a wobbly plank placed over a log. At the same time, he juggled three small leather balls, chanting French rhymes that made the audience burst out in laughter again and again.

Inyo found himself mesmerized by the juggler's performance and playful antics. But then something else caught his attention. A disheveled figure, half-hidden in the tightly packed crowd, reached for the leather pouch of a gray-bearded man in the circle of onlookers. A small knife cut the purse string, and the pouch disappeared in the blink of an eye.

Inyo frantically pointed and shouted, but most spectators were too engrossed in the performance, while some frowned at the disturbance. The thief dashed away and around a corner before anyone understood what was happening. Ignoring the puzzled faces staring at him, Inyo bolted away, chasing after the cutpurse. He hurtled around a street corner, swerving around lumbering carts, barrels, and vegetable crates. Ansa, running a few paces behind Inyo, pleaded breathlessly, "Come back, Inyo! It's no use—"

The thief rushed into an alley and through a narrow stone archway. Inyo, hard on his heels, came to an abrupt stop in a dark courtyard, alarmed to see the man had now turned to face him. Inyo hesitated, then lifted his trembling fists, panting, "You—you scum! Return that purse or—"

Startled by a flash of silver and a sudden sharp pain searing in his right forearm, Inyo recoiled, stumbled backward, and fell to the ground with a gasp.

Less than a heartbeat later, Ansa swept around the corner, colliding with the thief and getting knocked into the wall. The man escaped quickly. "Inyo!" Ansa wheezed, out of breath, his eyes wide in shock when he crawled closer to Inyo, casting about for what else to say.

While Ansa hovered over him, muttering, Inyo suppressed a groan and curled over his injured arm. Ansa pulled him to his feet. They staggered back out to the street. Inyo moaned, turning pale as he sank next to a wall with trembling limbs. He pressed his left hand over the gash. The bleeding wouldn't let up. Ansa finally urged, "Let me have a look."

Inyo shook his head. Surely, this would require sutures. He remembered seeing the nuns at the convent stitch up a patient once. An unpleasant memory.

"Let's get you back on board and see what we can do," Ansa suggested.

"No! No! I—maybe someone here in town can help," Inyo pleaded. He didn't want the crew to see him like this.

Ansa scratched the back of his neck and then said, "The barber!"

Inyo nodded. They had passed the shop earlier. When they arrived, the barber was finishing a transaction with a customer. Then he stared at the young, scruffy Spaniards with a lofty expression. Ansa asked, *"Monsieur, s'il vous plait?"* and mimed a sewing motion while pointing at Inyo's arm.

The barber nodded curtly and mumbled as he gathered a bottle, a spool of fine thread, and a slender, curved needle. He poured a clear liquid over the wound. It burned instantly, causing Inyo to wince in pain. The man then bent over Inyo's arm and deftly started the first suture. Inyo cursed and groaned while Ansa patted his back, watching the whole procedure intently. Inyo drowned in wave after wave of intense pain, hot tears brimming in his eyes.

After finishing the sutures and dressing the wound, the barber opened his hand and demanded, *"Trois livres, s'il vous plait."* Ansa and Inyo slowly emptied everything from their pouches. With a lifted eyebrow, the barber stared at them, huffed dramatically, and finally took the coins while shaking his head. He shooed them away with impatient grumbles.

Inyo pulled his sleeve down to hide the bandage. By the time they arrived back at the *Gaviota*, it was dusk. Two shipmates guarded the gangplank, playing cards by lantern light. Everyone else was at the tavern.

Inyo was surprised that Ansa not only helped him below deck but also kept him company.

"Can you move your fingers?" Ansa wanted to know.

Inyo tried to move his numb hand and curl his weak fingers, but a sharp pain shot from his wrist all the way into his shoulder. He shook his head and replied through clenched teeth, *"¡Mierda!* How am I to climb the rigging now—or carry loads?" Panic avalanched into his gut, and his breathing became shallow. What if there was permanent damage and he couldn't work for Bernardo, the carpenter, anymore? In the darkness of the lower deck, Inyo blinked back a tear, grateful for Ansa's hand resting on his shoulder.

Inyo lifted his face to meet Ansa's concerned gaze. "Ansa. I— thank you for everything."

"Don't mention it. But you know, that was a mighty foolish thing you did, running after a cutpurse!" Ansa scolded. Inyo hung his head. "Don't worry, it will heal," Ansa assured him.

Inyo wondered how long it would take to heal completely, dismayed at the realization that he couldn't pull his weight now, that he'd let down the entire crew, that Juan and Antonio would probably notice right away something was not right, and that he'd better catch them before work began early the next morning.

—

Juan narrowed his eyes when he saw Inyo in the morning. "By Neptune, you look like someone just dipped you into a frozen fjord!"

Inyo swallowed. "I have to tell you something," he confessed sheepishly, revealing his bandage and recounting the incident.

To his surprise, Antonio lifted an eyebrow and whistled. "Nice! Every sailor should have a few scars!" And while Juan chuckled approvingly, Antonio added, "We'll come up with a stirring yarn about how you got it."

"Um, confronting a thief in a dark alley isn't *stirring* enough?" Inyo wondered dryly, though secretly relieved they didn't harp on the obvious stupidity of his actions.

"You mean: *three hulking, dangerous criminals* you had to fight off all by yourself," Juan corrected him with a laugh.

Inyo's clumsy attempts at unloading cargo in Bordeaux and sitting out most of the work during the journey back to Coruña drew unwanted attention from his shipmates. Inyo didn't like being useless, a burden, wished he could disappear and never have to see the crew again after this. Pulling his blanket over his head at night, he brooded over the humiliation but then reminded himself of how much he had learned, how he loved being at sea with Juan and Antonio, and with Ansa.

When the *Gaviota* arrived back in Coruña, some of the wares were unloaded and sold, and repairs on board began. Inyo had already helped with caulking last year and had gotten the hang of using the mallet and caulking iron. This time, Juan tasked the entire crew with removing much of the old caulk. Diego grumbled loudly while picking out the disgusting material stuck between the planks, and Inyo was surprised that even Antonio muttered under his breath while they both hammered greasy oakum into the seams, a seemingly endless task.

At the end of the day, after the planks were sealed and the decks were tidy, Juan paid each member of the crew; they'd be having a day's rest before heading out to the Mediterranean. When Inyo was about to take his leave, Juan slapped him on the back and told him how proud he was that he had faced his fears and found his sea legs. "I hope, despite everything, you wanna join me again sometime. And tell Marina I'll come by tomorrow evening."

"I will." Inyo nodded, slung his satchel over his shoulder, and shuffled down the bouncy plank. He saw several of the crew already making for the tavern, Ansa in the back of the group, looking back, lifting his hand to farewell Inyo. Inyo felt the urge to run after him, tell him Sister Francisca was in town, maybe ask him to come meet Marina, but after waving at Ansa and mouthing a silent "Thank you again," he hesitated and watched Ansa follow Pedro and Diego into the tavern, the open door quickly swallowing the figures one after another.

The approaching rattle of a cart and the crack of a whip pulled Inyo out of his pondering and set his feet in motion. He was finally heading home. When he reached the bakery, Inyo stopped to wave to Clara through the window. She nodded briefly at him while kneading dough. Her torso, arms, and face were covered in flour, even a strand of hair that had escaped her cap and danced in the rhythm of her work. Clara's days in the bakery started when everyone else was still fast asleep. No wonder she wore a tired frown whenever Inyo saw her. But Clara was a different person in church on Sundays. She was flour-free. And her long, wavy hair was so interesting to glance at. The curves of her smooth, pale face were too. The problem was that she was older than Inyo and had always treated him with a mixture of indifference and mere sisterly tolerance.

Inyo swallowed, then headed across the street and entered his home, where voices drew him towards the garden. "We're back here!"

When Inyo stepped through the warehouse's back door into the garden, he swiftly landed in Marina's arms. *"¡Mi pequeño marinero!"* she half-laughed, half-sniffled.

Francisca rose and clapped her hands in delight. "Inyo! I'm so happy to see you!" She folded him into her arms. Her voice instantly transported him back to the *convento de Santa Columba* in Santiago, where tiny beds in neat rows slumbered in the orphanage's dorm, where stories of the saints and Aesop's fables came to life in the schoolroom, where basins of warm water, strips of linens, and prayers were delivered to the white-haired patients in the hospital wing, where the plates and bowls in the kitchen were filled, then served and washed and dried and put away, only to be filled and served again. Most vivid were the memories of the abbey's quiet and shaded garden, where Sister Francisca had shown him the various herbs, the myrtle, thyme, sage, and rosemary. Where he used to breathe in their fragrances and get a close-up look at each one, pretending his finger had become a beetle crawling over the leaves of various green plants, weaving through the tiny hairs on their stems, his imaginary insect legs stepping in time with the song Francisca had taught him. *Mirto, tomillo, salvia, romero. Mirto, tomillo, salvia, romero.* The melody had been—and still was—strangely mesmerizing, much like a prayer or an incantation.

"I can't wait to hear all about your adventure with Juan." Francisca interrupted Inyo's thoughts.

"Yes!" Marina said. "Tell us, which ports did you see? Did Juan turn you into a sailor? What did you learn?"

The kind faces and his comfortable surroundings washed away Inyo's exhaustion. He recounted the highlights of his voyage, the route, the towns, and the work of sailing and navigation. The three of them leaned back on the woven willow bench while a bird serenaded from one of the trees. Marina's eyes fell on Inyo's arm, which he had absentmindedly cradled awkwardly. "What happened to your arm?" she asked.

"Oh, um, it's nothing, I—" He tried to brush it aside. "I just ran into something."

He bit his lip, not wanting Marina to scold him or Francisca to worry about him. Juan was right; nobody needed to know about the injury. Inyo's thoughts drifted to the way Ansa helped him that day. Ansa, who seemed so cold and hostile at first, was now more than a shipmate; he had become his friend, and Inyo missed him already. He turned to Francisca. "One of Juan's hands is from Santiago. His name is Ansa. Do you remember him from the orphanage? He would have been a few years older than me."

Francisca paused to think, but then slowly shook her head. "No, there was no one by that name that I remember."

Inyo's eyebrows furrowed in bewilderment. Surely Francisca couldn't have just forgotten one of the children? Someone who'd been there as long as Ansa couldn't have failed to make an impression. *Something's not right*, Inyo thought. *What dismayed Ansa so much? Why can't Francisca remember him?* Maybe Ansa had a different nun in mind? Unlikely as it was, for now he stored the thought away and rejoined the conversation.

Rockfleet

CLEW BAY, IRELAND 1584

Leaving the open ocean in her wake, a skinny galley darted towards the gray coast of Connacht under full sail. Aloft in the main mast lookout, Finley's stomach grumbled while she braced herself on the rail.

Clare Island and Clew Bay came into focus. The sacred mountain of Cruach Phádraig, massive and veiled in wispy clouds, rose over the south shore of the bay. Weak sunlight skittered and danced on the waves. In moments like this, Finley wished she could be a painter, to capture the grandeur of it all, the many moods and colors of the sea, the white foamy spray dancing on dark rollers, the calm pastels of dawn, and especially the transparent and otherworldly hues near the coast, ranging from deep emerald to luminous light blue.

Finley shivered as the breeze blew her hair into her face. The day at sea aboard the *Dubhdara* had started early, the morning painting its own version of the bay with repeating patterns of lacy foam on the waves, flinging spray and fulmars into the clouds. The crew had ferried provisions to allies on Clare Island and Inis Toirc. Then they headed out into the Atlantic. Four French boats, part of a fishing fleet, heaved to quickly when the *Dubhdara* approached. The French paid their fishing permit without resistance, though their captains grumbled a few times.

Later, the *Dubhdara* pursued an English trader to press for the toll. The English sailors aboard their bobbing vessel were much more obstinate. They couldn't grasp how England ruled Ireland, yet the O'Malleys could tax the English. "Pirates, the lot o' you!" growled the merchant captain. "The governor ought to finish you, he should!"

"Maybe tomorrow," Finley's mamó laughed, gripping the hilt of her sword, "but today, you pay." She was as tall as Owen, and her curly hair, streaming out from beneath her cap, rippled like flames, much the same way Finley's did.

Finley's eyes now swept over the bay's familiar scenery, the folds and curves of the coast, the scattering of low sand islands. Owen climbed aloft towards her, steadied himself on the mast, and patted her on the back. "I'll take it from here, Fin."

"Looks like we'll reach Rockfleet in an hour," she said.

"About time. I'm starving!"

The wind coming from astern shifted, causing the sails to weaken briefly and then snap again as Finley started down the shrouds. She had come to Rockfleet several weeks before her parents, who had arrived by now to help with summer tasks. She would soon head back to Galway Bay with them. Finley was proud that this year, like last summer, her mamó and her uncles, Owen and Tibbot, had deemed her strong enough to work aboard the various ships. Most days, it meant fishing in the bay on smaller vessels, but now and then, she was aboard when they checked on foreign fishing fleets, as they did today, or traded up and down the coast.

Over the past two seasons at Rockfleet, Finley had developed a particular fondness for being at sea. To be aboard a ship on a steep roll, amid a symphony of roaring waves, flapping canvas, and creaking of timbers. The acceptance from the crew and the clan's courage had rubbed off on her, infused her with confidence and a sense of belonging, lifted her gaze out of melancholy waters up to life above the waves as she worked alongside her uncles and her mamó with the laughter of the gulls circling above her head.

Nevertheless, the old muffled grief still lurked deep inside her. Falkyn drifted through her mind often when she was at sea. After she was told about him last year, she never again spoke of him to anyone other than Owen, never confided even to her ma' that he haunted her dreams, stared up at her from the deep to this day, how learning of his death left her riddled and longing for something, for someone.

Lost in thought, she climbed down the ratlines and hadn't reached the main deck yet when Owen shouted, "Sail on starboard bow!"

Finley jumped off the shrouds and made her way to the bow of the *Dubhdara*, from where her mamó stared out to sea. "Can you make out who it is?" she asked.

They braced their boots firmly on the deck and narrowed their eyes. Owen eventually recognized the colorful masthead banner of the approaching ship. "I think it's the O'Neills!" he shouted.

Finley looked up into the stern eyes and leathery face of her grandma, who wondered out loud, "At this hour? Hm, must be something important."

For as long as Finley could remember, her mamó, Grace O'Malley, had been the fierce and charismatic chieftain of the O'Malley clan. Along with Owen and Tibbot, she resided in the clan's main seat, Rockfleet Castle, situated on the eastern shore of Clew Bay. The various clans making a living on Clew Bay's forested shores had successfully banded together for centuries, pushed back foreign influence, and carved out a prosperous life of fishing, farming, trading, and raiding.

Grace O'Malley didn't just command a large fishing fleet, several hundred loyal warriors, and numerous larger ships for trade and other enterprises; she was also a clever businesswoman and forged strategic political alliances, and was respected by the men and women of Connacht and beyond. Her voyages had taken her as far away as France and Spain, and she spoke several languages.

Many people only knew Grace by her nickname, Granuaile, which means "bald Grace." The tale of how she acquired that byname had already become one of the clan's proud legends: When Grace was a child, her father didn't want her to come along on a trading run to Spain. But the young girl was desperate to sail with her father, so she chopped off all her hair and made the journey disguised as a common sailor. Her boldness and tenacity continued to inspire the whole O'Malley clan and their allies.

But the O'Malleys' disrespect for the law was a thorn in the side of the English, so Finley had been told, who wanted the entirety of Ireland, wanted every inhabitant loyal to the Crown. The increasing flood of English settlers, who'd been given Irish land cheaply, were tasked with keeping the unruly clans in line. They also forced all of Ireland to conform to their strange new Protestant religion.

Finley watched the O'Neill ship draw close and then pull alongside the *Dubhdara*. Geoffrey O'Neill shouted, "We just got word that five MacDermot families are on their way from Cranford. There was an attack! Some are badly injured. They're coming to seek refuge at Rockfleet."

"All hands, make haste!" Grace thundered. The whole crew sprang into action.

Geoffrey brought his ship about. "We'll come with you!"

Finley dashed away to help Owen and Liam lay on extra sail while many hands readied the galley's oars. Less than an hour later, the ships docked at Rockfleet harbor, the evening heavy with the threat of rain and with the scent of earth, cattle, and fish being smoked. The crew scrambled to get off board. Geoffrey and his men ran up the hill to his home. "I'll get our farm hands. We'll be over shortly!"

With their capes streaming out behind them, Owen, Grace, and Finley sprinted to Rockfleet, a square tower house with small, narrow windows. There was one of the O'Neills next to a cart, unloading blankets and crates of food. And Finley's mother, Maeve, cradling baby Ronin in her arms, hurrying up to Grace. "Thank heavens you're here! The poor MacDermots! They're all upstairs waiting to talk to you."

Finley's heart was beating hard against her ribs. She took Ronin into her arms when Rockfleet's main door flung open. The ground-floor kitchen was already bustling with activity. Soup simmered in a kettle. Finley's brother, Teagan, deftly cut a loaf of bread into slices. Grace motioned for him to come along and ordered the kitchen staff to bring up the food as quickly as possible.

Finley and Teagan moved up the winding staircase with rapid feet and followed their grandma into the hall, the main living area of the tower house. More than a dozen weary adults, grimy and thin-lipped, and many children huddled around the large fireplace. Finley's father, Brian, was handing out blankets among them. They all turned when Grace approached them. "What happened?" she asked.

"English soldiers, about a hundred of them. They burned our barley and corn," one of the MacDermot women lamented, "the entire crop!"

"It was terrible! We tried to stop them, but there were so many."

"Armed to the gills with halberds and muskets!"

"They robbed our home, they took *everything!*"

One of the older men, his eyes tired and red, gripped Grace's arm and sobbed, "They—they took all of my cattle and sheep."

Grace's voice trembled with anger. "Will they never leave us in peace?"

"They said it's because we failed to pay taxes," one of the crestfallen MacDermots lamented. "We told them we didn't have the money yet. I promised to pay soon. We asked for a few more weeks, but they wouldn't hear of it!"

Grace shook her head slowly while the glow from the fireplace cast her face in a forbidding mask of hard lines. Someone in the huddle sobbed. Many times, Finley had overheard her parents discuss the tyranny of English monarchs who claimed Ireland for their own. Even though the Irish clans had tried to resist, English governors and lords destroyed the abbeys, burned fields, stole cattle, and seized any land they wanted. Every Irish chieftain was to be replaced by an English sheriff, forcing the clans to obey English laws and pay exorbitant taxes.

"How will we survive the winter?" one of the men sighed, his shoulders drooping. "Our farms are in complete ruin. They've left us nothing."

While the adults leaned towards each other with solemn faces, speaking in urgent tones to one another, Finley's forehead remained creased. She finished cleaning an older man's shoulder wound and wiped her hands on a towel just as the platters of food arrived. The mood in the hall lifted as everyone gathered around the bread and the bowls of fragrant soup, an abundance that wasn't taken for granted. Finley could still recall a full year of famine taking its toll when she was very young. There'd been no rain for months, the harvest failed, and gnawing hunger tormented her and everyone in Connacht. They said it was because of a comet. Finley shook her head, lost in thought. *First some comet, now the English!*

After the meal, Grace rose. "Friends," she began, "you are safe here for tonight. We will find new homes for each of you. The O'Neill, Bourke, and O'Malley farms surrounding Rockfleet, and our allies across Connacht, will all aid in this. Now, it may take us a while to find land and help you build farms, but I promise you will *not* go hungry this winter." Relieved murmuring filled the hall.

A moment later, a young man with a bow slung behind his back strode through the door. "Tibbot!" Maeve sighed, relieved, when she saw her brother. Tibbot was Grace's youngest son and just three years older than Finley. Owen and Maeve quickly filled him in on everything that had happened.

Tibbot's face hardened as he took off his bow. "The thieves and their shameless demands!" he growled. He huddled with Owen, Grace, and the older MacDermots to plan for the next day.

Finley helped Teagan arrange thick straw mats in groups for the families, then motioned the children over to sit with them close to the crackling flames. Orange shadows danced across their empty faces, some of them still sniffling. "Do you like songs?" Finley wanted to know.

The children nodded. Teagan asked, "Which one do you want to sing?"

One of the younger boys requested *Brian Boru.*

"That's my favorite!" said Tibbot as he approached, settling in next to Teagan. They lifted their voices, singing the ballad of King Brian Boru and how he outsmarted the Norse ruler of Limerick. The children hummed along and joined in the chorus. Finley was glad to see their smiles at the end of the song.

One of the youngest girls tugged on Finley's sleeve. "What's that on the mantle? The shell. Why does it have a mast and sails?" Everyone's eyes turned to where the girl was pointing. Above the fireplace sat a large, upside-down scallop shell that had been turned into a ship with a twig for a mast and small canvas squares for sails.

"Have you heard about Cleo and the scallop shell?" Finley asked.

"No. Can you tell us that story?"

"Of course." Finley contemplated for a moment, then smiled at the expectant faces surrounding her. "It all began in Galicia."

"Where's that?"

"Galicia is part of northern Spain," Finley explained. "Our village priest, Father Whelan, has been there many times. He told me it takes at least four days to sail there. He said that many of the clans in Galicia share the same legends we have in Ireland. This tale is about how our two nations came to be." Finley grinned and then continued in a low and dramatic voice.

"Long ago, a brother and sister went fishing out on the ocean. A terrible storm took them by surprise. Huge waves washed them both overboard, and they drifted apart. They were about to be pulled into the deep when the goddess of the ocean, Cleo, heard their shouts. She took pity on the drowning girl and placed her in a scallop shell. With the shell as her boat, the girl washed up on the shores of Ireland.

"Cleo also rescued the brother. She sent a dolphin that carried him to Spain. When he woke up, he realized he was alone. So he built a large tower and climbed to its highest part. From up there, he could see his sister on a beautiful, faraway island. But however much he waved and shouted, she could neither see nor hear him across the distance. When evening came, the brother ignited wood branches on the top of the tower. Soon, he saw a tiny light on the horizon. His sister had indeed glimpsed his fire and lit one on her far shore in response.

"From that day on, every evening, the brother set a fire on top of the tower so his sister would be able to see the flame and be comforted, knowing he was alive."

One of the little girls huffed. "My brother would never do that for me."

The children giggled. Finley continued, "And guess what! The tower still stands in Galicia to this day. It's a lighthouse. And when you're sailing near that coast, you can see the flame lighting up the night."

"Oh, so it's a real story then?" asked the little girl who had stayed at Finley's side all this time.

"Maybe." Finely winked at her. "But now it's time to sleep. Off you go."

"Good night!"

The youngest children scampered off, leaving Finley, Teagan, and Tibbot behind by the fire with an older girl who looked to be about Finley's age. She had long black hair and bruises on her cheek. "I love that story. By the way, my name's Ellis. Ellis MacDermot," the girl said.

Finley, Teagan, and Tibbot introduced themselves quietly, knowing that many in the great hall were already asleep. Ellis nodded, then gazed into the dimming embers. Finley had noticed earlier how she and her father helped take care of the other MacDermots, despite their own injuries. Finley whispered, "I'm so sorry about what happened to you, and . . . that you lost your farm. You had to walk a long way, didn't you?"

Ellis nodded again, still staring into the fire, her hair hanging like a dark curtain. "They destroyed everything." She turned to Finley, a tear streaking down her cheek. "But I'm so glad we're here now. I can't thank your grandma enough. My da' didn't think that . . . He was . . . Well, he has hope now that we'll make it through."

Finley placed her hand on Ellis' knee, and their eyes met. "I can't imagine what you went through, but I'm glad you're here," Finley whispered with a smile. Ellis squeezed her hand in return.

—

A rooster crowed in the distance as the morning sun painted a hint of warmth on the upper part of Rockfleet Castle. The stone tower house was situated at a strategic point, where a creek crossed under the road that curved towards the farms along the densely forested northern shore of Clew Bay. Farms and buildings with thatched roofs clustered around the fortress.

While the MacDermots still slept in the main hall, Finley stirred on her mat in a corner of the drawing room, the castle's upper floor. She yawned and rose to join Owen, Tibbot, and her mamó at a table. Her mother sat down with them, too, nursing Ronin. In the solemn looks on all their faces, Finley could see how much the MacDermots' plight troubled them. Her forehead creased. What would become of the O'Malley clan? The English had already killed Finley's grandfather. *They grab ever more of the land. And there's no end in sight.*

"Let's send word today to find homes for the families," Grace began.

Owen nodded. "One of them can stay here at Rockfleet."

"The O'Neills also offered to take in one of them," Tibbot said. "Geoffrey needs farm hands and fishermen, and he has some land where they can build a cottage in the spring."

Finley's eyebrows lifted in surprise when her mother added, "Brian and I will invite one of the families to come to Barna with us when we sail home. But we're worried for you, for Rockfleet, for Connacht. This attack likely won't be the last one . . ."

Owen squared his jaw. "I hope our alliances remain strong. We must remain united and vigilant."

Grace nodded slowly. A long and uncomfortable silence followed, causing Finley to shiver. Her great-grandfather, Black Oak O'Malley, had successfully united some of the clans in Connacht. And her mamó had made the alliance even stronger when she brought together many who had previously quarreled among themselves. Together, they had negotiated a contract with the English governor, committed to balanced rules and fair taxes, and had thus been able to live in peace and relative independence for the last few years. Why were things turning sour now? A fog of worry and premonition hung in the silence of the drawing room.

—

A few days later, Finley was in the harbor at first light, rain clouds, and the keening of gulls clinging to the sky. A breeze lifted off the bay and rustled her hair. Together with Teagan and her uncles, she loaded crates and barrels onto the *Gavilán*, a three-masted trading vessel that would take them all to Galway Bay, to the village of Barna and the Morris farm, and then continue on her customary trade run to Limerick before heading back to Rockfleet.

Her parents strode down the road to the harbor with Fergal MacDermot, his son Padraig, and his daughter Ellis. Finley had loved talking with Ellis since that first night by the fire. It would be great to have her company on the voyage and to help her build a new life in Barna.

Padraig was as tall as an adult, yet he was holding his father's hand as he was pulled along. He stared off into the distance as they gingerly stepped onto the plank. Finley turned to Ellis, whispering, "Why does your brother need to be led?"

"Padraig is blind," Ellis explained. "You didn't know?"

"Um, no," Finley admitted. Over the past few days, she had spent a lot of time with Ellis but had ignored Padraig entirely. How could she have been so oblivious?

Grace, awaiting them on the main deck, linked arms with her daughter Maeve when she came aboard. "Looks like we have favorable winds. We'll easily make it to Galway Bay before dark."

There was a contented and knowing smile on Maeve's face. The wind circled the two women and creased the surface of the bay behind them.

Finley watched Padraig's fingers haltingly explore the railing near him. Teagan had taken over leading him around, pointing out all sorts of things on board, and gently placed Padraig's hands on the helm, saying, here Padraig, that's the whipstaff, it's connected to the tiller below and controls the rudder, why yes of course you'll get a turn at the helm, it's easy, let me show you. Finley's eyebrows lifted, surprised by Teagan's kindness toward Padraig.

While Fergal tucked away their bundles, Ellis' awed gaze wandered up the masts and sails. With her hand trailing over the wooden belaying pins and the thick ropes, she asked Finley, "What does her name mean, the *Gavilán*?"

"It's Spanish for hawk."

"She's such a beautiful ship," Ellis sighed. "Did your grandma build her?"

"No, the O'Malleys captured her. My ma' was there when it happened," Finley chuckled.

Maeve continued the story with a mischievous grin, "Yes. It happened in Galway Bay one summer when I was about your age. More and more trading and fishing vessels from places like Portugal and Spain sailed up here. By and large, they adhered to the treaties with our clan. We raised fees, fishing permits, and taxes on their trading. We couldn't just let them take our fish without compensation.

"But the *Gavilán's* captain, a stubborn Spaniard, refused. He then tried to outrun my ma' and my grandpa. Like that's never been tried before! Our galleys hunted him down. Ma' took over the ship and Grandpa O'Malley marooned their entire crew on Inis Oírr."

"What happened to them after that?" Ellis wanted to know.

"Well, since we left them with nothing," Maeve grinned, "the islanders made them work their fields in exchange for food and lodging. A month later, the farmers of Inis Oírr took mercy on them and flagged down a Spanish merchantman. Told them to spread the word about us O'Malleys. That attempting to outsmart or outrun us was futile!"

Maeve and Brian broke out into laughter, along with the handful of Bourke and O'Neill women and men who made up the crew.

Rockfleet grew smaller and smaller in the distance behind them as the tide carried the *Gavilán* westward. Fulmars swirled above them, screeching in the wind. While Teagan and Padraig stood at the helm, Ellis and Finley helped Brian repair some of the spare sails. Ellis watched in awe as the crew climbed aloft and unfurled the main sail.

Clare Island, home to another O'Malley fortress, soon hovered directly to starboard. "Set a course for south by southwest!" Grace commanded.

Finley recalled one of her very first times at sea aboard this ship, back when she was very young and had to be lifted up to reach the first rungs of the shrouds from where she could have a good view over the vast, island-dotted bay. Everything had seemed so different back then, so simple. Her grandma and the O'Malley clan ruled the entire coast and the ocean, too, or so Finley thought. She never worried about the security and freedom of the O'Malley lands and hadn't been aware of any looming dangers. But over the past week, the darkened expressions of all the adults in her family betrayed the clan's vulnerability. The uneasy balance of peace they'd come to with the encroaching English appeared to be fracturing.

Finley's forehead wrinkled as she rose from her work to gaze over the bay one more time. Despite the clans' combined strength, despite her grandmother's resilience and Owen's optimism, doubts gnawed at the edges of Finley's mind, and she couldn't shake off a creeping dread about the future. Would the English keep pushing further into Connacht, into her mamó's homeland, threatening the freedom of the alliance? *What's the English queen's ultimate goal? What will happen to Rockfleet, to Mamó, Owen, and Tibbot?* Finley stared at the dull water below the hull. Ellis joined her and the two of them lingered by the rail, looking out over the bay, lost in thought, their hair two pennants, red and black, streaming and rippling in unison.

Elizabeth

GREENWICH PALACE, ENGLAND 1584

Elizabeth folded up a letter, her face darkened by the news it contained. "The Spanish!" The queen's richly bejeweled dress billowed as she paced back and forth in front of the large palace windows.

"What are they up to now?" Robin rose with a concerned expression, and he joined Elizabeth at the window. She handed him the report. While his eyes took in the note, Elizabeth allowed herself a moment to close her eyes and lean into him, savoring his calming presence. Robert, the Earl of Leicester, was her closest and most trusted advisor and a childhood friend. "Sweet Robin," she'd called him since they were young, and she still loved having him by her side. His unwavering loyalty and devotion had always infused her with strength.

Robin's grip on the letter tightened. "They're attempting to land troops in Ireland again?"

Gazing absentmindedly at the tapestried walls of her chamber, Elizabeth felt her composure falter. As before, her enemies were plotting against her. "How dare they!" She trembled. "Ireland, despite all the agonies it's causing me, is mine, is *England's* by law! Spain can't be allowed to send troops there!" Elizabeth paused to glance at the calm, wide ribbon of the Thames. She clearly had to stamp down any further unrest and uprisings in Ireland, for fear the Irish Catholics would join forces with Spain and allow King Philip to use Ireland as a launching point for an invasion of England. Elizabeth's fists tightened with the effort to control her fury. She knew from her informants that Spain had begun planning an attack on England. Her land. The country she'd pledged to protect, and the people she loved with all her heart.

"Bess, you've seen how Philip has become more and more radical over the years, considering it his life's work to bring all of Europe back to the Catholic fold—whether they like it or not." Robin reminded her.

Elizabeth shuddered at the memory of her first meeting with Philip. That was thirty years ago, when he married her half-sister, Mary Tudor, a Catholic who was England's Queen at the time. It was obvious even back then that he considered England his dominion.

Mary's shocking and violent attempts to restore England to Catholicism were in vain and had only increased distaste for the old church. Since Mary's death, England had grown even more solidly Protestant. But the pope had declared England's new queen, Elizabeth, an infidel. *An immoral heretic who must be removed*. And Spain, siding with the pope, agreed that she was an abomination. And her country, filled with witless farmers and lawless pirates, as they saw it, was too. The plotting against Elizabeth was constant, she knew from her spies at home and abroad.

Our small island against the greatest empire in the world! Elizabeth breathed a heavy sigh, then straightened her figure and lifted her head. She locked eyes with Robin, whose attentive and encouraging gaze instantly eased her tension.

Thirty years ago, Mary had suspected them both of involvement in a revolt. Elizabeth and Robin were locked in the Tower, imminent death hanging over them. Every hour, Robin and Elizabeth had realized, could be their last. They'd clung to each other, trembling, their friendship a raft keeping them afloat in the darkest and stormiest months of their lives. There was no one she could trust more than Robin.

A knock on the door interrupted Elizabeth's thoughts. Robin placed the letter on her desk while her principal minister entered and bowed. "Your Majesty, Sir Francis Drake has returned. He wishes to present to you the profits of his latest endeavor."

—

Her ladies and courtiers bowed as the queen entered Greenwich Palace's main hall and took her seat on the throne. For a moment, expectant silence filled the vast hall, with its richly painted vault ceiling and warm light filtering through windows of many-colored glass. At Elizabeth's gesture, the large portals swung open. Drake entered under a trumpet fanfare, dressed in a lavish, gold-embroidered vest. He held back his velveteen cape with one arm, swooped off his plumed hat, and lowered himself to one knee before Elizabeth.

She studied him, remembering when she'd knighted him a few years ago for his circumnavigation of the globe, a mighty achievement of seamanship. Drake was a talented and aggressive entrepreneur. All in all, he'd been very useful to England, and this latest exploit with two dozen ships had been carried out under her covert orders.

As servants followed behind him, parading captured Spanish treasure, dozens of laden chests of silver and gold, along with baskets full of sugar cane and tobacco, Drake's herald announced boldly, "A sample of our spoils from Hispaniola, Florida, and Colombia!"

Yet even as she smiled and inwardly thanked God for the profits that would fill her empty coffers, a vague flicker of concern creased Elizabeth's face. Drake, this English hero, was known in Spain as *el*

Draque, the dragon, a fearsome enemy. His deeds: crimes that enraged King Philip even further and undoubtedly deepened his desire for revenge. *Will this dragon's fire spark the flames of outright war?* Elizabeth worried. Behind her composure, restless thoughts rippled and swirled, agitating her much like the stiff and scratchy lace ruff around her neck.

The Castle of Perseverance

BARNA, IRELAND 1585

Springtime in Ireland carried the lush scent of awakening forests and fens. In the small stone church on the outskirts of Barna, less than a mile away from her home, Finley settled in next to Teagan when Father Whelan began his sermon. He was full of gentleness and humor, and the church was packed with dozens of regulars. Like all of them, Finley felt drawn to the charismatic priest. He loved to use props and objects to illustrate his messages. Today, he lifted a pilgrim's staff. "When the path becomes rocky or steep, what can help us? Right, a walking stick. Or a friend to lean on. This life is a journey, and we are all walking it together. Some fast, some slow . . ." he began.

Finley could already tell where his message was heading. He'd talk about how "if we walk in the light as He is in the light, we will have fellowship with one another," or maybe how believers ought to walk humbly, be guided and strengthened by the Spirit, lift the fallen and help one another, and how, above all, scripture was "a lamp on a dark path." Some of his favorite verses.

A few weeks ago, Father Whelan had encouraged all the younger people of Barna to consider joining him on a pilgrimage. "As you know, I sail to Spain every few years to walk the sacred trail to the tomb of Saint James. The *Camino de Santiago de Compostela*. Who wants to come along this year?" he had asked.

Finley, Ellis, and Padraig immediately said yes. Although Finley was looking forward to the pilgrimage, she'd never been away from Connacht, much less across the sea to a whole different country. While she was familiar with coastal sailing, such a long voyage, out of sight of land, out of reach of her mamó's protecting ships, would be filled with uncertainty and perils. To tamp down her concerns, she reminded herself that Father Whelan had made the journey many times, and half of Barna as well. *He must know what he's doing*, she comforted herself.

After the service, Father Whelan reminded his congregation, "Later today, there will be rehearsals for the play, but first: our weekly weapons practice." He had made it clear many times how much he believed practicing with swords, axes, and hunting bows was as essential as prayer and confession. Finley had asked her father once why the priest was so insistent on this.

"Not long ago, our coastal towns were constantly attacked and destroyed by invaders from many different lands," her father had explained. "You know, when Father Whelan was a boy, his village was raided by Barbary corsairs. The entire population was taken to Algiers and sold into slavery. Men, women, and children. They suffered terribly. Father Whelan was eventually freed by Spanish friars who regularly purchased captives in Tunis and Algiers. He was one of the lucky ones who was set free, but he never saw any of his family again."

After the service, Finley watched her parents stroll through the church portal into the sunlight, with her mother carrying two-year-old Ronin on her hip. Ronin squirmed, more than ready to run around with the other children.

Some of the villagers took weapons to a separate practice area behind the rectory, where they had built a wooden stall for throwing axes. There were bulging sacks of straw on poles for training with spears and halberds.

In the meadow behind the stone church, Finley joined the older children who were helping Father Whelan as he coordinated the setting up of targets.

With a less than enthusiastic expression, Finley sat slumped over in the grass next to Padraig and watched her mother help Teagan string his bow while Ellis and her father lined up with their bows. A row of women and men stood ready while Father Whelan checked the field and then shouted, "Ready? Shoot!" The archers aimed. A swarm of arrows soared at the targets. "Cease! Aaand retrieve!"

With excited chatter, they rushed to pull the arrows out of the targets and gather a few stray ones off the ground. The next group included Brendan, one of Barna's fishermen. Finley found herself sneaking a covert glance at him as he aimed with a confident, steadying breath. At nineteen, he was four years older than she was. Unlike her, he was an excellent marksman. Brendan's arrow hit the black, drawing cheers from several onlookers. Finley's gaze followed him as he trotted away to retrieve his arrow.

Teagan and Ellis lined up for another turn. Finley joined them apathetically. Her shoulders cramped, and her arms began to tremble when she pulled the bowstring. Father Whelan gave the command, and instantly, dozens of arrows whizzed through the air. Teagan and Ellis hit their targets, but Finley's arrow landed several yards off in the grass. She muttered angrily under her breath. When she retrieved her arrow and stomped back, Finley hoped no one—*especially not Brendan*—had seen her dismal shot. Why were her eyes suddenly brimming? Flinging herself into the grass with a huff, Finley sensed a bitter irritation rising in her throat. She quickly wiped away an annoying tear with her sleeve.

Ellis ran up to her and urged, "Come on, Fin, you gotta go again." Finley rose reluctantly and followed Ellis. They each tried a few more times, but Finley's aim was as wayward as her emotions.

After weapons practice, Finley, along with a group of other young villagers, ambled back into the church to rehearse the play with Father Whelan. Every year, he organized a dramatic stage production in the town center to celebrate Litha, the summer solstice.

This year's choice for the play was *The Castle of Perseverance*. A gabble of excited voices filled the church when they started rehearsing. Brendan took his position in the lead role as the allegorical hero *Mankind*. Padraig had been selected to star as the Good Angel. He had to put on an exceedingly pious and upright air, repeatedly showering Brendan with scripture and godly advice in Latin with his pale arms lifted high.

"Nicely done, Padraig," Father Whelan directed him. "Now try that line again with more pomp and a much haughtier look."

Teagan, the Bad Angel, sneaked up to Brendan with an impish waddle, delivering his grandiose lines with a devilish grin. "Ah, no need to feel guilty, *everyone* sins. You're so *young!* Just enjoy your life!"

The play followed Mankind's life, his failures and successes as he navigated different moral choices. Anytime he was on the straight and narrow, he stood in the castle, which still needed to be built. For now, they used a cluster of wooden chairs.

In all of the castle scenes, a few girls surrounded Brendan, symbolizing various Virtues, and Finley portrayed one of them. She didn't have any lines, as usual, and only participated as a sort of prop and to join in the songs.

As Penance, Ellis's part was much more interesting: she got to pierce Mankind's heart with her Lance of Conscience. Ellis lunged for him in such a convincingly sharp and threatening manner that it elicited a gasp from all of them watching. In turn, Brendan gripped the lance, bent over with wide eyes, sank dramatically to his knees, and exclaimed, "Ah, Penance, thou hast awakened my soul!" Finley found herself mesmerized by the lance scene, inwardly coveting Ellis' role.

Father Whelan looked on with a smile, obviously pleased with their progress. The second act opened with an eruption of chaos on stage —a dramatic fight between the handful of boys who portrayed the Deadly Sins. Finley and the other Virtues sang a pious hymn in an unsuccessful attempt to tame the Deadly Sins, to protect the castle and Brendan, but the Deadly Sins eventually overpowered them all and dragged Brendan away.

He returned to the castle after Mercy preached a poetic sermon, taking Brendan by the hand. Mercy was portrayed by Neasa, who was Brendan's age. Finley stared at her graceful movements and her impossibly shiny, golden hair. Neasa was beautiful in a tall and willowy way that made Finley feel like an oaf.

"Well done!" Father Whelan praised the actors. "Next week we'll continue from here."

After they put away the chairs and props, they all lingered in clusters in front of the church. Neasa bantered with Brendan. The older players were getting ready to head for the tavern with Father Whelan, and Finley watched Brendan linking arms with Neasa. The two of them looked like a fairytale king and queen, beaming at each other as they floated towards the harbor with the sun low on the horizon. Swallowing hard, Finley became aware of a strange dullness in her chest, a soreness, a pang that clung to her like the fog that lingered over the bay in winter.

She caught up to Teagan, Padraig, and Ellis. They followed the road from the church past a cottage and out of town. It turned into a dirt path snaking through the forest and past the ferns surrounding the old stone well. Ellis, Padraig, and Teagan carried on excitedly about the play's fight scenes, about the progress on their costumes, and about how much they were looking forward to the performance in a few weeks.

Finley, lost in thought, lumbered several steps behind them. Eventually, they strolled into the open meadow where the Morris farm, Finley and Teagan's home, was situated. Hugging Finley goodbye, Ellis promised, "I'll see you tomorrow!" before she headed up the path towards the MacDermot farm, a short walk further on.

It was two years ago when Ellis arrived with her father and brother. They'd all worked together to build the new cottage for them on the far side of the Morris' land. Ever since then, not a day went by that Finley and Ellis didn't meet up to ride the horses and to help each other with chores and errands. Ellis was more than a neighbor, more than a friend. She had practically become Finley's sister.

Brian sat at the big loom near the fireplace, watching Teagan and Finley have their evening meal. It was getting late, and while the wooden parts of the loom rattled, Teagan recounted the highlights of the rehearsal to Maeve. Finley yawned and soon headed for her bed. Ronin was already asleep in the cot near their parents' curtained bed.

Finley stared up into the gloomy shadows of her bed canopy, ruminating on the events of the day, telling herself she needed to practice her archery, get better at it, she just had to.

And then her thoughts drifted to Brendan. There was a mysterious chiming inside of her when she pictured his handsome face, his smile, and his sinewy arms. What would it be like to be wrapped in arms such as his? *He's at the tavern right now. With Neasa. Will someone ever look at me the way Brendan looks at her?* Was it all because she was so much younger than Neasa? Could someone as shrimpy as her ever turn into a graceful fairy queen? Was there a potion to change an unruly mane to golden softness? An internal dam slowly gave, gradually flooding Finley's vision, turning into a thin rivulet of tears that trickled down her cheek in the darkness.

—

Finley and Ellis saddled the horses early the next day. They mounted up and trotted away from the farm under a weak drizzle. When they reached the main road to Galway, they urged Cormac and Merla into a canter, their hair trailing out behind them. With Ellis by her side and Cormac's mane whipping under her nose, Finley left behind her low spirits. She inhaled deeply. Though the rain had now stopped, water still dripped from branches and ferns. Then, the weak springtime sun peeked out from behind scattered clouds as the forest fell away behind them, opening to tilled farmland. The horses' hoofs pounded the dirt road, flinging bits of mud in their wake.

Galway's western gate came into view, and soon they began to cross the stone bridge over the River Corrib. Finley caught a glimpse of flashing halberds bobbing out of the gate. *A patrol!* The English soldiers quickly crested the bridge, heading towards them, and the girls stopped to let them pass. The men strolled by with puffed chests and wide steps; a few had muskets slung over their backs. Some of them leered at Finley as they passed, sneering and nudging each other. Over the rushing of the river, she couldn't quite make out what was said, but the gestures were obvious enough. Her grip tightened on the reins, and a wild-eyed pressure in her throat strangled her breath. She'd never seen English soldiers this close before and kept her eyes fixed on the distance, pretending that she could neither see nor hear them.

She knew from her father that tensions were still high in the remote areas of Connacht, and she had heard more and more rumors about the English pestering the townspeople here. Finley turned her anxious gaze to Ellis, alarmed to see her utterly pale and trembling.

The sergeant in charge of the soldiers growled at his men, "That's enough, you lot, eyes forward!" As his men moved along, he paused and grinned at Finley with a mocking tilt of his head. "Don't worry, missies, they don't mean nothin' by it. Just lads bein' lads!" he boomed, then strode after the patrol.

The girls nudged their horses on. Finley desperately wanted to turn in her saddle and hurl an insult at the men, but she knew better than to do something foolish like that. Ellis' shoulders rose and fell rapidly. "Ellis?" Finley tried to get her attention, but her friend couldn't get her breath under control and seemed beyond reach, wiping her sleeve across her face repeatedly.

Once they crossed the bridge and were past the gate, they dismounted, and Ellis collapsed into Finley's embrace, sniffling angrily, "God, I *hate* them!"

Finley nodded, cradling Ellis. She had imagined many times what it must have been like for Ellis to witness the English attack on her farm a few years back. "I won't let anything happen to you, Ellis," Finley muttered, tightening her arms around Ellis.

Ellis suppressed a few more sobs, gradually calming down in Finley's arms. When they got sent on errands, they habitually roamed the market and took their time. Today, however, as soon as they were done purchasing the lye soap and sewing needles Finley's mother had sent them for, they mounted up again and made their way back over the bridge, hoping not to run into any other patrols. Across the bridge and out of town, Ellis seemed to breathe easier, but she begged Finley, "Let's take the coastal path home."

Finley nodded in agreement. It was a detour, a longer and more difficult path home compared to the main road, but Finley preferred it, too, and so she led the way.

Past the small fishing village of Claddagh, the overgrown path meandered along the shore for a long time. It then curved inland towards the O'Halloran keep, which sat hidden at the edge of an overgrown cove. The horses forded the shallow stream near the tower house and soon entered the shade of the cathedral-like woods, following the uphill path along the creek. A short way before a turn towards the small bridge that would take them home, the girls dismounted and led the horses off the trail, along another smaller creek to their secret spot, the Druid Tree. The old oak, with its mighty trunk and long, winding branches, looked like a wild, dancing giant, with large, moss-covered boulders strewn about. They had named him the Druid Tree a few years back.

After Merla and Cormac drank from the brook, Ellis and Finley tied them to a bush nearby, leaving them to lip at the nettles and grasses. They took off their shoes, waded into the refreshing waters, then sat down in a patch of moss at the creek's edge.

"What happened in town—" Finley began, "I'm—it was so scary. And you, are you well?"

Ellis nodded quietly and huffed, "I just don't like the soldiers."

"Next time, we should get Cormac to kick them. Real hard!" Finley said, relieved to hear Ellis chuckle in reply.

They smiled at each other, the tension slowly melting off their bodies. A few spots of sunlight glistened on the horses' backs as their tails flicked. Surrounded by the gurgle of the creek and the intermittent bird song, the girls exhaled deeply and lifted their faces to the green canopy above them. Ellis turned to Finley. "It seemed like something was bothering you yesterday . . ."

Finley's eyebrows lifted in surprise. "Oh, was it that obvious?"

"Fin, I've known you for long enough now, I can read your face. And you can't just hide things from me. Now tell me!"

"You're right," Finley admitted, "It was a rotten day. Because—" she paused and swallowed. Ellis wrapped her arm around Finley's shoulders. Finley took a deep breath and then huffed, "Archery practice was a disaster."

Ellis stared at her with one eyebrow lifted in disbelief. "You're all crabby because of archery practice? Come on, what's *really* going on?"

"Well," Finley sighed. "The truth is, I can't stop thinking about

Brendan."

"Brendan?" Ellis asked.

"Well, he—he's so handsome," Finley confessed with a sheepish half-grin, a redness flooding her face.

"Wait, are you—Are you falling in love?"

Finley nodded. Ellis' immediate look of surprise and her cheerful giggles were infectious. Finley couldn't help but smile. Finally, it felt like letting go of a burden, a misery she'd been bottling up for weeks.

"I don't know why! I feel all jittery when I'm near him. If only he would look at *me* the way he looks at Neasa. Oh, what I would give to have Neasa's hair! If I could just be as tall as Neasa, as mature—"Finley stopped herself and grabbed Ellis' arm. "You can't tell him. Don't tell anyone! Promise me you'll never—*never ever*— mention this to anyone. Please!"

"I promise." Ellis nodded loyally. "And let me know if I can do anything. Maybe my Lance of Conscience could 'accidentally' skewer Neasa," she chuckled.

Finley sighed, recalling all the times she'd worked alongside Brendan in Father Whelan's plays and out on fishing boats in the bay. He used to be just another villager. But then, a few weeks ago, Finley began noticing these strange longings. They unsettled her. She hadn't asked for them, hadn't imagined them, and now she desperately wished they would disappear on their own. The pilgrimage to Spain would be the answer, yes, she was sure of it. This momentous adventure would *have* to cure her—how could it not?—would flush Brendan from her mind forever, and would turn her into her old self.

For a long time, the two girls sat under the oak, Finley's head resting against her friend's despondently. "And you?" Finley asked. "Is there someone that you fancy?"

A hint of amusement lingered in the corner of Ellis' mouth. "Well, I might be in love with Cormac."

Cormac nickered and turned his head to Ellis. It was time to head home. They mounted up, found the main trail, and crossed the small stone bridge over the creek. The path soon emerged out of the woods, revealing smoke rising from the chimney of the Morris farm. The delicious aroma of freshly baked bread and simmering soup hung in the air. Ellis and Finley led the horses to the pasture, closed the gate, and hung up the tack in the barn.

Later that evening over supper, Finley told her parents about the encounter with the soldiers in Galway. "They've always been a pushy lot," Maeve huffed. "I'm glad nothing worse happened."

"They are going to get more than just pushy, I fear." Brian shook his head slowly. "There's a new governor on the way. Hard man, from what I've heard, fought with the Dutch against the Spanish. Seems they think he's the right kind to get us 'wild Irish' into line, as they see it." Brian settled back in his chair, turning a knife over and over in his fingers, a frown lingering on his face.

Libros y Cartografía

W here do you want it?" Inyo panted, shuffling backwards awkwardly, dragging a large table he had finished sanding earlier.

Marina pointed to the space with her broom. "Right here near the window."

Over the past months, the warehouse on the ground floor of their home had been cleared out, and Marina finally opened her bookbinding and cartography business. She laid out her materials on the new worktable while Inyo sipped water and then opened the door, allowing the warm springtime air to flood the shop. He stepped outside, placing his fists onto his hips, watching Marina burst out the door with a squeal of delight. They proudly gazed at her new enterprise.

Above the entrance, a large wooden sign that Inyo had carved proclaimed *Libros y cartografía*. In the window to the right of the entrance, Inyo had placed one of Marina's large books, opened up to a spread of flawless text and brilliant illuminations. In the other window, a magnificent, hand-drawn map of Spain hung suspended from twine.

One afternoon, a few days after they opened, Isabella, the mayor's wife, swept in and commissioned a small book of hours. "I've seen these adorable devotionals in Santiago. I want mine to be about *this* big," Isabella piped, forming a small rectangle with her two hands. She listed all her favorite prayers and the saints' legends she wanted included. "And lots of illustrations!" she added.

Marina took notes, calculating the number of required pages. "This should be done in two months' time," she said. Inyo was as excited as Marina to begin work on this unique and lavish project. Marina ordered the pages of text and picked them up from the printer a week later, then started adding the illustrations: colorful scenes from the scriptures. Angels, saints, the stations of the cross, flowers and flourishes, and even some local legends.

During the work, Marina's table held a collection of liquid paints in shells, colored powder in small jars, rags, ceramic plates used as palettes, a variety of brushes and quills, and a tiny stack of precious gold leaf. After the final painting for the book of hours was completely dry, Marina folded all the pages, stitched them together, and clamped the bundle between two planks to shave and smooth the edges. Then she carefully added a fine leather binding with gold leaf embellishments and a small clasp. The finished book looked like a treasure. Inyo knew such books were considered priceless belongings by those able to purchase them.

Over the following weeks, *Libros y cartografía* saw an increasing number of customers come through its doors. Inyo marveled at the books and maps Marina created. He found himself leaving Bernardo's carpentry workshop earlier and earlier each day, spending more time helping Marina with projects and errands.

And soon Inyo had to build a second worktable in the shop, a place where Marina wanted him to create his own maps. Francisca occasionally brought borrowed books and atlases from the convent's library, and Inyo spent much of his free time soaking up the Latin and Spanish texts, Ortelius' glorious atlas, and Ptolemy's astronomical charts.

Juan showed up one day, in between trading trips, with his ragged collection of maps and wrinkled sketches. "I saw a Flemish trader's set of charts once," he told Marina. "They were just gorgeous, and I wonder if you could consolidate these into a, um, a more *coherent* set. You know, these are almost as old as I am and—oh, look at that rag— it's getting hard to find anything in the jumble . . ." Juan's voice trailed off into embarrassed mumbling while he rifled through the mass of tattered pages, shaking his head, struggling to explain the "system" he used to make sense of his maps.

With a sisterly grin, Marina took the pile, placed it on Inyo's table, and assured Juan, "Don't worry. We will redraw, update, and consolidate them all."

Inyo's eyes glowed, eager to start the project. He was familiar with many of Juan's maps from his time aboard the *Gaviota*. When he studied the charts, he vividly remembered each coast and each port. A map was a road that wound through the complexities of time and space. A portal into the lofty perspectives reserved exclusively for birds and angels. A journey of weeks that could be understood at one glance.

Inyo curled himself over his table, dipped his quill into ink, and watched as coastlines formed on the parchment, instantly transporting him back onto the *Gaviota's* decks. He missed his time at sea and looked forward to joining Juan again, usually for one sailing in the spring and another in the summer. Despite the satisfaction he felt working for Bernardo and for Marina, in his heart, he craved the ocean, the soughing of waves, the briny air, and the euphoria of heading out into untold adventures at sea.

With the growth of the port, however, the workload at both *Libros y cartografía* and at the carpenter's shop had increased sharply. So when Juan asked Inyo if he wanted to work aboard the *Gaviota* this spring, as he had done in previous seasons, Inyo felt a twang of guilt for leaving Marina. He scratched his chin, contemplating what he should do, while both Marina and Juan waited expectantly for his answer.

"What routes are you planning this year?" Inyo asked.

Juan listed his spring and early summer schedule. "And then I'll head up to Ireland, latter part of July," he added. "Why don't you join me on that route?"

"Hm, I've never been to Ireland." Inyo nodded thoughtfully, then smiled. "Yes, count me in!"

Over the following weeks, as spring brought warmer temperatures, the port became ever more alive with all manner of vessels, including merchant carracks and towering galleons. Sailors from Italy, France, the Low Countries, Scotland, Ireland, and North Africa crowded the landings. Day after day, the ships disgorged their wares, merchandise from as far away as the Spice Islands to the east and the Americas to the west.

Sprinkled in between all that commercial activity were musicians, beggars, and, occasionally, small groups of solemn pilgrims. A heady mixture of languages pulsed in Coruña's bustling streets. Inyo often found himself at the harbor with Bernardo, repairing ships or delivering work to customers near the harbor front.

Traders and captains also sought out *Libros y cartografía* to purchase or commission detailed nautical charts of specific coastal regions. The dexterity and ability to carve even minute features, which Bernardo taught him well, directly translated to Inyo's accuracy and attention to detail on the valuable maps he created. Lacy curves of coastlines, scatterings of tiny letters and numbers, and a grid of thin lines indicating latitude and compass bearing.

The street outside *Libros y cartografía* was buzzing with activity as well. From his worktable at the window, Inyo watched the daily crowds of customers at the bakery. Clara had hired two young apprentices, and the bakery churned out ships' biscuits, bread, rolls, and cake from morning till evening.

And the printing press next to Marina's shop had been taken over by a new owner, an industrious young man by the name of Adrián. One day, when Adrián delivered a bundle of printed pages to Marina, Inyo stood on a ladder, stringing up lengths of twine across the shop. "Laundry time?" Adrián grinned.

Marina chuckled, and Inyo explained, "We can now hang the maps from the ceiling and our customers can look at all of them without having to shuffle them around."

"Oh, I see!" Adrián nodded. "Very clever."

The idea spread through nearly all the stores on their street. Adrián suspended his printed manuscripts and documents. Clara hung small wheel-shaped loaves from the ceiling in the bakery. Locals and foreigners marveled at the row of shops with their fabulous aerial displays. The blacksmith down at the corner, however, shook his head and declined to join the craze.

—

Just like every spring, Coruña celebrated the festival of the crosses. Festooned with flowers and colorful ribbons, wooden crosses were displayed on the plazas and in front of churches. The townspeople decorated their gardens, ready for a night of music and dancing.

In her own garden, Marina hung flower wreaths, while Juan and Inyo adorned one of the almond trees with fishnets and shells. They invited Francisca and Antonio, as well as their neighbors Clara, Adrián, and Bernardo, to join them for the celebrations.

The garden was festively lit with candles and lanterns as the guests arrived one by one, wearing their finest and most colorful clothing. Inyo caught himself staring at Clara. He didn't often see her like this, wearing a dress, her face clean and her hair open.

Adrián, Marina, and Juan clinked their mugs together, bantering next to a table that was piled high with fruit, pasties, meats, and jugs of wine. Clara passed around a large basket filled with small, savory loaves. Francisca had brought almond cakes, the tiny oval ones decorated with thin strips of quince paste to make them look like bees. Inyo knew them from his time at the orphanage. Tasting them conjured up memories of the sunny convent garden in Santiago, lessons with childhood friends, the large kitchen with its vaulted ceiling, and learning to bake these tiny bee cakes. Inyo smiled at Francisca as he savored his sweet bee, and she gave him a wink.

Surely Ansa would want to see her again one day, Inyo told himself, but he still hadn't brought it up with him because they saw each other at most a few times a year aboard the *Gaviota*, and they didn't talk about the orphanage days anymore.

After the meal, Bernardo played his *vihuela*. Inyo joined the circle that danced around the flower cross and the decorated tree. When Bernardo switched to a slower ballad, Adrián approached Clara and asked her for a dance. On top of the fine dress and lack of flour, Inyo had definitely never seen a smile of such euphoria on her face before. She and Adrián swayed and twirled, holding each other close. There was a mysterious energy between the two figures. Adrián looked like a prince in his white doublet and black jerkin. Clara's hair framed her radiant face, and, with her skirts billowing around her, she appeared to be floating.

Inyo couldn't bear to watch them any longer, but he didn't know why. He stuffed another bee cake into his mouth and plopped down next to Antonio, who chuckled knowingly and slapped his back, which annoyed Inyo even more.

El Camino de Santiago

When the first stars appeared in the evening sky over Galway Bay, the people of Barna gathered in the village center to celebrate Litha, marking the summer solstice. First up, as each year, was the play. Benches and bales of hay had been arranged in concentric semi-circles before the stage, which was framed by two wooden scaffolds. Suspended between them were rough drapes fashioned from old canvas.

Backstage, Finley peeked nervously at the audience through a gap in the curtains. She flashed a smile and lifted her hand briefly when she saw her parents and Ronin. Teagan practiced a few thrusts with his pitchfork, the fringes of his Bad Angel costume flapping excitedly. Padraig mouthed his lines absentmindedly. Ellis took a deep breath, smoothed her flowy pale gown with one hand, and gripped her lance with the other. Finley cast a very brief glance at Neasa, who was doting on Brendan and his costume. The backstage buzz fell silent when Father Whelan welcomed the crowd in his baritone voice and reminded them that yes, this was the old Celtic celebration of Litha, but it was also Saint John's Night. He started the festivities with a brief prayer in his usual genial manner, before inviting his flock to please enjoy tonight's performance, *The Castle of Perseverance.*

The audience cheered, laughed, and booed at all the right spots as the play proceeded, and Father Whelan doled out praise and encouragement behind the set following each scene. In the past, Finley used to enjoy the over-acted morality plays, but this year, it took effort to perform, to shift her facial expressions into the right shapes, to keep her mind from drifting away. She knew why, but what could she do?

After the players had taken a final bow to loud rounds of applause, everyone moved to the bonfire in the meadow behind the church. Several villagers raised their voices in song as lutes and drums played. Finley watched her parents dance in a circle around the fire, along with the other adults, Neasa and Brendan among them. She lifted herself on her toes, trying to appear taller and grown-up, but Brendan only had eyes for Neasa. He looked so elated, and the longer Finley stared at him, the more her face fell. Ronin ran up to her. "Fin, will you dance with me?"

She hesitated for a brief moment, her sadness still pulling on the corners of her mouth, but then she bent down to Ronin. "Of course, my sweet." Finley scooped him up, twirled him around, and they both giggled with their faces lifted to the wheeling stars in the night sky.

Later that evening, Ellis and Finley settled down on the edge of the meadow, watching the festivities from a distance. Finley absentmindedly plucked on blades of grass while her gaze kept flitting to Brendan and Neasa.

Ellis interrupted her brooding. "Just two more days, Fin!" she squealed. "I can't believe we're sailing to Spain!"

Of course, the pilgrimage! Finley felt herself swimming up from her dark mood as she looked into Ellis' exuberant face. She took a deep breath and resolved to focus on the future instead of *this Brendan thing*. After all, she was about to embark on the biggest adventure of her life, after which her heartache would pale into insignificance. Or so she hoped.

In the spring, when Finley's grandmother had heard about Father Whelan's plan, she clapped her hands and encouraged Owen and Tibbot to be part of it as well, saying, yes, it was time Tibbot and Finley should go, alluding to an O'Malley duty to walk the *Camino*.

Her ma' had explained to Finley its deep significance to their family: "My great-great-grandfather, Lorcan O'Malley, had a bad leg and limped all his life. He was to be chieftain, but no one respected him. In a dream, he was told to go on a pilgrimage to Santiago for healing, to walk there from whichever Spanish town his ship reached first. So he sailed to Coruña and walked the *Camino*. When he arrived in Santiago, he was healed!

"He became a great chieftain. And every year for as long as he lived, he either made or sponsored the sailing to Spain, often taking along men and women from neighboring clans. Now it's a tradition that if you're an O'Malley, you go to Santiago at least once in your life."

"Have you been there before?" Finley wanted to know.

"Of course! I went once when I was your age. Owen went too," Maeve said.

That evening, as they sat near the fireplace, she told Ellis and Finley everything she remembered about her journey to Spain. The cheerful and temperamental people. The language that sounded so much like Latin. The food and customs, the impressions of the towns she passed through, and her memories of the glorious cathedral in Santiago.

"It is said that pilgrims' sins are all forgiven when they arrive in Santiago. I'm not so sure about that part, but I firmly believe the pilgrimage can cleanse one's soul. Very often, the young people who go, find their calling, have a vision, or receive a divine answer to a problem. Miracles might be rare, but you never know," Maeve added with a wink.

Finley's eyes shone, and Ellis smiled at her, equally excited. Soon, they'd be aboard an O'Malley ship, forging south through the open ocean, a new land ahead of them, waiting to be explored.

The day after Litha, the *Gavilán* arrived in Barna with Owen, Tibbot, and a handful of Bourke, O'Neill, and MacDermot men and women. Geoffrey O'Neill, Grace's neighbor and closest ally, was a seasoned sailor and had been trading with Spain for years. He was thrilled to take the spacious *Gavilán* and rubbed his hands. "Got the hold loaded with cargo."

Owen told Finley and Ellis, "While we're on the *Camino*, Geoffrey and his crew will sail to San Sebastian and Bilbao before we all meet up again in Coruña."

Finley found it hard to sleep that night, squirming in anticipation. Tomorrow, she'd be on her way to Spain, sailing away from her home, the only land she had ever known. She'd miss her parents, and Teagan, and Ronin, and the horses. She sighed. Wouldn't it be better to back out after all? But then, what would Ellis do without her? No, despite her apprehension, she was determined to go.

—

The early morning sun filtered through the forest canopy when Finley and Ellis marched briskly down towards Barna harbor, with Tibbot and Owen in the lead. They soon saw Geoffrey and his crew as they readied the ship, Padraig, and Father Whelan already at the gunnel. Ellis' father, Fergal MacDermot, as well as Finley's parents and brothers, had come down to see them all off.

While Finley hugged her father, she overheard her mother whisper to Owen, "You make sure to keep good watch over my precious cargo, will you?"

"Don't worry. We'll be safe."

Ronin desperately clung to Finley's leg and pleaded, "I wanna come with you!"

She lifted him and hugged him tightly. "In a few years, you'll go to Spain too. But this year, I need you to stay here and do something for me. Will you take good care of Merla and Cormac while I'm gone? Feed them and brush them every day?"

Ronin nodded enthusiastically, then wrapped his arms around Finley's neck. "I will. Love you, Fin!"

After the lines were cast off and the ship pulled away from the dock, Ellis and Finley leaned over the stern rail, waving goodbye, watching the smiling faces of their families retreat into the distance.

While Geoffrey glanced at the compass, then at the crew's work on deck, Owen, Tibbot, and Finley studied the charts and discussed the plans for their route with Father Whelan. Weather and wind were sometimes unpredictable factors, but they hoped to arrive in Spain in three or four days. Not long after leaving Barna, they passed between the Cliffs of Moher and Inis Oírr, the smallest of the Aran islands. Galway Bay retreated in the distance behind them. Strong gusts pummeled the *Gavilán* as she kept a safe distance from the coast, sailing beam reach under gray skies.

Balancing on the swaying decks, Finley made her way to the bow where Ellis held herself in an alarmingly stiff manner, her white knuckles gripping the rail and her face hard as she scanned the startling infinity of the ocean before her.

"Being so far out at sea, God, I'm terrified," Ellis haltingly confessed.

Over the noise of the wind and the creaking timbers, Tibbot assured her, "Not to worry! We've sailed this route plenty of times, and the *Gavilán* has always carried us safely to Spain."

Owen added, "With the winds in our favor, we'll have land in sight within three days."

"Three days?" Ellis' face fell.

After a violent bout of seasickness, Ellis huddled in Finley's arms for over an hour, trembling and groaning. The days at sea didn't worry Finley at all, but she wondered what to expect on the walk to Santiago and what that journey would hold in store for them all. What would she get out of her pilgrimage? She didn't have an ailment that needed healing. *Well, maybe a love-sick heart, but pilgrimages aren't meant for such things. Or are they?*

For her grandmother and for Owen, the walk on the *Camino* had brought assurance, had strengthened their resolve to fight for the freedom of their land, and had made them determined leaders. For Father Whelan, the frequent pilgrimages were a reverent expression of gratitude to the Spanish, who had rescued him from slavery. Finley wondered how the *Camino* would affect her. Maybe unexpectedly change her? Would she find her calling? Or have a vision?

She glanced at Padraig, standing tall at the helm. What did he want out of this pilgrimage? A miracle to cure his blindness, surely! And then there was Tibbot. He'd once considered joining the clergy and was still undecided as to whether to remain in Rockfleet and follow in Owen's footsteps or forge his own path. Much to the dismay of Grace and Owen, Tibbot had recently also befriended several Dutch and English traders, learning about this new Protestant religion to "gain perspective," as he said. Finley was certain that Tibbot would have many deep conversations with Father Whelan in the coming weeks.

That night, they found a berth at Dingle Harbor, its small bay offering shelter from the wind. At dawn, Finley and Ellis pulled their hoods over their heads, yawning, and followed Father Whelan down the plank and through Dingle's sleepy streets to the church. He wanted to begin the day with mass, then whispered about the church's history, his voice trembling with reverence. "How incredible that Spanish believers built the church here, at this spot, so far from their own shores! And they named it Saint James, *Sant Iago* in their tongue. To this day, it is Ireland's most sacred departure point for pilgrims, the northern anchor of the route that connected one Santiago to another. It's a reminder of our joint ancestry and shared faith."

At the end of that day, Ireland disappeared on the horizon behind them as the *Gavilán* forged her way south with a school of silvery dolphins in her wake. Finley's gaze followed the creatures as they sliced and darted through the water, rising in exuberant arches, sending glitters of spray into the relentless wind. As she watched them fling themselves into the air, suspended for a fraction of a heartbeat, then plunge beneath the waves, inhabiting both the world above and below, Falkyn drifted through her mind. These seas were the last he saw. Once, when she'd asked Owen where exactly Falkyn had fallen overboard and disappeared, her uncle hesitated, then admitted he himself was so inebriated on that voyage that no clear memories remained. "Somewhere between Finisterre and Ireland," he'd said. That stretch of ocean, in its enigmatic wildness, had both frightened and fascinated Finley. In her childhood imagination, she had pictured its shadowy mysteries and her father's body floating amid its noiseless world of undulating turquoise light, dark skeletons of shipwrecks, canopies of kelp drifting overhead, Queen Cleo's seaweed castle, from where the goddess must be commanding an army of dolphins, sending them to rescue drowning sailors and fishermen. Well, obviously, not always. As a child, Falkyn's fate bewildered her. So many questions she couldn't articulate ebbed and surged between hope and anger, filling her with despair.

She became aware of Owen standing on the rail next to her. He turned to her with a solemn expression and gave her a knowing nod, the way he had done numerous times when he caught her lost in thought. She was grateful for his presence, for his quiet support.

After their supper on the main deck, while the crew of O'Neills and Bourkes rested nearby, Father Whelan, Tibbot, Padraig, Ellis, and Finley leaned back against the gunnel. Together, they marveled at the vast stretch of black velvet sky above them. The Milky Way rose as a blue spilling of light on the southeastern horizon. "Did you know the Spanish call the Milky Way *El Camino de Santiago?*" Father Whelan asked. "They say the pale ribbon up there is the trail of dust from the pilgrims on the road to Santiago."

Hadn't Tibbot once told Finley a similar tale when she was six or seven years old? He had explained that the Milky Way was made of thousands and thousands of rocks and pebbles. Why would pebbles be up there, she asked, and Tibbot said that one time the old god Lugh was fighting against Tureann, his enemy. Lugh loaded his sling with rocks and flung them at Tureann so hard that they became stuck up there. Now Finley was curious to hear Father Whelan's Milky Way story.

"James, the son of Zebedee, was said to be Jesus's cousin. He came to Spain to spread the faith and then returned to Jerusalem. His remains were later brought to Galicia in a magical stone boat. The ancient Celtic tribes of Galicia buried the sacred bones of Saint James at a place where they had observed the stars raining down that day. They called the place *Sant Iago*, Saint James. Then the tomb was nearly forgotten. Later, the land was occupied by the Saracens."

Father Whelan paused to draw in a long breath. "But when Charlemagne was emperor, Saint James appeared to him in a dream and urged him to find his tomb and to liberate Spain and Galicia from the Saracens.

"Charlemagne asked, 'Where is the tomb and how will I find the way?' In a dream, James advised him to simply follow the Milky Way. And so, Charlemagne led an army of warriors over the Pyrenees, following the path of the Milky Way from east to west. He freed many towns along his march across Spain, and upon arriving at the tomb of

Saint James, he built the first cathedral there. The town was named Santiago de Compostela from that day onward. *Campo stella*, meaning field of stars, because here the stars rained down."

—

The *Gavilán* reached Spain less than two days later. Finley and Ellis stood on tiptoes at the bow after land was sighted, watching its details materialize before their eyes, commenting on how the grayish-green coast looked a lot like Ireland. The tall stone tower, Coruña's ancient lighthouse, rose on a cape west of the harbor.

Ellis gaped at Finley. "The lighthouse! The story you told us at Rockfleet!"

"They call it Hercules' Tower," Tibbot shouted, which immediately prompted Owen to beat his fist on the gunnel in a rhythm. Finley and the crew belted out the chorus of the old "Tower of Hercules" shanty they had learned aboard Grace O'Malley's fleet.

The port sat in a curving embrace of land, and from the hill to their right, clusters of handsome stone houses tumbled down to the water. In the harbor, colorful banners danced high above a forest of masts. Crews on large and small ships hoisted and rolled their wares to and from the busy markets.

Once they were tied up, Geoffrey laid the gangplank, and Father Whelan was the first of the excited group to amble off the ship and onto Spanish soil. A moment later, Ellis and Finley found themselves surrounded by a flurry of foreign languages as Spanish, Italian, Flemish, Portuguese, and Galician merchants swarmed around them. Woodsmoke hung in the air, along with the aroma from meat vendors and bakeries.

The Irish pilgrims spent the first night at a *refugio* Father Whelan knew well from his previous pilgrimages. The brothers of the order of San Andres ran it. With radiant faces, they welcomed their old friend

Padre Whelan. After a delicious meal and communal singing in a large, candle-lit hall, the tired pilgrims fell asleep in an adjacent dorm.

Finley tossed and turned restlessly, trying to get comfortable on her cot. On the *Gavilán*, the swaying had always helped her fall asleep. A part of her missed home, yet she found herself filled with curiosity and anticipation. What would the upcoming days hold in store? She softly whispered Ellis' name, but her friend was already deeply asleep.

In the morning, they stepped into the sunlit streets, following Father Whelan. A few of the Spanish *padres* farewelled them warmly and handed each of them a staff and a large scallop shell on a leather necklace. "Here, for your walk on the *Camino*!"

"*¡Gracias!*" Finley said while she and Ellis marveled at the beautiful shells. Maeve had told Finley that the scallop shell serves to identify pilgrims to the locals and to others on the road, that it's an emblem, a lot like a clan's banner. *A clan of pilgrims*, Finley thought to herself while Ellis tied her shell to her satchel.

"What does the shell symbolize?" Padraig asked.

"Here, can you feel the grooves on the shell? They start from different directions, but all converge on the base of the shell. It's a metaphor for life," Father Whelan explained. "And for the many routes the pilgrims can walk. And how, despite different origins, we all journey to the same destination. It's also great for drinking from streams along the way, of course," Father Whelan explained.

"Or to scoop the biggest portion of oatmeal!" Tibbot joked.

Ellis led Padraig for the first few miles before Finley, then Tibbot, and finally Father Whelan took turns to guide him safely. The dusty gravel path wound away from Coruña and began the ascent into the hills, past scattered farms. Wildflowers nodded as they passed, and clusters of trees pushed against the intense heat of the sky. Covering the miles quickly, they followed the *Camino* south through small villages and stayed at *refugios* in abbeys along the route. The countryside around them soon turned dry and barren as they went. The crowd of pilgrims, speaking many different tongues, increased steadily. Father Whelan led mass every day, either in the wee hours of the morning or during their midday rest breaks.

—

In the sluggish afternoon of the fourth day, they found themselves barely a few miles from Santiago when Owen, wiping sweat from his face, called for a much-needed break near a creek. "Let's rest here and wait until it gets cooler."

With relieved sighs, Finley and Ellis plunged into the shade of the trees, staring tiredly at their grimy legs. Owen, Tibbot, and Padraig plopped down next to them. They had started walking early, but the surprising intensity of the Spanish sun had sapped all their energy. Finley caught Father Whelan's pale and tired expression as he leaned against a tree trunk, seemingly lost in thought.

When the late afternoon brought cooler temperatures, a group of pilgrims settled nearby. They started singing a simple, repetitive hymn in Latin and cheerfully encouraged the Irish to join in the chorus: "The path may be steep, dusty, and dry, onwards to Santiago. Soon we'll arrive, you and I, onwards to Santiago." The reverent music lifted everyone's mood and matched the otherworldly beauty of the afternoon sun that bathed the entire landscape before them in vivid and warm colors.

Then they rose, dusted themselves off, and resumed their pace, halting and stiff at first, then falling into the familiar rhythm, their anticipation growing with each step.

They covered the last miles quickly and flooded into the town of Santiago. After following the narrow alleys, a vast plaza opened up before them, a mighty cathedral in its center. Finley's jaw hung open in wonder at the towering structure with its ornately carved portal.

She'd never seen anything like it in Ireland. The warm-colored stone façade and the many ornaments and architectural details competed for her attention. Ellis and Tibbot excitedly described the sight to Padraig. His honest and knowing smile moved Finley; his expression of awe, despite not being able to see what she could.

"Mass begins in less than an hour. We can sit down here until then." Father Whelan motioned to a shaded part of the plaza. They were approached by two nuns and a few young children who wheeled a handcart filled with baked goods.

"Almond cakes!" Padraig cheered after catching the aroma wafting through the air. He had discovered this delicacy in a bakery in Coruña on the day of their arrival.

The children handed them the cakes and welcomed the pilgrims, *"Bienvenido, bienvenida!"*

"Why do they give away free cakes?" Ellis wondered.

"They see it as a privilege to live here in the presence of the tomb of the apostle," Father Whelan explained. "The hospitality towards all pilgrims, no matter where they're from, has a long tradition here."

Finley silently devoured the sweet cake as more pilgrims arrived, filling the plaza with multilingual chatter.

Father Whelan soon led them into the cathedral through the massive portico. Many other dusty pilgrims surrounded them, whispering with astonishment and awe. Ellis and Finley gawked at the decorated interior and the altar. All exhaustion dissolved as reverent silence spread over the international congregation. The service in Latin began.

During mass, the soaring pillars pulled Finley's gaze aloft. Her mind wandered to the promise they were given, that incredible things might happen here, and how, by walking the *Camino*, all their sins would be forgiven. She tried to remember her last sin. *Maybe those jealous thoughts about Neasa.* And the promised miracles? *Padraig,* she wondered, *will he be able to see again?* She cast a sideways glance at his bowed head, wondering if his blindness could be taken away and sight be magically bestowed on him right at this very moment.

And what about Owen and Tibbot? She knew what miracle they were praying for. Rockfleet and the freedom of Clew Bay, of course. Grace and her warriors. Their safety, the future of their lands. All the Bourkes, MacDermots, O'Neills, and the O'Malleys' other allies. Finley's chest tightened, but she willed herself to take a deep breath, close her eyes, and bundle her worries into a silent prayer for protection.

—

The Irish pilgrims arrived back in Coruña a few days later. The hospitality of Santiago, the food, the friendships with other pilgrims along the route, the honest conversations, and the communal singing had made quite an impression on Finley. Tired, worn, and grimy, fulfilled and smiling nevertheless, they all shuffled towards the harbor, eager to find the *Gavilán*. After the hot days on dusty roads, the seagulls' urgent wailing and the cool breeze rustling in her hair felt utterly refreshing.

"Finally, we made it!" Finley exhaled, looking forward to sailing home.

"Almost there. I can see the harbor," Owen panted as they hobbled through town.

Padraig, sniffing the air, stopped at a bakery. "Hmmm, almond cakes! Why don't we take some home with us?"

Before anyone could protest, Father Whelan and Padraig disappeared into the bakery, quick as weasels. Finley, Ellis, Tibbot, and Owen waited in the shade of a building across from the bakery, sighing and fanning themselves with their hats.

Above Finley's head hung a wooden sign. *Libros y cartografía.* Her eyes widened when she turned to the exquisite map in the shop window. She gasped and elbowed Tibbot to get his attention.

—

Marina lowered herself at her angled worktable and carefully drew quill and ink closer. Charts, rolled parchments, and books surrounded her. The map in front of her depicted the entire coastline of northern Spain and western France. The customer who commissioned the work requested an extensive, detailed map that included trade routes, mountain passes, abbeys, major towns, ports, rivers, and bridges.

Spread out on Inyo's worktable was a partially completed map of the Caribbean and South America. He was to combine already existing charts into a single map, with updated details of the continent's coast and ports. He dipped his slender brush into red paint and added tiny scales to the sea monster in the lower corner of the map, a horned creature with talons.

Inyo was so intensely focused that it was some time before he felt someone's eyes on his figure. The person standing on the other side of his worktable held an outrageously colorful bag adorned with a pilgrim's scallop shell. Inyo found himself face-to-face with a girl, her head adorned with astonishingly red hair, the likes of which he had never seen before. He wondered how long she had been watching him. And why. Her arms and her face were incredibly pale and dotted with freckles arranged like the innumerable stars in the night sky.

She studied his map with a tilted head, then whispered something to one of her companions, who uttered a few syllables in a strange language and nodded at the map approvingly. Inyo glanced at the companion, then back at the girl, shocked to see her now looking straight at him. There was a tangible current between them, a river that surged along the beams of their eyes. The floor beneath Inyo seemed to lift into a slow spin. His gaze zigzagged between her mesmerizing eyes and her hair, waves of fire, of burnished gold and sunset red.

The group then turned to Marina, who pointed out a few maps hanging further back and began a conversation with the tallest man of the group, who spoke Spanish quite well. *Maybe her father?* Inyo wondered while he watched them select two maps.

The girl turned her head one more time, glanced at Inyo's map, and then beamed at him. His cheeks instantly filled with warmth. He didn't know what to do, where to point his eyes, how to hold his body, or his hands. Unnoticed, a small tear of red paint dripped off his brush and splattered on the floor.

Another customer demanded Inyo's attention, and he had to fetch a roll of parchment from the storage cabinet near the stairs. By the time he handed it to the man and collected the payment, the group of pilgrims had disappeared. Inyo ran out into the street, whipping his head from side to side. Would they have gone right to the harbor or left toward Santiago? He didn't know. They were gone, and all he was left with was a pang of sadness.

Señora O'Malley

The *Gaviota* had been at sea for a few days, sailing due north on favorable summer breezes, as Juan said had been done for many generations.

"These are perfect weeks for sailing to Ireland, so long as we're back home before August ends. Bad storms up there, lemme tell you! Got caught up there once in *the worst gale* . . . almost didn't make it," Juan admitted to Inyo with a wry grin. "The sea is a fickle thing—gentle one day, out to kill you the next. When it comes to the Atlantic, between spring storms and autumn gales, we have maybe three or four good months for Ireland, that's it. And here's the most mysterious thing: the return trip always takes much longer. Always! Even with ideal winds. Must be some Celtic sea goddess trying to haul in our poor sailor souls. Wonder what she wants?" Juan shrugged, then elbowed Antonio. "Maybe a handsome young seafarer like you, hm?"

In preparation for their arrival in Ireland, Antonio, Ansa, and some of the others taught Inyo fragments of Gaeilge, the Irish language. *Good Day. Thank you. Where is the harbor? Where is the tavern?*

"Essential phrases all vagabond sailors and traders need," Antonio chuckled.

Shortly after dawn on the fourth day, they heard, "Land in sight!"

from the lookout. The coastline of Ireland hove into view, and Inyo's pulse quickened. He had never been this far from home. Juan's nice new set of maps showed the whole southwestern portion of Ireland as a fluttering of finger-like peninsulas and islands jutting out into the wild and vast Atlantic.

The details of the coast sharpened before Inyo's eyes. The route would take them west-by-northwest, past Mizen Head, between Scariff and the Skellig Islands, and finally into Dingle Bay. They would anchor there for the night and resupply the ship.

Inyo and Ansa leaned out over the gunnel and watched the coast to starboard, where sunbeams played on foaming white and emerald waves that crashed into the steep, gray headlands. The *Gaviota* rolled in the mighty swell. She made steady progress and soon turned into a large bay, where a few fishing vessels dotted the water.

The crew took in sail. Antonio leaned out over the bow, shouting course corrections as Juan piloted his ship through rocky narrows into a much smaller bay. The village of Dingle hugged its north shore with thatched-roofed cottages that huddled around the dock and the church.

Francisca had told Inyo once, "Most Irish pilgrims traditionally sail from Dingle. The church of Santiago in Dingle is a sacred place, the starting point for the *peregrinos* who travel from this part of Ireland to Spain. Ancient legends speak of Irish pilgrims bringing hope and healing with them from their island. You see, a few hundred years ago, while the Normans burned and plundered churches everywhere, our Irish brothers and sisters kept the faith alive and also hid many precious books and manuscripts."

Inyo's gaze wandered over to the market, to the fishermen selling their fresh catch, barrels of fish, salted and dried, the farmers with crates of produce, weavers and basket-makers offering their wares. A handful of merchants came up to them as soon as the *Gaviota* was docked.

After an hour, Juan had sold spices, casks of wine, and iron ingots. Meanwhile, Antonio, Diego, Pedro, and Inyo were sent to buy fresh food. The sun hung on the horizon by the time everything was finally stowed and tidied up. Juan scrutinized the decks, as meticulous as ever, then nodded with a satisfied grunt and dismissed the crew.

With his leather purse on his belt, Inyo followed his shipmates as they ambled toward the tavern. He joined Antonio and Ansa at a table inside, and their drinks soon appeared. Juan was the last one through the door, and when he entered, the innkeeper looked up and laughed, "Don Juan! You Old Salt!"

"¡Rory, *mi amigo*!" Juan cheered. They slapped each other's backs and carried on in roaring fragments of Spanish and Gaeilge.

Rory turned to the crew. "Welcome, my friends, welcome to Dingle!" He lifted a mug and thundered, "*¡Salud!*"

One of the patrons at a nearby table started beating a large drum while two others sang a cheerful tune. The strange and beautiful Gaeilge lyrics seemed to Inyo like a door into another realm. The musicians taught the Spaniards the chorus so they could join in. Swept up into the rousing rhythm, Ansa smiled at Inyo as they sang. When the musicians took a break, Inyo ordered a bowl of mutton and vegetable stew, which he shared with Ansa. The long journey had made them tired, though, and after just an hour of dining and singing, they headed back to the ship.

—

The crew weighed anchor at first light and got underway quickly. It would be less than a full day of sailing to get to Galway. The weather looked promising, and the westerly winds picked up as soon as they left the bay. Juan knew the currents well and confidently sailed between the western tip of Dingle Peninsula and an island with steep hills. The *Gaviota* followed the coast, running broad reach before the wind.

The bright sails contrasted strikingly against the rich blue of the sky above Inyo, while he lingered at the bow at the end of his morning watch. Impressive headwalls came into view to starboard. Juan had told him to watch for these remarkably tall, sheer cliffs and the fierce waves crashing into their bases. Undulating and massive walls of dark rock reached straight up to the heavens, where splatters of seabirds clouded their rims.

Inyo ambled to the larboard gunnel, watching three long, flat-topped islands to the north—the Aran Islands. Waves of incredible power crashed against their abrupt and imposing cliffs while the *Gaviota's* new heading took her into Galway Bay.

Inyo spotted movement in the distance. *A ship!* It darted out from behind one of the Arans, sailing swiftly towards them under full sail.

Pedro's voice rang from the lookout, "Sail ho! Just abaft port beam! Oh—there's more than one!"

Maybe a fishing crew or merchants? Inyo wondered. Antonio and Juan shot anxious glances at each other.

Eventually, Pedro caught a glimpse of one of their pennants and shouted, "They—they're O'Malley ships!"

Juan groaned. The mood on board shifted. Moments ago, there had been excited chatter about their arrival in Galway, but now dread hung over the decks and Diego hissed, "*¡Corsarios!*"

Inyo's insides tensed up. The possibility of pirates had been mentioned before they departed. "Galway trades the world's best hides, the finest wool, and pays us well for our wine and wares. But many of the merchants now report more and more attacks," Juan had warned the crew. "Remember Maldonado? Last year, half his cargo was taken! These marauders have several fast galleys and a system for waylaying Spanish vessels. Let's pray we'll be lucky this time."

Inyo watched the ships' progress. Both galleys sailed under canvas and oar. He had heard of the O'Malley clan more than once. Wild, uncivilized, ruthless, and unpredictable Irish thieves, Antonio had called them. Inyo made his way back to the bridge, where Diego argued with Juan and angrily pointed towards Galway. "Come on! Surely we can make it!"

Juan shook his head. "With our hold full of barrels and iron, sitting deep in the water ? While their skinny galleys are flying at us at twice the speed?"

"Let's run a shot across their bow, then they'll leave us alone," Diego growled.

"That could be risky. We're here to trade, not fight." Juan glanced over at the approaching vessels. "They probably have four times as many men as us, all of 'em armed. Besides, if we rile 'em, they'll ram and skewer us."

Inyo knew Juan was right, but had difficulty keeping his breathing under control. Many of the crew cursed loudly as they stayed the course, still making close to six knots. The wind was calmer here, east of the Arans, but the O'Malleys were sailing hard on their heels, and one of their bow chasers fired a warning shot. A sickening whistling sound followed the boom, and the *Gaviota's* crew ducked in shock. The cannon shot splashed into the waves nearby, missing them by a few yards. Inyo hesitated before pulling himself back up, legs trembling, turning to look at the enemy vessels closing in. From one of them came a shout in Spanish: "*Gaviota*! Heave to!"

Juan ordered the sails hove to. This time, instead of the usual frenzy, the shipmates seemed to dally deliberately. A fierce roar wafted from the O'Malley galley closest to the *Gaviota*. Some of the warriors were singing loudly while pounding their fists on the gunnel. The captain shouted orders, and the men hurried to work their sails, angle a cannon, pull in the oars, and ready grappling hooks.

It was a sturdy, brightly painted vessel, with a red stern canopy and carved flourishes of angular, tangled knots along its railings. The banners displayed the O'Malley coat of arms, a red boar on yellow ground. Inyo studied the warriors on the main deck, their varicolored garments, and practiced movements. Oddly, they didn't look as uncivilized as Inyo had imagined them.

And the captain . . .! There was something peculiar about his posture and shape. Inyo narrowed his eyes, confused. *A woman comandante?* Antonio, all pale-faced, uttered, "God help us. It's Señora O'Malley!"

Someone else shouted the name again until the entire crew had heard it. Most of them shook their heads and frowned. Ansa's face, however, was filled with awe and curiosity, rather than apprehension.

Grappling hooks whipped through the air and clawed into the *Gaviota's* bulwark with crunching thuds, making Juan writhe and groan. The bobbing vessels slowly drew close. Two heavy gangplanks were placed across the gunnels while several dozen O'Malley muskets pointed at the Spaniards. Inyo awkwardly glanced at the grim and rugged faces of the Irish women and men.

Señora O'Malley and two of her crew started making their way across on the plank. A formidable cutlass in her one hand and a pistol in her belt confirmed everyone's fears. When she spied Juan and Antonio, a leisurely grin, like that of a hunter, flashed across her weathered face.

And then Inyo noticed a few wavy strands of reddish hair streaming out from under her cap and down to her shoulders. It immediately lit up a memory inside Inyo. *Like the pilgrim girl last month!* Since that enigmatic encounter, he had often found himself thinking and wondering about her.

Inyo tumbled out of his daydream as Señora O'Malley deftly landed on their main deck with a thump. Adopting a proud stance and obstinate expression, she faced Juan, who drew his hat and bowed deeply. O'Malley greeted them in her native tongue. Pleasantries were exchanged; Juan spoke Gaeilge well enough after his many years of trading with Ireland.

To Inyo's surprise, Señora O'Malley answered in fluent Spanish. "*¡Bienvenidos a Irlanda, valientes marineros!* Welcome to beautiful Galway Bay, filled to the brim with fish. Welcome to Galway town, where upstanding sailors such as you will find true hospitality and the chance to sell your goods. Pray tell what treasures the *Gaviota* carries in her hold?"

"Señora O'Malley, our humble caravel carries merely some, um— some iron and wine."

"Ah, Spanish wine, excellent!" She paused with a genial grin and then exclaimed, "My friends, I must inform you of many *terrible dangers* lurking between here and Galway. But since Spain is our dear friend, we feel deeply obligated to assist you!"

O'Malley dramatically extended her sword out over the bay. "The water is shallow in places, with many hidden rocks. Dangerous currents have carried hundreds of ships onto the cliffs and many sailors to their deaths!" She continued with a well-rehearsed look of concern. "And some of the local clans have a habit of harassing innocent merchants such as you." With that, she winked at Juan, whose cheeks turned red.

"But fear not! I will provide my most experienced men as pilots for safe passage."

Inyo was alarmed by the sight of Diego's clenched fists and a growl escaping from under his breath, "What a disgrace of a woman! Should we stand here while she mocks and robs us?"

Antonio and Juan, however, stayed utterly calm. Inyo couldn't help but admire their composure. Juan gave a polite nod of agreement as he requested—so Inyo guessed—the price for that service. "*Cá mhéad atá air sin?*"

O'Malley answered benevolently, "*Es un peaje insignificante, nada del otro mundo.* It's but the tiniest of fees, it really is nothing at all." She waved over a young man who carried a small roll of parchment.

Juan took the list, read it, and nodded. "Inyo, Diego, bring up twenty casks of wine. Antonio, fetch my purse."

Diego growled and abruptly lunged at O'Malley, but Antonio had anticipated Diego's move, gripped his sleeve, and held him back firmly. Señora O'Malley glowered at Diego, shaking her head and clicking her tongue at his bad manners. Juan then passed her a handful of coins and received a hardy slap on his back that made him wobble.

Inyo was tasked with helping to load the wine. Along with his shipmates, he rolled the heavy casks across the plank and onto the O'Malley vessel while their pointed weapons ensured cooperation. When it was all done, he wiped the sweat off his forehead with shaky hands as the enemy galleys turned and retreated, sails unfurling under Señora O'Malley's commands, oars clawing at the waves in the rhythm of a shanty that the wind carried towards him.

Juan exhaled, "Could've been worse!" Diego and Inyo stared at him with incredulous expressions, shaking their heads. Less than two hours later, they finally arrived in Galway.

—

Earlier that day, Finley and her father hitched a cart behind Cormac, while Finley's mother, Fergal, and Padraig loaded crates of vegetables, bundles of fabric, sacks of fine wool, farm tools, and baskets. Ronin and Padraig rode in the cart, while Teagan, Ellis, and Finley led the way to Galway, followed by Maeve. Between spring and early autumn, they made the trip to town for market days twice a week.

The sun warmed their faces as they crossed the stone bridge over the Corrib and entered Galway. Its narrow alleys, tightly packed stone houses, and shops were encircled by a blocky wall that gave the city a rectangular, orderly appearance.

Foreign merchants and countless piles of cargo crowded the waterfront near the western gate. English soldiers patrolled the harbor and marched through town. In its center, a short walk from the river, Saint Nicholas church rose like a sentinel over the busy square.

Finley and Teagan set up the market stand. With harvest season upon them, the farm tools were in high demand along with Maeve's colorful blankets and wide-brimmed straw hats. Teagan's wooden figurines, which he had carved over the past weeks, were also on display. Many customers smiled when they held them up and studied the details of the small animals.

Ronin and Teagan scampered away to look at the ships while Ellis, Finley, and her mother manned the table. In the afternoon, it was Finley's and Ellis' turn to have a break. They hurried out of the city gate, back across the stone bridge over the rushing river, and down to the shore. There was a short stretch of beach where waves caressed the sheen of sand and seagulls squalled above their heads. More and more clouds had drifted in from the west, obscuring the sun.

They glanced over their shoulders, across the river, where a gathering of ships was docked next to the city wall. French and Spanish traders swarmed the landing, and the bay was filled with even more anchored ships, awaiting their turn. Finley paused several times to admire the vessels. Beautiful caravels and carracks. "You and ships!" Ellis teased her jokingly while she pulled on Finley's arm.

Inwardly, Finley smiled. When they returned from their pilgrimage last month, Ellis's first words upon stepping onto Barna's dock were, "Never again!" Ellis had been horribly seasick on the return trip and had raged, wailed, and cursed for days on end. The memory made Finley's lips twitch in silent laughter.

"What's so funny?" Ellis wondered.

"Nothing, I just remembered something from the *Camino*."

"Hm." Ellis glanced suspiciously at Finley, but then her expression became thoughtful. "You know, I was really expecting a miracle for Padraig . . ."

"I'd had the same hope." Finley nodded as she relived the pilgrimage and her fervent prayers, especially for *that* miracle. However, Padraig was still blind.

"It doesn't seem to bother him, though." Ellis shrugged. "At least not as much as before."

For Finley, however, the unanswered prayer had led to disappointment, a stirring of nagging doubts and anger. If Padraig hadn't been cured, hadn't been given the miracle everyone so fervently prayed for, would all their other prayers also go unanswered? Was God selectively healing and protecting certain people and ignoring others for some reason? Did he have favorites who were given all the blessings, like Neasa, while others, like Padraig, were left out? Where was the justice in all of this?

Finley's thoughts drifted back to that summer up in Clew Bay, the attacks on the MacDermots, the cruelty of it all, the gloomy expressions of everyone at Rockfleet, and how paralyzed she had felt that day. She didn't know what to do with the fear, with her questions and doubts, her bewilderment and disappointment. The helplessness had morphed into a strange rage deep inside of her, one she kept tucked away, trying to stifle it. The pilgrimage didn't bring her the calm and inner strength she'd hoped it might. And over the past year, the English hadn't just raised taxes and enforced stricter laws; their numbers had also increased. More patrols were out and about now. Finley's eyes fell on the English governor's mansion on the other side of Galway as she kept brooding.

On top of all of this, Brendan and Neasa's wedding was coming up. It loomed, unavoidably, and agitated Finley endlessly. The entire village was invited. She dreaded that day, dreaded having to will her feet to walk into that church and to compel her face to smile.

"Oh, Fin, you won't believe this," Ellis interrupted her thoughts. "The other day my da' asked if Padraig would be the first one of us getting married, or me."

"My parents brought up the marriage thing not too long ago as well," Finley huffed, then imitated the deep voice of her father, "'Well, now that you're all grown, Finley, isn't it about time to find a hardworking and handsome lad?'" The girls snickered. "So, how about it, Ellis, who do you have your eye on?"

Ellis shook her head with a mock shudder. "To be honest, I—um, I'm not going to marry."

"Ever?"

Ellis shrugged. "I don't know why, but I just don't *want* to be married."

"But Ellis, what if *Cormac* asks you?" Finley joked.

Ellis quickly flipped over on her hands and knees, nodded passionately, and stomped her hands as if they were hoofs. Finley laughed out loud at Ellis' wild antics, the way she shook her hair and her convincing whinny.

"Come on then, time to get you back to your *one true love!*" Finley rose and brushed the dirt off her pants.

They ambled back towards the town and crossed the bridge. Finley glanced briefly at the harbor where an older Spanish trading vessel cast off, the crew bustling about on the decks. Finley's gaze fell on one of the figures, a young sailor. A vague hint of recognition dawned on her. She hesitated, unaware that Ellis continued over the bridge, leaving her behind. The Spaniard turned to look in her direction. *Could it be—?* She leaned out over the bridge's rail, lifted her hand halfway, hesitated, then raised it high into the air, waving, looking at him, willing him to see her, to lock eyes with her. But the force of the river rushing beneath her propelled the ship into the bay, farther and farther away. Soon, the figures were so small she couldn't tell anymore which one of them was him. She lowered her hand and felt herself flooded with sudden sadness. Ellis called to her, urging Finley to catch up.

—

At the very same time, another set of eyes ranged over the ships and the bay. Galway's newly appointed English governor, Sir Aldred Bensbury, lingered near the windows of his office in the governor's mansion, located on a slope outside the city walls, not far from the docks. The anemic afternoon light cast his face in a pale mask of stern lines. His young wife, Sarah, approached haltingly, puzzled by the rigid gaze on her husband's face as he took in the town and the port.

They had arrived two days ago, and Sarah had already explored the town and met the servants of her new home. She had written to her father earlier that day, telling him about Galway. *I love it here already. It's a surprisingly prosperous and cultured town, a busy trading center*, she wrote. *The mansion is quite large and stylishly furnished. The staff are polite and so very friendly, and from what I can see, the townsfolk are loyal to our Queen. I think Aldred will find it an easy assignment.*

Aldred ignored Sarah while his two senior advisors entered and joined him at the window. "I see now what you mean," Aldred commented while he studied the pennants of the merchant vessels dotting the bay. "So many Spanish and Portuguese."

"Commerce with Portugal and Spain has flourished for decades, sir," one of Aldred's advisors replied. "The people of Galway thrive, especially the wealthier merchants. We have their cooperation and they do pay their taxes, but . . ."

Aldred's eyebrows lifted as he turned to his advisors. "But what?"

"Outside of the city wall, it's an entirely different situation. The

Connacht countryside is home to wild clans. Primitive farmers and fishermen who obstinately resist English law," one of the men huffed defeatedly.

With an obvious air of superiority, the other advisor spat, "Damn these filthy hordes and their rebellious ways!"

Aldred's silent and heavy brooding filled the room. Sarah remembered how the queen had made it quite clear when she appointed him that he was to make obedient subjects of the inhabitants of this part of Ireland as quickly as possible. He'd been given the order to enforce absolute allegiance to England in all of Connacht.

"Though Ireland is part of the Queen's kingdom, many Irish still defy her authority. They cling to the Catholic faith and scheme with our enemies," Aldred had explained to Sarah on their way from London to Galway. The foreign vessels in the port symbolized flourishing trade, which generated more tax revenue for England. However, Queen Elizabeth was also concerned about strengthening economic and political relations between Ireland and Spain.

During their courtship, her husband had dazzled Sarah with tales of his naval assignments in his younger years. He'd told her about the time when the Spanish landed troops in the southwest of Ireland, when he was a naval captain under Admiral Winter, and how he had defeated the invaders. Aldred then described the Spanish surrender at Smerwick, how hundreds of Spaniards and their Irish allies were put to the sword. She remembered being taken aback by the way in which he seemed to enjoy the recollection of that bloody day.

"Above all," Aldred told Sarah, "the Crown counts on *me* to ensure that Connacht complies and that the Irish rebels cannot join forces with the Spaniards. King Philip's desire to overthrow Queen Elizabeth is well known. A base in Ireland could be a big step in that direction and must be prevented at all costs."

Sarah had nodded fervently, filled with patriotic fervor, brimming with the desire to be supportive of Aldred, of Queen Elizabeth, of England. But now Ireland would be her home. And the people she'd met so far didn't look and sound like the heinous and heathen foes she had envisioned. In fact, they all seemed law-abiding and exceedingly kind.

The Gathering Storm

GREENWICH PALACE, ENGLAND 1587

Elizabeth swung herself into the saddle and drew herself up to her full height. "I shall take my leave now. Tom, ride with me," she demanded, glancing back at her courtiers and the men of the hunting party who were bent over the stag, preparing to return with it to the palace. Her stallion reared and then took off in a loping run.

"Yes, Your Majesty!" Thomas McDarren shouted as he hurried to mount his horse.

The hoofs of McDarren's mount thundered behind her, but she was already far in the lead, riding her favorite charger, Apollo, a white and gray bundle of speed and agility. Elizabeth had always been a natural on horseback, proud to be a skilled huntress still. Even though being an accomplished equestrian was required of royalty, she also had an innate, intuitive connection with the animal.

While she was in residence at Greenwich, her favorite palace and place of birth, she made it a point to ride almost every day, usually with Robin at her side. But now that Robin was abroad, leading her troops in the Low Countries, she enjoyed having Thomas as her companion instead. He had become Master of the Hunt at Greenwich two years ago, and there was no one she trusted more with the horses. He had been on outings and hunts with her and Robin many times, and she valued his company.

Elizabeth ripped off her cap, allowing her hair to stream out behind her as she galloped through the forest of the sprawling estate. Hunting and horseback riding meant unsupervised time away from court, away from the stiff and suffocating conventions of royal life. Here in the woods of Greenwich, flying through the wilderness like an arrow, she was free.

Thomas finally caught up with her, and they slowed down upon reaching a stream. "Your Majesty and her esteemed companions did very well indeed today," he flattered her.

"Thank you, Tom," she replied with an affable smile. "How is your daughter?"

"Oh, she is well, thank you, ma'am. I receive frequent letters," he said.

In a clearing between the trees, Elizabeth noticed a scattered herd of deer drinking from the creek. For a few moments, all she could hear was birdsong, the horses' breath, and the gentle wind in the branches that danced above her head. She inhaled deeply, savoring the peacefulness of the moment. Apollo shook his mane and whickered. The deer, sensing danger, lifted their heads and flicked their ears. Elizabeth watched them bound away.

Here I am, she thought, *a hunter stalking unsuspecting beasts of the forest, but in Spain's eyes, I am the prey.* She was acutely aware of how underestimated she was, at home and abroad. Scrutinized, attacked, and hunted. The pope had declared her an infidel and heretic, an abomination in the eyes of God. Constant dangers overshadowed her reign and her realm.

Her shoulders stiffened as she contemplated the imminent prospect of war. Tensions with Spain had been simmering for years, although the earlier threat of Spanish troops landing in Ireland hadn't come to pass. Yet.

King Philip's violent efforts to suppress the Protestant faith in the Spanish-controlled Low Countries and his unreasonable taxes on the Dutch led to bloody and armed rebellions there. But despite using increasing force with brutal abandon for twenty years, Philip had been unable to defeat the Dutch. However, he showed no signs of giving up. *They keep him distracted for now, but if he ever succeeds there, my own kingdom will be the next target for Philip's crusade*, Elizabeth worried.

She remembered the terrible news she received a year ago when the Spanish army, led by the Duke of Parma with forty thousand men, laid siege to Antwerp. The threat not only endangered English trade, but having a major seaport like Antwerp under Spanish control was like a dagger aimed straight at England.

She pledged military support to the Dutch rebels and sent Robin to lead her armies there, but Antwerp fell despite her intervention. Her spies now warned her that King Philip of Spain was in a boiling rage over her involvement and openly spoke of wanting to topple her from the throne.

His Army of Flanders, the mightiest in all of Europe, is already in Antwerp, right across the Channel from England! Elizabeth shuddered when she remembered the detailed reports of bloodshed and terror that Philip's troops had inflicted in the Low Countries. He could easily invade her kingdom at any moment.

It was imperative to prevent that by any means necessary. Again and again, she had authorized Francis Drake and other privateers to raid Spanish ports and ships in the Caribbean, robbing them on the high seas to disrupt the endless flow of wealth bringing Spanish gold to England. But it wasn't enough. Even Drake's most successful forays had failed to derail or delay Philip's war effort.

Then, in the spring, Drake attacked Cadiz in southern Spain. Elizabeth had read the reports of the many large armed galleons that had been sunk and the vast amount of supplies that Drake had successfully destroyed. These ships and provisions served one purpose only: to invade England and to harm her.

Apollo turned his velvety ears towards her as if to ask a question, as if to discern her hesitation. "The day is coming to an end, Tom. Let us return to the palace." Elizabeth gathered the reins and wheeled Apollo away from the stream.

"Yes, Your Majesty."

Later, when Elizabeth arrived in her privy chambers, her ladies rose. "Leave me, please," she commanded. When the door finally closed, she allowed herself to collapse at her desk. "Oh Robin," she whispered, "I wish you were here!"

Not having her closest friend by her side during all this turmoil left her feeling more alone and vulnerable than ever before. He would have calmed her, advised her, and given her the clarity of mind to face what was coming. She unfolded his last letter, reveled in his words, soaked up the comfort they offered, and pressed the parchment to her chest.

—

A few hours later, Elizabeth had regained her composure and entered the main hall with a determined stride. Her chief advisor and her principal secretary were waiting for her.

"Your Majesty, our spies have intercepted communications between King Philip and the Duke of Parma. The King intends to send a large naval force to bring Parma's troops over to England. There are many reports of frantic activity in Spain's ports and shipyards. King Philip has assembled and armed every seaworthy vessel he could find, gathered thousands of troops, and stockpiled provisions in Lisbon. Our sources have never seen anything like it."

Elizabeth's fists balled up, and her face darkened. *So it's finally happening.* She straightened herself, despite the knot of apprehension in her stomach. "Raise the Royal Standard—we'll muster the trained bands, and anyone else who can stand and fight. But pray God, we can stop them at sea where we have a chance!" She turned to her chief minister with a strengthened resolve. "Summon Lord Effingham and Lord Howard, along with Drake and Frobisher. And any captains they deem should attend us. Time to plan a *proper* welcome for Spain's navy!"

Duende

IRELAND, MAY 1588

Ronin tumbled into the workshop, laughing, "Uncle Tibbot is here!"

"Excellent!" Finley looked up from a basket she was weaving.

Maeve rose from her workbench near the window. "Go, tell Da' and Teagan," she said, placing down her carving knife and wooden bowl. They both released themselves into the warm spring sunshine, stretched their backs, and watched Ronin rush off as fast as his tiny legs allowed.

Finley smiled. The sheep shearing was Tibbot's favorite chore, and he had come down to Barna last spring for it as well. She saw her uncle ride through the meadow towards them on his horse, Arlyn. From this distance, he looked like a young version of Owen.

Tibbot shouted cheerfully, "Finley, Maeve, I'm so glad to see you!"

Finley reached for Arlyn's bridle while Tibbot dismounted.

"So good that you're here!" Maeve hugged him tightly.

"Arlyn doesn't even seem tired." Finley patted the horse's dark-brown neck.

"Well, you know how he loves to stretch his legs. I don't think all of Connacht is big enough to wear him out." Tibbot grinned as he gently punched Finley's shoulder.

"How are things at Rockfleet?" Maeve asked.

"Owen and Ma' are busy with the fields, the cattle, and sheep. The ships are in good shape, and they'll start heading out soon."

"I hope it goes well for them." Maeve nodded. "Galway's having a slow start to spring trading so far. Not many merchants have made it up here yet."

Tibbot's eyebrows lifted. "Strange. On the other hand, it's understandable. Tariffs have gone up for everyone, locals and traders alike. And tensions between England and Spain keep rising. There's even talk of imminent war."

"We've heard that, too," Maeve remarked.

"The English are clamping down hard everywhere," Tibbot huffed. "But they have to be careful not to escalate things in Ireland. They can't afford open rebellion here since their main focus is to defend the realm against Spain. But we are next, that's for sure. You probably heard that the governor arrested a few O'Connors and Bourkes not too far from Cranford. We think he had inside help."

An uncomfortable silence followed. Finley had seen how the new English governor had made life hard for everyone in Connacht, had increased taxes and fees, threatened more violence, and kept sending out increasingly aggressive and suspicious patrols.

"Well, let's hope for a few calm months," Tibbot said.

Finley asked him, "How long will you stay?"

"At least until harvest is done, or until my sister can't stand me anymore," he chuckled.

Finley nodded with a smile. From spring planting until harvest season, the more hands there were on the farm, the better. Tibbot made for the workshop that stood adjacent to the barn, where he found a pair of shears near the forge and then took off to join Brian and Fergal. Finley led Arlyn into the barn, where he dipped his muzzle into the trough next to Merla and Cormac.

—

At the end of the day, Ronin and Finley huddled next to Tibbot near the fire and watched him whittle a small, ugly gnome with a wide-brimmed cap and pointy beard. Tibbot inclined his head to Ronin and whispered, "Do you know what this is?"

Ronin shook his head with a look of suspicion.

"That's a Spanish house gnome, a *duende!*" Tibbot continued, "The *duendes* come out late at night to help people finish their work or to clean up. But if they find any children who forgot to wash their hands or feet, they might bite off a finger or a toe!"

"Really?" Ronin gasped with wide eyes.

"Don't worry. *Duendes* only live in Spain!" Tibbot laughed as he placed the wooden goblin next to several other figurines that he, Finley, and Teagan had carved. "For market day," he said.

Ronin still stared at the figurine with a shudder and pouting lips.

—

In the governor's mansion on the other side of Galway, Sarah Bensbury's chambermaid, Aisling, opened a set of heavy curtains, bowed to her mistress as she wished her a good morning, and then scurried out of the room. Sarah awoke with a roaring headache and the dull soreness of bruises around her neck, on her face, and on her arms. Tiny flutters of trapped emotions stirred hopelessly in her ribcage, and she labored to draw a ragged breath. How could she have foreseen . . .?

Over the past year, Aldred had started drinking heavily, and Sarah had become the target of his unpredictability and wrath. The first time his hand had hit her face, she was utterly stunned. Then she had dutifully forgiven him, had tried to convince herself it didn't actually happen, and that it wouldn't happen again. What else could she do? *He's a busy, overworked man,* she kept telling herself, *the wine made him do it, he didn't mean to hurt me, he just can't control himself. I must devote myself to him more, and then things will be like they used to be, surely they will, they must!*

This morning, however, something had shifted. She realized she was only fooling herself as she stared in the mirror. Her swollen face spoke of the hopelessness of her predicament, and the thick ice of despondency permeated her limbs. A door closed inside of her. Gone were sweet memories of their courtship, when she was taken by Aldred's seemingly polite manners and the prospect of his promotion to governor of Connacht. Gone were the times when she had completely trusted him. She moved here with him right after the wedding, and now she was alone in a faraway country, where she missed her father more and more.

Sarah glanced at her wedding band. She used to love it, but now it revolted her, seemed to choke the life out of her. She pulled it off her finger and slipped it into the drawer of her desk. After quickly dressing, Sarah covered her bruises with powder and then headed downstairs to check in with the servants in the kitchen. They smiled and curtsied as they uttered their "Good morning, milady" in broken English. As always, they were kind and amiable to her. Sarah had found a friend in Aisling, her chambermaid, and had learned Gaeilge from her over the past years. Feeling Aisling's warm hand on her arm, Sarah managed a gracious nod before she turned her face to hide the welling up of tears.

She wrapped her cloak around her shoulders, pulled the hood far over her red eyes, and headed out into the streets. It wasn't seemly for her to be without an escort, but her husband was too busy to notice, and others in the household never commented on it. Wandering down into Galway town, past the church, and along the row of shops, she came to the tables that were already being set up for market day. After exchanging a timid greeting with the butcher, she crossed the stone bridge over the Corrib and headed west along the shore.

Sarah paused near the tiny hamlet of Claddagh and turned her face to take in the panorama of the river, the bay, the gray stone town, and the even grayer governor's mansion situated less than a hundred yards beyond its walls. There was still plenty of time before the evening meal, so Sarah walked briskly further along the shore. The soothing soughing of the waves and the rhythm of her steps formed a trance-like drumbeat as she leaned into the strong breeze and inhaled the chilling mist of freedom.

Eventually, though, she turned back. There was no place for her here, and she had no one to turn to. She tried to slow her pace as she retraced her steps, but the wind pressed urgently into her back and didn't let up.

Later in the afternoon, as clouds from the west raced overhead, Sarah finally crossed over the stone bridge, slowly trudged through the gate, and was back in Galway. Several vendors were already packing up their goods when she paused at a table piled high with woven items and something she hadn't seen at the market before: small wooden figurines of ducks, seals, and gnomes.

The large farm family selling them was bantering among themselves. Sarah smiled while she admired the figurines, the colorful shawls, gorgeous cloaks, and blankets. Her fingers lightly trailed over the soft materials of the wares and then paused on a cloak. One of the vendors, a young man, set aside his whittling project and rose. His eyebrows lifted in surprise when she asked timidly in slow Gaeilge fragments if they would allow her to try on this cloak.

"Of course," the young man answered in English and helped Sarah take off the black one she was wearing. She flung the new garment over her shoulders and studied the delightful fringes, a unique curly metal clasp, and the colorful design. She couldn't help but smile and, for the length of several heartbeats, her eyes locked with those of the tall young man. She found herself caught in a dazzling moment of unexpected connection, so much so that she didn't realize the entire family had fallen silent as they stared at her. Flustered, she dropped her gaze, wondering what they must think of the bruises and her clumsy attempt at speaking in their tongue.

Sarah studied the fabric and asked, "Are you the weavers who make these beautiful cloaks?" They answered, yes, this is how we dye the wool and weave the fabric. At first, they all spoke English, obviously accustomed to it, but she was so eager to learn more Gaeilge and specifically asked them to teach her. They nodded, surprised, then spoke slowly, allowing her to repeat the Gaeilge words carefully to ensure her pronunciation was correct. The language lesson and the warm conversation brought a smile to her face and loosened the tension in her frame. The attractive young man, who introduced himself to her as Tibbot, was the one she enjoyed talking to the most. She eventually took her leave and continued toward the governor's mansion.

With her purchase under her arm, Sarah entered through the gate, passed the guards, and continued to the front door. Entering the hall, she was unaware of the chill swirling around her feet because her thoughts still lingered with the farmers at the market. *Especially Tibbot.* Most Irish, even here in Galway, tended to keep their distance from Sarah because she was English, and so it had been a treat to get to know the artisans.

Sarah abruptly halted her steps. The door to Aldred's office stood slightly ajar. Several muffled voices drew her closer. What were Aldred and his advisors up to this late in the afternoon? She held her breath.

". . . will be sentenced to death for disloyalty to the Crown tomorrow."

"Good. Then the gallows are set up?"

"Yes, my Lord. And may I introduce the trustworthy informant who singlehandedly helped us catch the rebels: Murrough Bourke."

"Sir, it's a pleasure to make your acquaintance," said a rough voice with a heavy accent.

Aldred replied, "Likewise. Your reward, Murrough." There was a clink of coins before Aldred continued, "We are looking forward to your continued service concerning Galway and its vicinity, but I'm also concerned about Connacht's far western region. I've been told the clans around Clew Bay harbor countless other outlaws."

"Yes, sir, they do. All the clans there are united in their obstinate efforts to resist the law. They have numerous strongholds and fast ships."

"They have outfoxed every single one of my predecessors." The timbre of Aldred's voice betrayed his frustration.

Murrough added, "Some of my kin, a branch of the Bourke family, are allied with them. I myself have attended their gatherings a few times. Could never get myself to join, though, too much bad blood between me and Granuaile."

"Is that the name of their leader?"

"Yes, sir. She is the worst of the lot and—"

Aldred interjected, "*She?* Their chieftain is a *woman?*" Sarah could hear the incredulity in her husband's shrieking voice, could imagine the look on his face amid his advisors' gasps and growls.

One of them spat, "Despicable!"

"Indeed, sir," Murrough agreed. "She is vile and ruthless. An abomination if you ask me!"

There was a loud bang when something wooden—a cup, perhaps—landed on a desk. A flaring of voices raged in feverish tremors between Aldred, his advisors, and Murrough, then turned into a hissing torrent, making Sarah shrink away from the door. Her heart was pounding, and her head filled with images of wild rebels led by a fierce woman.

Who are they talking about? She'd never had an interest in Aldred's way of governing Connacht, yet she wondered about this Granuaile, "leader of rebels and notorious outlaw." Sarah was filled with an inexplicable sense of awe as she tiptoed upstairs. She locked her door and reached into her bundle. Wrapped inside the new cloak, she found a small wooden figurine. A smile flickered across her face as she studied the details of the goblin, then placed it on her desk. She opened the cloak out fully and wrapped herself in its lush wool, so remarkably warm and comforting. The memory of her interaction with Tibbot sped up her heart rate.

Sarah noticed a throbbing of recklessness, courage, and fearlessness pulsing through her body and her will, a phoenix yearning to unfold her wings and fly. With fierce eyes, she glared at her reflection in the mirror, drew herself up to her full height, and wondered what it would be like to be daring. To be free. To be a chieftain, a rebel, an *outlaw*.

Felicísima Armada

CORUÑA, MAY 1588

Inyo shuddered as he entered the *Delfin*. Coruña cowered under lead-colored clouds, howling winds, and frigid rains. Brutal storms had raged for several days now, and the harbor was unusually quiet. In the tavern, Inyo found Marina at their favorite table. Juan and Bernardo were there, too. A year ago, much to Marina's delight, Juan had sold the *Gaviota* and now worked with his sister at *Libros y cartografía.*

Adrián and Clara soon entered with their young daughter, little Margarita, and joined them at the table where candles cast a warm glow, contrasting the dull light that fell through the windows. Adrián bounced Margarita on his knees while Clara and Marina laughed at Bernardo and Juan's jokes. Inyo had noticed that Marina was spending more and more time with Bernardo over the past weeks. She stretched her arms out to little Margarita, taking her from Adrián.

Inyo had fond memories of Adrián and Clara's wedding two years ago on a sunny day in the cathedral near the convent. Clara had moved in with Adrián, the two of them running the printing press. Just before the birth of their daughter, she had finally sold the bakery, trading her days of exhausting drudgery for family life. Which improved her mood a great deal, Inyo noted.

Marina interrupted Inyo's thoughts when she handed him Margarita. "Here, she wants to hear you sing that song again."

While Margarita settled in on the bench next to him with expectant eyes, Inyo obliged and began Margarita's favorite shanty. *"Valiente marinera, marinera en el mar . . ."* The child squealed with delight, clapping her hands in time. At that moment, Antonio wandered into the tavern, shook the rain out of his hair, and took his place at the table next to Inyo.

"Suits you well, Inyo!" Antonio joked, but before he could blink, Inyo handed him Margarita with a grin.

"Your turn!"

"Marina, what news have you heard about the Armada?" Adrián wanted to know. Marina had become close friends with the mayor and his wife, Isabella. As a result, she got a daily dose of official state news, as well as all the town gossip.

"Nothing new. King Philip sent them on their way from Lisbon several weeks ago, and his advisors assume that by now they must have linked up with Parma and his troops in the Low Countries. It wouldn't surprise me if they've already taken London."

"That could very well be," Juan agreed.

"But the weather wasn't in their favor," Antonio pointed out.

Bernardo scratched his chin. "Hm, right. Who knows where they are . . ."

"Oh, don't worry!" Adrián laughed, "With the most experienced officers and the world's best ships, what could a bit of poor weather do to the Invincible Armada?"

"I agree! How exciting to think that England will soon be free of that immoral queen," Clara chimed in, and everyone nodded in agreement.

Antonio, however, cautioned quietly, "I've seen the English navy. Their new ships are built skinny and low. Swift, like fish. When Drake assaulted Cadiz last year, our galleons were helpless against his lightning-fast attack and furious cannons . . ."

All of them had heard about the horrors of Drake's attack, since Antonio had had the misfortune of being there. He'd relayed the shocking details: "*El Draque* and his fleet swooped in so quickly, bombarded and destroyed thirty warships, plundered the town without mercy, and wiped out all the provisions in the stores and on the landings." After the attack, Antonio's vessel needed repairs, and half his crew vanished or were injured. He returned broke.

The news that Diego and Ansa were among the missing left Inyo and Juan with a deep sorrow. Inyo still wondered what might have happened to Ansa. Did the English capture him? He secretly clung to the hope that he could still be alive somewhere.

Antonio was convinced that the loss of so many ships and provisions would delay the planned invasion fleet for years. It was surprising when King Philip, seemingly unperturbed, pushed on stubbornly, built more vessels, and replenished cannons, troops, and provisions as quickly as possible—no doubt funded by the steady flow of silver and gold coming in from the New World.

Heavy-hearted, Antonio had eventually sold his trading vessel to pay off his debts. He found employment in Cantabria for the entire summer, where thick oak forests provided strong timbers for the warships. In the busy shipyards there, he had heard of the frenzied restocking and rearming of the King's mighty navy, which was quickly known as the Invincible Armada.

"From what I've been told, it's an impressive force of one hundred and thirty ships, eight thousand sailors, and close to twenty thousand soldiers," Antonio had reported. "Parma has an additional thirty thousand troops."

Bernardo raised his drink in a toast. "To King Philip, the Most Fortunate Armada, and to victory!"

"To victory!" They all lifted their tankards in agreement. Little Margarita mimicked their solemn expressions and piped, "Amen!"

—

The rain clouds and fierce winds of the previous days finally gave way to much calmer weather by morning. On the dock, Inyo bent over a timber, swinging his adze. The cadence was always the same. A slow, precise first chip with the grain, then a few large ones to shave the wood off completely and smooth the timber. Coming from the lower deck of the French trading caravel that blocked his view, Inyo could hear the muffled voices of the busy crew while he watched Antonio climb aboard the vessel with his tools.

Church bells began to ring in the upper town. A murmur rose from a few nearby ships. "What's going on?" Antonio paused his work. Inyo shrugged, wondering the same.

One of the French sailors stared out to sea, pointed, and shouted, *"Mon dieu!"*

Inyo clambered up to the vessel's main deck. He gasped in disbelief. The sea was teeming with hundreds of sails, many of them emblazoned with red crosses. Large galleons, galleys under canvas and oars, loaded carracks and caravels, and scores of smaller messenger ships were drawing closer and closer. Shudders of goosebumps rippled over Inyo's skin. He had never seen anything like it in his entire life. *So many ships!*

"The Armada!" someone shouted. A spectacle of billowing sails and colorful banners danced above the crowded decks of the approaching vessels. Inyo couldn't believe he got to witness the concentrated might of King Philip's fleet. But then his forehead creased. "What are they doing here? Shouldn't they be in London?"

Antonio scratched his head. "Maybe they've already completed the mission and they're coming home?"

Inyo wondered if they could have actually sailed to England, helped Parma's troops to London, and made it back here so quickly. It seemed impossible.

A few of the large galleons pulled up slowly while most of the other warships and smaller vessels dropped anchor in the bay. Upon closer inspection, Inyo noticed the tattered sails and the ships' general state of disrepair.

"Oh dear!" Antonio muttered. "Looks like the English gave them quite a fight!" Inyo couldn't shake the suspicion that something wasn't quite right.

By now, locals flooded the harbor front and nearby streets, awe-struck by the festive scene of towering hulls, fluttering pennants, and trumpet fanfares. Coruña's mayor, adorned in lace ruff and velvet, arrived with his entourage of advisors and servants. He waved and shouted his welcome as he waddled towards the biggest one of the galleons, the *San Martin*. "It's Admiral Medina-Sidonia's flagship!" Antonio exclaimed, his voice betraying his awe.

The massive *San Martin* towered over the harbor. Inyo's eyes widened as he took in the tall masts, the streaming banners, and the regal decorations on her massive hull. A long stripe of red and gold chevrons ran from her bow to her stern. The tall aft castle featured more painted patterns and a canopy of green velvet. A string of brightly colored shields displaying coats of arms decorated the gunnels and the gun ports.

Soldiers crowded the castles, dressed in every hue under the sun, their caps adorned with plumes. On the yards, sailors hurried to furl the sails. Inyo winced when he noticed the damage to the *San Martin*'s rigging.

Trumpets sounded as the Duke of Medina-Sidonia, an imposing man dressed in a richly decorated vest and cloak, strode down the gangplank. A giant golden chain of office hung around his neck, and his gait and posture spoke of a man acutely aware of his own significance. The ship's priests, a few officers, and two dozen aristocrats followed him.

The mayor took off his large hat, bowing deeply. "Welcome, Your Excellence! I'm delighted to hear what news you might bring us. Our humble town is at your service."

"Thank you. I'm afraid I don't have pleasant news," the admiral began. "We were surprised by powerful gales and adverse weather off Finisterre. While we waited out last night's storm, we suffered great damage. My guests demand suitable accommodations, all ships require urgent repairs, and we need fresh provisions." With a quiet voice, he added, "Most of our food has spoiled."

Inyo's eyebrows lifted in shock. They hadn't even reached England yet? Their provisions had already turned bad?

The admiral handed the mayor a letter, commanding, "Urgent message to King Philip. You will see to it that it gets to Madrid as fast as possible!"

Medina-Sidonia's officers fanned out, mumbling about their plans to secure provisions. Then the *San Martin*'s master carpenter planted himself on the gangplank and shouted, "To assist King Philip's Armada, and his holy mission, all carpenters of the town are hereby summoned to the docks without delay!"

Antonio, who already had tools with him, prepared himself to be sent wherever needed. He urged Inyo, "Quick, go find Bernardo! Looks like we'll have a lot to do over the next week."

—

The amount of work awaiting Inyo, Bernardo, and Antonio was staggering. The fore topmast of a warship named *Santa Catalina* had snapped, and the remains now had to be removed, which required a hastily constructed pulley system on sheerlegs. On another vessel, the storm completely ripped off the spritsail and its yard. Bernardo and

Antonio helped heave up the new yard, and Inyo was among the hands tasked with securing it in place while clinging to the bowsprit.

As Inyo inspected the storm damage further and worked alongside the tired and strangely unmotivated crews, doubts about the Armada's supposed ordained status trickled into his thoughts and dampened his patriotic mood.

After a busy day filled with hard labor, Inyo, Bernardo, and Antonio met up with Marina and Juan at *Libros y cartografía*. Armada officers dressed in varicolored velvet and silk filled the shop. Inyo noticed the officers' forlorn expressions and overheard fragments of their quiet discussions while they stared at the maps on display.

"The storms and lousy food are making it difficult to keep my crew in line. Morale aboard my ship is currently even lower than it was after Drake's attack last year."

"When my men opened the first casks of water, we found nothing but green slime!"

"The same was true for every vessel as far as I've heard. Even the *San Martin*."

"And we had to throw overboard all of our salted pork and bacon. All of it was rotting before we had even departed Lisbon. We have no meat left."

"I don't know where they bought the ship's biscuits, but my men won't eat them. They taste like poison!"

"Ours too. I had to cut rations just a day after leaving Lisbon."

Rushing in through the door came Isabella, the mayor's wife, her eyes wide in shock as she grabbed Marina's arm. Inyo was burning to know what was going on, so he leaned in closer to hear Isabella whisper, "I can't believe it! In the letter that Medina-Sidonia is sending to King Philip, he's advising him to *abandon* the entire mission!" Marina gasped while Isabella continued, "He writes that obviously God has different plans!"

Inyo was surprised the mayor would have the audacity to open the admiral's letter, but couldn't dwell on it too long, because Isabella now detailed several blunt portions in the letter about the weakness of the Armada, that the admiral sees no way they could ever invade England, and that most men aboard have no knowledge or ability to perform the duties entrusted to them.

Later that night, when Inyo joined Juan, Antonio, and Bernardo in Marina's garden, where they could finally speak freely, Marina wondered out loud, "How will the King perceive such a letter?"

Bernardo shook his head with a forlorn expression. "King Philip won't listen to the admiral's advice." Spain's sovereign supposedly lived like a hermit, alone at the Escorial, his monastery-like palace near Madrid. It was well known that he brooded in solitude and prayed for hours each day, like a monk. Many devout believers were impressed by his display of faith, firmly believing that the King's every decision and command was ordained and blessed by God.

At the Escorial and throughout Spain, there was such a haughty confidence in the Armada's superior strength that the success of the enterprise was considered a given. Spain's mighty and wealthy empire, after all, stretched across the globe. What resistance would an insignificant, mist-strewn isle under an excommunicated queen pose? Inyo, along with the rest of Spain, had been led to believe that it would be easy to invade England, remove its wicked ruler, the bastard, the great heretic, and restore the true faith to the suffering English people.

But there had been rumors not too long ago that advice from commanders, diplomats, or military leaders rarely reached the King. His closest advisors filtered out which messages should reach him and which ones needed to be modified for his ears.

Bernardo quietly forewarned, "The King *says* that God's on our side, but . . ."

Marina stared at him, shocked. "Shh! If anyone hears you!"

They all knew that any open criticism of the church or doubts about Spain's ruler could easily mean death if reported. That night, Inyo mulled over everything he'd heard the officers say. *Maybe Juan and Bernardo are right to be skeptical. What if God isn't speaking to and through the King?*

Early the next morning, Inyo, Antonio, and Bernardo carried their tools to the docks. The blacksmith and the cooper were already at work too, harrying their apprentices. Overloaded carts rattled up and down the harbor front to the sounds of shouting and whip cracks. In the harbor, smaller vessels plied back and forth in the gentle breeze, ferrying provisions to the anchored galleons and supply ships.

They ran into Francisca on their way, her sleeves and apron covered in flour. She carried a basket overflowing with fresh bread and cake. "I've been up all night," Francisca reported. "It's such an honor to do something for the brave men aboard the Armada."

—

The admiral, while awaiting the King's reply, had ordered even stricter enforcement of the already austere discipline aboard each vessel. "This, after all, is a '*sacred mission*,'" Bernardo huffed and rolled his eyes. "Aboard the King's ships, gambling and foul language are strictly forbidden. Attendance at morning and evening mass is now obligatory, and no one is allowed to go ashore anymore. Except for priests and officers."

One day, while Inyo, Antonio, and Bernardo helped with repairs aboard a galleon, they noticed the soldiers crammed together below deck, guarded by armed troops. "To prevent them from deserting," one of the officers admitted under his breath.

"Is that why the admiral ordered most of the warships to be at anchor, to prevent desertion?" Inyo asked.

The officer nodded with a frown.

"I see," Antonio said. "Most soldiers and sailors can't swim . . ."

"I guarantee that the sailors who *can* swim won't be here for long," Bernardo whispered so only Inyo and Antonio could hear him.

Having foreseen that the tavern would be overcrowded while the Armada was in port, Marina suggested meeting at *Libros y cartografía* after work to discuss the latest developments. Francisca, Juan, and Marina cleared a workbench, lit candles, and served wine, cheese, and bread when Inyo and Bernardo arrived with Antonio.

"One of the *comandantes* told me today that the admiral actually begged King Philip several times not to place him in command of the Armada. Because he has no naval experience, none at all," Juan updated them.

Inyo wondered what prompted the King to place someone *this* inept in command of his entire fleet. Marina argued, "The duke may not have his sea legs yet, but Isabella says he's a good man."

"And he is the most respected noble in all of Spain," Francisca added.

Bernardo snorted. "It also helped that he is the *richest* noble in all of Spain, and that twenty years ago, King Philip offered him his own very young, very illegitimate daughter to be his wife."

"Who told you such things?" Marina demanded.

"It's true. The Duke of Medina-Sidonia married the child of one of the King's mistresses . . . when the girl was only four years old. And then consummated the marriage when she was just ten."

Shocked silence and unease fell over the gathering. The candles flickered, unable to defeat the shadows in the darkest corners of the shop. Inyo shuddered. How could anyone think it fitting to marry off a child, a young girl? He couldn't help but think of little Margarita. The faces of the children at the orphanage in Santiago came to his mind, too. Inyo remembered what it was like to be that small. He clenched his jaw, clamped his hands into tight fists, and was overcome by the urge to punch something.

What intensified Inyo's disgust was the fact that *outwardly*, King Philip, Medina-Sidonia, and the clergy and aristocracy of Spain paraded and celebrated their own supposed holiness, ordering the people to follow their pious example. *And then it turns out they live such vile lives! Having mistresses, trading their illegitimate children for political gain, giving a daughter away, knowing she'll suffer!* Thinking of the filth behind these religious façades revolted Inyo as he tried to suppress a cynical huff.

A progression of images from his childhood flashed in his mind. The gentle and honest echoes under the convent's vaulted ceilings, the kind and cheerful nuns. The hymns, the respect for the work of the clergy, and his own sincere and simple devotion. God's quiet voice that he heard in his own heartbeat amid the bowed heads, incense, and soothing silence. Charity. The work of the hospital. *That is faith*, Inyo thought to himself. To learn that people who claimed to believe in the same religion and speak for the same God could behave in such ways? A string of expletives rose inside him, but he reminded himself that Sister Francisca was there and so bit his tongue. The simmering anger, the disillusionment, and, with it, the doubts, bewildered and upset him as he stared out the window, where twilight had turned to complete darkness.

—

Over the following weeks, the summer heat intensified and repairs continued. Bernardo, Antonio, and Inyo were taken from one ship to another. Aboard each vessel, they were instructed by the ship's carpenters on what work needed to be done. Sometimes they even helped with re-rigging, mending sails, or caulking work below decks. They carved replacements for deadeyes and blocks. On one of the ships was a heavily damaged fighting top. Its topmast rigging required careful reattaching, which took several days. The new foremast for the *Santa Catalina* also arrived, and the ship's master carpenter looked pleased when he watched Bernardo and Inyo plane the timber.

The town's coopers and blacksmiths labored from early morning until late into each night. The Armada's barrels were taken apart and the staves piled up shipside, while better barrels and water casks were purchased. The landings and streets were alive with horses, carts, and cargo, merchants, messengers, officers, priests, beggars, musicians, and dancers. Fresh provisions and supplies continued to flow to the ships while the admiral and his staff awaited word from the Escorial.

Then, early one morning, Isabella pulled Marina aside inside *Libros y cartografía*. "King Philip's message arrived yesterday! My husband was called aboard the *San Martin* late last evening, where Medina-Sidonia met with his senior officers and some of the nobles. The King insists that God Almighty commands the enterprise, would most certainly ensure the Armada's victory, and that therefore everyone ought to pull themselves together and do their part."

After the orders to proceed as planned were passed down the chain of command, Inyo noticed many more grim faces and resigned stares aboard the ships of the fleet. The crews had only received pay for their first month, which in most cases was April. The Armada was to land in England in May or early June, by which time more pay was expected, on top of a share in the plunder of any English wealth captured. But now, it was already July, and the ships were still stranded in Spain.

In response to the darkening mood, the ships' priests, under the admiral's directive, ordered even more prayer times and obligatory confession. Every night, more and more deserters jumped overboard, abandoning their ships.

One morning, Bernardo, Antonio, and Inyo were ferried to their next assignment on the *San Francisco*, a massive galleon fitted with twenty-one guns. They were not surprised when they saw the decimated number of sailors aboard. One of the ship's junior officers pulled Inyo and Antonio aside after they replaced a broken spar. "You both have sailing experience, yes?"

"We do indeed, sir." Antonio nodded.

"I've watched you work. You should know that my *comandante* and the ship's master will recruit locals starting tomorrow. Over half of our hands have run away, and we can't safely put to sea with a crew of just twenty men."

Inyo's eyes lit up. "You're saying they'll hire us to sail aboard the *San Francisco*?"

The officer nodded and encouraged them, "Be here at first light, they'll have a table set up near the *San Martin*."

Antonio and Inyo looked at each other in confounded silence. So much had already gone wrong with the Armada, and those in command obviously didn't inspire confidence. But here was the rare chance to serve in the most formidable fleet in the world. Despite the hesitation, despite Marina's worried expression at supper that evening, Inyo was firm in his decision. Juan boxed his shoulder approvingly. "Always knew you had it in you! Remember when you started with me aboard the *Gaviota*? Now look at you!"

When dawn painted its first vague orange glow on the eastern horizon, Antonio and Inyo hurried towards the flagship, where officers and guards were setting up tables. Word must have spread quickly because soon after Inyo got in line behind Antonio, clusters of local dockhands streamed towards them.

Then the *San Francisco's* captain sat down with his first officer, who opened a roll of parchment. They sternly glanced at the line of men, and the *comandante* shouted, "My name is Don Matías de Villagar. This is the consecrated and ordained mission to oppose and quash our enemy. I am proud to command the *San Francisco*. We're looking for reliable and strong men to join our crew. Tell us about your sailing experience, the vessels you've worked on, which oceans you know, and about any other additional skills you have, especially in the areas of ropemaking, sail-making, and carpentry. If we hire you today, you will become a King's man and vow to serve valiantly. Payment for your first month will be issued to you aboard this evening; the remainder and other rich rewards will be issued upon arrival in England. Let's begin!"

De Villagar motioned for Antonio to step closer. Antonio's chest swelled as he pulled himself up to his full height and listed his achievements. "Sir, I have sailed the coasts of Africa, Italy, Spain, Ireland, Flanders, and France as a trader on a carrack for over seven years. I also captained my own trading vessel for two years. In addition, I have been employed in Cantabria's shipyards during the building of the *San Esteban* and the *San Salvador*."

The ship's master quietly conversed with de Villagar, while both men nodded with thoughtful expressions. Then he proclaimed, "Hired as sailing master. Please sign here."

Antonio scribbled his name on the parchment, saluted his commanders, made a crisp about-face, and winked at Inyo. Inyo blinked furiously. This was all happening so quickly.

It was his turn now. The officers stared at him. Inyo rummaged for a confident expression and pinned it in place, commanding his knees to stop wobbling this instance. "Sir, my name is Inyo. I'm a carpenter. Oh, and a cartographer, and, um—" he stammered, "and I have experience sailing aboard the same merchant vessel as Antonio. I've sailed the Bay of Biscay on a few occasions and have sailed to Ireland once."

Again, the officers conferred with each other, this time rather briefly. Enlisted as a sailor. Be prepared to assist our carpenter as needed."

Hired! Aboard the San Francisco*!* An overwhelming sense of pride welled up in Inyo while Antonio slapped his back enthusiastically.

Sarah

IRELAND, JUNE 1588

Haunting cries of seagulls and melancholy clouds slumped over Galway Bay. Summer refused to reach its full richness. Cold winds prevailed. That particular day, Sarah's tears had long run dry before she reached the city gate and stormed across the bridge. Her sorrow morphed into burning fury as she marched westward with her new cloak fluttering behind her like a rebel banner. Because of the early start, she wandered much farther than on any of her previous walks.

Life at the governor's mansion was altogether unbearable. Aldred had grown increasingly paranoid about rebellions simmering across Connacht and about rumors that the Spanish were poised to launch their invasion forces. On occasion, he received official visitors from Dublin or met with local chieftains who assured him of their loyalty, but he was never satisfied with progress. He mainly stayed in his office, veiled in a constant drunken stench, brooding and raging about not having enough men to patrol the county, smashing the dishes brought to him by the staff. He ignored Sarah during the day, but late at night, his ranting fists hammered against her door, and he unleashed his curses and unintelligible slurs, terrorizing her.

In her desperation, she had written to her father. A cryptic message, only vaguely hinting at the despair she found herself in. Why had she not received an answer?

In her loneliness, Sarah began spending even more time with the staff at the governor's mansion. She took an interest in them, asked them about their families, hummed along when they sang in their native tongue, and steadily became more fluent in it herself. Deidre, head of the kitchen staff, often shook her head in astonishment when Sarah spoke Gaeilge. Aisling seemed especially elated about Sarah's ability to comprehend so many words and phrases of the Irish language.

On market days, Sarah loved to visit her favorite craftspeople and merchants, and the Morris farm stand was one of her regular stops. Tibbot was usually there, and his presence was pure sunshine in an otherwise gloomy life.

There was no market today, so she hiked the familiar path out of Galway along the shore and pushed ceaselessly onwards. After an hour, the trail narrowed and curved away from the bay. Heavily overgrown, it followed a small inlet towards a tall tower house. In its shadow, Sarah crossed a creek and then climbed a steep section of dense forest. As the trail leveled out, she paused to inhale the aroma of the warming day. The fern-lined path invited her into the quiet and green sanctuary of towering trees and mossy boulders. Birdsong beckoned her deeper into the woods.

Sarah had just crossed a small stone bridge and now paused, tilting her head. There was faint music in the distance. The sounds of a lute, drums, and singing drew her closer. She carefully moved towards the music, hid behind a tree, and curiously gazed at a gathering of locals in a meadow. It looked like one of the ancient Celtic celebrations she'd heard about that mark the different seasons. At least twenty dancers circled in the meadow, accompanied by musicians. There were clusters of farm families and tables laden with food. A dog barked and ran towards Sarah, its ears flapping cheerfully. Several heads turned to look at her, and the music stopped as she emerged from the trees.

"*Dia daoibh*," Sarah greeted the group with a tremble in her voice. She worried how her intrusion might be received, but then she recognized several of the farmers whom she'd met at the market in Galway. Fergal, Brian, and Maeve were there. And one of the dancers was Tibbot.

"Sarah!" Tibbot's eyebrows lifted in surprise, and he was by her side with quick strides. Slightly out of breath, he reached for her hand. "I am so happy you're here! Welcome!"

She reluctantly followed Tibbot into the meadow. "I hope I'm not interrupting?"

"No, not at all! Guests are always welcome," Tibbot replied, and his smile put Sarah at ease.

"Is this your farm?"

"It's my sister's farm," Tibbot explained.

"Sarah, good to see you!" Maeve greeted her with a wink. "You look stunning in that cloak."

The music resumed, and Tibbot pulled her along into the circle to dance. When Sarah found herself in Tibbot's arms, whirling about, her heart flooded with astonishing warmth and a profound sense of belonging. In the back of her head, however, was a gnawing sense of guilt. Tibbot and his sister didn't know that she was married. To the governor, no less. *Surely if they knew, they wouldn't be so welcoming,* Sarah worried. But when she looked into Tibbot's brown eyes, all those unpleasant thoughts vanished.

Maeve gently placed a hand on Sarah's arm at the end of the evening, briefly glancing at her bruises, whispering in a motherly way, "Please know you were *always* welcome here."

Sarah nodded gratefully. "Thank you, Maeve." When she was

about to take her leave, Tibbot ran after her. "Sarah, wait! It's a long way to Galway from here, and it will be dark soon."

"Oh, right . . ." She bit her lip.

"You can't go all by yourself. We can take my horse." Tibbot must have seen her hesitation because he added, "Just to the city gate, perhaps?"

Jittery and excited, she blinked under Tibbot's warm gaze. A smile slowly dawned across her face, and she nodded. Tibbot motioned her to follow him to the barn. While he saddled his horse, Sarah's heart was about to leap to the heavens. But was it proper for her to ride with him? What if someone saw her?

Tibbot, unaware of her inner turmoil, handed her a lantern and smiled at her in a way that melted all her worries away. When she was seated behind him on his horse, holding on to his torso and pressing her cheek against his leather jerkin, she found herself completely at ease.

"Ready?" he asked, and they quickly took off into the night.

Santa Catalina

CORUÑA, JULY 1588

In Marina's garden, Inyo lifted his eyes to the first full moon of July as it hovered low in the pastel evening sky. Francisca, Juan, Bernardo, Adrián, Clara, and little Margarita gathered there to see Inyo and Antonio off. The Armada's repairs had been completed, and Medina-Sidonia had sent messages to each captain. Aboard the *San Francisco*, Captain de Villagar announced to his crew that they'd put to sea the next day. He granted Inyo and Antonio evening leave as an exception after Francisca, Marina, and Isabella, armed with an enormous pile of almond cakes, had personally requested the favor.

Juan counseled Antonio and Inyo, "Remember everything you've learned. Have courage and be there for your shipmates."

Bernardo had carved a small wooden model of the *San Francisco* for Marina and passed it around the table. "This ship will be a reminder in this house while you are gone. Whenever we look at it, we will pray for protection and for your safe return," Bernardo said.

"Yes, to your safe return!" Juan raised his mug, and everyone joined him.

"*¡Salud!*"

When it was time for Antonio and Inyo to take their leave, Marina hugged Inyo tightly. "Be safe, *mi querido. Ve con Dios.*"

"I'll be home soon," Inyo promised, trying to keep his voice strong and assured.

Francisca gripped Antonio's hand. *"Que Dios lo proteja!"* Antonio nodded appreciatively.

When tears welled up in Marina's eyes, Bernardo draped his arm around her shoulder to comfort her, a sweet gesture that warmed Inyo's heart.

Inyo and Antonio then hurried to the harbor. They were about to climb into one of the longboats when Inyo halted. "Oh no, I forgot my vest!"

"Be quick, you know Villagar wants us aboard before dark," Antonio warned him.

"Right, I know. Don't wait for me, I'll catch up to you!" With that, Inyo sprinted away.

By the time he raced back down to the harbor again with his jerkin, it was dark. Up ahead, the lanterns of the longboats illuminated several officers clambering aboard. Inyo sped up, but suddenly, odd noises snaked out from behind a large pile of wooden crates and broken barrels to his right —vile snickering and a whimper —bringing him to an abrupt stop. There was a slap followed by a sickening thud, as if something—or someone—had fallen hard on the cobblestones. "You first," a voice hissed.

Inyo crept closer. Dim light fell through a gap between the crates, and he could see the long black curls of a woman writhing on the ground. Blood smudged her face and her hair. A hand covered her mouth, and another hand strangled her neck.

Something inside of Inyo snapped, and he bolted forward with a roar. *"No!"* He grabbed a barrel stave and rushed around the pile. "Get away from her, you bastard!" He swung the stave and hit a man, who shrieked and tumbled backward. There was another man, a lanky one, who struggled to get off the ground. Inyo jumped on top of him. *A priest?* Inyo punched his face with all the strength he could muster. With a moan, the priest rolled down the embankment, blood gushing from his nose.

In shock, Inyo turned to see the first man back on his feet. It was also a *padre*, armed with a crate, and he was rushing at him with a gargoyleish scowl. Inyo ducked to escape the swing. The red-faced priest flung the crate into the harbor, missing Inyo, then lost his balance. Inyo didn't take any time to watch him tumble into the water; instead, he turned to the woman. Inyo had seen her before. *One of the dancers!* He pulled her to her feet, while the splashing and cursing behind him made his heart gallop wildly. Inyo yelled, "Run!"

The girl wiped a bloodied hand across her pale face and staggered away, coughing and weeping. Inyo wheeled around to see one of the *padres* hoisting himself out of the water, screaming, "Guards! Guards!" Inyo froze for a terrifying fraction of a heartbeat, but then rammed and tackled the man, who crashed into the pile of barrel staves, still shouting, "Help! Guards, arrest him! This devil's attacking us!"

Footsteps approached, unleashing even more terror in Inyo's heart. He knew in an instant that his life was in danger. No one would believe him. No one would question the words of two priests. And he had no proof of their crime. Inyo's thoughts shrank and narrowed, reduced to just one desperate idea. He took a running start and plunged into the black waters of the harbor with a splash. The angry shouts behind him urged him on, and he swam away as fast as he could. Someone ordered, "A boat, quickly!"

"Don't let him get away!" shrieked one of the priests.

Inyo took a deep breath and ducked. With smooth strokes, he swam underwater, further and further away from the docks. Finally, his head popped up again. There was the longboat sent to look for him, but it was heading south. Inyo quietly turned north. In the murk, he slipped past the towering shapes of the warships. Where was the *San Francisco*? There were so many vessels, and aside from the glow of a few stern lanterns, the entire harbor was dark.

The frigid water pulled on Inyo's clothing and slowed his movements. To catch his breath, he paused at the anchor cable of one of the vessels, his fingers gripping the soggy rope. A menacing voice startled him, "Don't move!" Inyo's shocked eyes shot up. Several armed soldiers aimed their muskets right at him.

"A deserter," one of them sneered.

"Shoot him!" spat another.

"No! Please—I'm not a deserter!" Inyo yelled. "I'm trying to find the *San Francisco*!"

"Ha! That's a good one!" one of the men snorted.

"P—Please, I beg you," Inyo gasped, clutching the thick cable, the dull pounding in his chest turning into a frantic drumbeat, "I need to get to my ship!"

"Here, catch!" one of the sailors shouted, throwing a rope. Inyo was pulled towards the ship, then hoisted himself up, hand over hand on the wet rope, his feet scrambling up the side of the hull.

Strong hands grabbed him and dragged him over the gunnel. "Look what we caught! A herring!" laughed one of the men. Inyo wiped the wetness out of his face, shuddering. Half a dozen weapons were pointed directly at him. "Please, I am assigned to the *San Francisco!*"

"No, you're under arrest!" barked one of the men.

Inyo's arms got yanked behind his back. "I'm not a deserter! Ouch! No, please!" Inyo's voice drowned under the laughter of the crew. They pushed him forward, and he hit the deck with a breath-shattering thud. Inyo struggled to his hands and knees, his shallow breaths quickening.

"Get up, you bastard!" a sailor growled, alarmingly close, an unbearable stench of sour ale on his breath. Inyo's heart clenched with fear.

"Step aside! Make way for your *comandante*!" someone shouted as heavy footsteps reverberated on the timbers. The captain approached with two officers in the light of torches and lanterns. "What is the meaning of this?" one of them demanded.

Inyo opened his mouth to defend himself, but the crew started yelling, "We caught a deserter!"

"Fished him out of the harbor."

The captain abruptly ordered, "Hang him!" and turned on his heel.

The words fell like daggers, unleashing a surging panic in Inyo. "No, I'm not a deserter, sir, *please!*" Inyo tried to shout, but his raspy voice drowned in the chaos. As the crew manhandled him and dragged him away, he struggled to escape, but found himself unable to breathe, to get another word out of his deflated lungs. Tiny dots began to dance at the edges of his vision as a rope was tightened around his neck.

Just then, someone jostled through the crowd and ran after the captain, yelling, "Sir! Sir, I know this man. He's a local carpenter!" Inyo instantly recognized the man who was speaking on his behalf. It was the master carpenter of the *Santa Catalina.*

The captain had already disappeared, but one of the officers paused. "A carpenter, you say?"

"*Sí*, Señor Martínez. A carpenter! An extremely skilled one! And as you know . . ."

"Hm. I see. Well, we cannot risk him escaping while we're still in port. He must remain interned until we're well underway. If he is useful to you, Sabado, you may then take him on."

Inyo collapsed onto the ground, trembling, still unable to speak. His hearing had changed, overpowered by the pulsating rush of his own blood, letting in only a few vague scraps of the conversation between the officer and the carpenter. Someone freed him from the ropes and pulled him to his feet. Martínez and Sabado escorted Inyo down into the gloomy and crowded hold of the *Santa Catalina*. The stench of mold and feces wafted through the dark space. By the glow of lanterns, Martínez placed shackles around Inyo's feet, the chain encircling a post.

After the officer turned and left, the carpenter placed a hand on Inyo's shoulder. "Don't worry. I'll have this sorted by tomorrow," the carpenter promised. "But you'll have to wait it out until we've set sail."

Inyo nodded, grateful to be alive as he looked into the carpenter's round and friendly face. "By the way, that was Martínez, the captain's right-hand man and sailing master. And my name's Miguel Sabado. Master carpenter. I remember you from your work on our foremast. Your name was—?"

A shudder gripped Inyo's chest, further clamping down on his throat, but he forced himself to take a deep breath. "Inyo," his voice finally rasped.

"Ah, right, Inyo." Sabado steadied himself on the hull. "You mentioned you're assigned to the *San Francisco*?"

Inyo nodded. "Yes, as a sailor. My friend Antonio is her sailing master and—" Inyo's voice gave out again. He shook his head.

Sabado nodded thoughtfully. "I'll speak to Sandoval about it," he promised while Inyo shivered. "Oh, goodness! I'll be right back." When Sabado bustled away, Inyo's ears picked up the squeaks and scurrying feet of rats nearby, restlessly hunting in the murk between the barrels and crates. Sabado returned with a blanket, another lantern, and a plate of food.

"Thank you, Señor Sabado."

"Call me Miguel. You rest now. Tomorrow, I'll get you out as soon as I can."

Miguel clambered up the ladder, leaving Inyo in the claustrophobic hold where he struggled to breathe, overpowered by the stench. Images of the assault on the girl flooded his mind while the iron shackles constricted his ankles and the ropes cut into his wrists. He leaned back on the timbers with a gloomy sigh, wrapped the blanket tightly around himself, and squeezed his eyes shut.

The hull groaned and creaked while Inyo's thoughts drifted to the *San Francisco*. What would Antonio think of him? Would he suspect Inyo of desertion? All he desperately wanted was a transfer to the *San Francisco*, where he belonged, as soon as possible. Eventually, the swaying amber glow of the lantern and the muffled rhythm of water lapping against the hull lulled Inyo to sleep.

—

Trumpets sounded for morning prayers, followed by the rumble of footsteps on the deck above him. Inyo, still bound in the hold, heard the crew's indistinct voices as they joined the ship's priest in prayer and chanting. He felt utterly detached from the music, shivering involuntarily instead.

When the *Santa Catalina's* crew weighed anchor and set sail, the hull creaked, and Inyo sensed the ship slowly turning. Now that the Armada was finally underway, Inyo imagined many of the people of Coruña in the harbor, watching the departure of the fleet—Marina, Juan, Francisca, and Bernardo among them, entirely unaware of his misfortune.

Inyo curled in on himself, his stomach growling. Time crawled along at a snail's pace, and the tight ropes itched more and more. *Where's Miguel?* Finally, the carpenter clambered down the ladder and quickly freed Inyo's limbs. "That was the longest night of my entire life," Inyo sighed as he unfolded himself slowly and rubbed his wrists. His hopeful eyes met Sabado's.

"Well," the carpenter began, "I was interrogated by our captain, Don Luis de Sandoval, and I had to vouch for you. That you'll be a hard worker and won't even think of desertion. And I'm so sorry, but Sandoval disapproved of you being transshipped." Inyo's face fell. Miguel added quickly, "You're now officially assigned to the *Santa Catalina* as carpenter's mate." Miguel explained that they'd also be required if any tasks needed extra hands, even though carpenters and sailmakers were usually excused from rotating watches or labor at night like regular sailors. "With our crew already low in numbers, everyone will be given additional duties," Miguel warned Inyo with a huff. "Nothing we can do about that."

Inyo climbed up the companionways behind Miguel and shielded his eyes as he stumbled into the shockingly bright daylight. They headed towards the starboard rail, Inyo wanting to take one more look at his hometown. His attention was instantly drawn to the multitude of ships that made up the Armada. All around him, the ocean was festooned with warships, their crews laying on sail. There were large, awe-inspiring galleons, smaller transport and supply vessels, impressive galleys in their orange and red war paint, the entire fleet under scores of colorful pennants, all unfurled and rippling like flames.

"And up ahead," Miguel shouted over the wind, ushering Inyo over to port side, "that's the flagship of our squadron, the *Rosario*." Her mighty sails, emblazoned with large red crosses and heraldic symbols, flexed like muscles of an enormous animal. Surprisingly, and despite what had happened to him, Inyo felt awe and pride well up inside of him. Surely, the world had never seen a sight such as this.

"The *San Francisco*!" Inyo exclaimed when he noticed her astern of the *Rosario*. But now that all hope of a transfer was gone, his face darkened. Miguel slapped Inyo's back to cheer him up.

Inyo's gaze followed the barefoot sailors working on the yards above him while a rough string of commands rang from the quarterdeck. He turned to study the sailing master, Martínez, the way his eyes shot up each mast, and how he carefully checked the ship's position in relation to the fleet. His perpetually stern face, thick eyebrows, and tall figure gave the man an air of innate authority.

Behind Martínez stood the richly dressed *comandante*, Don Luis de Sandoval, and another nobleman, along with the priest, seated under a canopy, where they were enjoying an elaborate meal. There were also two ladies in ornate dresses.

Miguel, having noticed Inyo's surprised look, explained, "Yes. Sandoval and his guest are accompanied by their wives. And half a dozen servants each to attend to them."

"What?" Inyo gasped. "We're going to war! Why would anyone bring wives and servants?"

"Don't ask me, but every Armada officer is an aristocrat and therefore has the King's permission to bring family members, guests, and as many servants as he desires. I heard that at least twenty personal servants accompany Admiral Medina-Sidonia himself."

Baffled, Inyo wondered where the logic was in all of this. The Armada was short on crew, short on food, and they all knew they were heading into dangerous waters. Yet there were people aboard each galleon who had no function, who took up resources and space. Spectators. *Is our endeavor just entertainment for them? Like the ancient Roman gladiator contests?*

"Come, time to get to work." Miguel led the way below deck. They climbed down past the gun deck to the lantern-lit lower deck, where Miguel pointed to his carpenter's store, wedged between the surgeon's room and a storage area for barrels of provisions. The thick scent of hemp, tar, and mold filled Inyo's nostrils. Lanterns and candles illuminated Miguel's work area in the tightly packed space, which also housed the sailmaker's tools.

"Here." Miguel waved at a stack of shims and thick wooden plugs. "You know what these are for?" Inyo shook his head. "Thought so," Miguel continued. "We'll use them to plug cannon holes and leaks.

You have to fit the hole quickly, hammer it in, and seal any remaining gaps with material. Whatever you can grab quickly. Canvas, oakum, pitch." Miguel rambled on while Inyo lifted his candle and carefully studied the materials. Behind him, the sailmaker bustled in with a big bolt of canvas.

The gun deck above them trembled under footsteps. Now that there was no longer a need to tightly herd and guard the soldiers, they practiced their drills. In the afternoon, Inyo watched the pikemen, arquebusiers, and musketeers, a total of two hundred sixty soldiers. Under the strident command of the military captains, the two battalions of soldiers perfected their formations and firing lines along the upper decks and in the castles, readying themselves for war.

Enemy in Sight

JULY 1588

The Armada sailed in a loose formation centered around the admiral's ship, *San Martin*. One day of adverse winds halted progress and put them behind schedule, but five days after leaving Coruña, a strong westerly wind brought back more assured smiles to the crew of the *Catalina*. They could sense that they were finally closing in on England.

That day, Miguel and Inyo constructed a new chicken coop and carried it up to the main deck, where the livestock was kept. A company of tired soldiers, cleaning their weapons, huddled nearby while Miguel and Inyo gently dropped the flustered chickens into their new coop. "Inyo? What are *you* doing here?"

Inyo, puzzled, turned to face the soldier who'd addressed him and was beaming at him. He was nearly unrecognizable in a crested helmet and a little lost in his overpowering uniform —a thick, dark-blue jerkin and puffy red pantaloons. He carried a musket, and from a leather bandolier across his chest hung several powder flasks. "Ansa!" Inyo gasped. He hadn't seen him since their last voyage to Ireland and had feared him dead after hearing about his disappearance at Cadiz.

"I'm so happy to see you!" Ansa said as they fell into each other's arms, laughing.

"Have you been on the *Santa Catalina* all this time?" Inyo wanted to know.

"Since Lisbon. And you?"

"Well, I was—"

"Back to work, soldier!" the army captain scolded with a frown.

Ansa ducked his head and whispered, "Meet me at the beakhead latrines before the next watch."

When the ship's bell rang to mark the end of the watch, Inyo hurried to the beakhead, where Ansa awaited him. Inyo shook his head in awe. "You're one of the musketeers!"

Ansa puffed his chest and nodded with evident pride. "And you?" he asked.

Inyo briefly explained what had happened, how he ended up here under unfortunate circumstances, and that Antonio was aboard the *San Francisco.*

Ansa frowned absentmindedly, "Antonio . . . last time I saw him was in Cadiz."

"What happened to you there? Why did you disappear?"

"I don't have clear memories." Ansa rubbed his forehead and closed his eyes. "All I remember from that day was that Drake attacked. There was so much terror and chaos . . . the hellish English cannons . . . fires in the warehouses . . . I woke up face down on a pile of dead men in the harbor when it was dark. No idea how long I'd been there. After that, I worked at the docks in Cadiz for a few months. It was hard. The drivers were mean. It wasn't like working for Juan or Antonio.

"But then the King's recruiters showed up. They promised regular food and a salary. Well, there's been no pay since April, but they say we get to plunder the heretic queen's palaces when—"

"Land in sight!" a lookout shouted from high above them. Ansa and Inyo stared at each other open-mouthed.

"*Inglaterra!*" Ansa whispered, and then they raced up to the forecastle's open deck.

A low gray coastline swayed far in the distance to the northeast. The wind filled Inyo's ears while he gripped the rail, but then a boom drew his attention to the *San Martin*. She had fired her cannon, signaling that they should form the defensive crescent shape that Medina-Sidonia and his senior officers had devised. The fleet had practiced falling into this all-important formation more than once. Every squadron knew its assignment, and every ship had a designated spot.

Sailing crews swarmed into the rigging in answer to Martinez' commands. Then Sandoval's booming voice cut through the air, "All hands! Clear for action!"

Ansa's captain ordered the battalion to take their position on the forecastle while trumpets and drums heralded the imminent battle. Inyo scurried to the main deck and was about to head back down to Miguel when Martínez' eyes bore into him, his voice a caustic whip. "You! To the bilge, sailor. Now!"

Inyo startled but did as commanded, heading down to the gun deck where a scruffy sailor was already working one of the bilge pumps. Inyo joined him and had his first real look at the gun deck, a packed warehouse. The dark space was filled with towering stacks of casks and crates.

"Where are the cannons?" Inyo wondered as he struggled to lift and lower the squeaking handle of the pump. The exhausted shipmate pointed vaguely, but Inyo couldn't see any cannons, guessing that they were all hidden between the supplies.

"Everything we need for the siege of London. And the soldiers sleep here, too."

Inyo shook his head. "Shouldn't the gunners run regular drills here?"

"Why? The soldiers know how to fire the cannons. They'll do it when the time comes," his shipmate assured him.

"What, *the soldiers?*" Inyo hissed. "But aren't they needed in the firing lines? And to board enemy vessels?"

"Yep, they'll fire the cannons once before boarding, then rejoin their formations upstairs."

Hadn't Antonio reported how the English gunners had fired volley after volley during their attack last year in Cadiz? Their gun crews had perfected rapid firing and quick reloading. Weren't the Spanish officers aware of that by now? Or was the old-fashioned Spanish strategy deemed superior and thus remained unchanged? Inyo stared at the overcrowded gun deck with a sense of unease and foreboding.

After his watch, he headed to a single open gunport. *The coast is so close!* Inyo gasped.

Just then, Miguel sidled up to him. "Any enemy vessels?"

Inyo shook his head. No sight of the English anywhere, not a single warship or fishing vessel. The admiral had ordered the fleet to sail close to the coast in battle formation to frighten them, Miguel had explained, so they won't dare come near and to keep the handful of ships the English call their *Navy Royal* cowering in one of their pitiful fishing ports. Miguel was proud that Spain's fleet was considered the mightiest in the world —the best there would ever be —and that Spanish fighting and boarding skills were feared throughout Europe. "And on top of it all, the English have no real militia, no trained army, just bands of farmers and half-wits. The simpletons and their pitchforks will pose no hindrance to our soldiers and Parma's well-trained troops once they march on London."

Inyo, however, scratched his chin as he studied the southern shore of England. From what Antonio told him, the English navy was definitely fearsome and well-trained; how else could Drake's fleet have caused such mayhem in Cadiz and in the Caribbean?

When night fell, the southwesterly wind became erratic and blew against them all night. The storm whipped the sea into a frenzy, and angry swells beat into the hulls, halting the Armada's progress. In the morning, the fleet was scattered and labored to get back into formation. Five ships had mysteriously disappeared overnight: the four war galleys and one large galleon. Inyo noticed the incredulous faces around him as rumors began to circulate.

"*El Draque* sunk 'em!" one of the older hands whispered.

"The English are in league with the devil himself!"

"There are sea monsters in these waters—I've seen one with my own eyes!"

Inyo was ordered to the main mast lookout that day. Miguel shrugged. "Martínez sure knows how to keep you busy." Inyo quickly climbed the shrouds to the fighting top, and his eyes widened at the incredible sight before him. To the southeast was the enormous fleet formation, fanned out into a wide arc with its two tips pointing westward. Like the menacing horns of a bull, ready to fend off any attacks.

In the center of the formation, the slower supply and transport ships were surrounded and protected by the flagship and the admiral's main squadron. Other large galleons and heavily armed warships were assigned as defense along the two curving flanks. The *Santa Catalina* and the *San Francisco* belonged to the squadron of Andalusia. Led by the *Rosario*, this squadron was assigned to the left flank of the formation, closest to the English coast.

Inyo scanned the horizon and the undulating coastline, a mere league away. Remnants of smoke rose from a string of fire beacons. *Those must have been lit when they first saw us yesterday, which means by now the queen knows the Armada has arrived. But where's the English fleet?*

The sailor next to Inyo exclaimed, "There, Plymouth!" He pointed. "Look, the tide!"

Inyo couldn't believe his eyes. The English fleet, a mere twenty or thirty ships strong from what he could see, was trapped in Plymouth harbor. "Wind and the tide are against them," Inyo gasped. "They won't be able to head out for hours." His gaze fell on several messenger ships swarming from his squadron towards the *San Martin*. Inyo leaned over the rail, peering down at Sandoval and Martínez, whose stern faces were trained on Plymouth.

Martínez slapped the gunnel and shouted, "What good fortune! No doubt the admiral will take advantage of this opportunity and order an attack on the English!"

"True," Sandoval scratched his beard and added, "currently they are easy prey, but I wonder . . ."

"Once the English fleet is defeated, bringing Parma's troops across the channel will be a breeze."

"Hm. King Philip's orders are rather explicit. We are *not* to attack or engage with the English navy unless necessary."

Inyo's head snapped up. "What?"

"Shh! You'll get us in trouble!" His shipmate pulled Inyo back.

Sandoval reminded Martínez, "The Armada is here strictly as a defensive escort for the barges that will bring the troops from the Low Countries to England." Sandoval then shrugged his shoulders and lowered his voice; the rest of the conversation was lost in a gust of wind.

Inyo was fuming. Here was a golden opportunity to take out the enemy, to ensure the Armada wouldn't be attacked in hostile waters, to pave a path to victory. *And what's the admiral doing? Nothing! Clinging to rigid orders from someone who knows nothing of naval warfare, a fool hiding in a solitary cocoon hundreds of miles away!*

Inyo's fury made it hard for him to concentrate as he lurched down the shrouds at the end of his watch. Serious misgivings growled deep inside of him while he ate his evening meal, a vile stew that he washed down with repulsive wine that stung like vinegar and left a revolting aftertaste in his throat. He flung himself into his berth next to Miguel in the carpenter's store, but he couldn't fall asleep. Was it the rotten food or the anger that was eating away at his insides?

—

Horrible cramps startled Inyo awake shortly before dawn. He grabbed a lantern and hurried up to the main deck, where he reached the gunnel barely in time to violently hurl the repulsive contents of his stomach into English waters. With a grimace of disgust, the officer of the watch averted his gaze. Inyo leaned on the railing for a long time, faint and contorted in misery, his breath edging carefully around the angry, clenching pain in his stomach.

The darkness weakened slowly, lifted away by a faint pastel streak on the horizon that heralded the morning. While the rigging above him creaked dissonantly with the stiffening breeze, the seascape around him began to brighten. Inyo lifted his eyes towards the southwest. What was that cluster of tiny white shapes reflecting the dawn? *Were those sails?* He shook his head and narrowed his eyes, unsure of what he was seeing.

"Enemy in sight!" a lookout on a nearby vessel screamed, alarm distorting his voice.

The *Santa Catalina's* own lookouts startled, then sprang into action, cursing and muttering. Finally, one of them hollered, "Quarterdeck, ho! Enemy approaching on port quarter! *And* on starboard quarter!"

Inyo caught sight of Sandoval, tightening his sword to his side with fumbling hands as he clambered up to the quarterdeck. "Unbelievable! How is this possible?" he roared while Martínez and the two army captains stormed up to join him. They stared out to sea in disbelief.

"All hands!" Sandoval's voice boomed. "Battle stations!"

A moment later, the ship exploded into a frenzy, the decks trembling under footsteps. Sailors raced up the shrouds while others awakened the rigging under Martínez' tense commands. Soldiers rushed to take their positions, their helmets and weapons gleaming in the morning light. The hatches of the gun deck banged loudly while gunners prepared and aimed the swivel guns on the upper decks.

One of Sandoval's guests, the overdressed nobleman whom Inyo had seen dining with the captain, reluctantly climbed up to the quarterdeck with a mask of terror. "You said the winds wouldn't allow the English to sail to windward, to attack us *from behind*, that it's all but impossible."

"It was impossible indeed," Sandoval grumbled. "The wind was against them all night."

"Maria is *distraught*!"

"Don Álvaro, you have nothing to fear," Sandoval tried to calm him, his voice strained, "but please stay in the cabin with Maria and Ana."

Inyo had expected that the tiny English fleet would be too scared to sally out. Instead, they'd departed Plymouth, sailed against both tide and wind, and were now threatening the Armada from behind. Being upwind, they had a considerable advantage, allowing them to control the pace of battle and the angles of attack.

Inyo overheard Fra Rodrigo attempting to convince Sandoval, "Sir, the day *must* start with mass! It's the King's order and—"

Sandoval cut him off. "We don't have time!" he growled as he turned away and defiantly glowered out at the English fleet, gripping the hilt of his sword. The English now positioned a cluster of ships directly astern of the Armada's seaward wing and another smaller one astern of the landward wing to which the *Santa Catalina* belonged.

While hatches crashed open, Inyo rushed below deck, where Miguel was stuffing tools and plugs into large canvas satchels. "Inyo, glad to see you're feeling better. I'll keep an eye on the lower deck. You cover the gun deck. Here, your bag!"

Inyo nodded tautly; he knew what to do. A few days ago, Miguel had pointed out the critical areas on the gun deck and on the lower deck where a leak from cannon shot could mean disaster. "Most importantly, take care of any damage closest to the waterline. Second, repairs to masts, yards, and rigging. Everything else will have to wait."

The low ceiling of the gun deck constricted Inyo's breathing and posture, while the master gunner ordered the cannons to be angled. Strong arms hauled and adjusted the tackle to aim the guns while the wind, rushing through the gun ports, drowned out terse mutters. The gunners readied powder and cannon shot in the cramped space.

"There!" exclaimed one of the soldiers assigned to the starboard battery. Inyo peered out the hatch closest to him. A mile off to starboard, a single small ship raced towards the center of the Armada, sailing at a dead run right between the flanks. A few hundred yards from the center squadron, which included the massive San Martin, the tiny English vessel presented her broadside, fired one cannon—a declaration of war—then swiftly turned and beat away.

The soldiers on the main deck above Inyo laughed out loud, but then Fra Rodrigo started a hymn. The crew's voices wafted and trailed the song in fickle unison. It was mandatory to join in anytime the priest led a prayer or a song. Inyo, however, couldn't get a single note out, which confused him. He knew the song. He used to love it. But while the reverent words of the familiar hymn fill the muffled air, images of the attack on the dancer in Coruña pulsated in his mind again. Invisible hands strangled his own neck.

He closed his eyes, struggled to draw a breath, and was overcome by intense revulsion for those *padres*.

As the first cannons boomed in the distance, one of the officers hurried down the ladder and warned the master gunner, "Line of enemy vessels approaching on port quarter! Ready your men!"

The master gunner peered out the center gun port, then turned to look windward, his expression rigid. Inyo's hands trembled. The enemy was closing in, and he was facing his very first time in battle.

A soldier near him tilted a powder horn over the touchhole, then stepped back. Another stood ready with his linstock as the master gunner lifted one arm high, watching the approach of the first enemy ship. He reined in his men's nerves with a sonorous, "Steady, men!" Then he whipped his arm down. *"Fire!"*

On the cannon closest to Inyo, the linstock fell, a spark hissed, and a deafening boom ripped through the tense air. All port-side cannons fired and bucked under the recoil. The gun deck trembled and became engulfed in heavy smoke. Then the soldiers were ordered to their positions in the castles above. Inyo's ears rang and his eyes stung as he waited for the coughing men to rush past him.

The English cannons thundered in return. After a discordant whistling that shredded the air, a salvo of hard knocks thudded against the *Catalina's* hull. A devastating scream of a man on the upper decks tore through Inyo's bones. With his heart pounding wildly, he rushed along the length of the gun deck, inspecting for damage. *Nothing, thank God! Our hull is too strong for their shot!*

Inyo glanced out of one of the hatches at the English vessels, which were all sailing in a line. They were new race-built galleons whose sleek profiles, with much lower fore- and stern castles, were a startling contrast to the towering, slow Spanish warships.

The English ship that had fired at them spun around a few hundred yards away on port beam, fired her stern-chasers, and then brought her other broadside to bear. Inyo gasped at the terrifying sight of the gaping cannon maws all aimed at him, at Ansa, at their ship. He stumbled backward in fear of the next assault. And it came. First, a deep and menacing tremble in the distance, a furious searing in the tense air between the ships, then the heavy thuds of cannon shot against the hull, a volley that took its toll on another man on the upper decks. Inyo whispered a prayer for Ansa's safety.

But now, surely, we'll close in, grapple the enemy, and begin boarding, Inyo hoped, but the English ship dashed away too quickly, while above him his shipmates screamed their anger into the wind. "You bastards, come back here and fight like men!"

The *Catalina* clearly wasn't able to close in. Instead, another nimble English vessel increased to battle tempo, brought her starboard broadside to bear, and fired. She came about, unleashed the larboard battery, and quickly retreated before the *Catalina* could react, let alone get close enough to attempt boarding.

Heavy gun smoke obscured the sea. Inyo coughed, closed his stinging eyes in the darkness, and wiped the sweat out of his face, trying to comprehend the outlandish speed of the attacks. He peered through one of the starboard hatches. Two miles south was a second line of enemy ships attacking the Armada's seaward flank. It appeared that both lines intended to remain upwind of the Armada.

So, this is their strategy! Attacking our flanks from a distance . . .

As quickly as the crowded conditions allowed, Inyo staggered along the length of the smoke-filled gun deck again, inspecting each section. He hurried down to Miguel and reported, "No damage on the gun deck!"

"Good!" Miguel's voice was filled with grim determination as he stumbled towards Inyo, his lantern illuminating the timbers near him. "No damage or leaks here either. The hull is intact!"

"It looks like the English just want to fire on our flanks, one ship after another. But they won't come close enough for boarding."

"Cowards, all of them," Miguel huffed.

"Seems they're desperate and this is the only thing they can think to do," Inyo speculated.

"As long as we can hold our formation, they are nothing but dung flies to us," Miguel grunted obstinately and stepped aside as a group of men carried a moaning soldier past them to the surgery. Inyo turned pale and quiet when he saw the soldier's anguished face, his blood-soaked vest, and the surgeon readying a table.

A shipmate appeared on the ladder, shouting, "Carpenter, the captain needs you!"

Miguel and Inyo clambered up to the quarterdeck and had their first look at the damage. There were several holes in the *Santa Catalina's* sails and shattered portions of the railing. Sandoval and Martínez stared at the line of English ships to windward, none of which were currently in firing range.

Sandoval turned to Miguel. "Sabado, how quickly can you repair this damage?" The captain pointed out several limp strands of the mizzen shrouds, their heavy deadeyes and chains damaged by shot. Inyo knew what that meant: the mizzen mast was weakened, in danger of toppling into the other sails and masts, hampering their agility.

Before Miguel could answer, however, gasps from the crew drew everyone's attention out to sea. "What in God's name?" Martínez yelled, rushing to the rail, his eyebrows deeply furrowed. Everyone's eyes were glued to the *Rosario*. She had broken formation and now veered north in an attempt to pursue the English vessel closest to her. Despite her towering size, she managed to turn, heeling in defiance against the wind.

"*¡Dios mío!* It's the *Revenge*! El Draque's ship!" Sandoval shouted. "She is going after Drake!" Inyo wondered how Sandoval could know this was Drake's ship. Had the captain been in Cadiz during Drake's attack, like Antonio? Sandoval slapped the gunnel. "They're going to board!"

"Yes!" Inyo yelled. He clenched his fists tightly. They'd take the *Revenge* and force Drake to surrender!

Don Álvaro appeared next to Inyo and leaned over the rail,

enthralled by the *Rosario's* gallant maneuver while all around them the crew cheered loudly.

But then Medina-Sidonia's flagship fired a cannon as a signal to stay in the assigned positions. As if to emphasize the urgency of the order, additional flag signals rose quickly on the *San Martin*, ordering everyone to remain in formation.

The *Rosario* fired her bow chasers at Drake's galleon, but they were too far away to cause any damage. Then the ship quivered, struggling in the wind as she came about and attempted to re-take her position. She was barely fifty yards away from the *Catalina* when a gust of cold wind pushed against her tall castles and her riddled courses, indifferent to the hectic shreds of shouting and running feet between her damaged rigging. Sandoval and Martínez brushed past Inyo, panicked muttering flying between them, as they stared at the *Rosario's* approach.

"No!" Sandoval roared. The *Rosario* couldn't complete her full turn. Instead, she now sharply veered towards them and sliced helplessly through the choppy waves, her bowsprit aimed right at the *Catalina*.

His expression and voice tinged with raw panic, Martínez shouted to the helmsman, "Hard a-starboard!"

But it was too late. With a sickening creak, the *Rosario's* bowsprit clipped a back corner of the *Catalina's* tall stern castle, tearing into the railing and obliterating a chunk of the deck. The decks beneath Inyo shuddered, Martínez fell, and both crews screamed their panic and anger at each other. In the agitated waves, the two vessels grated, reared, rose, and fell like stags in a fight until the *Rosario's* bowsprit broke off. Her spritsail and tangled ropes raked over the *Catalina's* stern castle, ripping away more of the rail. Inyo ducked beneath a swoosh of wet canvas, but quickly became engulfed in the chaos of ropes, a frenzy of running feet, and panicked shouting.

"Álvaro!" Sandoval screamed. "*Álvaro!* Man overboard!"

Inyo and Martínez staggered to the railing, shocked to see Don Álvaro's head in the furious waves between the two ships as he thrashed about. Inyo found himself paralyzed, the scene before him entirely unreal. The *Rosario* attempted to veer away, but she was still dangerously close. The ocean swelled between the vessels, pushing them apart, and in the widening chasm, Álvaro swirled helplessly and drifted away. Sandoval and Martínez were unable to speak and instead cast a glance of resignation at each other.

After a few wingbeats of hesitation, for reasons he couldn't quite explain, Francisca's voice echoed in Inyo's mind, a song she used to sing, and the words took on meaning as if they had waited for precisely this moment. When Álvaro screamed again, a jolt of determination fired through Inyo's body.

"A rope!" Inyo roared, groping around in the mayhem that surrounded him. He found a coil and, with cold, trembling hands, pulled out one end. With a hard stare, Martínez approached, glowering at him. "What the—? Are you mad?"

Inyo, wide-eyed, shouted back, "I have to try!" He finished tying the rope around his waist while Sandoval and Martínez muttered angrily, but they didn't stop him. They secured the other end of the rope around the mizzen mast. "We have you. Go!" Sandoval's voice trembled.

Inyo scurried down the damaged hull and lowered himself to the stern gallery. He paused as Don Álvaro bobbed away. Sandoval was right. Martinez was right. It was hopeless. But Francisca's song inside of him took over all his reasoning. *I was lifted out of the pit of despair. Out of the mud and the mire. My feet are set on solid ground. My eyes are set on the sky.*

The fire in his heart burned away all fear, and he flung himself into the frigid waves. His lungs constricted; an icy grip pulled on his limbs. He sputtered and gasped when he popped up next to the *Catalina's* towering hull and swam against the onslaught of the wild sea. Don Álvaro's head disappeared behind wave after wave. The heavy rope pulled on Inyo's hips.

A woman's piercing scream tore from the gallery above him. In the distance, an enemy vessel came into view, and her cannons started firing at a Spanish ship that sailed a few hundred yards astern of the *Santa Catalina*. Water and fear barreled over Inyo. Fighting against both forces, he kicked his legs hard and crawled through the cold sea.

He was within reach when Don Álvaro went under again. A wave pulled them apart. Inyo took a deep breath, ducked, angrily kicked against the resistance of the rope, and reached out his arms. Miraculously, two heartbeats later, he found and tightly gripped Álvaro's arm. When they came up for air, Don Álvaro screamed, wild-eyed, and clawed at Inyo. "The rope! Grab the *r*—" Inyo sputtered as he got pushed under. Álvaro's leg kicked him; Inyo struggled to come up for air, gasped, and spun around. Don Álvaro clung to the rope, white-faced and in shock, while the crew frantically hauled them both in.

Cannons thundered nearby. Shot whistled through the air and tore into the waves near them, causing columns of water to explode skywards.

Maria, leaning over the stern gallery, was still screaming, her arms outstretched, while another woman tried to pull her back inside. As the *Catalina* wildly heaved, a rope ladder was lowered for Don Álvaro, and he slowly pulled himself up.

As Inyo began his climb, the enemy vessel was directly abeam and fired her broadside. Inyo froze. The sailors above him shouted. Then the whistle of inbound shot pierced the air. Two heavy thuds violently boomed against the hull near Inyo, and another shot hit the stern gallery above him. The structure exploded into a cloud of chunks and splinters. Something heavy hit Inyo's head, and everything plunged into ink.

—

There were low voices in the darkness when Inyo's eyes slowly fluttered open. In the flickering glow of candles, the barber-surgeon turned to him and smiled, "Ah, he's awake!"

Inyo became aware of a spot on his head that ached. "What happened? Is Don Álvaro safe?" he asked weakly.

"Yes, all is well!" the surgeon assured him.

Inyo struggled to sit up. "Miguel, he needs me, the *Catalina*—"

"Shh. It's quite all right, lie back down and rest."

Inyo glanced at the blood-stained apron of the surgeon and two injured soldiers next to him. At that moment, Miguel appeared in the doorframe, exhaling in relief. "Am I glad to see you awake, Inyo! You scared us all when you wouldn't come to."

"The damage, Miguel, what—"

"Don't worry, Inyo. All leaks are plugged, the mizzen is secure, and the repairs on the stern can wait until tomorrow."

"The English?" Inyo wondered.

"They retreated to windward," Miguel snorted. "Maybe they're all out of ammunition. Or maybe they realize we're unstoppable."

One of Sandoval's servants showed up behind Miguel. He carried a large platter of food and handed it to Inyo. "Compliments of Captain Sandoval. He insists you dine with him tomorrow."

—

The Armada remained in its defensive formation the entire next day. Under the hot July sun and with just a weak northwesterly breeze, both fleets bobbed along at a snail's pace all day long. The *Rosario* was the only missing ship, presumed captured. Strangely enough, much of the English fleet had scattered for some unknown reason and didn't make any attempts to attack that day.

The admiral, obviously displeased with the *Rosario's* independent action, sent messenger ships to every warship in the fleet. Under pain of death, every captain was explicitly ordered to hold his ship's position from now on, no matter what.

Sandoval dispatched a company of soldiers to assist Miguel and Inyo with the repairs to the stern. When the sun stood high, Inyo's head started to throb, and he retreated into the shade of Miguel's store. Ansa showed up after his morning watch. "That was so brave, what you did," Ansa said. "I watched you from amidships." After a pause, he asked, "Why did you do it? Why would you risk your life for this man?"

Inyo slowly lifted his eyes to Ansa. "Do you remember that song they taught us in Santiago, the one about being rescued 'out of the pit of despair, out of the muck and the mire . . .?'"

Ansa nodded. "I remember it . . . But I don't think any of the sisters would have wanted you to risk your life like that."

Inyo contemplated again why Francisca couldn't remember Ansa, but his thoughts were interrupted when trumpets sounded for evening prayers. Ansa rose. "We have to hurry."

Inyo knew that attendance was obligatory, but he mumbled, "I'm—I'm too weak to get up right now," he blurted, seizing upon an excuse. "You go on ahead."

Soon afterward, Miguel and a few shipmates huddled in a cluster nearby, eating their meager rations of bland wine, hard biscuits, and salt cod.

Late in the evening, as Inyo readied himself for his supper with the captain, Miguel beamed at him like a proud parent. The carpenter had pulled clothes out of his chest earlier that day and began altering a dark-blue jerkin, then fussed over Inyo's disheveled hair, muttering,

"Want to make sure you look presentable!"

The sweat and grime wiped out of his face, dressed in a clean doublet and Miguel's fancy vest, Inyo stiffly found his way to the stern. He skirted around the helmsman and went past the officers' quarters. In front of a wooden door, ornately carved and painted, a guardsman indicated to Inyo to wait while he knocked and awaited an answer.

"*¡Sí, adelante!*"

Inyo entered the captain's cabin, a small but splendid room with fine wood panels along the walls and window drapes made of maroon damask. Candles illuminated the richly set table in the center of the cabin. Sandoval, Don Álvaro, and their wives rose when Inyo entered and bowed. His breathing turned shallow as he approached the table.

"Inyo. I'm *so* happy to see you. Please, join us." Sandoval motioned to a chair next to Don Álvaro. Inyo took in his host's richly embroidered outfit. The ladies, adorned in colorful satin dresses and lace, smiled graciously when Sandoval introduced them. "My wife, Doña Ana. And Don Álvaro's wife, Doña Maria de Benavente."

Inyo bowed his head politely, trying to suppress the uncomfortable memory of Doña Maria's unsettling screams.

A servant poured wine into the silver goblets. "I owe you my life, Inyo," Don Álvaro began. "I still can't believe you were able to reach me!"

Maria shook her head, dabbed a dainty handkerchief at her eyes, and sobbed, "When I saw him drift away . . . my heart just broke!" Ana placed her hand on Maria's heaving shoulder.

Sandoval explained, "A man overboard is as good as dead even in the best of circumstances. I must admit that I had very little hope. It was a miracle how you braved the waves and the enemy."

Murmurs of agreement rose. "A toast to Inyo, who selflessly risked his life to save mine!" Álvaro raised his goblet. "To Inyo!"

"To Inyo!" they all exclaimed.

The servants brought meat and pastries on silver plates. The women inquired about Inyo's place of birth and upbringing. "I was raised in Santiago and later Coruña, where I learned to be a carpenter. I also worked in my mother's shop, *Libros y cartografía*."

Sandoval's eyebrows lifted in surprise. "I know *Libros y cartografía* in Coruña well." He rose, pulled out a map from his desk, and unrolled it. "Your mother creates excellent work!"

Doña Ana leaned in to admire the map and asked, "Is this one of her creations?"

Inyo nodded, buoyant from all the admiring glances. He already pictured Marina's face when he'd come home to describe this moment to her. The conversation and delicious food lifted Inyo's spirits, and he enjoyed the oasis of calm refinement, a sharp contrast to the previous day's chaos of battle.

"In a few weeks, when we're back in Spain, you must come stay with us," Maria insisted. "You will *always* be welcome at our family's castle at Benavente."

Don Álvaro nodded in agreement and asked, "How can we ever thank you enough for your valorous deed? Is there anything you wish for, Inyo?"

Inyo hesitated briefly, then lifted his eyes to Sandoval. "Sir, may I send a message to the sailing master of the *San Francisco*? He is a close friend of mine from Coruña, and I believe he needs to know about my whereabouts."

"Of course!" Sandoval opened his private desk, pulled out parchment and quill, and invited Inyo to take a seat. "We will send your letter by messenger ship this very evening!"

Inyo began to write.

Estimado Antonio,

I'm safe on the Santa Catalina. She is low on crew, and thus I plan to remain. I will explain everything when I see you in London. Buena suerte!

Con Dios,

Inyo

Inyo folded the parchment. Sandoval sealed the letter and handed it to a servant. "Have a messenger ship deliver this to the *San Francisco* right away!" With a nod, the servant took off.

"Thank you," Inyo said as he took his seat at the table again.

Doña Maria asked, "Is there anything else we can do for you, Inyo?"

"Well, I—" Inyo hesitated.

"Whatever it is, you must tell us!"

"Sir, one of your musketeers, Ansa, is another close friend of mine. In the battle, I noticed—" Inyo bit his lip. Should he really bring up military advice to professional officers? He plunged on quickly, before he could stop himself again. "The English have no soldiers on their ships. They won't come close enough for boarding. But our soldiers . . . standing up on deck—They're so exposed and easy targets for their cannons. I fear for them." Inyo was dizzy, realizing he had forgotten to breathe. Criticizing his superiors, especially on something so outside his expertise, could easily get him flogged or worse.

To Inyo's relief, though, Sandoval and Álvaro listened quietly and glanced at each other briefly. "Your concern for your shipmates is admirable, Inyo. Indeed, the English fight quite differently than anyone else we've faced." Sandoval scratched his chin absentmindedly. "I will confer with my officers on this matter." He cast a thoughtful gaze at Inyo, then motioned a servant to pour him more wine.

Meanwhile, Doña Maria and her husband had inclined to each other, whispering, then turned to Inyo. "Inyo," Don Álvaro began, "we also want to thank you from the depths of our hearts, and we hope that you will accept this small token of our eternal regard and respect."

Maria held out a golden ring. "May I?" she asked with a smile.

Inyo hesitated, then allowed Doña Maria to take his hand. Inyo was at a loss for words when she placed the ring on his finger. It fit. In the warm glow of the candles, he stared at the gorgeous design of the ring: It depicted a handshake. Two elegant hands clasped each other from sleeves adorned with thin floral swirls.

Inyo had seen such rings before when wealthy merchants and officials had visited *Libros y cartografía*. Marina had once explained that these rings, with a design of two clasping hands, were given as symbols of loyalty between political allies, brothers, close friends, or even as wedding bands.

"Your hand reaching out to rescue mine," remarked Don Álvaro. "I can't think of a better way to symbolize and express my gratitude."

At the end of the evening watch, when Ansa and Inyo met each other at their usual spot at the beakhead, Inyo recounted the evening in Sandoval's cabin. Ansa whistled as he admired the ring in the glow of his lantern. "That's real gold! You're a rich man, Inyo!"

Though She Be But Little, She Is Fierce.

AUGUST 1588

U nder a warm summer sun, Finley and Ellis wandered along the shore of the bay, not too far from Galway's western gate. A warm burst of heather and ocean swirled past them. It was market day, a welcome reprieve after a week of harvesting. Finley's arms and shoulders still ached. "Isn't that Tibbot?" Ellis wondered aloud with her face turned away from the shore. Finley's eyes followed her gaze. Half-hidden behind tall grasses and ferns, Tibbot and Sarah lingered in a shady stand of oaks. They were whispering and chuckling while Tibbot played with one of Sarah's locks.

A pang lanced sharply at Finley's chest. Why did it both bewitch and sting to see Tibbot in love, to see the happiness in his face? She closed her eyes. Images of Brendan and Neasa's wedding rose in her, and then, quite unexpectedly, memories of the handsome cartographer in Coruña. When she opened her eyes again, she wondered what it would be like to stand face to face with someone who gazed at her the way Tibbot looked at Sarah. Finley tried to insert herself into the scene at the edge of the woods, wondering what it would feel like to be seen, truly seen, entirely treasured and loved. She couldn't take her eyes off Sarah and Tibbot and the magic that pulsated between them. They stood so close, basking in the moment. Then Tibbot handed Sarah a small pouch, and her eyes lit up as she pulled out a bracelet, admired it, placed it on her wrist, and leaned in to kiss Tibbot.

Finley swallowed. She had seen enough. "I think we should go."

Ellis agreed, "Yes. Teagan and Ronin are probably waiting for us."

A few weeks ago, Finley had started noticing that Tibbot was distracted and inattentive on market days, and had been wandering alone more and more. Now she knew why. Her eyebrows creased. She knew little about Sarah, other than that she was English and often came by to chat when she bought their woven goods and carved figurines. Her family was probably among the town's wealthy merchants.

But what if she's close with the governor or his officials? And what if she finds out who Tibbot really is? No one in Galway knew that Finley and Tibbot were related to the O'Malley clan. It had remained a secret on purpose all these years. To guard it had become especially crucial when the English started targeting the clans neighboring Clew Bay. Finley couldn't help but worry. Tibbot was obviously enchanted, and it was none of her business who he wanted to court, but she couldn't shake off her unease about it all.

—

Elizabeth tightened the polished silver cuirass around her torso, then took up the reins. The energetic white steed below her whickered and shifted eagerly from one leg to the other. Her eyes wandered down the road to the fortifications and the troops' tents, behind which rose a forest of flags, pikes, and halberds. She turned to glance at the incoming tide that relentlessly pushed against the rippling flow of the Thames. No Spanish ships anywhere. She exhaled in relief.

Under Robin's command, her troops had fortified Tilbury and the fort across the river at Gravesend, less than an hour downriver from Greenwich Palace. Cannons had been readied, and an army assembled. She reminded herself that sailing past this defense would be near impossible, at least for the first handful of enemy vessels. But after that, there'd be well over one hundred more ships. Hundreds! With heavy artillery and thousands of troops. The threats loomed like low-hanging clouds. Raw fear sent a tremor through Elizabeth's limbs.

Reports of the Armada approaching the southern coast had flowed in a week earlier. Elizabeth trusted her admirals' plan to engage the enemy at sea, aiming to decimate their numbers. But ever since then, the daily updates painted a bleak picture. Howard and Drake had been largely unsuccessful, and the Armada kept sailing up the Channel, undeterred. They could ferry Parma's troops across the sea and invade London any day now. Nothing stood in their way. Nothing except this defense at Tilbury and these men. England's finest. But could they stand up to Parma's experienced veterans?

Elizabeth had arrived by barge early that day, greeted by Robin and his officers. The troops were assembled, and she was ready to inspect them, to rally and encourage them.

"They're waiting for you, Bess." Robin handed her a bejeweled sword. He was mounted on his war horse, wearing his armor and helmet.

Elizabeth spurred on her charger and led the procession, her white dress billowing out from underneath her armor, cascading down elegantly over the ornate saddle. Robin followed her as she rode up and down before the companies and battalions of troops. Like her, they all knew of the enemy's superiority, their large number and their skill, the hellfire of inquisition that would ravage the land, the looming darkness, and imminent dangers.

And yet, Elizabeth saw a steely fearlessness in her soldiers' eyes, in the way their fists gripped the weapons, a resolute will to prevent the enemy from taking even a single pebble of their homeland. *Like me*, she realized. She had to do for them what she had done for herself, will herself to believe in the impossible, raise determination over fear.

In the center of camp, she reined in her horse, straightened her back, and glanced at the men surrounding her. With thousands of eyes on her, she inhaled and addressed her army.

"My companions in arms! My fellow soldiers!

"Our tyrannical enemy, Spain, is intent on invading our realm, but I have faith in you, knowing you to be as determined to foil their evil plans as I am. That is why I have come in person, to be here in your midst, to be your general, and to ask you to do what I myself am willing to do: defend our freedom, defend England!

"I am just a woman, but make no mistake, I have the heart and courage of a king. I will not allow this invasion to succeed. You know as well as I do that God is on our side." She briefly lifted her gaze to the sky above in a silent prayer, trying to calm her racing heart. "Of that we can be certain!"

The soldiers cheered, some banging their fists against their armor. Elizabeth motioned Robin to her side and announced, "While we're at war, my trusted Lieutenant General, the Earl of Leicester, will be acting on my behalf. His commands are mine, and he will lead you to victory. Follow him, be valiant, and you will be honored and rewarded.

"Now fight for God, for your Queen," she raised her sword and bellowed, "and for England!"

The troops, swept up in her rousing speech, raised their weapons and fists, shouting, "For England!" The chant continued, the words "For England" repeated over and over again. The roaring had a buoyant effect on Elizabeth, lifting her out of dread, sparking a fire of hope, and giving her wings.

Robin escorted her to the headquarters in the fort's blockhouse, overlooking the Thames. The officers and guards huddled over a table overtaken by reports and maps, allowing Elizabeth a few private moments with Robin in his adjoining office. She had taken off her armor when they entered the fort and now stood before him, dressed all in gleaming white, like a virgin bride, reaching for his hands. Robin stared at her; the luminous hue of her dress reflected in his pale face. He lifted her hands to his chest, and she raised herself on her toes to reach for a kiss. When they pulled apart, hands entwined, Elizabeth drank in the silent poems that filled his eyes. "Bess," he whispered as he pulled her into another embrace.

Momentarily free from the need to project strength, she melted into Robin's frame and wrapped her arms around him. Why had he lost weight? Why was his face so gaunt today? She mumbled, "Oh Robin, why are you trembling?" It couldn't be fear. He had never been openly afraid.

He avoided answering her question and instead murmured, "Have courage, Bess. We will not let them pass."

She swallowed, hoping he'd be right. Spain's troops wouldn't show mercy to him, nor to anyone. And when they'd reach London, her head would be under their henchman's axe. A tremor had taken over her entire body, and tears were brimming in her eyes. But Robin's words and his warm embrace reassured her. "Have courage," he repeated. She nodded bravely, wiped away a tear, released her grip on him, and straightened herself to face the uncertain future.

Brothers

A week after sighting the English coast, the Armada neared Calais, preparing to rendezvous with the Duke of Parma in Flanders and to escort the troops to England. In the entire previous week, the Spanish fleet had two more skirmishes with the enemy, running battles during which the English stuck to their strategy of firing at the Armada's flanks from afar, sailing in their predictable line astern formation, always turning away swiftly before getting in grappling range.

Whenever enemy shot raked over the decks, Sandoval kept the soldiers to a minimum, with most sheltered in the castles or below deck. Inyo was relieved and grateful that the captain had taken heed of his suggestion, ensuring Ansa would be safely out of the firing line, for now, and fewer lives would be needlessly lost to the English cannons.

As they approached Calais, the English fleet remained two leagues west. Inyo felt a new confidence building in him and in the shipmates around him. Despite having the upwind advantage, the English had been unable to inflict any severe damage. After losing only two vessels, the Armada still had well over one hundred and twenty ships, while the English fleet consisted of only forty.

Medina-Sidonia had gathered his captains together for a war council aboard the flagship. There were rumors that many officers were concerned for the Armada's safety while waiting for Parma's troops. "The Dutch rebels have well-armed ships that patrol their shallow seas. Parma might be unable to sail out on the barges to join us. And we can't sail into the shallows. Until he's ready to move, we're stuck on this open coast, without a suitable harbor, exposed to the weather and to English attacks," Miguel had explained.

Soon, doubts seeped into the initially confident mood aboard the *Catalina*. No one knew when Parma's army might be ready, but the admiral apparently believed that it would only be a matter of a day or two, and therefore gave the order to drop anchor.

Later that evening, Miguel muttered, "We're sitting ducks!"

"I'm sure Parma's troops are ready," Inyo tried to cheer him up.

"Well, as far as I've heard, there haven't been *any* dispatches from Parma."

Inyo was stunned by this. Why did Parma not coordinate with the fleet? Was he not ready? Did something happen?

The *Catalina* swayed rhythmically on her anchor as Inyo and Ansa met up at the end of the evening watch again. In the lantern light near the beakhead, Inyo asked, "When all of this is over, will you remain in the army or come back to Coruña?"

"I don't know yet." Ansa absentmindedly picked at a stain on his sleeve, then whispered, "Inyo, there's something I have to tell you." Inyo tilted his head, perplexed. Ansa continued, "Well, two things actually. The first thing is . . . I need to ask for your forgiveness. When we first met, and I recognized you from the orphanage, I was—I was angry . . ."

"You were angry? Why?"

Ansa lifted his large eyes. "You don't know?"

"No, tell me!"

"You ended up being chosen by—by a real mother, going to live in a real home and having Juan as your uncle. And Antonio mentoring you from the start. And I—well . . ." Ansa's voice turned to a whisper. "So, at first, I didn't mind how Diego treated you."

Inyo's heart sank as understanding dawned. While he ended up in Marina's home, with all the love and opportunities that came with it, Ansa had to find his own way in life. No uncle, no mother, no Sister Francisca to support him.

"Forgive me," Ansa whispered. "I truly wanted to be happy for you, but it wasn't easy for me."

"There's nothing to forgive, Ansa," Inyo assured him. "I would have felt the same way!"

Inyo stared at Ansa's skinny and deflated figure as lantern light bobbed towards them through the dark forecastle and past the shapes of sleeping soldiers. After the shipmate edged around them on his way to the latrines, Inyo turned his face to Ansa again. "We're both from the same place," Inyo whispered. "Santiago is our home. You and I, we—we'll always be Sister Francisca's little bees. In a way, that makes us brothers." While he spoke, though, Francisca's voice troubled his thoughts again, the way she had said, "No, I never knew an Ansa."

He wondered whether Ansa might be lying, and, if so, why. Nevertheless, Inyo drew him into an embrace, and they clutched each other tightly. Ansa suppressed a strangely high-pitched sob and then inhaled, as if he was about to say something. But right at that moment, a shout from the lookout above them ripped through the night. "Fireship! *¡Dios mío!* Fireship dead ahead to windward!"

Inyo and Ansa were among the first to reach the gunnel; behind them, sailors muttered and screamed. Half a mile away, the English had set a ship alight—a towering monster of flames, a floating embodiment of evil that sent shudders through Inyo's limbs. The strong wind bore the glowing ship right towards the Armada's exposed anchorage. Inyo gasped when several smaller flames near the main fireship flickered in the darkness and grew quickly. Seven more fireships ignited and now drifted closer and closer.

"All hands!" Sandoval's thundering voice awakened the *Santa Catalina* and urged the crew into frantic action. "Weigh anchor! Martínez, quickly!"

"*¡Sí, mi Comandante!*" Martínez shouted. Waves of panicked footsteps reverberated on the timbers.

As Inyo rushed below deck with Ansa, several shipmates already labored at the capstan, attempting to heave up the heavy anchor cable. Inyo hurried down the ladder and into the carpenter's store to shake Miguel awake. Inyo panted, "Fireships. Heading straight towards us!"

"*¡Santa madre de Dios!*" Miguel gasped. Inyo's attention was suddenly drawn to panicked shouts that echoed from the deck above.

"Stop! Drop that axe! I forbid you to cut the cable!"

"We don't have time, sir!"

"Get your hands off me!"

Inyo stuck his head up the companionway. An agitated crowd of sailors held Martínez back from the capstan while two men feverishly axed the anchor cable.

"You will hang for this!" Martínez threatened, struggling against the powerful arms that held him. One of the sailors, an axe in his grip, stared hard at him and growled, "Hang me if you must, but I will *not* allow the *Catalina* to burn!"

"We've lost our main anchor!" Inyo gulped, huddling next to Miguel.

The carpenter's shocked face mirrored his dread. "Without an anchor, we won't be able to ride out another storm safely," Miguel said, shaking his head despondently. Inyo soon sensed the tilting of the decks as the *Catalina* leaned over in the wind, moving away to escape the attack. "We're at the mercy of the elements now," Miguel whispered.

Inyo later learned that in the darkest hours of that night, the confusion and fear of the approaching fireships propelled the frightened crews on most ships to disobey the admiral's order, cut their anchors, and abandon their position.

Driven by strong westerly winds, the Armada scattered far and wide. They miraculously evaded the fireships unharmed. But what would the morning bring?

—

As the vague glow of dawn lifted the night away, the admiral fired his cannon, signaling the fleet to retake their position in the defensive formation. The Spanish squadrons, however, were widely flung out and utterly disorganized. Inyo had been on duty on the foremast lookout since the early morning hours, when Sandoval and Martínez rallied the crew to sail into the fierce gusts, desperate to return to the anchorage near Calais. Far away was the admiral's flagship, the *San Martin*, and four other galleons surrounding her. But the *Catalina* and most other ships weren't able to make sufficient headway against the blustery wind to join them. For hours, the squadrons valiantly fought on at desperate angles, sailing as close to the wind as they could, trying to restore the fleet's formation.

Most concerning was the sight of the English fleet lurking on the western horizon. Their number had doubled overnight, and they now sallied out, a pack of them quickly surrounding the *San Martin* group, others heading right towards the other vulnerable remnants of the Armada. Tension hung over the decks as the salt-ridden gusts lashed Inyo's face.

Martínez's series of commands whipped over the sailing crews, urging them on. The *Catalina* heeled over hard, yielding to the elements, fighting on, too far away from the main body of the Armada to the south. Inyo's eyebrows furrowed as he stared out to sea, his eyes beginning to water. Several of the agile English galleons darted towards them from northwest. Inyo shouted, "Enemy approaching on starboard bow!" *If they keep their distance as before, their guns won't be able to do too much damage*, he tried to assert himself, striving to ignore the searing fear in his chest.

"All hands! Battle stations!" Sandoval's voice cut through the air.

The military officers bellowed their commands. Trumpets and drums clashed above the trembling of hundreds of footsteps. Inyo hurried down the shrouds. Ansa rushed past him, and they slapped each other's shoulders with a quick nod of encouragement. The musketeers and arquebusiers flooded the fighting tops and the castles. Gunners loaded and aimed the swivel guns.

As Inyo scrambled down the ladder to join Miguel, the air around him was charged with danger, lifting the hairs along the back of his neck. The formation wasn't tight enough, Inyo realized. The *Catalina* was utterly isolated, and the English were closing in quickly.

Miguel and the sailmaker readied their gear in the stores. Inyo grabbed his materials and uttered, "I'll cover the gun deck again."

"Inyo, I'll join you," said the sailmaker while he lit the lanterns. Miguel nodded appreciatively. "Good. The more hands, the better!"

The hatches crashed open, and the master gunner readied his men.

English salvos boomed in the distance, and Inyo could feel his quickening pulse in his temples. The *Catalina's* cannons were primed and ready. With tight muscles, the soldiers leaned forward, their eyes darting out to sea. *Will the English use the same strategy again, or will they come close enough for boarding this time?*

The master gunner raised his hand. Through the gun ports, Inyo saw an enemy vessel approach and fire her bow chasers. Judging from the sound of the thuds, the shot hit the forecastle. Then the English swooped into position and presented their broadside barely sixty yards away. *Good God, they've never come this close before!*

"*¡Fuego!*" roared the master gunner. The cannons near Inyo thundered and recoiled. The decks bucked violently, quickly becoming engulfed in dirty gun smoke.

Then the loud English cannons fired back and instantly timbers exploded all around Inyo. Stunned, he ducked under a deadly whirlwind of splinters that slashed his exposed skin. He couldn't comprehend the bewildering chaos surrounding him. The world tilted. A soldier nearby screamed and fell. Inyo opened his eyes to the sight of wreckage, splattered blood, and four gaping holes in the hull.

The master gunner detailed two soldiers to carry the wounded man below, then shouted at his company, "Take your fighting stations, now!"

The soldiers rushed past Inyo. In the confusion, only one shipmate had remained to carry the wounded gunner, and he struggled under the load. Inyo dropped his tools, draped the injured man's arm around his shoulder, and helped get him to the infirmary. Inyo gasped when the surgeon ripped open the man's bloody pants. A dagger-sized splinter sat in his thigh.

Inyo's stomach lurched, and, mumbling about being needed elsewhere, he dashed away, trying to locate Miguel. He found him in the gloomy cable tier near a leak, firmly pressing both hands on a plug. In the lantern light, water hissed and squirted through the frayed timbers. "Hurry, Inyo, help me with this one!" Swinging the mallets, they pounded and pounded the plug, their ragged breaths turning to gasps. Finally, they were able to fill the seams with canvas, oakum, and pitch.

Enemy cannons thundered again while Miguel and Inyo clambered up to the gun deck, where they frantically plugged several more leaks, holding back the invasion of the ocean. From above, guns crackled angrily. "The jackals are within musket range!" Miguel shouted. Inyo imagined the brave companies of arquebusiers and musketeers in the fighting tops and in the castles above him, giving their utmost. And indeed, when he glanced through an open hatch, he saw gunfire peppering the enemy ship and her crew. An English sailor fell out of a fighting top with a terrifying shriek.

Enemy cannons roared again, punching through the hull ten paces away from Inyo, obliterating the timbers that instantly exploded into dusty shards. Inyo stumbled along the blurry gun deck to find further leaks. Then came Martínez's muffled shout, "Helmsman, hard a-starboard!"

The hull creaked and shuddered in the erratic wind. Inyo paused and stared at Miguel. "We're going after them!" he uttered, wide-eyed. The vessel beneath him tilted sharply to engage in her attack.

Sandoval's voice roared, "Prepare for boarding!" Through the port-side hatches, Inyo saw the stern of the enemy ship, now less than thirty yards away. Inyo's heart sped up. What would it be like to board the enemy vessel? The English obviously would stand no chance against the overwhelming power of the *Catalina's* soldiers. Inyo was nevertheless concerned for Ansa.

They sailed broad reach with the wind and closed in quickly. Inyo's face fell when the English galleon abruptly changed course and sailed out of reach. "No!" he roared in a rage of helplessness. The *Catalina* was too slow, too difficult to maneuver; she'd *never* be able to get close enough to grapple and take over an English galleon, no one ever would.

A moment later, the escaped enemy galleon came about and pursued the *Catalina* once more. Muzzles flashed behind the gloomy veil of smoke that hung over the waves. The English cannons thundered and shot ripped into the Catalina's hull again.

Trying to ignore the chaos, Inyo clenched his jaw and continued to work feverishly. As one hole got plugged, two others exploded near him. He furrowed his brow against the rivulets of sweat that ran down his face. *They dance around us like wolves around sheep. They fire again and again, while our cannons sit silent and useless.* Inyo couldn't hold back his angry tears any longer.

A violent impact rocked the *Catalina*, knocking Inyo off his feet, while timbers exploded loudly near him. Dazed, Inyo sat up. Pale splinters surrounded him. His hands were bloodied. What was that strange ringing in his ears? He glanced up to one of the small, square gun ports that had been shredded into a jagged panoramic window, revealing a menacing scene of smoke and enemy vessels. The wails of the injured men on the upper decks pierced Inyo to the core. Sea spray and blood rained down in red curtains from the decks above.

He slowly rose, swayed, lost his balance, and stumbled into a cannon where a shipmate lay motionless at his feet. Thunder grumbled outside, and rain started reluctantly. It soon turned into a roaring deluge, forming shadowy drapes over the sea. For what seemed like an eternity, Inyo stared at the chaos around him, a hollowness weighing on his senses. He was only vaguely aware of Sandoval's muffled voice from above ordering a course adjustment.

The English finally retreated, but the driving rain continued as evening fell, obscuring the sea while Inyo and Miguel worked for hours. Would the *Catalina* be able to join the cluster of other vessels that had started forming up to the south earlier? How could anyone possibly navigate or guess their position in relation to the fleet in such conditions?

Inyo needed to get more caulking supplies from the hold. He sidled past the two dozen injured men waiting near the infirmary. Some looked immobile, already dead, while others sat with drooping shoulders and blood-drenched uniforms. There was a small, limp figure among them.

"Ansa!" Inyo gasped. Ansa's eyes were half-closed, and he moaned weakly. Dark crimson blotches stained his garments. With trembling fingers, Inyo unbuttoned Ansa's jerkin and doublet, revealing a large wooden splinter thrust deep into his right shoulder. Blood had soaked into a wide linen strap that was tightly wound around Ansa's chest like a huge bandage. Inyo looked up when the barber-surgeon and his mate stepped out of the surgery, assessed the injuries, then saw Ansa's bloody figure and Inyo's pleading face.

"That one," the surgeon motioned.

"Let me help." Inyo lifted Ansa's legs while the surgeon's mate carried his torso. In the glow of lanterns, the surgeon's smudged instruments glistened weakly. The pile of bloody garments on the ground, soggy and black, contrasted with Ansa's pale face. Inyo held his hand.

"Looks like it's just that one splinter," the surgeon noted as he wiped the front of Ansa's shoulder, "and with a little luck, it won't have cut into the bone too deeply. We'll see." He then tugged on the blood-stained linen strap on Ansa's chest. "Hm, what's this here?"

Ansa mumbled and held his left hand over his chest while Inyo stared at the tight bandage. The surgeon raised an eyebrow while he gazed at Ansa's face and then nodded briefly. "Oh, I see. So, we have a brave young soldier here, hm? How long have you worked like this?" he asked with a knowing expression.

Ansa's raspy voice quaked, "Eight years, sir."

Their conversation confused Inyo, but the urgency of the moment and his concern for Ansa drove out all other thoughts. Ansa's grip on his hand tightened as the surgeon removed the splinter, cleaned out the area, and then applied sutures. Ansa remained entirely still throughout the whole procedure. Inyo's thoughts drifted to the knife attack in Saint-Nazaire and being given stitches. Ansa smiled wryly at Inyo, as if the same memory had crossed his mind as well.

Inyo watched the surgeon move on to the next man, working

tirelessly in the tightly packed space, attempting to save as many of the injured as he could. Near the infirmary, the surviving wounded stayed under his care all night, while Fra Rodrigo was on hand to offer last rites. Inyo brought extra food and rested next to Ansa, who tossed and squirmed himself into a fretful sleep.

At the end of the evening watch, Sandoval appeared below deck to offer words of encouragement to the injured and to get an update. "We have eight dead, sir," the surgeon admitted with a tired voice, "and about forty wounded. I think half of them have a good chance of making it."

Sandoval nodded solemnly. "We will have the funerals at morning prayer."

Inyo stared at the face of a fallen shipmate, pale as a ghost, while the sailmaker stitched him into a rectangle of old canvas with cannon shot placed by the feet as a weight.

Miguel and Inyo then labored on through the night. Before the end of the first watch, while the sky was still a dark slate, trumpets called to morning prayer. This time, demoralized shipmates gathered around the eight cocoons and after short eulogies, one by one, the bodies were released into the sea.

—

In the morning light, the Dutch coast to the south revealed itself slowly to Inyo's tired and shocked eyes. All through the night, the scattered Armada had been pushed closer and closer to the sand banks of Flanders. Relentless winds pummeled the *Catalina*, driving her towards the deadly shoals. Under Martínez' urging, the sail crews fought to steer away from the dangerous shallows. Port tack, starboard tack, port again, agonizingly slow against the stiffening northwesterly breeze with a main sail riddled with holes from enemy shot.

Inyo was alarmed to see how little headway the *Catalina* was making and feared she'd run aground soon, to be dashed to pieces by the powerful waves. He nervously glanced at the telltale breakers of the sandbanks.

A shipmate nearby took a depth sounding. "Six fathoms!"

Inyo shuddered. While the enemy fleet threatened the Spanish ships from windward, the merciless winds drove them ever closer to the sandbanks to leeward. The English obviously waited to let nature finish off their foes.

"Five fathoms!"

Sailors stopped working and turned their exhausted eyes towards their inevitable death. Some fell to their knees, shoulders drooping, praying quietly. A few desperately clung to the priest's cloak, panic marking their postures as they asked for final absolution.

Sandoval's pale and defeated face spoke of the hardships of the previous days. When he kneeled at the main mast next to Don Álvaro, they both pulled off their hats and bowed their heads. Doña Ana and Doña Maria, their hands entangled in a trembling grasp, hovered behind their husbands like ghosts. The priest's sorrowful chanting swirled around the mainmast and over the decks.

"Four fathoms!"

Any moment now, the keel would rasp against the sea floor. But suddenly, the wind let up, and Inyo's eyes shot up to the drooping main mast banner. A moment later, amid lost hopes and mumbled prayers, the flag unfurled again and—miraculously—this time, it pointed away from the shore.

"Wind coming up from southwest!" the lookout called. Around Inyo, surprised murmurs slowly rose.

"The wind's changing!" Martínez shouted.

Sandoval jumped up and ordered, "Helm to north-north-east. Martínez, lay on sail!"

"Aye, Captain!"

Sailors sprang into action. "It's a miracle!" someone uttered. With teary eyes, Fra Rodrigo glanced around at the jubilant crew.

The *Catalina's* courses unfurled with loud and relieved cracks. Every stitch of sail was quickly set. Inyo stared south at another galleon, maybe half a league away, which hadn't been as fortunate as them and had instead run aground. Her masts were damaged beyond recognition, and the ocean slowly began to devour her hull.

Will the Armada, or what's left of it, still be expected to escort the invasion forces over from Flanders to England? Inyo wondered. For now, though, he knew that Sandoval had to focus on getting them into deeper waters, repairing as much of the battle damage as possible, and finding the flagship to await further orders.

Inyo rubbed his tired eyes as he slowly found his way below deck. He wanted to check on Ansa before his next watch. Inyo's lantern flickered warmly as he approached Ansa, who was fast asleep, his bloody clothes replaced with fresh garments. The surgeon waved Inyo over into his room. "Is Ansa your friend?" he whispered tensely. Inyo nodded. "It's none of my business, but you should know that Ansa's secret, if found out, could mean his death."

Inyo stared at the surgeon, vague shreds of suspicion stirring in him again. So much about Ansa had seemed odd. "*What* secret?"

"You noticed his tight chest bandage yesterday, yes?"

"I did. Is it an injury?"

"No, there's no injury."

"Well, why would he have it then?"

"Think about it." The surgeon gave a pointed look at Inyo's own torso. "Who would want to wrap their chest that way?"

Inyo gaped at him. "Ansa is a *girl?*"

"*Shh!* We can't let anyone find out. I've known plenty of women disguised as sailors in my time. Tough and sea-hardy, all of them. But if the crew or the officers discover this, or—heaven forbid—the church, Ansa will be flogged for sure, and imprisoned, and most likely executed."

Everything began to make sense to Inyo. Ansa had always been a loner, secretive, shrouded in loose and oversized clothing. And Francisca didn't remember an orphan named Ansa when Inyo had told her about him. The surgeon assured Inyo that he wouldn't disclose the discovery to anyone, and that he shouldn't either.

Inyo put his hand to Ansa's forehead, which felt extremely hot, and the wound had now become badly swollen. He stayed by his side, holding watch over him and wiping his sweaty forehead, wondering what all Ansa had to endure—with no family to turn to, living under this assumed identity. A sadness gripped Inyo. How he wished he could have helped Ansa earlier. Eventually, he drifted off to sleep.

Miguel had to shake him awake. "Inyo, we need you. There are still so many leaks."

The repairs would take days, as far as Inyo could see, and would only maintain the ship in a ragged version of her former glory. At the end of his watch, as he staggered to the beakhead latrines, he caught his first glimpse of the loose formation of other damaged warships surrounding the *Catalina*—ghost ships, with shredded rigging, riddled sails, and decimated crews.

Inyo frowned when he spied enemy sails lurking on the horizon. *Why don't they attack and get it over with? After the last battle, they can't have any more fear of us.*

On his way back to the infirmary, he paused to glance at Sandoval and Martínez up on the quarterdeck. Both men were slumped over, their movements slow and labored. The *Catalina* followed the flagship all day, awaiting orders, but Inyo was too tired to keep wondering if, when, and how the admiral planned to return to Flanders.

For the evening meal, Inyo settled in next to Ansa, whose eyes were now open. "Look! We get a double ration of wine tonight. Captain's orders."

"How long was I asleep?" Ansa mumbled.

"All day long," grinned Inyo while he checked on the state of Ansa's injury. Ansa winced as Inyo carefully lifted the dressing. In the glow of the candles, Inyo stared at the swollen, angry, red wound. That, along with the fever and Ansa's pale face, worried him, but he gave Ansa an encouraging smile.

"I wanted to tell you—" Ansa began in a low tone, only for Inyo's ears.

"I know," Inyo whispered. "The surgeon and I, we know. But we're the only ones."

"No one was to find out. I never wanted to get caught," Ansa sighed with a hint of guilt in his voice.

"I promise, we're not going to give your secret away!" Inyo replied. "I was just surprised. With your short hair—well, to be honest, I had a few suspicions. And when I told Sister Francisca about you, she couldn't remember any orphan called Ansa. So, what's your *real* name, my friend?"

"They named me Anisa. It's a very nice name, for sure. But when I started work at the docks at age seven, I always went in disguise, as a boy. Life's easier that way. Told everyone my name was Ansa. And that's who I became and have been ever since."

Inyo nodded. They finished their meal in the comfortable silence of trust and friendship, of a secret unburdened. Ansa then fell asleep quickly and Inyo settled in next to him. He still meant what he'd said: they were brothers and nothing would change that.

Inyo woke up a few times to wipe his friend's forehead, while Ansa tossed his damp head in a feverish sleep. The trembling increased. The surgeon kept coming to check up on Ansa and the other recovering shipmates throughout the night as well.

—

In the morning, Inyo made his way to the main deck. An unknown transport ship bobbed nearby. Maybe they had come to deliver supplies? Inyo's eyes narrowed when he saw their small crew laying on sail, ready to turn westward. There was a man and two women aboard, and Inyo recognized them instantly: Doña Ana, along with Don Álvaro and Doña Maria, gaunt figures with unkempt hair. Captain Sandoval waved at his wife from the *Catalina's* quarterdeck. A shipmate nearby, inclined to Inyo, whispered that the nobility was being plucked from the warships, all of them, and that there was a covert plan to return them to safety, to France or Spain immediately. Inyo frowned, watching the transport vessel beat away slowly. This was all wrong. Weren't they supposed to witness the Armada's victory? And how long would it take them to reach a friendly shore? He could see no land anywhere. The winds must have carried the Armada far into the North Sea. Juan had always said it was a savage ocean that was best avoided. The enemy fleet also still loomed to the south, neither relenting their pursuit nor attacking, just herding them farther and farther away from England.

With furrowed brows, Sandoval paced the quarterdeck late in the afternoon, anxiously looking out over the gray sea with its foggy patches that lifted only intermittently. Half a mile away, Medina-Sidonia met with his senior officers aboard the flagship. After an endless wait, the *Catalina's* crew finally saw the small messenger ships fan out from the flagship, swerving under the looming shadows of the tattered warships, delivering the admiral's orders to each captain.

One such messenger climbed aboard the *Santa Catalina* and handed over a letter. Sandoval read the orders and passed the roll of parchment to Martínez. Both men gave each other a hard glance, lips pressed together in an effort to stifle their fury. After the messenger ship darted away again, they motioned for Inyo to join them. Puzzled, he followed them as they marched to Sandoval's cabin under a cloud of snarls, sharp and angry. What was going on? When Inyo heard Sandoval muttering about the "need to confirm the map's accuracy," a panic caught fire in him.

Once the door was closed behind them, Martínez uttered, "He's abandoning the entire mission?" Sandoval rifled through the charts on the rack while Martínez read the orders with shocked eyes.

"Sir, what—" Inyo began, but Sandoval interrupted him, thrusting a chart at him.

"This map of Scotland and Ireland, Inyo, how accurate is it?"

Inyo was startled to hear they were to head for such northern latitudes, and then he saw the flawed chart, the vague and distorted coastlines of Scotland and Ireland. *Good God, how old are these maps? Why hadn't the captains been given updated ones?* Inyo inhaled sharply, recalling Marina working on a Scotland map not too long ago. "Sir, may I?" he blurted. Making for Sandoval's desk, dipping the quill into ink, he began to redraw the coastline of Ireland and Scotland, as best as his memory allowed, from having seen Marina's work.

Sandoval explained, "The admiral has decided the winds are too strong to attempt a return to Flanders, so we are to sail north around Scotland instead, then south past Ireland and back to Spain."

"Without resupplying in Denmark, Norway, or Scotland?" Martínez asked, the order quivering in his grip.

"All Protestant—can't trust them," Sandoval grumbled and took the parchment from Martínez, rereading it. "Ireland is also ruled out, too many English troops and garrisons there. Instead, we are to remain in battle formation and cut rations further." Sandoval's shoulders slumped as he exhaled. Then he abruptly crushed the order in his hand and threw it against the door.

"Sir, that route will take us at least a month. Or longer," Martínez warned grimly.

"Right. Without resupply, it's madness!" Sandoval's anger

darkened his face. "We have water and food for, what, a few days at most?"

The pained voices of the officers brought a tremble to Inyo's hands as he tried to concentrate on his work. Sandoval only had two choices, Inyo realized: break official orders and risk execution, or follow the admiral's orders and sacrifice the lives of the crew.

Inyo finished the map, then headed above deck, where he shuddered in the freezing gusts. He huddled up with the crew for evening mass, where half a dozen more dead shipmates were released into the deep. Numbed by hopelessness, Inyo gazed out at the tattered sails and damaged hulls of the ships closest to him as the sky darkened.

When the main body of the Armada reached Scotland's Firth of Forth, the English fleet that had been snapping at their heels all this time finally disappeared. The experienced sailors warned about how dangerous autumn could be in these latitudes.

And indeed, storms, illness, uncertainty, and starvation in the constant thick fogs awaited them. Aboard the *Catalina*, the grim elements hardened the crew's faces. The arduous work of sailing, pumping, and repairs had to continue. Foul water, filthy conditions, and shortened rations began to show their effects. Diseases spread aboard the ship like wildfire, taking the injured first, then the old. Inyo guessed that it was the same aboard all the other vessels, too. Ansa's fever peaked, and he became weaker and skinnier by the day.

The temperature plummeted, and every day, more men had to be buried at sea; Fra Rodrigo and the barber-surgeon were among them. The crew's pace became ever more sluggish and labored. Morale deteriorated completely. In a state of perpetual hunger, Inyo hammered material into weakening seams, toiling in the dark below deck. He pulled extra duty above deck, rarely getting any sleep.

—

Late in August, the *Santa Catalina* doubled around the island of Orkney. Scores of worn-down soldiers and sailors crowded together in the darkness of the decks among an overwhelming stench and the moaning of the sick. The meager meals affected even the most robust and hardy of them, with now half a dozen or more shipmates dying every day.

Miguel and Inyo sat at Ansa's side in the gloom of the infirmary, slumped over, their tired eyes staring into space. Ansa was completely unresponsive. When Inyo tried to give him some water, he didn't come to. Inyo shook his frail shoulders, gently at first but then more desperately. He called his name, but Ansa's eyes still didn't open, and his breathing faded away completely.

"Ansa! No! *Ansa!* Please! Oh God, not Ansa, please!" With tears streaming out of his burning eyes, Inyo wrapped Ansa's limp body into an embrace and cradled him on the damp timbers of the miserable lower deck. A dull pain gripped Inyo's chest as he sobbed for hours, refusing to release his friend's body. Ansa's skin turned cold, and a blind rage took over Inyo's mind. *This isn't fair! This is the admiral's fault, the cursed King's fault!* Lines of fury and grief furrowed Inyo's face, and tears clouded his vision.

The next day, under black clouds and lashed by bitter winds, Inyo stood on the main deck with his head bowed. He couldn't bear to see his friend's tiny body wrapped in the pale burial cocoon. With Miguel at his side, Inyo wept while Sandoval prayed over Ansa. Then they gave him over to the sea.

Lugh and Tureann

SEPTEMBER 1588

One storm after another barreled towards the Armada. The coasts, other ships, the stars, and even the sun vanished for days, turning navigation into desperate guesswork. Depth soundings showed they were likely in the safety of deep waters, so they kept their course. It wasn't until September first that a break in the clouds allowed Martinez to log their position at fifty-seven degrees north. Though occasional clusters of sails appeared here and there, it was clear to Inyo that the Armada was no longer a cohesive fleet but a forlorn scattering of ships, each fending for herself. They had finished rounding Scotland, and following the admiral's sailing orders, Sandoval directed them on a southwesterly course.

During the first week of September, more storms and rain reduced visibility to near nothing. While freezing rain beaded up in his scruffy beard and disheveled hair, Inyo, along with the exhausted crew, struggled under the shortened sails and shredded rigging, attempting to stay the course despite the ferocious winds. He now only spotted the sails of one or two other vessels. Most days, the *Catalina* was completely alone, and no one knew how far ahead or behind the flagship was, or if any new orders had been issued.

Provisions and water, which they'd stretched beyond what was thought possible, were now running dangerously low. The only food left was a barrel of peas and a handful of ship's biscuits that the maggots had reduced to crumbs. Many of the crew were sprawled in the forecastle and below deck, half-dead, utterly resigned, their bodies tortured by illness, fever tremors, and stupor. The drinking water would run out in a few days. Of the original number of hands aboard, less than half remained. Day after day, more fell ill and passed away.

Sandoval and Martínez, getting paler and skinnier by the day, took turns on the quarterdeck as the *Catalina* struggled in the heavy seas. Relentless winds clawed at her sails and rigging, progressively debilitating the strength of her masts. Below deck, the caulkers and pumpmen toiled hour after hour. Inyo taught a score of soldiers how to check the plugs and fill the weakening seams, but the water in the hold kept rising as the crew's strength waned.

Then one morning, when Inyo was part of the main mast sail crew, the lookout above him croaked, *"¡Tierra a la vista!"* Inyo's eyes shot over to the east in sheer disbelief. A break in the fog revealed a coastline. *Must be Ireland . . . looks like it's less than a league away.*

Martínez wheezed, "We're far too close!"

The plan had been to stay well west of Ireland's dangerous coast. With the relentless storms and no references for navigation, they'd been pushed to leeward unnoticed. Inyo swallowed hard, aware that they couldn't do anything about their situation. The *Catalina* had no anchor left. She couldn't ride out the storm and was therefore entirely at the mercy of the wind.

Martínez immediately ordered a course change, a desperate attempt at a beam-reach escape, maybe their only way to avoid being driven against the rocks. But sailing an unwieldy warship like the *Catalina* this close to the wind? In her battered state, with a weakened crew, and in these conditions? Her bow sliced through the crest of the swell and plunged hard into the trough of an enormous wave. Numb and shocked, Inyo watched the thick fog swallow the coast.

Extreme winds gusted from the west, bringing frigid, driving rain. The shredded sails flapped loudly in protest as they were furled. Furious swells beat the hull, and icy sea spray blasted over the bow. The dismal weather quickly turned into a horrific tempest unlike any the men had ever experienced. Martínez commanded the entire crew to tie into the safety line. Inyo wrapped a rope tightly around his waist and braced himself for the wild and unpredictable upswing of another monster wave. With each terrifying fall off the towering rollers, his body was lifted into the air, then slammed down hard on the slippery deck. The gale was driving the *Santa Catalina* ever closer to the coast.

"Helm over!" Martínez shouted to the sailor at the whipstaff, his voice tinged with fear. Inyo staggered after his shipmates and swayed on the tilting deck when the sea's onslaught caught the *Catalina* on her way into a trough, bucking her sideways. Inyo fell hard and barreled into the gunnel. The pain of the impact wrenched a scream from him and instantly lit up his senses. He scrambled to his hands and knees while the wind screamed in the rigging. Seawater washed over the deck and ran out the scuppers.

With a jolt, the *Catalina's* bow was pushed to larboard. Through the curtains of rain, Inyo, horrified, caught a brief glimpse of a wailing shipmate being flung overboard. A rope high above Inyo snapped loudly. Then a mast creaked and toppled. Canvas and rigging collapsed, and a wall of spray blasted over the decks. The *Catalina* leaned over, unable to escape the ocean, the gale's powerful will and single-minded rage. The surge devoured the world around Inyo. It quickly engulfed him, and swept away the deck beneath him. The icy weight of the sea clamped down on his lungs and burned in his throat. Ensnared by ropes, he struggled to stay above water as the ocean lifted him and then abruptly pulled him under.

—

In Barna, Finley was wrenched from her sleep by the howling gale. After a few disorienting moments in the darkness, jolted by the drumbeat of rain on the wooden shutters, she wrapped her blanket tightly around her shoulders and scurried to the hearth, where a few weak flames still flickered and cast an amber glow in her face. She added a log to the fire and shuddered. Unseasonable storms with freezing winds and endless rain had battered Galway Bay for days. Her father shuffled past her, lit a lantern, and raised it as he slowly and methodically checked the roof's underside. "Haven't had a storm like this in a long time," he said.

"Any leaks?" Finley asked.

"No, thank God. I think we'll be alright," Brian concluded after making his round. He headed back to bed after nodding at her in his usual calming way.

She continued to stare into the flames. When the shrieking outside escalated, Ronin woke up too. He dashed to her, climbed under her blanket, and curled himself into her embrace, muttering, "I'm so scared . . ."

Finley ruffled his hair. "Don't worry, my sweet. It's just rain and wind."

Ronin pressed his tiny hands over his ears, asking, "But why is it *so* loud?"

"Well, you know Tureann, the god of thunder, right?"

Ronin nodded, his eyes growing wide with anticipation.

Finley said, "He's a mean one. Always in a sour and jealous mood, always looking for a fight, especially with Lugh. You know who that is, right?"

"Lugh is the sun god," Ronin said.

Finley nodded. "You see, whenever Tureann and Lugh quarrel up in the heavens, that's when we have weather like this, with thunder and lightning. The meaner the fight, the worse the storm."

Ronin contemplated her story for a while. "They need to stop fighting," he mumbled.

Finley nodded. "Don't worry, they'll wear each other out real soon."

The siblings remained huddled together, watching the fire, hoping the daunting roar outside would let up. Eventually, Ronin's little body relaxed, and he fell asleep. Finley carried him over to his cot and tucked him in. She then climbed into her bed, closed the drapes, curled up under her blanket, and waited for sleep to come.

The horses! She sat up. Tibbot and Teagan had fed and watered them before the evening meal, but Finley wanted to check on them again. She slipped on her cloak, reached for the lantern, then sidled through the well room and into the barn. The storm rattled the barn door in a menacing way. She placed the lantern on one of the high windowsills to illuminate as much of the shadowy barn as possible. The horses shifted their weight restlessly from one hoof to another with wide eyes, lifted heads, and flicking tails. She spoke to them in a low tone and stroked Arlyn's flank until he snorted and relaxed his frame. She brushed her hands down Cormac's neck, trying to block out the raging outside. Then she melted into Merla's fur, inhaling the sunny aroma of hay while the mare rounded her head, lipping at her cloak. With every deep breath she took in the calming huddle, Finley sensed her pulse slowing.

—

Inyo's strength vanished as wave after icy wave pulled him under, forcing him to repeatedly struggle up for air, shuddering and sputtering and gasping desperately while his limbs stiffened and his movements slowed. There was a piece of wreckage he managed to grab. Clamping down on its edges as it was tossed about, he felt for its shape: a broad plank. He was terrified of losing his grip on the plank as he was being hurled about.

With every labored gasp, Inyo's lungs seared in pain, his breathing turned to crackling wheezes and his mind spiraled into a daze. Pictures of home sparked in his mind, shreds of memories that faded quickly, lost color, fell silent under the churning of the ocean. How long had he been holding on now? An icy fog took over his thoughts, and a heavy numbness pulsed through his hands. Slowly, and almost gratefully, he surrendered to the inevitable.

But then the roaring changed. It now included a deep, crashing rhythm, its alarming thunder getting louder and louder. A surge of panic gripped Inyo, frightening images of towering cliffs in the dark, of rocky headlands, and churning waves. Then his plank rose upwards in one long swoop up onto chafing grit, onto a strange firmness under him. What was it? Sand? He scrambled to his knees, dumbfounded. Was this all a bizarre dream? A wave barreled him over from behind, and he landed, face-first, on cold, hard sand. The plank slammed into his shoulder. He labored to rise and take a step forward when the surf crashed into his legs again and toppled him over. The menacing roars of the waves behind him instilled urgency into his jerky movements as he got up on all fours and crawled over sand, seaweed, pebbles, and jagged boulders.

The ocean finally released its grip. Inyo's entire body trembled in the frigid night as he sank into a stand of reeds with a heaving chest, hoping the dizziness would let up. But instead, the cold now stung even more, and the sideways rain, pelting relentlessly, propelled him to scramble back up and head further into the darkness. He navigated away from the shore with a spinning head, wind tearing at his hair and clothes. The sea's roaring grew fainter as he stumbled through grass, brambles, and dripping bushes, trudging on through the darkness. His breath grew ragged, forcing him to hunker down a few more times before he plodded onwards. Soon, he stumbled over the gnarled ankles of a tree. He rose again and staggered through a disorienting forest of ferns, uneven ground, and branches that whipped into his face. The howling around him was unchanged, his breathing was still labored, but the trees soon disappeared, and the ground beneath him began to squelch. And then he froze at the sight of something so surreal and unexpected.

Just ahead of him, a skinny sliver of amber hovered behind curtains of rain. He could see nothing else, only this enchanting shape. Inyo blinked, his mind searching in vain for an explanation. He lurched forward, swaying, reaching out one trembling hand until he bumped into something hard and cold. A stone wall, perhaps. Inyo steadied himself, wiping the rain out of his eyes, trying to make sense of what was in front of him: a slice of light falling through a gap in what appeared to be a shuttered window.

With his hands braced against the building, Inyo peeked through the crack, making out the ears of a horse. The flickering glow inside the stable moved, dimmed, and then faded completely. How risky would it be to hide here? If someone found him, he might be killed on the spot or given over to the English. But he was desperate for warmth, for sleep. And so he edged along the wall, his frozen hands grating on the rough surface, until he reached a handle. He opened a wide, wooden door, paused to listen, then staggered out of the rain into the muffled darkness. He inhaled the warm scent of animals and pulled the door shut behind him.

A sob of relief and gratitude involuntarily welled up in his chest as he shuffled along the inside wall, with one hand stretched out in front of him, until he reached a pile of crunchy hay. He crawled into the fragrant hay, covered himself with it, and wrapped his arms around his knees. A horse nickered and the wind whistled through the thatch above his head. The storm's howling outside slowly faded as Inyo fell asleep.

Haven

The rain and wind kept everyone inside all morning. Brian worked at the loom while Finley whittled wood with Ronin and Teagan. In the afternoon, Finley and Tibbot kneaded a few small loaves of barley bread and placed them on the hot stones near the fire. It was time to feed the horses, and Finley motioned Teagan to follow her.

Their lanterns lit up the barn walls and the horses. Teagan began scooping oats, and Finley headed into the well room. She shivered as she cranked the handle. Once her bucket was filled, she shuffled back to the horses with it.

While Merla, Cormac, and Arlyn munched on hay and oats, Teagan started mucking out behind them. He worked quickly, humming, while Finley filled the trough with more water.

—

Inyo woke up, aware of voices speaking in a foreign tongue. From his cave in the pile of hay, he could see the glow of a lantern as well as weak light coming through the windows. He tried to breathe as quietly as he could and remained motionless.

—

Finley whispered into the horse's fur, "Merla, my sweet. Maybe tomorrow will be better, and you can go out to pasture."

Teagan placed the shovel and bucket back into the corner, then stumbled over something protruding from the hay.

"What the—?" He brushed the hay aside, revealing a boot. Then someone sat up in the hay, a wild-looking creature. "Finley!" Teagan yelled.

—

Horrified, Inyo stared up at the screaming and frantic boy, when another figure with a shovel rushed towards him with a savage battle cry.

—

Finley's panic unleashed a fury inside of her. *Teagan! Who is this man?* A wild roar exploded out of her, one she had never heard herself make before. She lifted the shovel, ready to swing it down with all her might, desperate to smash the intruder before he could attack her brother.

—

The shovel! Inyo threw his hands above his head. "*¡No, no! ¡Por favor, no!*" he croaked.

—

Finley halted her attack when she heard the pleas, recognizing the language. *Spanish?* She lowered her shovel, breathing sharply. "Teagan, bring the light over here!"

Teagan edged towards her with the lantern, and Finley's hands trembled as she scrutinized the man's pain-filled face. He was all tangles of black hair, an unkempt beard, and tattered remnants of a shirt. "Good God—I'll get Da'," Teagan stuttered.

Finley tightened the grip on the shovel. "Tell him to bring his sword!"

Teagan hurried away while Arlyn whinnied and stomped a hoof. Finley studied the gaunt figure in front of her. His ripped clothing, pleading eyes, and the dried blood in his dirty hair. *Why would a Spaniard be here?* Finley wondered. The lantern light flickered, casting shadows on the barn wall as Finley edged closer and asked, *"¿España, tu?"*

—

Inyo's face lit up, surprised to hear the girl speak Spanish. He nodded. *"Sí. España.* Mee, Spain. I . . ." Cloudy thoughts obscured his tired brain, and he struggled to remember any of the Gaeilge he'd learned aboard the *Gaviota.* Why could he not remember more? All he was able to mutter was a weak "gracias." He pressed his hands together and glanced at the girl's red hair. A foggy image began to stir in him, an obscure memory. A mane of red hair framing a face adorned with a beautiful smile.

Three adults stormed into the barn with raised swords and grim faces. The girl whirled around, shielding Inyo with her outstretched arms. She shouted at the adults over and over again. It was a clipped exchange he didn't understand, but the girl obviously defended him, arguing with the adults, her pale hands gesturing wildly. The intensity of their conversation eventually eased, but then Inyo had to watch helplessly as the girl was sent away. The two men and the woman closed in on him, the blades of their swords glinting. *Now what? Will they finish me off? Months of starvation and misery at sea, the English cannons, the hellish storm, the shipwreck, and now this . . .*

Lifting both his hands, Inyo stammered, "Help, please! Mee, friend." He was surprised when the woman knelt in front of him, spoke to him, and gently touched his head where he could feel a tender spot underneath the crusty blood that had caked his hair together.

After another brief exchange, one of the men took off his cloak, swung it behind Inyo's back, and helped him wrap it over his shoulders while the woman reached for his arms. Relieved and astonished, Inyo stared at them and croaked another "gracias" while his eyes involuntarily filled with moisture. They slowly pulled him up. Inyo was dizzy and sore, and his head began to throb again when he shuffled out of the barn and through a small well room, supported by several arms.

They entered a large, warm cottage. In one corner, the girl comforted a young boy who clung to her and hid his face. Inyo was invited to sit by the hearth and was handed a blanket for his legs. His shuddering eased. The comfort of the cloak, the blanket, and the warmth of the fireplace worked their magic. His limbs relaxed and his mind eased. He didn't understand most of what the Irish family talked about, but it had something to do with food. He was given warm bread while the older of the two men sat down next to him and encouragingly patted his back. Inyo broke a piece off the loaf and slowly chewed the first bite. He had never tasted anything so delicious, so heavenly.

He turned to look at the girl, and their eyes met briefly. That mysterious spark of recognition flooded him with undeniable excitement once more. Where had he seen her before? She and her father were heating one kettle of water after another, then pouring them into a wooden tub in a small washroom behind him. The younger man smiled at Inyo, mimed a few washing motions, and pointed to the tub.

Grateful, Inyo limped into the washroom, closed the drapes behind him, shed his damp shirt and shredded pants, and lowered himself into the bath. The hot water felt shocking and wonderful at the same time. He hadn't washed himself since leaving Coruña, an eternity ago. With the water shortage aboard the *Santa Catalina*, all bathing and washing had been out of the question for anyone.

Inyo frowned at the gashes and bruises covering his scrawny body and began to wash away the grime, blood, and salt. He grimaced when his hand grazed against the gash above his left temple. Despite the initial sting of the hot water on his wounds, a ripple of goosebumps spread over him as he leaned back in the warm water, inhaling the deeply soothing aroma of the herbs floating in the tub. He recognized hyssop and rosemary among them. *Like Marina's garden!* The thought gave him a sharp pang of longing to be home. *Mirto, tomillo, salvia, romero.*

He massaged his aching knees, the skin slick in the warm water, and his gaze settled on the back of his hand. There was no ring. He swept his hands across the bottom of the tub. Nothing. *The ring is gone! Did it slip off in the cold sea?* His only possession of worth that could have been traded for safe passage back to Spain was now most likely at the bottom of the ocean. With the *Catalina*. With his shipmates. Inyo drew a ragged breath, fighting back tears.

The clutter of cutlery intruded on his sorrow, along with the aroma of soup and the family's melodic conversation in Gaeilge. While his stomach grumbled, Inyo dried himself off and slipped into the luxuriously dry garments they'd left out for him.

—

While they set the table and the Spaniard bathed, Teagan added a log to the fire. Ronin grabbed his arm and hissed, "Why didn't Da' kill the stinky stranger?"

Teagan shrugged. "Maybe he wants *you* to do it."

"Not funny!" Ronin grunted, sliding his hands into his armpits, pouting.

Finley wondered, "How did he get here?"

"After supper, we can hear his story," Finley's father replied while her mother turned to Tibbot. "I don't remember much of my Spanish. You?" Maeve asked.

Tibbot shrugged. "I'll try. Maybe Finley can help me."

Finley shook her head. "I actually didn't learn that much. I wish Mamó was here!"

"Aye, she could certainly help us," Brian agreed. "Well, she'll be here for the harvest festival."

Ronin's brows furrowed deeply. "Da', will the stranger stay here *that* long?"

Brian scooped him up and sat him on his lap. "What if it was you? Alone in a foreign country, in need of help?"

Ronin hesitated, biting his lower lip, then nodded slowly. "Alright, I guess he can stay here till harvest festival... But Da', if he's from Spain, you need to burn his old clothes! There might be *duendes* hiding in there."

—

When Inyo stepped out from the washroom, the family cheerfully motioned him to one of the wooden stools, and he sat down. Their table was covered with a colorful cloth. He had seen this fabric before, but where? They all bowed their heads, and the older man prayed in Latin. The familiarity of the words flooded Inyo's starving soul. He smiled and joined them in the "amen." Unexpectedly, in this cold and savage land, he was now safe and dry, enveloped by words that reminded him of home. After the terror and misery of the last three months at sea, here was a place of peace, a haven for his body and soul, and the strangers who fed and sheltered him inexplicably felt like kin. He dipped his spoon into the fragrant stew and savored the warm meal, lifting his gaze to the timbers that supported the roof of their home—massive beams whose curves created the appearance of an upside-down hull, strong and resilient.

After a few moments, his eyes darted to the pale and freckled arm of the girl seated next to him. Inyo cast a sideways glance at her, trying not to be obvious. *Why does she seem so familiar? Where have I seen her before?* Could his mind be playing tricks on him, sleep-deprived and exhausted as he was?

—

Finley handed the Spaniard a platter of bread. "*¿Tu nombre?*" she asked.

"Mee—name—Inyo."

"Inyo?" There was something about the stranger that seemed familiar.

"*Sí*, Inyo. Ignatio Fernández de Santiago. And you?"

"I'm Finley." She then introduced her parents, her uncle Tibbot, and her brothers. Inyo quietly repeated each name with a smile and a nod.

"*Señor y señora* Morris, thank you verry, verry much," he said.

His Gaeilge sounded rough and unsure, but she was surprised that he could speak it at all, and the way her parents arched their eyebrows at each other indicated that they were equally impressed. Finley chewed quietly, wondering if she had seen him somewhere before. On her pilgrimage, perhaps? She offered to pour him another mug of ale, glancing at him as he nodded. This time, she looked beyond the beard and wild hair, focusing on his warm, dark eyes. They were not the eyes of a stranger.

Meanwhile, Tibbot attempted to ask Inyo in broken Spanish

where he was from. *"¿Qué—qué parte de España?"*

"Mee from Galicia, from Coruña," Inyo answered.

Finley stared at him. *He's from Coruña? Could it be . . .?* Images flashed in her mind. The handsome boy at work in the shop. That one singular figure, bent over his table. And the beautiful map he leaned over. She had been so mesmerized by the careful movements of the quill in his tanned hands, by his lovely, concentrated face, by the way he suddenly stared right at her. In those wide eyes, Finley had sensed a trace of bewilderment. Or was it shock? Trepidation? Curiosity?

Although the beard made him nearly unrecognizable, Finley felt certain now that he was the young mapmaker she remembered. She turned to her parents, blurting, "I think I know him."

Her father glanced at her, puzzled. "What do you mean, how would you—"

"I recognize him. I have seen him before! At the end of my pilgrimage, in Coruña. Owen, Tibbot, and I went to purchase maps in a shop in town. Inyo was there; he's a cartographer!"

—

Inyo stared at Finley, understanding some of what she'd said despite the distracting dance of freckles in her face. *She's been to Coruña! She saw me there.* Could it be her? The red-headed pilgrim girl who visited *Libros y cartografía?*

She turned to him, speaking slowly, "You are a mapmaker, yes?" She mimed a drawing motion with her hand. *"¿Cartografía, sí?"* Her warm smile made his heart stutter. *Dios mío.* Yes, he could indeed trust his memory. It was her! He wasn't imagining it.

Inyo nodded and gestured with his hands to indicate that drawing maps was his trade. His cheeks turned warm as memories and emotions danced round and round in his head: the group of Irish pilgrims and her —her smile, her satchel with the scallop shell. "You, *peregrina?*"

—

Finley pointed at herself. *"Sí. Mi, peregrina en el Camino de Santiago."* Images of the pilgrimage whirled in her memory. The voyage, the walk, and the arrival in Santiago. Her impressions of the harbor of Coruña, and of course, his shop, the way he worked on his map, surrounded by paints and rolls of parchment. She had hundreds of questions. *If he's a cartographer, then how did he end up here in Ireland?*

There had been odd talk for some time in Galway. Tense whispers about Spain's plans to send a mighty invasion force to England and to overthrow Queen Elizabeth. A few months ago, foreign sailors spoke openly about a mighty Spanish fleet being underway. Awestruck, rumors flew regarding its size and power—several hundred ships, a thousand, an innumerable Armada, all of it made possible by the legendary wealth of King Philip. By now, the fleet must have reached England.

Strangely conflicting rumors followed: a few indicated that the Spanish had succeeded and taken London, while others said that England had defeated the Spaniards. Hopes and fears collided, and no one seemed to know for sure. But here in Connacht, the English governor in Galway feared parts of the Armada could attempt to land in Ireland and begin their invasion of England from the west. What that meant, again, no one was sure.

Finley turned to Inyo. "You, *tu*, Armada?"

"Sí."

"Where is your ship?" Finley's father wanted to know.

"Donde es tu—" she attempted to translate, casting about for the words.

Tibbot added, "*Tu barco?*"

"Mee ship . . ." Inyo shook his head slowly. He described what happened with brief phrases and a few gestures. "Armada in *Canal Inglés*, Plymouth, Calais, Drake, *sus cañones—*" He paused to swallow, "Battles. Many, many dead. Then, *Norte, Scotlanda, Irlanda.*" He drew an imaginary map on the tablecloth and traced his route with a shaky finger, explaining, "Bad wind, verry bad storm!" A trembling overtook his hands, and he had to pause again. He squeezed the bridge of his nose with his fingers. "Night, ship sink down. And mee . . ." he pointed at himself, then swooped his arms through the air in a swimming motion.

Finley stared at Inyo, openmouthed. He had sailed all this way, all these many months. Despite uncertain reports, the Armada had clearly not succeeded, hadn't landed in England at all, but instead had sailed up north. Around Scotland and Ireland. Tibbot muttered, "Why did they take the most dangerous route to get back home?" Apparently, Inyo's ship had been wrecked in the worst storm anyone could remember. And yet he'd survived. It was unbelievable.

As she studied Inyo's pale expression and the vague tremor in his hands, Finley wondered what that shipwreck must have been like. The shrieking winds, the press of the cold, churning ocean on his body, constricting his lungs, pulling him into the deep, swallowing him, drowning him. Without hesitation, she placed her hand on his.

—

Inyo lifted his gaze, surprised by the unexpected touch and moved by the kindness of the angel next to him. On top of being safe and well fed, something deep inside of him came alive. His soul mysteriously responded to the warm gesture, awakening and ascending from a watery abyss.

—

Finley breathed in the warm aroma lifting from his freshly washed body while she gazed at him. He smiled at her; his dark eyes blazed warmly. There were so many questions she wanted to ask him. About Coruña and his store, the sailing of the Armada, and what happened to his ship. But it was getting late. While they prepared Teagan's bed for Inyo, her parents and Tibbot whispered among themselves, wondering if there might be other survivors and how to help Inyo, knowing his life was in great danger here. After the latest rumors, Bensbury had grown more panicked and sent his troops to the far reaches of Connacht. Hundreds and hundreds of English soldiers now patrolled the coast and the roads.

"So, this half-dead Spaniard, is *this* what Bensbury and his men are so afraid of?" Brian wondered while he secured the door and the shutters.

"We have to help him get to safety, back to Spain," Maeve whispered. "But how?"

—

Inyo sensed the tension in the family's hushed conversation and the deep frowns, realizing the danger his presence posed to them all. He resolved to rest here for a day or two, then find his way off this island and back home as quickly as possible. He had no idea how he'd do that, though. They motioned him to a four-poster bed on the other side of the hearth. Endlessly grateful, Inyo crawled under the covers, turned his face to glance at Finley one more time, watched her close the drapes, and hoped she'd appear in his dreams.

Ian

Inyo's eyes fluttered open. It took him a moment to remember where he was and why his limbs were sore. With a dry throat, he groaned quietly as he sat up, opened the drapes of his bed, and was welcomed by the sight of the fire in the hearth. Daylight flooded through the windows nearby, and he noticed a bag hanging on a peg between his bed and the next, a colorful satchel adorned with a large scallop shell. A smile spread across Inyo's face as he remembered where he had first seen that bag.

No one was here, and Inyo wondered where Señor and Señora Morris might be. And Finley. He slowly ambled through the cottage, the wooden floorboards pressing their rough veins into the soles of his sore feet. On the table were a cup, a pitcher of water, and a loaf of bread, next to a wood shaving adorned with his name in charcoal. Inyo smiled gratefully as he ate and drank near the crackling fire. His eyes paused on the swords on the wall, then wandered past the bundled herbs hanging in one of the windows, down to the basket full of carved wooden toys next to him, then to the spinning wheel and the patterned fabric in the big loom, with its spindles of colored wool.

One of the shutters creaked in the wind, shifting Inyo's thoughts towards the sea. To the fleet. To the *Catalina*, and especially Ansa. Inyo buried his face in his hands, overcome by grief. Echoes of the howling gale flooded his mind. Haunting memories of the furious ocean, the horrors of the past months, and his shipmates. He could clearly see the crew's faces. Miguel, Martínez, and Captain Sandoval. As Inyo listened to the fire's crackle with its sporadic pops, his figure deflated, and tears dripped into his lap. Here he was, safe and warm, but oddly, being safe and warm now felt so very wrong. Inside him churned an ocean of sorrow, a gnawing sense of guilt, and an intense longing for home.

And yet, as he held his hands towards the fire, a sense of peace and relief permeated his body and soul. He closed his eyes and reminded himself of how lucky he was to be alive, to be here. That his desperate prayers out at sea had been answered. This home was undeniably the refuge he had prayed for. Even more astonishing was the extraordinary fate that brought him to Finley, the girl he thought he'd never see again.

Just as he started to wonder whether he should find and help the farmers, crunching footsteps and laughter approached from outside. Teagan came tumbling through the door, breathing heavily. "I win!" he shouted back, hung up his cloak, and turned to Inyo with a grin. "Ah, look who's finally awake." Ronin was next in through the door, followed by Finley and her parents.

—

Finley had worked with her family all morning. Fergal's barn needed repairs on the damaged roof, and after that, they all set about threshing the barley. Tibbot left around noon, mentioning that he had "things to do in Galway." The way he grinned indicated to Finley that his main reason for going was to see Sarah again.

Finley's parents had decided in the morning that no one should mention Inyo yet, to keep his presence a secret, but Ellis must have noticed something because she asked Finley several times what was going on. Indeed, Finley had found herself smiling for no reason over and over again, her gaze turned towards the road leading home. Her thoughts were filled with Inyo. She wanted to talk to him, but the repairs needed to be done first.

Now they were finally home again. "We should show him the farm," Maeve suggested. Finley nodded and smiled at Inyo. "*Mira—nuestro animales y estable.*" She motioned for Inyo to join them, while her mother pointed to a pair of boots and handed Inyo a cloak.

"Teagan and I'll start supper," Brian said, "and you, Ronin? Show our guest around or help me?"

"I'll help with supper," Ronin grumbled, making Finley chuckle. He definitely did not enjoy cooking, but he still wasn't at ease with the foreigner in their midst either.

She watched Inyo inhale deeply as he headed out into the mild afternoon. Gone were the cold rains and winds; instead, the air was infused with early autumn's wealth, the song of a lone bird, and the lush fragrance of rain-soaked earth. They showed Inyo the sheep enclosure, the meadow, the workshop, and then the barn, speaking slowly and clearly, "Sheep . . . meadow . . . barn." Inyo studiously repeated the words and translated so that Finley could learn the Spanish terms.

"You two can take care of the horses and then come in for supper," Maeve said, leaving Finley and Inyo behind in the barn. When Finley was about to disappear between the horses, she noticed Inyo glancing back at the hay in the corner, his hiding spot, before he turned to join her in the tight space between the animals.

"Our horses. This is Merla and Cormac," she explained, "and Tibbot's horse, Arlyn."

Inyo repeated, "Horses, Merla, Cormac, Arlyn."

She grinned, caressing Merla's neck, giving Inyo an encouraging nod as she placed his hand on her horse. Inyo stroked the fur slowly and gently, whispering, *"Qué yegua más linda."*

Finley watched him out of the corner of her eyes and drank in his words. They did something unexpected to her knees, weakening them. In a pleasant sort of way. And she felt a flush on her cheeks and a spark rise from deep within, throwing her heart into a wild jig.

—

Inyo struggled to control his breathing and keep his eyes on the horse, for in this glorious moment, he found himself alone with Finley. He wanted to lose himself in her eyes, in her freckles, but she wrapped her arms around Merla's neck and hid her face. Inyo awkwardly shuffled a little closer and fixed his gaze on Finley's striking red curls. The barn, oddly, expanded to the size of a jubilant midnight sky, filled with hushed breathing.

Finley released herself from Merla and smiled at him timidly. He inhaled sharply when their eyes locked. He felt his face blush uncontrollably. Finley's cheeks changed color too. For a moment, no words were needed, and he was transported back to their chance encounter three years ago at *Libros y cartografía.*

—

Cormac's snort startled Finley out of her trance. "Oh, we need to feed them, um, *alimento—por caballos,*" she uttered as she skirted around Inyo and pointed to the sack of oats and the bucket. She showed Inyo the well. They filled the troughs, bustling about in the tight space, and she caught him glancing at her several times. "Lastly, we muck out behind them," she explained as she handed him a bucket, grabbed a shovel, and continued teaching him new vocabulary. "Shovel," she pronounced, holding it up.

"Shovel," Inyo repeated. Suddenly, with exaggerated panic in his face, he ducked, pretending to escape an imaginary shovel attack.

"Shovel—no! Ahhhh!" he gasped. Finley giggled nervously at the memory of the previous day's close call in the barn.

After the evening meal, her father explained to Inyo in slow sentences, "I'll head to the harbor in Galway in the morning. Maybe I can locate a merchant ship, *un barco*, headed to France or Spain." Inyo nodded gratefully. But then he cast a sideways glance at Finley with a somber expression. Yes, he wanted to get home, but that meant leaving her.

—

The fire had burned low, and everyone had turned in for the night, except for Finley's mother, who worked the spinning wheel in the glow of a lantern. Inyo lay awake under his warm blanket, the worries in his mind chasing each other round and round in time with the low, rhythmic whirr of the spinning wheel. He was in enemy territory, and his life was in danger. He had to find a ship bound for Spain as soon as possible. But, oh, Finley! He hadn't forgotten the girl. All these years, he'd wondered about her, had wished and hoped and prayed that he would see her again. And now, against all odds, his life had been spared, he'd been led here, and reunited with her. It all filled him with elation. But under these circumstances? Having to leave her just as soon as he found her again? Hopelessness flooded him as he draped an arm over his eyes.

—

An arm's length away from Inyo, Finley stared at the drapes of her bed. She tried to make sense of the raging blizzard inside of her, the excitement, the weak knees, the worries, and the warring emotions. Inyo's life was at risk, and they would do everything in their power to help him escape. But the stars had miraculously aligned, and he was here, so close to her. This couldn't be a coincidence—surely it was meant to be, it had to be! How, then, was she to wholeheartedly support his effort to flee, when all she wanted was for him to stay?

In the morning, Maeve insisted on keeping Inyo at the farm. "It's too dangerous for him on the road. Bensbury's patrols are everywhere," she cautioned, and so it was decided that only Brian and Finley would ride to Galway.

"What's your plan?" Finley asked her father while they saddled the horses.

"We need to see if we can secure passage for Inyo on a merchantman. If we can find one."

"But is it safe for Inyo on a ship?"

"Let's hope we find a trustworthy captain willing to make a good deal," Brian said as he tied his purse to his side, "and if it's too dangerous to get Inyo aboard in Galway, maybe we can row him out to the ship as she sails past Barna."

When they mounted up, they caught a glimpse of Inyo's frown. "We'll be back as quickly as possible," Brian assured him as they took off.

As soon as they reached the turnoff to Galway, they saw the backs of English soldiers on the road heading west towards the village of Barna. Finley and Brian quietly turned east and briskly continued past forests and farms. They were close to the city walls when they dismounted their horses and led them across the stone bridge over the swollen river.

Finley gasped, "There are still no ships!" Shocked, she gazed over the harbor and the bay. Her father's eyebrows furrowed deeply. September days in Galway were usually abuzz with commercial activity at the waterfront. But not this year. Trade had dwindled dramatically, and now only local fishermen were at work in the bay and along the river.

They entered the town through the city gate and led Merla and

Cormac along the road past Saint Nicholas' church. The stands of a few local craftspeople, farmers, and fishermen dotted the square. Finley and her father ambled through the thin crowd, eavesdropping on fragments of conversations. The words "Spanish Armada" were everywhere, in the breaths of gossip between the locals, inclining their heads to each other, in the whispers between the bustling merchants.

"Did you hear? A Spanish ship ran aground at Carickeen! My cousin told me about it. The ship belonged to the Armada."

"God's knees, that's just twelve miles west of here. What happened?"

"A few survivors made it to shore. But Bensbury's troops shot them all. And the villagers got to loot the entire wreckage. There was gold aboard that ship and coins sewn into the clothing of the Spaniards. My cousin is a rich man now."

Someone nearby whispered, "Did they have weapons?"

"Aye, cannons and muskets. But the English confiscated those."

Finley shuddered. She was horrified to hear about the murder of Spanish survivors, and it angered and troubled her that the locals were only concerned with weapons and money. But was it any wonder, as desperate and poor as some of them were?

Brian soon spotted a familiar figure. Father Whelan. The priest waved when he saw him and Finley. "Brian, Fin, good to see you!" He lowered his voice. "You heard about Carickeen? Someone told me two more Spanish warships were sighted off the Arans last week, another galleon near Tralee and one that sailed into the mouth of the Shannon."

Brian put on a flawless veneer of surprise. "Wow, the Spanish, hm? And that many sightings!" He glanced sideways at Finley.

When Father Whelan turned towards an acquaintance, she whispered urgently, "Da', maybe one of those Spanish ships is anchored somewhere safe! How can we—"

Finley was interrupted by a loud trumpet fanfare. A company of helmeted English soldiers cleared a path for mounted riders. "Bensbury!" a merchant uttered as the governor and his advisors entered the square. Apprehension filled the air. The foot soldiers' pikes and halberds gleamed in the morning sun, and the ones on horseback all wore full armor over their brown and red uniforms. Finley's breath caught in fear, and the crowd around her shifted uncertainly. Governor Bensbury, adorned in a plumed helmet and stiff ruff, swept his piercing, scowling eyes over the townsfolk as he reined in his mount.

"Citizens of Galway!" he shouted. "As you know, the Spanish sent a fleet against our good Queen Elizabeth. They were defeated by the will of God and by her Majesty's navy. Remnants of this Armada have now been sighted along our shores. You are hereby ordered to report all sightings of enemy ships immediately. Any Spaniards coming ashore *must* be killed on sight." There was something menacing in the governor's voice. "Anyone aiding the Spanish will be executed for disloyalty to the Crown. God save the Queen!"

Finley began to tremble and steadied herself on Brian's arm. He hurriedly waved goodbye to Father Whelan as they headed to the horses. Finley was unable to hold back her tears any longer. "What are we going to do?" she sobbed.

Brian wrapped her in a tight embrace. "Don't worry, Fin, we— we'll figure it out."

They mounted up and quickly headed out of town, but just after the bridge, a patrol blocked the road. The English soldiers glared at them, their weapons at the ready. Finley's stomach cramped violently.

"Halt!" the sergeant ordered them. "Where are you headed?"

"We live in Barna, just two miles west," Brian stated calmly, his voice assured.

"Do you carry weapons?"

"No, sir."

"Open your satchels!"

Finley's bag was ripped from her unsure hand. She had to stifle her revulsion and panic, keeping her face expressionless while the soldiers rifled through their belongings. They snorted, shamelessly grabbed a few errant coins, then threw the bags back at them.

Brian grumbled after the tense encounter, anger mottling his face crimson. The English were everywhere now. Their apparent fear of a Spanish landing made them paranoid and dangerous. Finley found herself so shaken and overwhelmed that the ride home felt like a trance, the sun much higher than she realized when they finally arrived. "Da', what should we tell Inyo? Would it be best to—to keep him in the dark about Bensbury's orders and what happened to those other survivors?"

Brian took off Cormac's tack and paused. "Hm, I don't know. If you were in his shoes, wouldn't you want to know the truth?"

Tibbot, Maeve, Ronin, and Teagan poured out of the cottage, and Brian filled them in on the latest developments in Galway. A drumbeat of steady pounding had rung out from the forge all this time, but it now stopped. A figure appeared in the open door of the workshop. Finley narrowed her eyes. Who was that?

"Good day, milady!" Inyo greeted her with a bow, eyes dancing with amusement. He wore a set of her father's work clothes, the beard was gone, and his black hair was hidden under a wide-brimmed cap.

Finley's lips twitched into a smile, the burden of fear and trepidation set aside for a moment. Teagan excitedly told them the disguise was his idea, that Inyo could conceal himself as a local farmer, and that's how they'd keep him safe. And that he also taught Inyo more Gaeilge words, and how, together with Tibbot, they had forged hooks and axes.

While Teagan rambled on, Inyo motioned Finley inside the

workshop, showing her the result of his work. She gawked at the iron tools and then back at Inyo, who stood so close now that she could hear his soft breathing. He looked at her the same way he did in the barn, his dark eyes intensely focused on her.

Her heart sputtered when Inyo slowly reached for her hair and mumbled, ". . . *tan hermosa* . . ." Swarms of wintery goosebumps began to purl up and down her back when he spoke, his gaze swooping from her hair back to her eyes. But as the crunch of footsteps approached the workshop, she broke eye contact, quickly took a step backward, and turned her face to the axes.

Teagan and Brian showed up in the workshop. "Da', let's name him Ian Morris. We can pretend he's our cousin," Teagan suggested and added details on how he and Tibbot had taught Inyo the basics of using the forge and the anvil.

"Well done!" Brian held up the tools and turned each one over with an approving nod while Inyo's cheeks turned red. Then, however, Brian's smile faded when he had to explain to Inyo that there were no ships bound for Spain. "And the English soldiers in Galway . . ."

"*Soldados inglés*," Finley attempted to translate. Inyo's frame sagged, and the color drained from his face.

"Don't give up hope, Inyo," her father said. "You're safe here, and I'm sure we'll find a way for you to flee. We'll keep looking for Spanish or French traders."

"*Un—un barco a España, mañana, es possible*," Finley encouraged Inyo, but there was doubt in her voice and apprehension in the way Inyo nodded in response.

Later that evening, he whittled wood with Teagan and Tibbot, learning more Gaeilge phrases and songs. Ronin's eyes widened when he saw the small, beautiful ship in Inyo's hands.

Her mother turned to Finley. "We helped Fergal finish the

threshing today. Ellis asked if you have time to go see her this evening." Maeve winked.

—

After supper, Finley wrapped a cloak around her shoulders as she took off, relieved that her parents had decided that Fergal, Padraig, and Ellis could be let in on Inyo's true identity. Ellis was in the garden in front of their house, a few turnips and leeks in her basket. She shrieked in delight when she saw Finley. They hugged and then got to work, pulling up a few more vegetables. "Your ma' said you have something very extraordinary to tell me?" Ellis asked.

"Aye." Finley nodded. "Do you remember that store in Coruña?"

"The bakery?"

"No, the one with the books and maps!"

"Ah, yes, *that* shop. Filled with beautiful things. Books. Maps. And a handsome boy, if I remember it right?" Ellis elbowed Finley teasingly.

Finley sighed at the memory while she shook damp crumbs off a turnip.

"How could I ever forget!" Ellis shook her head with a grin. "You wouldn't shut up about him for days—the entire journey back."

After a pause, Finley sighed, "His name is Inyo."

Ellis startled. "What?"

"Aye, and we're hiding him."

Ellis gaped at her with a look of incredulity while Finley explained Inyo's whole ordeal, as far as she understood it. That he would hide here until a vessel could be found to take him home. Her voice turned weak when she mentioned Bensbury's harsh orders and the patrols on the main roads. "For now, we're pretending he's our cousin Ian. We *have* to keep him safe," Finley explained.

"Of course, that makes sense." Ellis rose and wiped her hands on her apron. "So, can I meet 'your cousin Ian?' Tomorrow?"

"My da' said we need to go fishing tomorrow."

"That's what we have to do, too. See you in the morning, then!"

—

The vast bay with its green embrace of coastline stretched out before Inyo's eyes. It all reminded him of the approach into Coruña. *Albeit with much less sunlight*, Inyo thought to himself. He focused on his task, rowing the fishing boat while Finley and Teagan managed the nets. The calm waters beneath his oars betrayed the fact that, less than a week ago, the horrible gale had sunk the *Santa Catalina* right here and nearly taken his life. He scanned the entire bay, but there were no trading vessels anywhere to be seen, only fishing boats. For the length of several deep sighs, he mulled over the uncertainty of his future. Tibbot, Finley, and her parents had assured him that a ship would be found to take him home. Inyo tried to remain hopeful, but his patience was dissipating under the weight of the lurking dangers, perils that might affect not only him, but Finley and her entire family as well.

For now, he was determined to help them with their work. In the wee hours of that morning, while it was still dark, he was introduced to the neighbors, Fergal, Padraig, and Ellis MacDermot, having Finley's assurance that all of them could be trusted to keep his real identity a secret. Inyo had followed them all down the forested path to the village and the shore. Standing on the beach next to the small harbor, he scanned the reeds and seaweed-covered boulders with dozens of seagulls *eek-eek-eeking* in circles above his head, but there was no sign of wreckage anywhere, just the sleepy fishing boats waiting to be put to sea.

When Inyo helped ready the nets and boats, other villagers emerged from the dawn, along with a priest, whose kind smile warmed the chill of the early morning. As planned, Brian introduced

Inyo as Ian to the villagers. "Meet Ian, my nephew visiting from Ennis. He, um . . . He's coming down with a cold or something. And he lost his voice yesterday."

Inyo nodded and smiled, glad that no one asked questions. They were all too busy preparing to launch their boats after the long spell of storms and dreadful weather of the previous weeks. At noon, they pulled the boats ashore for a rest break.

Tibbot rose, stretching his back with a smile, and then took his leave. Inyo didn't understand his words, but Finley explained that her uncle needed to head to Galway and that he'd keep a lookout for Spanish or French ships. The afternoon was filled with more work at sea, and now, finally, the sun was blanketing the sparkling bay with a bit more warmth. While Teagan and Finley pulled in the nets, their excited conversation circled a person by the name of Mamó. "Who eez Mamó?" Inyo wanted to know.

"My mamó. That's my grandmother, *mí abuela*. Her name is Grace. She's coming for a visit," Finley answered. Judging from everyone's reaction, Inyo could tell that this visit was something they were all looking forward to.

Harvest

Sarah hurried through Galway's darkening streets, smoothing her ruffled hair. She felt so alive, as light as a bird. Her cheeks were aglow, and she couldn't stop smiling after her secret meeting with Tibbot. She had been giddy all morning before she went to meet him outside the city gate. They had again strolled along the shore and past Claddagh, their favorite walk. When they paused in a shaded spot out of sight of the village, their hands had found each other. Their nest among the bushes allowed for a long, tender embrace, and their murmurs rippled on mysterious undercurrents of inexplicable cravings. Sweet, untethered moments and rich emotions she had never experienced before.

The door to the governor's mansion opened with a creaking moan. Holding her breath, Sarah tiptoed past the muffled sounds coming from the kitchen, through the quiet hall, then up the stairs. In the solitude of her room, she sank her face into her cloak and inhaled Tibbot's lingering scent with closed eyes. Dancing in her head were the words Tibbot had whispered when they parted, that he wanted to meet her again tomorrow. He'd also invited her to a harvest festival at his sister's farm.

Sarah's smile faded, and she bit her lip. She still hadn't told Tibbot who she actually was, had fibbed that she was *just the daughter of an English merchant*. She flung herself onto her bed and stared at the ceiling, still clutching her cloak. The immediate joy of being with him was all she had cared about, but now a darkness in the back of her head began to growl. She was a liar. Why did she let it get this far? Tibbot would be livid. He would certainly reject her. And she still had to figure out how to plan her escape from Galway, from Aldred.

Sarah was unaware that in the courtyard below her window, a figure moved unnoticed in the shadows. Someone had followed her on her little excursion.

—

Inyo woke to murmuring voices and the crackle of the fire. It was the day before the harvest feast, Mabon, which—as Finley had explained—was an annual celebration of gratitude for the harvest, for the abundance that would hopefully get everyone through winter. As far as he understood it, their mamó would arrive by ship, along with clan and family members from someplace called Rockfleet. While they waited, Inyo helped Teagan pile up branches for a bonfire in the meadow. Brian and Fergal prepared a spit and then went to select a pig, while Finley and her siblings were cooking and baking with Maeve. Soon, Ellis showed up with Padraig to see where help was needed.

Maeve appeared in the door frame, her hands covered in bits of dough, sending Finley and Ronin on an errand. They disappeared into the forest with baskets. Ellis had joined them, too. Curious, Inyo ran after them. He hadn't understood what Finley's mother asked them to do, but it became clear as soon as he caught up to them: they were picking mushrooms. Ellis and Finley were carrying on in the airy, fluttery bantering that reminded him of Marina and Francisca. Helping them, he smiled absentmindedly, drinking in the fragrant autumn air of the woods.

The baskets filled up quickly with the small mushrooms as they wandered from one shaded spot to another. As they knelt in moss and damp soil at the base of a thicket of oaks, Ellis grinned mischievously, whispered something to Finley with a wink, then grabbed one of the baskets and steered Ronin towards a patch of mushrooms in the distance.

Inyo watched them amble away, leaving him alone behind the grove of trees with Finley. Just like him, she also stopped work, and she gazed at him, her faint smile widening. Ronin's voice retreated further into the subdued morning light of the woods. The task for which they were sent was utterly forgotten. Inyo rose to his feet, helping Finley to her feet. She held his hand firmly, in a way that indicated she didn't want him to let go. Her eyes shimmered with a breathtaking luminosity and, as in a trance, he pulled her into an embrace, tightening his grip on the curve of her back, keenly aware of how wonderfully close they suddenly were. A hint of her breath caressed his chin, and his heart rate exploded like wildly crashing waves. As Inyo lifted his face to the dense canopy above, inhaling the freshness of the forest surrounding them, he felt Finley's head burrowing into his chest. Her hands held on to him so firmly, and her body melted into his. When he dipped his face into her curls and closed his eyes, a deep peace washed over him, enveloping him completely, calming his breath. The unexpected sweetness of the moment lifted him into a weightless realm. He couldn't feel the ground anymore. The two of them had become soaring hawks, slowly circling each other high above the trees.

Ellis and Ronin's voices, just a murmur in the distance all this time, drew closer, causing Inyo's eyes to flutter open. Finley withdrew with a timid smile, frantically smoothing her dress. With flushed faces and exuberant smiles, they watched Ellis and Ronin approach.

Shortly after they all arrived back at the farm, a commotion in the distance pulled Inyo's gaze towards the lower slope of the meadow. A cluster of sailors lumbered towards them. A tall man and a lady led the group. That must be Grace, their *abuela*, Inyo guessed.

"*Mamó!*" Ronin ran towards her, followed by Finley.

"Uncle Owen!" Teagan shouted.

Inyo watched the bedlam of excited greetings, backs being slapped, heartfelt embraces, banter, Ronin being swung around by the sailors, Brian helping with a few bundles, and Maeve linking arms with her mother, Grace.

The group was coming closer. Inyo's forehead wrinkled above his narrowed eyes. "*Santa madre . . .*" Inyo whispered to himself, his pulse quickening. *It's Señora O'Malley!*

Finley skipped toward him and grabbed his arm, oblivious to Inyo's inner turmoil. "Come, meet Mamó!" she said.

Señora O'Malley, the corsair, is Finley's grandmother! Inyo pulled his cap down to hide his ashen face. He stared at Finley as she dragged him towards Señora O'Malley. She introduced him to them all, explaining his ordeal and how he had ended up hiding here.

Her Uncle Owen uttered a few syllables, clearly baffled, then slapped Inyo's shoulder with unintelligible exclamations. Inyo startled when Señora O'Malley shook his limp hand and addressed him in near-fluent Spanish: "*¡ Qué Milagro!* I am so pleased to meet you, Inyo. You're fortunate to have found your way here."

"Se—señora O'Malley," Inyo stuttered, "it's a pleasure to meet you again."

"You may call me Grace. So, we've met before?" She took a step backward, eyeing him with a half grin.

"I once sailed aboard the *Gaviota* with my uncle Juan when we—"

"The *Gaviota*? Oh, I remember! A beautiful little merchantman. And how's Juan, the old rascal?" Grace asked. One of the sailors leaned in closer at the mention of the *Gaviota*. "Inyo, this is one of my best hands," she introduced him, "Liam O'Neill. His brother, Geoffrey, is on watch down in the cove."

The way she bantered with Liam made Inyo wonder if they might have been aboard one of the galleys that day when the O'Malleys raided the *Gaviota*. Inyo felt Finley's hand reaching for his while she listened intently to the Spanish conversation.

—

Finley leaned in close as Inyo answered her mamó's questions, talking about his growing up in Coruña and how he had met Finley briefly once before on her pilgrimage, which earned them both a raised eyebrow and a chuckle from Mamó. Inyo described the sailing of the Armada, the battles, his ship sinking, how he washed ashore and found the barn that night, and the plans Brian had made to get him home again to Spain.

"Well," Owen cautioned with a frown, "we can hope the Spanish merchantmen come up here again soon, but to be realistic, with autumn coming, trade may not resume until spring. Inyo should come with us to Rockfleet. From there, we can send him to our allies in Scotland at an opportune time."

"Excellent idea." Grace nodded.

Finley, however, bit her lower lip while her grandma and her uncle discussed their idea further. Spiriting Inyo away to Scotland? That was not what her heart wanted. But she felt reluctant to object, since it was probably his best chance to make it home safely.

"Was the *Gavilán* searched on your way down here?" Brian wondered. In times of danger, Grace's ships regularly sailed disguised as simple traders and not under O'Malley colors.

"Yes, we were stopped and searched by two English patrol ships. They seemed very concerned with possible supplies or weapons coming from or heading to Spain or Portugal," Owen reported. "But even if we're searched again on our return trip, if Inyo stays mute, he'll blend right in aboard. It's the fastest and safest way to get him to

Rockfleet."

Her grandma translated for Inyo, and his face lit up with hope. Once in Scotland, a Catholic ally, he'd be able to find safe passage from there to Spain. Finley told herself she should be glad he had this chance, but something inside of her cracked and splintered. She couldn't bear the idea of having to bid Inyo farewell, and as she watched him talk to Owen, an idea sprouted in her mind, a way to have a little bit more time with him. She blurted, "Mamó, I'll come along to Rockfleet."

Later that evening, though, she stared absentmindedly into the fire, trying hard not to think of the moment when Inyo would sail away from Rockfleet, heading to Scotland, leaving her behind—an unbearable thought. But wait! Hadn't her parents and Mamó always encouraged her to be the captain of her own destiny? She was filled with the singular longing to remain close to Inyo. *What if I sail with him to Scotland? And maybe from there to Spain?* she wondered. The thought seemed overwhelming. The journey would be filled with risks, their future shrouded in unknowns. And what if Inyo didn't want her to come with him? She was reluctant to ask him, afraid of what he might say.

Finley startled when her grandma wrapped an arm around her, encouraging her, "Not to worry, my love. It will all work itself out. Now, let's get everything ready for tomorrow. By the way, where's Tibbot?"

Maeve sighed. "There's a certain someone in Galway who occupies his heart and much of his time. Sarah is her name. I think she'll be here tomorrow."

"Oh? I see. But you don't look happy about that."

"Sarah is English."

"Oh dear!" Grace's forehead turned into a stormy seascape. Finley knew that many across Connacht would struggle this coming winter.

The clans were burdened with ever-increasing taxes because of the English. Entire farms had been burned to the ground, and innocent people sent to the gallows. And what would the Clew Bay alliance have to face in the years ahead? Tibbot's interest in an English lady would not sit well with anyone and would even be considered treason.

But Finley remembered how elated she'd seen Tibbot with Sarah, and a sudden understanding dawned in her heart. Love sometimes just happens, eluding rules and leaping over great divides, defying even vast distances, oceans, and nations at war. Her gaze returned to Inyo. He had been at the loom, where her father showed him its moving parts and the use of the shuttles. Inyo rose with a grateful nod to her father and made his way to sit next to Finley, reaching for her hand.

When Teagan, Ronin, Owen, and Liam started singing and dancing near the fire, Finley turned to her grandma. "Mamó, will you translate for me?" Grace nodded and headed outside with Inyo and Finley. They ambled through the meadow under the evening sky where the first stars emerged. With her grandma serving as translator and interpreter, Finley was finally able to ask about Inyo's family, his home in Coruña, and how he ended up with the Armada.

"La Armada necesitaba semanas de reparaciones en Coruña, ahí es donde me contrataron," Inyo began. Grace translated, "The Armada needed weeks of repairs in Coruña, which was where they hired him. He was to be aboard the *San Francisco* with his friend Antonio, but then ran into a bit of trouble and ended up as a carpenter on the *Santa Catalina.*"

Inyo outlined his time aboard, his work, the battles in the Channel, and the death of a friend named Ansa. With a halting voice, he spoke of weeks of intense hunger and diseases, the death of so many shipmates, the storms, and the horrific night the *Catalina* sank.

Grace and Finley stared at him, dismayed about the wretched conditions the Spanish sailors had had to endure for months.

In turn, Inyo asked about the pilgrimage, about Finley's companions, and if she had liked the maps and books in the shop.

"I *really* loved the map you were working on." Finley noticed Inyo's appreciative nod when Grace translated her answer.

Then Inyo wanted to know more about the O'Malleys and Rockfleet. With pride in her voice, Finley described Clew Bay, the clan's history, and the O'Malley fleet.

Paying close attention to her mamó's translation, she then learned about Marina and Juan, and how Inyo became a carpenter. "Ask him how he got into cartography, and—"

A crackle of breaking twigs coming from the forest interrupted them. Bobbing lantern light approached through the dark and emerged between the tree trunks. "It's me!"

"Tibbot, there you are!" Finley sighed with relief when she recognized him. Her grandma pulled him aside. "What is this I hear about you and an *English* woman?" Grace muttered sternly, steering Tibbot towards the cottage.

Inyo and Finley circled the meadow slowly one more time. They found that her rapidly improving Spanish, supplemented with some Latin and many hand gestures, was sufficient for their continued conversation. In the crispness of the evening, surrounded by muffled singing coming from the cottage and the hooting of an owl in the forest, Finley's hand intertwined with Inyo's. He pulled her close to him, sending a warmth to her cheeks as she blinked under his gaze. The moment in the forest earlier that day had awakened a deep longing in her, had set a mysterious fire at the base of her spine that now burned whenever she was near him.

They melted into a tender embrace, and their faces drew closer and closer, until the only space left was a delicate veil of anticipation. The kiss began gently, leaving starry tingles on Finley's lips. She pulled away for the length of a few heartbeats, wondering if this wasn't all just a dream, but Inyo's arms around her were warm and real, and their next kiss was even more so.

When Inyo pulled away, his shoulders were heaving and he cupped her face with both hands. *"Te adoro . . . Finley,"* he whispered.

Tears brimmed in Finley's eyes, tears of joy. His words, though she didn't quite understand them all, were gifts, blessings. Inyo tucked her under his chin, and a profound feeling of trust and peace infused her, erasing her earlier doubts and strengthening her resolve to find a way to stay with him.

Finley didn't notice Ronin, who had come to look for them. "What are you *doing?*" Ronin huffed when he saw them. "Ma' says it's time to feed Merla and Cormac!" He shook his head furiously and stomped back inside, while Inyo's shoulders trembled with silent laughter.

Owen, Grace, and the crew traditionally got the beds in the cottage when they visited, and so, after the horses were taken care of, Teagan, Ronin, Finley, and Inyo settled into the hay of the barn with blankets. Hoping that Teagan and Ronin would fall asleep quickly, Finley lay quietly, shoulder to shoulder with Inyo. With hushed breathing, they turned to face each other, knees touching, the hay crackling softly beneath them. "I want to stay here . . . with you," Inyo whispered, his fingers interlacing with hers. "For always."

"I want that, too. But—" Finley drew a ragged breath. "You *must* leave."

"No." Inyo shook his head.

"You *have* to! I will sail with you to Rockfleet. Me and you, *navegamos . . . juntos . . . a Rockfleet.*" Finley hesitated, wondering how to let him know that she wanted to come with him all the way to Spain. *But that would be selfish*, she reminded herself, *and very likely endanger his life needlessly*. Besides, the fear that he might not want her to go with him came back to gnaw at her newfound happiness. While she blinked away a lurking tear, Inyo shifted closer in the crunching hay. His lips nuzzled her hair while his arm tenderly wound around her torso, replacing her doubts with his warmth. Wrapped in his embrace, her cheek nestled to his chest, Finley soon drifted off to sleep.

—

Early morning sunlight filtered through the nearby trees and undulated on the calm waters of the small bay. Inyo's hands trailed over the smooth railing of the *Gavilán* while his eyes ranged over the clean decks and the neatly organized rigging. It was a beautiful ship. Tomorrow, she would take him to freedom, so Owen had explained.

He had woken them up a half hour ago, and Inyo followed him and Finley through the woods, across a bramble-lined stream, and down a steep bank. Overgrown shrubs and trees encircled the small bay, its entrance well hidden from Galway Bay. Surrounded by birdsong and the gentle lapping of water, they stood on the shore when Owen explained, "Even most locals don't know O'Halloran's cove. We anchor here if we don't need to be in Barna Harbor or in Galway. And especially if we need to avoid the English."

A man appeared at the ship's gunnel. Finley turned to Inyo. "This is Liam's brother, Geoffrey O'Neill, one of Mamó's hands." Geoffrey clambered down the hull, jumped into the boat, and rowed it ashore, humming a tune. Finley and Owen introduced Inyo, and then Geoffrey took off quickly up the hill for his breakfast at the Morris farm.

Once aboard, Owen and Finley disappeared below deck, and Inyo lingered near the main mast, lost in thought. The cut of the *Gavilán* reminded him of Juan's *Gaviota* and the time when Antonio taught him how to sail and navigate. Inyo inhaled sharply, worried about Antonio and whether he and the *San Francisco* made it back to Spain.

When his thoughts drifted to Ansa, Inyo struggled to clear a heaviness from his throat, unaware that tears were obscuring his vision. He hadn't noticed Finley appear by his side until she took his hand.

Inyo wiped away the moisture on his cheeks; he didn't want her to worry. They only had today, tomorrow, and a few days left together at Rockfleet. He tried to make each moment count, to focus on her, and to block out everything else. She wrapped her arms around him, filling him with calm.

Owen brought up a crate containing several bottles of wine, packed in straw. "Take that up to the farm with you," he said, then rowed Inyo and Finley back to shore.

—

Finley's breathing was labored. With the heavy crate between her and Inyo, she slowly trudged up the steep path. They eventually reached the forest's level part, trying to catch their breath and sinking into the ferns for a break.

"Oh, I want to show you something!" Finley said. "We have time."

They stowed the crate behind fern fronds just off the trail, then headed deeper into the woods and over a creek. Finley pointed out a massive oak. "This is the Druid Tree—*el árbol druida.*"

—

Inyo's eyes widened as he marveled at the twisted branches and the massive trunk of the old tree. *The Druid Tree.* He smiled. Following Finley, he circled the tree slowly and glanced at the sky. He was surrounded by a fairy realm filled with the gentle noises of the forest, a thousand worlds away from cannons, shipwrecks, agony, and loss. "Do you like him, the druid?" Finley asked. Inyo nodded and took in her smile, her fiery curls that danced with and against the green of the moss-covered bark of the oak behind her. He reached for her hand.

How beautiful her smile was, her ivory arms, the delicate flare of her hips, the curves of her torso.

—

Finley watched his gaze, silent and unabashed, range from her hands and arms to her entire body and up to her face. She felt a fire rising in her cheeks, hypnotized by his eyes and the enigmatic energy that vibrated between them. Inyo stepped closer and placed his hand on her chin, gently stroking her cheek. Why did her knees turn weak again? She had to lean back into the Druid Tree, had to close her eyes for a moment, aware of Inyo's slow, rhythmic breathing. His arms now wound around her torso, and he pulled her closer. "Keep your eyes closed, *mi amor*," he said, which made her smile. He placed a kiss on her eyelashes, then another on her forehead, soft and feathery, leaving a trail of bubbly cravings under her skin.

Finley opened her eyes, pressed herself into his embrace, and lifted herself on her toes when his lips found hers. She didn't want to let go of him anymore. She sighed breathlessly in the rhythm of their embrace, their kisses, his insistent hands on the small of her back, an intoxicating and wordless dance between his body and hers.

—

Inyo dissolved into the spell-binding ebb and flow of the moment, into a craving taking over his senses. One of Finley's legs wrapped itself around him, the movement dreamlike and fluid, pulling an involuntary gasp from his mouth. He pulled away, trying to catch his breath. Then, as if controlled by an invisible power, he placed a kiss on her neck and pulled her knee up to his hips, desperate to elicit more of her lovely, ethereal sighs. A tremor took over his body, and he found himself engulfed in a novel and undeniable ecstasy. Her closeness, her curves, and her warm skin tasted and felt unlike anything Inyo had ever dared to dream of. Sweet fruit wine, dancing at a *fiesta*, fresh grilled fish, a calm day at sea, a French castle, the towering *San Martin*, almond cakes, a beautiful map, a ring of gold—nothing, nothing, *absolutely nothing* compared to this!

—

They were completely unaware of how much time had passed. With chapped and tender lips, they finally slowed, released each other with shy grins, forest fragrances swirling around them. Inyo cleared his throat. "The feast," he mumbled vaguely.

"Right." Finley nodded. "They're probably waiting for the wine." She knew someone might be wondering what took them so long, but she didn't care one bit. She was still way too charged, and she could tell Inyo felt the same way.

With red faces and remnants of moss clinging to their hair and clothing, Finley and Inyo strolled into the meadow towards the farm, but no one noticed or commented on their late arrival. Liam and Geoffrey were setting up tables while Fergal prepared the spit over the fire. Ellis, Ronin, and Teagan carried platters and baskets of food to the tables, and Maeve fussed over decorations while Brian stacked more firewood.

When Father Whelan arrived, the harvest feast began with a devotion and a chanted blessing as he lifted his hands above the table piled high with vegetables and a barley sheaf.

Padraig, Ellis, and Fergal pulled out their drum, flute, and lute and began to play. Finley took Inyo's hand. Together with her parents, Mamó, Ronin, Teagan, and Geoffrey, they danced around the fire to the fast-paced music.

As the afternoon warmth started to fade, Geoffrey headed down to the *Gavilán* to relieve Owen. When Owen arrived in the meadow, he asked, "Where's Tibbot? He left so early. I thought he wanted to bring

Sarah to the feast. I'm getting worried."

Grace shrugged. "I imagine he doesn't want me to meet this Sarah. It's probably better that way. I just hope he makes it back before morning. He knows we plan to sail out with the tide."

Finley watched a steep frown crease her mother's forehead, but at that very moment, Inyo reached for her hand.

—

Inyo pulled Finley back towards the bonfire, back into the dance. The celebration reminded him of the end-of-harvest feasts in Galicia, where bonfires were lit in groves and squares, and the music of tambourines and bagpipes spurred on high-spirited circle dances for hours.

The aroma of the roasting food filled the air when Fergal, Ellis, and Padraig started another song. Inyo smiled at Finley, dancing with her to the rhythm, captivated by the chorus that Ellis' voice repeated several times.

The birds in the apple tree sing this song
After the harvest, when work is done.
Wherever you fly, this promise is true:
We'll fly together, me and you.

Inyo paused in mid-dance, fervently pulled Finley into his arms, and gazed into her eyes, repeating the words, "Wherever you fly, this promise is true: We'll fly together, me and you."

—

That morning, with her cap pulled far down over her face, Sarah had rushed into town to meet Tibbot again at their usual spot at Galway's western gate. They wanted to walk along the shore, and Tibbot intended to bring her to the celebration at Maeve's farm. Sarah flew into Tibbot's arms, then they briskly strode across the bridge and turned towards the shore. But suddenly, a patrol of soldiers blocked their path, and riders on horseback approached from behind. Sarah's smile faltered. "Arrest him!" a voice, cold as steel, growled from behind them. Sarah instantly recognized it. Aldred.

Startled, Tibbot bolted away, but the soldiers surrounded him too swiftly, muskets and sharp halberds bristling and glinting. Sarah screamed, straining against the arms that held her back. As Tibbot was being dragged away, she pleaded, "No! *No!* Please, I beg you —let him go! Oh God! Tibbot!"

When they reached the governor's mansion, Sarah was jostled and steered inside, having to watch helplessly as Tibbot was wrestled towards the prison. With tears streaming down her face and Aldred's musket pressed into her back, she stumbled up the stairs, where the guards pushed her into her room. "Please, he didn't do anything!" she sobbed, staring at Aldred, who lowered his weapon. "Set him free! Lock me up instead!" Sarah pleaded, unable to read the cold mask on her husband's face. She trembled, and her eyes locked on Aldred like an animal unsure of what would happen now. He rounded on her, face taut with fury, and punched her head with such force that she lost her balance and collapsed into a heap of uncontrollable weeping and despair.

Aldred paused triumphantly in the doorway. "The bastard will pay for this!" He turned to his advisors and sneered, "And so will this slut." His words dropped all around Sarah, like a violent hailstorm, leaving her shivering. As he marched away, she heard his command to the captain of the guard. "Lock the door. She is forbidden to leave!"

Sarah tried to get off the floor, all hope shriveling up inside her, blood oozing from her nose. Her shoulders throbbed from where the soldiers had brutally pushed her around; she couldn't open her swollen left eye, but most of all, she felt an emptiness in her soul, a pain she'd never known. *This is all my fault!* The guilt over Tibbot's imprisonment pressed down on her like a lead weight, and she couldn't stop the tears.

—

Inyo's eyes fluttered open when one of the horses snorted and stomped a muffled hoof into the straw-covered floor. It was Merla. Strangely, Inyo couldn't see Cormac anywhere. Finley was still asleep, curled up next to him with the morning light caressing the drowsy shape of her head in the hay. Inyo yawned, smiling inwardly as he recalled last night's celebrations.

The bonfire had burned for a long time. Finley finally revealed Inyo's true identity to Father Whelan, who spoke Spanish quite well and was elated to meet him. Inyo felt relieved that he didn't need to pretend to be "Ian" anymore.

He danced with Finley over and over again, then swung Ronin through the air. When he arm-wrestled Brian, Grace, Teagan, and Geoffrey in turn, Finley cheered him on, jumping up and down. Later, he flung himself into the grass next to her to rest and banter. The carefree evening put him in a vastly jubilant mood. His worries over the future had dimmed as he fell asleep contentedly in the barn next to Finley, overcome by fatigue.

And today he would sail to Rockfleet, together with Finley. As soon as he envisioned the journey, however, dormant worries awakened inside him. With autumn, there was always the possibility of heavy seas. And what if the English intercepted and searched them on their way? Inyo's pulse quickened while his eyes wandered to the empty spots in the hay where Teagan and Ronin had rested. *They're all getting ready. I should probably wake Fin*, Inyo thought to himself. He reached for her hair when muffled voices wafted from the house and became louder. The door leading from the well room to the barn sprang open.

Wide-eyed, Inyo stared at the pain-filled faces of Grace, Maeve, and Owen. Next to him, Finley stirred. "What's going on?" she asked in a sleepy voice.

"We have dreadful news," Maeve wept. "They've arrested Tibbot."

Inyo didn't quite understand Maeve's sobs, but while Finley scrambled to her feet, Grace turned to him, explaining in Spanish, "Early this morning, when Tibbot still hadn't returned, Maeve rode to Galway. At the market, she heard from someone who saw Tibbot yesterday. He was with Sarah, an Englishwoman. Apparently, Tibbot was arrested and is being held for a serious crime, but we don't know the exact nature of the supposed crime or what they might be accusing him of."

"We need to free him!" Inyo gasped.

Brian's head appeared in the doorframe. "Fergal and Father Whelan just arrived, and they have more news!"

Moments later, Inyo found himself in the main house, amid a chaotic gale of shouting, frantic gestures, pale faces, and weeping. *Why was Tibbot arrested?* he wondered. *Why was he with an Englishwoman?* A sick feeling spread in Inyo's stomach, a dark unease. *The English! What might they be able to get out of Tibbot?* he worried.

Grace finally turned to him to translate, "Fergal and Father Whelan were at the market and saw Maeve, then went to the governor's mansion. That's where the prison is. They were told that Tibbot is charged with treason and that he'll be executed unless a ransom is paid."

"The governor demands one hundred shillings for his release. The execution is scheduled for tomorrow," Fergal added with a flat tone. A heavy silence fell over the entire group.

—

Finley's heart pounded as she stared at the surreal scene before her. Her father was consoling her mother; her mamó sat with her head in her hands. A hollowness clamped down on Finley, leaving her thoughts fractured, scattered, useless. Even Owen, Geoffrey, and Liam were at a loss for words. Inyo reached for her hand when she began to blink back her tears. Father Whelan and Teagan consoled Ronin and ushered him outside. When Fergal left to fetch Ellis and Padraig, Finley's parents, Grace, Owen, Geoffrey, and Liam huddled up. Quickly, the room flared with angry mutters and shouts.

"Why did they arrest him? Do they know he's an O'Malley?"

"No, they have no way of knowing that unless Sarah—"

"Tibbot would never give away that he's an O'Malley!"

"I don't know. He is head over heels for this Sarah."

"It doesn't matter. What matters is that we free Tibbot, and soon!"

"Let's break him out of prison!"

"No, that's madness! There are hundreds of soldiers—"

"Listen! The governor has already stated the amount he wants."

"I agree, we have to pay the ransom, there's no other way!"

"What? Give in, just like that?"

"Tibbot's life depends on it!"

The whirlwind of rising aggravation, tinged with raw panic, reminded Finley of the time when the MacDermots were attacked near Rockfleet. No one knew what to do back then, either. Her mamó's brows furrowed deeper. "How can we get this much money in such a short amount of time?"

One hundred shillings? Finley worried. No one she knew had *that* much money on hand.

Tears were still streaming down her mother's face while her father clenched his fists tightly. "What can we sell?" he wondered.

Finley explained to Inyo what was going on when her mamó abruptly turned to Owen. "We can go on a raid! The ship can be readied in less than an hour."

Liam and Geoffrey nodded furiously in agreement, but Owen shook his head. "No, we don't have time! Besides, who are we going to raid? The harbor is empty . . ."

"Owen is right," Brian agreed. "Here, I have four shillings and a few pennies on me." He emptied his purse on the table. Finley gasped when she saw her mother slip her beloved golden bracelet off her wrist and place it on top of the coins.

Looking at the heap on the table, Grace turned to Owen. "The stash!"

Owen's face lit up. "Of course!" He motioned for Finley and Inyo to come with him. They took off quickly and rushed through the woods down to the cove.

"What stash, Owen? What was Mamó talking about?"

"You'll see!"

When they reached the *Gavilán*, Owen headed straight for Grace's cabin, Inyo and Finley close behind him. They lifted the mattress off the bed frame, revealing a wooden hatch, and opened it. In the storage compartment lay a folded blanket and a few candles, which Owen cleared out. Then his hand searched for a small lever in a recess at the foot end of the storage. There was a *click*. The wooden board that was the base of the compartment released. Owen slid it slightly towards the wall, then lifted it out completely, revealing a secret hollow filled with valuables. There were muskets with silver-inlaid stocks, a few pouches of coins, a jeweled sword, and a fancy vest with embroidery and gold buttons. Owen held up the vest. "Ah, I'd forgotten about this one," he mumbled, offering no further explanation. "Quickly now, let's take it all!"

They piled the valuables into sacks while Owen sliced about a dozen gold buttons off the embroidered vest. Finley watched them scatter across the cabin floor and hurriedly scooped them up.

—

When they arrived back at the farm, everything was quickly piled on the table—the coins, the weapons, the jewelry, Owen's fine sword, and his gold buttons. But would it be enough for the ransom? There was a knock on the door. Father Whelan, Fergal, Ellis, and Padraig tumbled in, and Finley quickly updated them on the plans, her voice quavering. Ellis hugged Finley tightly. "Don't worry, Fin. Surely this is enough to free Tibbot!"

Brian hitched Arlyn to the cart as everything was loaded. Grace had decided that Owen should be the one to negotiate Tibbot's release because he spoke English fluently. "It's safer if he is the only one to enter the governor's mansion. We'll wait nearby in case there's any trouble."

With Ronin clinging to her tightly, Finley tried to give him a calming look, desperate to hold back her tears, while her mamó, her parents, Geoffrey, and Fergal prepared to escort Owen and the ransom to Galway. She was glad that Inyo, Teagan, Ellis, Padraig, Liam, and Father Whelan remained at the farm with her, but unease clawed at her insides as she stared at the departing cart, rattling along the path, growing smaller and smaller in the distance.

Traitor

Sarah stared at her reflection in the mirror, adjusting the white cap over her hair. The convincing disguise made her appear like a young kitchen maid. Several weeks ago, when she had first formulated a vague escape plan, she had started to pirate away servant clothes. Her swollen face and the black bruise surrounding her blood-tinged eye made her unrecognizable. In her mind, she ran through her plan one more time. *Escape the mansion, make my way to Maeve's farm, and get them to help me find a way to rescue Tibbot.* Sarah pulled a coil of rope out from behind her wardrobe and tied one end around the foot of the heavy bed. A glance out the window told her this was an opportune time, the courtyard below empty. She opened the window, wincing at its squeak, then lowered the rope and swung her legs over the windowsill. Her breathing turned ragged. Clutching the rope tightly, she lowered herself as swiftly as her sore arms allowed.

She crouched behind a large hedge, panting and trembling with fear. Faint voices wafted from somewhere close, Aldred's among them, oozing with arrogance. Tibbot's name was mentioned, and something about a ransom. Sarah couldn't get herself to start running, as she had initially planned, she could not. What were Aldred and his advisors talking about? She scuttled around the corner of the building, ducking low behind the hedges, and then paused right underneath her husband's office window.

A wooden door creaked, followed by footsteps, and then she heard Murrough's voice. "Sir, a man named Owen has arrived. He says he is the prisoner's brother and wants to pay the ransom. But before you bring him in, there's something you need to know."

"What is it? He has the money, right?" Aldred asked.

"He does," Murrough continued, "but this man, Owen, he's Grace O'Malley's heir and oldest son."

Between the mumbles and muted exclamations of triumph, one voice cheered, "Sir, what great fortune! Both of O'Malley's sons are at your mercy today."

"You have her now!"

Murrough added, "Yes, sir, she would do *anything* for her brood."

After a tense pause, Aldred chuckled, then shared his despicable plan with his council. They would talk to Owen, then send him to lure Grace O'Malley into his office under the pretense of signing treaties in exchange for Tibbot's release. "Once she's inside," Bensbury snarled, "I'll arrest them all! The O'Malley offspring will be sent to the Tower of London for a public beheading. Our Queen will be most pleased. The outlaw O'Malley herself shall be executed right here in Galway. God, I can't wait to see her hang in the square!"

Sarah wrenched herself out of a frozen panic, reeling, covering her mouth to suppress a whimper. Not only was Tibbot's life in danger, but now his whole family would be executed as well. All because of her frivolous carelessness. Inundated by panic and guilt, Sarah fought against the turmoil threatening to overwhelm her senses. Finally, she willed her legs to move. She scrambled out from the hedges and breathlessly staggered towards the back gate.

"Where do you think you're going, maid? Back to work!" one of the guards roared, pointing his halberd at her.

Sarah stumbled and fell, rose with jerky movements, and finally trotted around the building to the servant's kitchen entrance. She cowered, trembling, her eyes swimming. She grabbed a basket from the pile, then made for the front gate, face lowered, footsteps firm, pretending she was on errands, willing herself to appear small and insignificant. Her heart pounded against her ribs like a blacksmith's hammer. She was sure the soldiers at the front gate could hear it. But no one recognized her as she slipped out into the street.

I have to get to Maeve's farm as fast as possible! Sarah gathered her skirts and started running into town. At Galway's eastern gate, she glanced back one more time. Her face fell when she saw a group of locals approaching the mansion, Maeve and Brian among them. There were several others in the group, and Sarah guessed that Grace O'Malley was one of them, too. *They must have all been waiting nearby!*

"No!" Sarah gasped with a feeble voice, but it was too late. The group disappeared through the doors, and two companies of soldiers streamed out of the barracks and formed up in front of the mansion.

In her panic, she dropped the basket, sank to her knees, and sobbed, "No, no! Tibbot! Oh God!" She hunkered on the hard-packed dirt of the street, trying to get her frozen thoughts in order. She eventually reached for the stone archway of the gate, slowly pulled herself up, and wiped away her tears.

Flaming anger seared in Sarah's chest, replacing the sorrow and helplessness. She lurched forward, step by step, while an idea formed in the turmoil of her mind. An unexpected confidence flooded her, seemingly out of nowhere, giving her resolution and strength. Sarah knew what she would have to do and how much depended on her composure now. Gripping the basket and taking a deep breath, she strode back to the mansion with determination, nodded to the guards at the entrance with her head low, wearing a grim mask, and entered the busy kitchen. With her disfigured face, the staff didn't recognize her at first, but when she reached for Aisling's arm with a pleading look, the chambermaid's eyes widened in recognition. Deidre, head of the kitchen staff, was startled to see the stranger until Aisling beckoned her over and began to whisper in her ear. Deidre straightened herself, glanced around, placed her finger to her lips, and ordered, "Shh! Everyone, back to work!"

"I *have* to know what's going on in the office!" Sarah pleaded.

Aisling nodded and handed her a bucket and rag. "We can go there and clean the hallway floor."

Amid an icy tension that swirled around Sarah's limbs, they huddled on the ground near Bensbury's office. In the hallway next to them, an armed company of at least fifty soldiers waited, while the muffled negotiations wafted through the closed doors.

Sarah could make out her husband's voice in his haughty manner. Then, suddenly, a roar: "Now!" Instantly, the armed officers flung open the door and stormed inside, the thunder of hundreds of boots at speed echoing. Amid startled shouts, shuffling, and toppling furniture, Sarah heard repeated pleading and screaming.

"No!"

"What the—"

"Surrender! All of you!" Aldred Bensbury's voice roared amid the chaos.

Shots rang out. Sarah saw the body of a man on the ground, but between the fighting and the shuffling legs, she couldn't make out who it was.

Sarah watched helplessly as Brian and Maeve were tied up and dragged away. She also caught a glimpse of someone who she believed to be Grace O'Malley on the ground, manhandled by the soldiers. Aldred's office emptied out, and Aisling quickly pulled Sarah to her feet. "We can't let your husband see you here!" They ran through the kitchen, out the back door, and to the servants' quarters, located right next door to the prison. "Stay here, Sarah," Aisling whispered, "I'll be back soon!"

"Don't leave me alone! I'm scared!"

"No one will find you here. I promise, I'll be back soon!"

Sarah huddled in a corner, clutching her skirt, when she heard pleading, shouting, and screaming coming from the courtyard. Several rough commands rang out above the mayhem of shuffling, cracking of whips, sounds of approaching carriage wheels, squeaking hinges, doors banging closed, whickering horses, and clomping hoofs. Sarah's heart pounded against her ribs as she tiptoed to one of the windows and caught a glimpse of a transport carriage leaving through the back gate. Meanwhile, several soldiers had gagged Grace O'Malley, tied her hands behind her back, and were dragging her towards the entrance of the adjacent prison.

Aldred strode behind them into the prison. Sarah could hear his sneering voice booming loudly through the walls. "Finally! The outlaw is where she belongs! Your days of pirating, inciting rebellions, and making a mockery of our laws are over. Tomorrow, the citizens of Galway will witness your execution. And in a few short weeks, the same fate awaits your offspring. In London, at the Tower."

A door banged shut, and a metal lock groaned behind Bensbury's cold laughter. Sarah slid down the wall she'd been leaning on, curling her head over her knees as she sobbed.

Soon, Aisling entered the servants' quarters and quietly closed the door behind her. Sarah whispered, "Tibbot, they are sending him to London! They're going to kill him! What am I going to do? And what if my husband finds out I've run away?"

Aisling grasped Sarah's arm. "No one knows you're gone. I discarded the rope and closed your window when I delivered your meal. Pretended to talk to you so the guards wouldn't get suspicious. Most of the prisoners were taken away, and I saw that two of the men were bleeding badly."

Sarah gasped.

"I don't know who, but one person is in prison."

"That's Grace O'Malley, Tibbot's mother," Sarah said miserably.

"*Grace O'Malley?*" Aisling arched an eyebrow, then started pacing, lost in thought. Finally, she lifted her gaze. "Oh, Sarah—I have an idea how we can free her! Deidre speaks English fluently, and she could—But we must wait until evening. The courtyards will be empty and only two guards will have duty at the prison—"

—

When it was finally dark outside, Aisling and Deidre showed up with a bundle of clothes they'd pulled out of the garrison laundry. Sarah asked, "What's your plan?"

"Take off your caps and ruffle your hair so it covers your face." Deidre winked at her and filled them in on her plan. She poured wine into two bottles and added a few drops of amber-colored liquid from a small vial. Then she put on a uniform, pulled her hair back, and hid it under a plumed cap. With her tall figure and angular face, Deidre's disguise as an officer was perfect.

They marched over to the prison's guard room, where two soldiers were playing cards by the glow of a few lanterns. The guards quickly rose to salute Deidre—the officer—who towered in the door frame with a stern face. "Just arrested this scum in town," Deidre's deep voice boomed. "They were disturbing the peace!"

Aisling and Sarah, pretending to be drunk, slumped behind Deidre. Their heads lolled from one side to another while they drooled and burped behind their wild tangles of hair. Sarah talked gibberish to the bottle in her hand, while Aisling had pulled down her shirt, exposing one shoulder. She croaked a shanty and clumsily wrapped herself around Deidre in a seductive way. Pretending to be annoyed, Deidre shook her off.

"Oh, *s'cuuuse* me, good sir, I didn' mean ter—" Aisling babbled in broken English, suppressing a hiccup, her eyes at half-mast.

"Governor's orders, they need to stay in prison until they're sober," Deidre barked.

"Yes, sir!" one of the guards replied.

"I don't know if they actually need to be locked up, seeing the state they are in," Deidre snorted. "Might be best if you simply stow them in a corner and let them sleep it off."

"That's a good idea, sir. Really good idea. We'll do that." The soldiers eyed each other briefly, holding themselves at attention in a stiff manner.

Deidre marched away. Sarah and Aisling, swaying on their unsteady legs, beamed crookedly at the guards. "So, ya want sum compa—companee?" Aisling teased and lifted the hem of her skirt with a coy smile while she handed her bottle to one of the men, whose grin was crenelated with several missing teeth, watching him eagerly take a swig.

The other guard followed suit with the second bottle, draining it in quick swallows, then pulled Sarah into his rough arms. "Ohh, hansum!" she purred as she caressed his chest with a lopsided grin. His eyes closed slowly, and his embrace weakened. A few heartbeats later, both guards had passed out and their bodies slithered to the ground.

Aisling reached for the keys hanging on the wall, and Sarah rushed to the two cell doors. One cell was open and empty; the other door unlocked quickly. Sarah pulled the metal door open and gasped when she stared into the small, shadowy room. Grace O'Malley cowered in a corner with ripped clothing, straining against iron shackles. Her eyes were puffy, her jaw purple and swollen.

Sarah quickly untied her gag while Aisling unlocked the shackles.

"Ms. O'Malley, can you walk?" Sarah reached for her hand.

"Aye, I think so. Who are you?" Grace asked as she slowly got off the ground, suppressing a moan.

"I'm Sarah. Tibbot and I—" Sarah began, unsure about what she should tell his mother.

"You have to hurry!" Aisling pleaded, sidling past the sleeping guards.

Sarah led Tibbot's mother out of the cell. Aisling found a hooded cloak on a chair, flung it over Ms. O'Malley's shoulders, then turned to hug Sarah. Sarah couldn't stop her eyes from brimming with gratitude. "Thank you, Aisling!" she whispered.

"Good luck, Sarah! Now go, quickly!" Aisling urged them. She retreated to the servants' quarters while Sarah and Grace opened the door and staggered out into the courtyard. Sarah realized, shocked, that with Ms. O'Malley's limp, they might not be able to hurry at all.

She pointed to the bushes in the courtyard. "Let's hide here!"

Ms. O'Malley quickly pulled the hood over her head when they sank, crouching under the cloak of night. The crunch of footsteps approached. It was the night guard on his rounds through the courtyard. They watched him stride past the main gate, then circle to the right where he disappeared behind the mansion.

"Now!" Sarah whispered, leading Tibbot's mother as the glow of the courtyard's torches fell away behind them, leaving them to scurry out the gate and into the darkness.

—

At the Morris farm, Inyo rose restlessly from the chair and paced across the floorboards, glancing at Finley's persistent frown. Ellis, Teagan, and Liam hunkered near the fireplace with forlorn stares, while Father Whelan and Padraig bowed their heads in prayer. Finley cradled Ronin. "What's taking so long?" she wondered. "It's dark! Shouldn't someone be home by now?"

No one knew what to do or what to say. Inyo sat down next to Finley. The flames of the fire reflected warmly in her face. "With horses, ride Galway, *rápido*. You and me?" he asked.

Finley shook her head. "No, it's too dangerous! You have to stay here, but I'll go."

"Wherever you go, I will go, too," Inyo urged, his eyes blazing.

Hesitation and uncertainty flickered across her face, but after a wingbeat of silence, she nodded and rose, handing Ronin to Father Whelan. He attempted to stop them, reaching for Finley's arm, but she insisted, "We're going to see what's going on. We'll be careful, I promise. It's better if it's just us, we'll be faster."

While everyone was distracted by Finley's explanation, Inyo took the two swords off the wall and made for the barn. He helped Finley saddle Merla and Cormac and handed her one of the swords. They nodded at each other, silently tucked the weapons into their belts, mounted up quickly, and took off.

Night had wrapped itself around them, its deep shade of ink flooding the even deeper black of the forests. The horses thundered along the empty main road, carrying Inyo and Finley to the edge of Galway. Inyo followed Finley across the bridge, his clammy hands tightening on the reins as the echo of the horses' hoofs began to drown under the rushing of the river below. They entered through the gate while the town slumbered, then rode along the dark streets, past the church and the deserted square.

When they reached the town's eastern gate, Finley motioned Inyo to a shadowy alley next to the open archway where she dismounted. "Let's leave the horses further back where they can't be seen," she whispered. "The governor's mansion is outside the gate."

Inyo nodded and jumped off Cormac. After the horses were tied up to a rail further down the alley, he and Finley crept back to the gate, ducking in the shadows. They peeked out past the city wall. The main road curved away from them and uphill towards the governor's mansion. A guard with a halberd strode across the fenced courtyard.

He paused at the mansion's main gate, then continued, disappearing behind the building.

Suddenly, two figures popped up from behind the bushes next to the building. They didn't look like soldiers. *Maybe servants?* Inyo wondered. The larger of them, wearing a hooded cape, limped next to a smaller figure, a maid with disheveled hair. They both crossed the courtyard and staggered out the gate, towards the town.

Finley whispered, "What's going on? Who is that?" Inyo narrowed his eyes, wondering why the limping figure, the taller of the two servants, seemed oddly familiar. But a movement drew his attention back to the governor's mansion. It was a bearded man, carrying a sword. He started chasing the servants. "We mustn't be seen!" Finley whispered, pulling Inyo back into the darkness of the alley. They pressed themselves flat, backs against the wall. Inyo held his breath, listening intently. While the crunch of footsteps drew closer and closer, he slowly unsheathed his sword.

A startled scream shredded the air, followed by a thud, shuffling, and heavy breathing. Then a deep voice cut through the darkness. "Freeze!"

Finley's grip on Inyo tightened as the larger of the two servants limped into view with her back turned. The figure stumbled and fell as the man approached with his drawn sword. He had the smaller maid by her arm, dragging her while she struggled and sobbed. He kicked her hard, knocking her out, and then whipped his sword towards the servant on the ground. "No need to wait until tomorrow to see you on the gallows," he sneered, his voice like a sharp dagger. "Let's take care of business right here and right now, Granuaile!"

Finley gasped. "It's Mamó!" she whispered.

Grace growled, "Murrough, you traitor!"

Murrough inhaled and swung his sword, his expletives as hard as the weapon in his hand.

Inyo reacted purely on instinct. He charged swiftly, sword in hand. He hurled himself out of the alley with a roar. Startled, Murrough staggered backward, his weapon a flash of silver that quickly changed direction as he advanced with a growl. Inyo threw his sword up into the air, barely in time to arrest Murrough's blade crashing upon his, steel grating against steel. Inyo's every muscle flexed. With all the resolve he could muster, he thrust Murrough far enough to retreat a step. Murrough lunged at him again, his sword aiming for his torso. But in one fluid move, Inyo dodged and rolled, then plunged his weapon into Murrough's thigh from the side, sending him to the ground with a gasp of disbelief. Inyo yanked his sword out with both hands and then swung it like a scythe at harvest time, slashing it through Murrough's throat, striking the fatal blow.

Inyo staggered backward, trembling and breathing heavily, staring at the surreal scene before him. His eyes shifted away from the pool of inky blood under the dead man to Finley as she rushed to her mamó and embraced her, sobbing. Inyo's chest tightened, making it hard to breathe, and the sword slipped from his hand. But then a warmth flooded him, the heat summoning him out of the trance and back into his body. Finley had wrapped her arms around him, embracing him tightly, shaking and sobbing.

Grace rose haltingly, at a loss for words. She regained control over her ragged breathing and eventually reached for Inyo's arm, giving him a weak squeeze, whispering, "Thank you."

"Mamó—who is that?" Finley asked, rushing to the limp figure on the ground. "Sarah?" The Englishwoman's eyes fluttered open, and they helped her sit up as she moaned, blood oozing sluggishly through the fabric on the back of her shoulder. "Tibbot . . ." she mumbled, still dazed. While they assessed her injury, Finley whispered with a quaking voice, "Mamó, what happened? Where are Ma' and Da'? Where is everyone? Fergal? Owen and Tibbot?"

"It was a trap. Bensbury arrested us all." Grace quickly explained to her, and in Spanish to Inyo, what had happened and that all the prisoners were already en route to London, to the Tower.

Finley gasped. She was on the brink of slipping into an icy pool of shock, but instead she balled up her fists. "We have to stop them! Do you know where—which road did they—?"

Sarah shook her head and mumbled, "It's too late. The transport left over six hours ago."

There was no way to intercept or catch up to the transport on the road now. The English forces had a well-guarded, efficient network of land and sea lanes. The gloomy silence threatened to choke all hope. But then Grace gasped, "The *Gavilán*! We must sail for London!"

"Yes! We can get her ready before morning, but we have to hurry," Finley urged. They helped Sarah off the ground and made for the horses. Finley turned to Sarah, explaining about the *Gavilán*, their ship, that she wasn't far from here, near Barna. She saw Sarah give a determined nod as she helped her mount up behind Grace in a flurry of jerky movements, of torn and blood-stained fabric flapping about. Inyo reached down to clasp his arm in Finley's as she swung herself up behind him. With her arms wrapped around his waist, he dug his heels into Cormac's sides, hoofs sparking to a clatter, before they all disappeared into the night.

The Flight of the Hawk

Several lanterns flickered in the darkness of O'Halloran's cove. Finley, Inyo, and Ellis dragged the last few crates down the steep path while the moon drifted in and out behind shredded clouds and fog. Teagan, Liam, and Geoffrey had refilled all the freshwater casks, and all night long the supplies were rowed over to the *Gavilán*. Despite feeling tired and numb, Finley was eager for the ship to be outward bound. When they'd first started loading, she insisted that her mamó should rest in her cabin along with Sarah, whose wound was still bleeding sluggishly. The Englishwoman had alluded to the need to flee Galway and asked to come along to London, although she hadn't been specific or forthcoming about her reasons.

The worry for her parents threatened to overpower Finley's focus, and several times in the middle of the frantic work, tears ran freely down her cheeks. What dangers awaited them? Would they reach London in time? Could they rescue everyone? The daunting weight of night hovered above, all around her, and even inside her.

When it was time to set sail, Finley kissed Ronin and then climbed into the rowboat with the last load. It was a massive relief that Padraig, Teagan, and Father Whelan insisted on taking care of Ronin and both farms. They waved at her in the glow of their lanterns as she pulled on the oars.

Finley glanced over her shoulder at the *Gavilán* where Inyo, clinging to the hull, awaited with an outstretched hand. She was so grateful he was here, but realized he was sailing straight into hostile waters. "How will Inyo get to safety now?" she had asked her grandmother earlier that night when she helped her limp into her cabin.

"He needs to come with us. If we happen upon any French or Spanish traders, they can take him to safety. Chances are we'll be able to do that in the English Channel," her mamó said, and Finley nodded reluctantly.

The tide was in their favor, and the new day dawned gently on the horizon behind the O'Halloran tower house. As soon as Finley flung herself over the gunnel, the crew weighed anchor. Ellis and Finley hoisted a French ensign, a dark-blue flag with three yellow fleurs-de-lis. "In disguise as a French merchant, we'll be able to get past patrols and ports without raising suspicion," Geoffrey had explained when he unfolded the bundle. *Good thing Mamó keeps such flags on board. One never knows when they'll come in handy!*

Together with Inyo, Finley trimmed and tied off the mizzen, then she braced herself on the bridge as the *Gavilán* passed the Arans. With a stiff northerly wind, they hurried along the coast. The autumn sun glistened brightly on the open ocean. In contrast to the splendid day, however, Finley's face remained dark, so filled was she with fear and with a fiery wrath burning against Bensbury. The wind rose, seemingly in response to her mood and to the urgent pace of work aboard. Finley's eyes fell on Inyo as he carefully checked the compass and charts, and then joined Geoffrey and Liam as they adjusted the sails.

Liam and Geoffrey O'Neill, having long been among Grace's most trusted and experienced sailors, had been concerned about the small size of the crew. "It's not impossible, but it'll be challenging." With just seven hands on board, every single person was vital.

Later in the afternoon, Finley was breathing heavily underneath the billowing canvas, wedged between Liam and Ellis, their arms and backs straining in unison as they worked the ropes. When Ellis glanced at her briefly, Finley gave her an encouraging smile. It more than astonished her that Ellis had insisted on coming along when it would have been easy, even expected, for her to remain in Barna with Padraig. The journey to Coruña came to Finley's mind, especially Ellis' panicked expression as they had lost sight of land and headed across the open ocean. When they'd arrived back in Barna after the pilgrimage, Ellis had gotten on her knees, kissed the ground, and vowed never to step aboard a ship again.

After the sails were trimmed and braced, Finley rubbed her tired eyes. She wondered how Mamó and Sarah were doing and made her way to the cabin. Mamó was fast asleep in her bed. Sarah lay curled up on a mat on the ground and opened her eyes.

"How is your shoulder, Sarah?" Finley whispered.

"It's not bleeding anymore. But . . ."

Sarah's lip quivered. Her face and neck were covered in dark bruises, which, Finley guessed, were Murrough's doing. She was grateful that the young Englishwoman had freed her grandma. Last night she had insisted—begged—to come along to London, to join the rescue mission. *It's probably because she loves Tibbot*, Finley thought to herself, though she couldn't shake the feeling that there was more, a despair that propelled Sarah away from Galway.

"You need to rest," Finley told her in a gentle tone as she patted her shoulder, then headed back out to help the crew.

—

Sarah curled up again, acclimating to the rolling of the ship, watching a hanging lantern sway back and forth. She tried to stretch out her limbs, but her body was filled with tension and pain. Cold and heavy in the pit of her stomach sat the agonizing shame over what happened to Tibbot and over the many lives that were in danger because of her carelessness. Tears ran from her face into the straw mat underneath her head, tears of shame, but also tears of gratitude. Because, despite her role in all of this, Tibbot's mother and the crew had welcomed her aboard, and now she was on her way to London. *But will we make it in time?* Her chest tightened.

Although she was tired to the bones, she couldn't sleep. She wiped the moisture out of her eyes and sniffled. After a few hours of praying silently amid the low creaking of the timbers, Sarah rose and pulled a chair next to the bed when she heard Tibbot's mother stir. "Ms. O'Malley?"

Ms. O'Malley opened her eyes and yawned. "Sarah, oh I—" she began as she maneuvered her legs out of bed. "What you did last night was so very courageous. Thank you. I owe you my life!"

"Please, don't thank me. I'm the reason Tibbot was arrested and all of this happened, and—I just hope we'll make it to London in time —that there's still something we can do—" Sarah's chest heaved with the effort to suppress her tears. "All of it is my fault! I was foolish to think … but I swear if I had known—" She hung her head, sobbing, her hands clenching the fabric of her vest, as though she wanted to carve out the guilt in her heart.

Ms. O'Malley assured her, "We'll get them out, *all* of them, we'll find a way." There was certainty in the woman's voice, but Sarah couldn't shake her sense of dread. *All of them. How will we rescue them all? It's impossible.*

Tibbot's mother contemplated her. "That face of yours. May I ask what happened?"

Sarah unbuttoned her vest and pulled down the collar of her chemise to reveal even more ghastly blotches of black, yellowish-green, and purple that had grown angrier by the day. "This is the reason I have to get away. My husband's handiwork."

"Oh," Ms. O'Malley exhaled, shifting uncomfortably in the silence. Sarah couldn't get herself to look back up, afraid to face the woman's anger. After all, she was Tibbot's mother. And indeed, Ms. O'Malley's voice had turned clipped and dry. "Who is your husband?"

"I—" Sarah choked. She just shook her head, hand covering her mouth. How would Grace O'Malley take to the news that Sarah was, in fact, the governor's wife, after all that he had inflicted on the O'Malleys?

"And Tibbot," Grace wanted to know, "does he know you're taken?"

"No. I meant to tell him, honestly, I did. I—" Sarah sank her head into her hands. She whispered with a trembling voice, "I know what I did was wrong, but I love him." She didn't know what else to say or how to apologize, stuck in guilt and despair. But she was utterly surprised when Grace's hand settled on her arm. Sarah's head lifted.

"Courage, Sarah! Don't lose hope," Tibbot's mother nodded with a gentle smile.

Sarah's breath came haltingly. She knew she'd have *a lot* of explaining to do. To Tibbot, to her new Irish allies, and to her father. After all, he had been so elated about her marriage to Bensbury and had given an extraordinarily lavish dowry. Would her father's love for her allow him to see past the disgrace of her failed marriage? Would he understand her? Forgive her?

While she hung her head and sniffled, she noticed glimmers on the floor. The cabin's lantern light reflected off two tiny, golden items under the table next to her. She reached for the small objects. Two buttons. Sarah picked them up and handed them to Tibbot's mother, whose eyes widened when she looked at them and then clutched them to her chest.

—

Over the following days, a northerly wind carried the *Gavilán* briskly along the coast. Inyo, along with the entire crew, scurried from task to task, between helm, lookout, and sails. Soon, they rounded Mizen Head and set a south-easterly course. With every inch of canvas set, the ship forged on through the waves as low-hanging clouds chased each other in the sky.

The elements continued to conspire in their favor, helping the *Gavilán* round the southwestern tip of Cornwall, then enter the English Channel. With their French flag hoisted, and a course that kept them at least a league away from land, they made swift progress without any interference.

Inyo gazed out at the calm horizon. Were these really the same waters that a few months prior had relentlessly battered the Armada? He was sailing the same route he had aboard the *Santa Catalina*. In a strange way, his life had come full circle. How was he to know back then that he would indeed be heading for London, not as part of King Philip's endeavor, but instead under Señora O'Malley's command, and for entirely different reasons.

—

Finley hovered over the map and compass on the quarterdeck next to her mamó. "Here: Boulogne and Calais." Grace pointed at the narrowest part of the Channel, "We'll be there in three days. Let's keep a lookout for traders we can flag down."

Finley swallowed, her heart in agony, knowing this would be Inyo's best chance to make it home. She desperately wanted him to stay, wanted to cling to him, no matter what, even though it was dangerous and selfish. But she remained quiet and stoic in the wind, stifling anything that might give her emotions away, while her grandma summoned Inyo and shared their plan.

"No!" Inyo insisted angrily. "I will come with you to London!" His eyebrows furrowed deeply. He pointedly explained to them that he would not allow himself to be dropped off while their future was still uncertain and while Finley's parents were imprisoned.

Finley could see how it infuriated him that they wanted to send him ashore, just like that, without any attempt at convincing him to stay. She was taken aback by the storm in Inyo's pained face as he gripped the shrouds, his brooding gaze turned to the far-off horizon. "Inyo, I want you to have a chance at returning to your home," she earnestly whispered. The taut lines in his face relaxed.

"And I—" Inyo countered, pulling her into a fervent embrace, "I don't *want* to go home, I just want . . . *you!*" The strength of his grip around her torso matched the burning intensity of his words. "I want us to stay together," he urged.

Finley admitted, "I want that, too, but . . ." Inyo should be heading to Antwerp or to Spain. Instead, he was insistent on helping to rescue her family, filling her with hope and strength.

But then what? What would their futures look like? Hers in Ireland. His in Spain. Separated by warring empires and endless ocean. All this uncertainty, all the questions and fears, the dread of approaching London, the worry over her parents and uncles, collided and knotted up in her chest like a giant tangle of lost fishing nets in a storm, constricting her breathing and dulling her senses. She desperately wanted to think herself away from all the distress and hid her face in Inyo's vest. Wrapping her arms around him, she melted into his body's contours, savoring the soothing rhythm of his heartbeat, a deep and steady ba-bom ba-bom ba-bom.

Inyo murmured, *"Estoy aqui para ti."*

She nodded bravely, relishing his words, the assurance that he'd be by her side. There was such wealth of emotion in the way he spoke, such depth to his promise. Lifting her face, she whispered, *"¡Te amo!"*

"Oh, Fin!" Inyo lowered his face to hers. "And I—I love you!"

—

Later, Inyo joined Finley and her mamó, huddling around the maps again. Inyo began, "We'll pass Plymouth soon. I'm worried about the English navy."

"We have to keep our wits about us for sure," Grace agreed. "They might still lurk in the Channel, protecting the approach to London, checking on trade. But I don't think we'll encounter many of them. The campaign against the Armada has very likely depleted their resources and supplies. Most of their ships are likely under repair right now."

Inyo swallowed. Even though he hoped Grace was right, he was apprehensive about sailing along England's southern coast. His decision to stay aboard, all the way into London, could endanger everyone aboard if it were discovered that he's a Spaniard. Inyo's brow creased. He wanted to help save Finley's family, not put them in more danger than they already were.

Grace assured him that if he stayed mute and remained in his Ian disguise, he'd have nothing to worry about. "And there's also the hiding place in my cabin," she reminded him. Inyo nodded. *The secret compartment!* He would hide there when necessary.

As darkness fell, the wind picked up, and a drizzle showered the sea. Inyo and Finley allowed themselves a rare few hours of sleep below deck. Inyo's arms wound around Finley as they curled up next to each other, surrounded by dissonant creaking and the scent of damp hemp.

Finley was getting more and more exhausted. Every day, she cried over her parents and her uncles, not knowing if they could be rescued from their inevitable deaths in time. When Inyo saw her like that, a dagger plunged into his heart. How he wished he had answers, wished he could give her certainty and guarantees. But he couldn't, and now his own fears about the English began to affect him. In those moments when he cradled Finley, when they clung to each other silently, he could sense her desperation and his own as well.

Restlessly, Inyo drifted in and out of sleep. Shredded scenes from the Armada's first morning near Plymouth flickered in his subconscious. It was the day the English had managed to defy the elements, had presented themselves to windward to hunt and harass the Armada. Battle scenes flashed through Inyo's dreams: his shipmates' anguished faces, approaching enemy galleons, thundering salvos of cannons, furious explosions of shredded timbers, splattering blood.

"Inyo? Inyo, are you well? Breathe!" Finley whispered in the darkness near him. "You had a bad dream."

A sob bubbled up from deep inside him. Finley pulled him up into her arms, and their limbs knotted around each other while the lingering clouds of his nightmare slowly dissipated. "Shh. All is well, my love. I'm here. Breathe," Finley repeated softly.

Inyo didn't know what to say, suspended between the terror of the nightmare and the embarrassment of having to be comforted. *I need to be strong for Fin! She's the one who needs solace, not the other way around.*

Finley hugged him tightly. Slowly, they both relaxed before settling back down.

For two days, strong gusts and gray skies with cold drizzles shadowed the *Gavilán* as she forged through the swell, frigid spray lashing any exposed skin. Inyo shivered on the rolling deck. Next to him, Geoffrey wrung out his sopping shirt and snorted, "We're making excellent progress *and* we're getting clean in the process."

—

That evening, Sarah found her way to Ms. O'Malley's cabin. From the bits of conversation between the crew over the past week, Sarah had gathered that once they'd reach London, they intended to head directly to the Tower. Crazy strategies and ideas had been tossed back and forth. Direct attacks, infiltration in disguise, none of them feasible. The obvious problem was their small number. Realistically, what could the seven of them achieve? Tibbot's mother had settled on the idea of a prisoner swap, where she'd offer herself in exchange for the release of her people. She seemed set entirely on sacrificing her life and saw no other option.

Sarah knocked on the cabin door.

"Come in."

Ms. O'Malley motioned Sarah to her desk, where a chart of southeastern England was spread out. Grace absentmindedly uttered, "London . . ." as they both studied the map.

"When will we arrive?" Sarah asked.

"In less than two days," Ms. O'Malley estimated. "You said you wanted to talk to me about an idea?"

Sarah nodded while her eyes followed the snaking curves of the Thames. Then she pointed to Greenwich on the map. Grace lifted an eyebrow as Sarah began to lay out her plan.

—

Finley was relieved that they'd only sighted a few traders on their journey, and not a single vessel of the English navy. After rounding Margate Head, the *Gavilán* started her approach to London, up the Thames. As expected, they were soon flagged down by a patrol.

Grace frowned as the ship drew closer. She rushed down to the main deck. "Liam, Geoffrey, *le stratagème français s'il vous plaît!*" She added with a taut voice, "Finley, Ellis, you know what to do!" Finley quickly hid her hair under her cap and helped Ellis do the same. They then rubbed her hands on the blackest, most tarred parts of the ropes, and smudged their cheeks and chins for a scruff beard effect. In the meantime, Grace pulled Sarah aside, whispering, and sent her to her cabin. When Sarah returned, she wore a fine skirt. Part of her freshly combed hair now covered her black eye, and she held a fan in such a way to hide the bruises on her neck.

In the meantime, Grace had ordered everyone else, "Make yourself appear as half-baked as you can. Liam and Geoffrey will take it from here."

The English pulled alongside the Gavilán when both vessels were hove to. "French merchantman, prepare for inspection!" they barked. Finley swallowed hard. An elderly English officer, his uniform exceedingly clean, climbed up and over the Gavilán's side, followed by two soldiers with muskets.

"*Ah, bonjour, messieurs!*" Geoffrey chimed. With a heavy French accent, he continued, "Welcome, ze sheep and our 'umble crew, we eez at your service!" With Liam by his side, Geoffrey played a convincing captain as he bowed to the officers.

Finley, Inyo, Ellis, and Grace had formed a ragged line behind them and kept their heads bowed, while the stern official glanced at them with a crinkled nose. "What brings you to England? What merchandise do you carry?" he asked Liam and Geoffrey.

"Well monsieur, we 'ave come all ze way from Bordeaux, but oh, *mon dieu*, we were robbed by ze most terrible corsairs near Saint-Malo!" Liam whined.

"Zey took everyzing! All ze wine! We 'ave nozing left. But we 'ave to sail to London, we do! Zis fine lady bought passage to London." Geoffrey pointed to Sarah. "And of course we are keeping our promeez."

"Is that true, milady?"

"Yes, sir. Indeed, it's true," Sarah tweeted, fluttering her fan, "These brave sailors are bringing me home."

Finley cast a sideways glance at Inyo, who had turned ashen, his breathing shallow. Two soldiers were sent to search the hold. When they returned, they confirmed that there was nothing aboard. "No weapons either, sir, just a few barrels of foul provisions."

The English officer snorted derisively and took his leave. "Remember to obey our laws and depart as soon as you're done delivering your passenger. Good day."

Liam and Geoffrey bowed deeply; their *'yes, sir'* and *'au revoir'* tinged with slightly overdone reverence. As soon as the English vessel beat away, Finley exhaled, doubling over. The main deck was aswirl with relieved murmurs and praise for Geoffrey and Liam's performance.

"Inyo," Finley whispered, grabbing his arm, "next time, just hide in mamó's cabin, in the secret compartment." She did not want him to come face-to-face with another English officer. Inyo, still pale and trembling, agreed.

With the help of the flood tide, the *Gavilán* closed in on London under leaden skies. Fields, brambles, and small fishing hamlets drifted past them. The crew watched exotic wares and riches from across the globe get ferried up the Thames on all manner of ships.

By late afternoon, they rounded another bend in the narrowing river, then anchored near the docks of the village of Greenwich. Columns of smoke rose from the vendors of the waterfront market and out of the ornate, half-timbered homes that lined the busy alleys. The scent of fish and woodsmoke lingered over the river. A group of soldiers on horseback followed a carriage, hoofs clomping on the cobbles, making their way to a long and impressive palace that sat upriver from the town. Its reddish brick façade was adorned with contrasting, white window frames, several flanking towers, a massive gate, and endless, festive crenellations.

"Greenwich Palace—oh, look!" Sarah pointed to the large flag above the tallest tower. "The Queen is in residence!" Lazy ripples danced over the pennant that featured the Queen's blue and red coat of arms, flanked by a lion and a red dragon.

Finley stared at the palace and the banner while her mamó asked Sarah, "And you're sure my letter will be delivered directly?"

"I have no doubt!" Sarah assured her as she climbed down into the rowboat with Liam and Geoffrey at the oars. Finley watched the boat head to the landing. Sarah leaped off and then dashed through the village streets and towards the palace.

Two Queens

GREENWICH PALACE, ENGLAND, OCTOBER 1588

The forest surrounding Greenwich Palace had erupted into festive autumn colors when a group of hunters on horseback neared the stables after a successful outing. Elizabeth and Thomas McDarren were among them. They slowed their mounts.

Ever since the defeat of the Armada, the country had been in a jubilant mood, celebrating with numerous feasts and hunts. The dark burden of the previous year had fallen off Elizabeth's shoulders after the surprising victory. Her life was spared. England remained free.

But just six weeks ago, she received word about Robin's death. Her heart had shattered. At first, she refused to believe the news, thinking it was her enemies' cruel plot to weaken her. But the mournful messenger was Robin's personal servant, someone she had known for years. He described Robin's declining health during his last days and that he refused to let anyone see the severity of his condition until it was too late.

In shock and grief, Elizabeth locked herself in her chambers for days. The tears had flowed as ceaselessly as the river outside her windows. She didn't want to continue without Robin; couldn't face the world; a reality that required her to be an unfeeling statue, to wear a stifling façade that smothered everything about her that was real and alive. All she wanted was to stand before Robin, far away in a country churchyard, to exchange vows and rings, lay her cheek against him, then live a quiet and anonymous life with him. But it could never be. The shouting and banging on her door was incessant, and she had no choice but to suit up in her dreaded stoic armor and mask. The grief was a constant, dark-feathered presence that wheeled above her head.

Thomas, who rode next to her as they neared the stables, gave her a knowing glance filled with kindness and encouragement. He had seen how much she'd loved Robin, and how deeply she grieved, how she needed solitude and quiet outings on horseback under the gentle canopy of autumn woods. Because he was a widower himself, Thomas understood what she'd been through, had become an unexpected source of comfort to her, a rock, since Robin passed away.

Thomas and Elizabeth dismounted at the stable gate when Elizabeth's mount, Apollo, lifted his head unexpectedly, turning his ears towards the open stable door, out of which a person appeared, a bruised and disheveled rag of a figure that barreled towards Thomas, startling him with a croak, "Papa!"

"Sarah?" Thomas caught her as she flung herself into his arms, her cap falling off, revealing her long hair. "Sarah! Oh, my love!" He cradled her limp body as she collapsed, overcome by weeping. "What in the world . . . what are you doing here, in such a state? My sweet Sarah! Good God, what happened to your face?"

"I—I—did you not get my letters? I left Galway. I ran away!"

"Why in God's name would you do that? Your husband—"

"Aldred beat me." The words cascaded out of her. "Almost every day, I couldn't stand it any longer! The Irish who rescued me and brought me here, they are led by the chieftain Grace O'Malley—her daughter and sons are currently in the Tower! They're innocent. Aldred arrested them and—" Sarah tried to catch her breath, suppressing a sob, "and Grace O'Malley is here to plead for their lives.

Here, this letter explains everything. Could you please—oh, Papa, if our Good Queen Elizabeth would only read her letter and if Ms. O'Malley could be granted an audience, then—"

Elizabeth, watching the scene from behind Apollo, took a step forward. Tom's daughter startled, staring at her with a pale, tear-filled face. "Tom, is this your daughter?" Elizabeth asked.

"Yes, ma'am, this is Sarah."

Shocked, Sarah dropped to one knee while hastily wiping her tears away. "Your Majesty!"

"Rise, Sarah. Let me see your face." Elizabeth studied the young woman, her bruised face, her haggard frame. "You say that you just sailed here all the way from Ireland?"

"From Galway, Your Highness."

Elizabeth raised an intrigued brow. "And you carry an important letter?"

"Yes, Your Majesty." Sarah curtsied and handed her the folded-up parchment.

Elizabeth turned the letter over to find it sealed with a golden button, neatly sewn on. Her eyes widened, and her fingers paused for a moment before she gently grasped the button, ripped it off, and unfolded the crackling page. She carefully scanned the letter, blinked absentmindedly, then straightened her frame. "Sarah, let Grace O'Malley know that I will arrange a meeting in the coming days."

———

Inyo had been hiding under the captain's bed in the secret hollow, the conditions in the cramped space as torturous, dank, and dismal as his first night aboard the *Catalina* when he was in chains. The hours dragged on and on while he labored to breathe. *What a coward I am!* What good was it for him to be safe while none of the others were? In a fit of impatience, he shoved the wooden board and the mattress out of the way and crawled out of the compartment with stiff limbs.

"What the—" Finley spluttered when he appeared on the main deck. She raised her voice in protest, "Are you mad?" She pleaded with him to reconsider, fearing for his safety.

Inyo's decision, however, was firm, his voice a tight and determined growl: "I don't care if we get searched again. I will not leave your side."

They joined Ellis at the rail of the *Gavilán* with grumbling stomachs, awaiting Sarah's return. When evening colored the sky in purple hues, the *Gavilán* slowly swung around on her anchor with the flow of the tide. In the alleys of Greenwich, shop doors banged closed, a handcart rattled away from the landing, the market emptied, and the windows of nearby homes lit up in the dusk. Liam and Geoffrey had passed the time by casting a few lines, and soon everyone gathered around the few bites of fish and the meager remnants of the ale.

The chill hanging over the Thames made their faces and hands clammy and seeped into their thoughts and sluggish conversation. Might Sarah have already abandoned them? Was her love for Tibbot strong enough to make her keep her promise to help, and what in Neptune's name was taking so long? A faint sound of footsteps caught everyone's attention in the dimly lit square. Sarah approached the landing with a man, both loaded with several baskets and bundles. They climbed into the boat with Liam and Geoffrey's help. As the oars dipped into the dark river, Inyo's pulse raced.

"Ms. O'Malley, I have good news!" Sarah panted when she climbed aboard. "The Queen read your letter and will send word tomorrow about the audience you requested!" Sarah's words tumbled out of her into the collective astonishment around her, prompting gasps and relieved murmurs. Grace, speechless with gratitude, reached for Sarah's hand when the man who accompanied Sarah swung himself over the rail, straightened his fine hunting outfit, and ran a hand over his graying hair. Sarah beamed from ear to ear when she introduced him, "My father, Thomas McDarren." She took his arm and whispered enthusiastically, "Papa, this is Grace O'Malley."

Thomas bowed, then shook Grace's hand. "Ms. O'Malley, you have brought me back my daughter, you have—delivered her from danger. How can I ever thank you enough?"

"Oh, Thomas, I need to thank *you*. It was your daughter who saved my life." Grace filled him in on Sarah's role in freeing her from Galway prison. Then she invited Thomas and Sarah into her cabin while Liam and Geoffrey finished hoisting up a bundle of folded blankets and two baskets filled with fresh bread, pastries, ale, and vegetables.

Liam smiled. "Gifts for us, they said."

Once Sarah and her father had taken their leave, Inyo curled up with Finley on the lantern-lit main deck under one of the new blankets. After the uncertainty and grief of the previous week, the more hopeful news of today and the McDarrens' kindness were beacons of hope that had flared up in the dark. But what would the coming days bring? How could Finley's parents, Tibbot, Owen, and Fergal be freed? Would Grace have to give up her freedom or even her life for their release?

—

While the low autumn sun hovered behind a veil of fog, the village of Greenwich slowly came to life. Sarah and her father, clutching a sealed royal message, approached the landing with rapid feet, clambered into the boat, set over, and climbed aboard the *Gavilán*. Expectant silence hung over the gathered crew while Grace took the letter, broke the seal, and read with trembling hands. She finally lifted her face, announcing that the Queen would see her the next day.

Shouts of astonishment erupted, the crew gasping and clasping each other. Their joy was catching and reflected in Sarah's face as she smiled first at Ms. O'Malley, then her father. They both led Grace off to the side and handed her a bulging leather pouch. "I want you to have this," Sarah's father whispered. "For your crew and for the voyage home." Grace stared at the purse in her hands and frowned, inhaling sharply to voice her protest, but Thomas McDarren continued, "No, don't say a word, I won't hear any of it. This is yours; I insist!"

Grace scratched the nape of her neck. "Thomas, you may not know this, but the English have been my enemies for decades. This—this truly unexpected generosity from you, a stranger, an Englishman, is turning my world upside down. Thank you, Thomas. I just hope—"

She cast her apprehensive eyes towards Greenwich Palace, and during the few breaths of silence, Sarah tried to imagine what would await the chieftain at court. Would she end up imprisoned, along with Tibbot and everyone else in her family? Sarah squeezed Ms. O'Malley's arm gently, at a loss for words. Her father cleared his throat, saying, "I know you are afraid . . . and while it's true that our Queen is a lioness, I know her to be just, kind, and merciful. So, have courage!"

—

The sun had placed long strands of pale light over the tiled floor below the palace windows. While her ladies decorated the curls of her wig with pearls, Elizabeth glanced at the letter in her hands one more time. The chieftain's language was eloquent and flowery, but underneath it all, the essence of the request was bold. Grace O'Malley was bold. *An extraordinary piece of writing*, Elizabeth admitted to herself. This determined woman was clearly well-versed in the art of diplomacy and international negotiations. Despite the obvious differences in nationality, class, and religion, Elizabeth wondered whether they might not have more in common than first appeared. Two women who found themselves in unexpected leadership positions, roles the fates had placed them in against the odds. Two rulers whose task it was to protect their people in a world where precisely that duty was a daily struggle bordering on the impossible.

Aside from the letter's content, something else caught her attention—O'Malley's handwriting. The entire page resembled a seascape. The sentences: wave after wave of undulating ocean dotted with vessels. The upward flourishes of her ascenders: masts and pennants fluttering in erratic winds.

What intrigued Elizabeth the most, however, was the gold button. She held it between her delicate fingers and lovingly gazed at the small bird etched into the shiny surface. She knew, of course, whose button this was. There was no doubt.

"A storm, Captain!" Her own voice echoed in a vivid childhood memory of the sun-dappled garden at Hatfield House. Both Robin and she were nine years old. He smiled at her while he held fast to a tree trunk as if it were a mast, pretending they were on a ship out in high seas.

Standing tall, Robin pointed his wooden sword. "There, Bess! Our island!" He still had that sweet boyish face back then, but his voice was already full of resolve, as it was throughout his entire life. So too were his eyes, forever glancing at her with kindness and loyalty. A friendship as rare as a gem. "Helm hard a-larboard!"

"Aye, Captain!" Elizabeth shouted as she gripped a tree limb.

It had been a childhood of loneliness, horrors, and unanswered questions. Years filled with intense mistrust and uncertainty, lacking the warmth of a real family, overshadowed by the brutal execution of her mother, Anne Boleyn, when Elizabeth was just three years old. Yes, the guardians and tutors throughout the years had been so very kind. But the relationship with Robert Dudley, her sweet Robin, was one of her life's richest joys, one of her greatest sources of strength. Having him at her side from the beginning of her reign had made the daunting task of ruling less lonely, less overwhelming.

Elizabeth had showered him with favors, and on one occasion, given him a finely tailored black velvet jerkin adorned with these very buttons. She had them specifically designed for him, each of the eight buttons engraved with the bird that carried his name.

But now, he was gone, taken from her much too soon. When the news of his death reached her, she locked herself away for days, plunged into grief. Oh, how she missed him! Her heart had never known pain as intense as this. How could he pass away when she still needed him more than ever? She squeezed her eyes to hold back her tears and lifted the button to her trembling lips.

Elizabeth glanced up at the mirror in front of her again as her ladies finished fluttering about her. She rose and turned to her principal secretary, who bowed to her and announced, "Your Majesty. The Irish chieftain O'Malley is here to see you."

Courtiers and ladies lined both sides of the great hall, where audiences took place on a near-daily basis. Today, there was unusual tension in the air. Heads eagerly turned from the throne to the heavy wooden doors that swung open, causing the many candles to flicker.

With her own curiosity hidden behind a well-trained exterior, Elizabeth watched from the throne as Thomas entered with his daughter, followed by Grace O'Malley. The Irish chieftain stood tall, wearing a nut-brown dress with touches of embroidery.

Behind her were three young clan members, and Elizabeth immediately noticed two of them clutching each other's hands, pale-faced and stiff. A small red-haired woman, so very young, and a handsome man with dark hair. He glanced at his beloved with such purity and protectiveness, held her hand as if he'd never let go. The two of them reminded Elizabeth of Robin and herself, many years ago, utterly scared in the Tower, clinging to each other with skinny and trembling limbs. If it had been their last day, at least they would have been together, the love between them an unbreakable and eternal bond. So everlasting, she could still feel it to this day. Despite Robin's death, his spirit and his love lived within her.

While everyone kneeled in a synchronized rustling of fabric, Grace O'Malley remained upright. The chieftain stared at Elizabeth and bowed her head briefly. "Your Majesty, forgive me for not kneeling in front of you as I was instructed to do. I'm afraid with these bad knees, I wouldn't be able to get back up again, and instead would have to remain permanently affixed to this fine palace floor."

The entire hall quieted. A few crackles from the large fireplace echoed in the tense silence while ladies and courtiers glanced at each other with bated breath.

Elizabeth remained still, then inhaled and arched one eyebrow ever so slightly. "My lady, 'tis an understandable predicament. I'm afraid there's indeed a shortage of good knees for women our age in all the lands."

O'Malley might have seen the hint of a smile play around the Queen's mouth, and with a dash more warmth in her voice, the Irish chieftain said, "Your Majesty, thank you for receiving me for an audience."

They exchanged a few more platitudes while carefully sizing each other up. Then Elizabeth rose from her throne and pointed to a round table off to the side, where a large map was rolled open. "Tell me about your journey here, Grace O'Malley." When she and Grace ambled toward the chart, Elizabeth asked her entourage to remain behind, so their conversation would remain private.

"Your Majesty, my crew and I sailed here on my ship," O'Malley began. Elizabeth studied the chieftain's face, the way her intelligent eyes took in Ortelius' map of *Anglia, Scotiae, and Hiberniae*. O'Malley's fingers trace a route on the map. "We sailed from Galway right after Sarah freed me."

Elizabeth circled Grace to get a closer look at the western coast of Ireland, a jagged, meandering line with dozens of small bays and inlets. "Your clan's territory?" Elizabeth asked, her finger on one of the small bays. Grace nodded. Clew Bay appeared as a minuscule and insignificant inlet in the shape of an elongated teardrop, the clan's name, O Mayle, noted next to the bay.

Elizabeth inhaled deeply, holding on to her composure as she contemplated her next move. She had intended to subdue O'Malley and her rebellious band. The voice of one of her advisors still echoed within her: *The rule of law is the road to the kingdom's unity, and it may have to be paved with stringent measures*. After all the grief Ireland had given her, she now had the upper hand. She could make an example that would resound forcefully.

On the other hand, her curiosity about the chieftain of the O'Malleys had come alive. Why did she risk so much for an audience? And above all, one question burned brightest in Elizabeth's heart. She placed Grace's letter on the edge of the map and revealed the golden button that had been hidden in the palm of her hand. "Grace, how did you come into possession of this?"

"It belonged to my son, Owen. Aldred Bensbury arrested him and all of us. This and several more gold buttons used to grace my son's vest, Your Majesty."

"Your—your son's vest?" Elizabeth swallowed.

Grace explained, "A little over ten years ago, my Owen received it as a gift from Robert Dudley, the Earl of Leicester. His ship, the *Antelope*, ran into trouble off my coast as he accompanied the Lord Deputy on a survey of the land. They needed help. My men and I found them with several leaks, a damaged rudder, and no knowledge of the dangerous coasts."

Elizabeth nodded slightly. That mission twelve years ago had been her idea, and she'd sent Robin because she intended to place him in charge of her armies eventually. When Robin returned from the survey, he'd recounted the "wild, treacherous and untamable coast" and the equally untamable clans making the frigid lands their home. "Tell me more about the damage to the *Antelope* and what happened."

"Her crew had never sailed Ireland's western coast. They were lucky they survived. While my men repaired his vessel, 'Robin,' as he told me you preferred to call him, was a guest at my castle for a week. He was most generous in his show of gratitude to my men, and he gifted this vest to Owen. The memory of his visit and the many praises he sang of his Queen have remained with me through the years. I daresay his devotion to you was as evident as the sun's heat on a summer day.

"Your Majesty, when I heard of his untimely death, I wept for your loss, knowing how close you were to your dear friend. Surely your heart must ache still . . ."

Grace's sympathy was evident in her expression. Elizabeth blinked back the moisture in her eyes, trying to push down the acute sorrow that bubbled up whenever Robin's name was mentioned. She picked up the button absentmindedly, curled her fingers around it, and pressed it tenderly against her shredded, grieving heart.

That morning, in preparation for this audience, she had reviewed a lengthy list of Grace O'Malley's crimes. Numerous incidents of piracy and rebellion against English officials and merchants. In a letter, Bensbury described this Irish chieftain as the "mastermind behind all rebellion," an "abominable criminal," and "the greatest menace in all the land." Elizabeth couldn't understand where the menacing criminal was, though. All she saw was a desperate, bruised, and weathered woman. A chieftain whose territory was smaller than an ant in a vast meadow, a mere speck on the edge of England's realm.

Ireland belongs to me, Elizabeth reminded herself. She had to insist on loyalty and compliance. But burning crops and farms? Murders? Surely there had to be better ways. Very recently, Elizabeth had read several disturbing reports about Aldred Bensbury's vicious methods. O'Malley's letter described how English armies had taken much of the clan's lands through the years and also made Grace a widow twice over.

Elizabeth couldn't help but reflect on her own anguished summer, the harrowing despair over what would have become of her home, her beloved England, if the mighty Spanish empire had succeeded in landing its powerful army. Her forlorn gaze lingered on the part of the map that delineated the coast closest to Dover.

Grace O'Malley quietly interrupted Elizabeth's thoughts. "Your Majesty, your very own realm was recently the target of invasion plans. Had Spain—"

"Had Spain succeeded," Elizabeth finished the chieftain's sentence, "my country would have lost its sovereignty. The liberty and the very lives of my people would have been in danger." After a moment of silence, she added in a dry tone, "And I most certainly would have lost my head."

Their eyes locked briefly, and an invisible filament of understanding and respect bridged the divide between them. After a long silence, Elizabeth asked, "In your letter, you mention five of your people currently imprisoned in the Tower?"

"Yes, Your Majesty. My sons, Owen and Tibbot. My daughter, Maeve, and her husband, Brian. And their neighbor, Fergal MacDermot. I am here to plead for their release."

—

All this time, Finley had clutched Inyo's hand tightly, Ellis next to them, staring wide-eyed at the splendid and surreal tableau before them: A large hall filled with vibrant tapestries, candelabras, and ornately dressed nobility, entirely bathed in festive light streaming through the many-colored glass of the windows. Above it all, a vaulted ceiling soared. The majestic spectacle of the English queen, covered in gold, silk, lace, pearls, jewels, and velvet, seated in regal posture on her throne, took Finley's breath away. What amount of grit and wit had chiseled the monarch's face? And what might have turned her eyes so wise, guarded, and fierce, all at the same time, much like Finley's grandma's?

Finley's gaze followed them both, her mamó and the English monarch, lingering over the map, their mesmerizing gestures those of two admirals plotting their agreement with whole oceans and countries under their fingers. They circled the table slowly and deliberately. Currently, the Queen had her back turned, so the lace halo of her huge ruff, fan-shaped and pearl-studded, formed a privacy screen during their negotiations. What might they be discussing? Could an agreement be reached, and at what price? So much was at stake. Finley wondered what would become of her parents, her uncles, and Ellis's father. *What will the Queen demand? Will Mamó pay with her life? Or be locked away forever and be forced to give up her lands, her fortress, and her ships if that is what the English demand for the release of the prisoners?*

The Queen signaled her principal secretary to the map table. He bowed, readying his quill and ledger. The slender man with a pointy mustache took notes, his face an expressionless mask, before he bowed and strode away.

Then the Queen took her place on the throne again. Finley anxiously glanced at her mamó, who now stood alone. All eyes in the hall were expectantly trained on the two women. Finally, Queen Elizabeth solemnly announced, "Grace O'Malley, since you vow that you and your alliance shall from here on refrain from any further rebellion against us, swearing absolute loyalty instead, I will see to it that all your lands are returned to you. Sir Aldred Bensbury, governor of Galway, will be replaced. The ransom he took is to be refunded to you, and the prisoners will be freed immediately."

Finley gasped. Could she trust her ears? Her eyes narrowed as she examined the Queen's face closely. Did she really mean what she said? Surprised voices quickly rose around Finley, drawing her attention to the elated faces of the courtiers and ladies lining the room. Her mamó stood frozen in place, her stunned expression shifting to an exhale and a smile. Finley hurriedly crossed to her and threw herself into her arms, overwhelmed with emotion. In the whirlwind of joy and relief, Finley barely noticed the tears in Ellis' eyes and her astonished whisper, "My da', they'll free my da'!" But when Inyo finally pulled Finley into his arms, a final warm certainty flooded her. She could finally exhale. Then they both turned their faces to the English queen, who looked at them warmly and nodded knowingly, holding eye contact. The moment cemented an unexpected connection between them: the young, scrappy lovers and the regal English queen. An hour later, Finley and Inyo walked out of Greenwich Palace behind her mamó, who clutched the signed treaty and the royal pardon.

That evening, under a brilliant night sky, the Queen's barge pushed off from the palace landing and drifted down the river like a gilded swan. Elizabeth reclined on her large velveteen settee, while several theater musicians at the bow raised their crystal-clear voices to the gentle melody of lutes.

Her barge followed a transport vessel that carried the prisoners from the Tower downriver to Greenwich. She'd tasked Sarah and Thomas McDarren with this mission. The vessel pulled up alongside Grace O'Malley's ship, and several figures climbed aboard. Elated voices and euphoric shouting greeted them, and every person on the ship was swept up in a jubilant whirl of relieved cheering and tearful hugs. Elizabeth smiled when she saw Thomas's daughter, Sarah, in the arms of a handsome young Irishman. Grace O'Malley embraced one prisoner after another, and the obvious joy aboard that vessel lit up the night and ignited a bonfire deep inside Elizabeth's heart.

—

Francisca clutched the abbey gate that she had just opened, her eyebrows lifted in surprise at Marina and Juan wanting to see her in the middle of the day. "Marina, what is it?" Francisca uttered when she saw their radiant faces and a letter in Marina's grasp.

"A letter from Inyo!" Juan smiled.

A sob of joy welled up in Francisca when she unfolded the parchment.

London, October 1588

Querida Marina,

I hope this letter reaches you soon and that you're well. You have probably heard of the Armada's fate. I fervently hope Antonio made it back to Spain safely.

Despite the terrors of the past season, I am relieved to be in very fortunate circumstances. So much has happened to me! It was the greatest of miracles that I survived a shipwreck and found shelter with farmers near Galway.

I'm currently in London as part of an endeavor to free Irish prisoners. It's a very long story, and I will tell you everything about my incredible journey when I come to Coruña in the spring, which I am determined to do. For now, however, I am heading back to Ireland to help my hosts on their farm.

To be honest, that's not the only reason why I am returning there. I have fallen in love with a young woman named Finley. Even though I don't know what the weeks and months ahead have in store for us, we want to find a way to remain together. I might ask her to come to Spain with me, but her family has also offered me work and they have taken me in as one of their own. Who knows, maybe there is a future for me in Ireland after all?

I can't wait to see you in April or May, to wrap you in my arms and introduce you to Finley. Please send my love to Francisca and Juan, to Antonio, Bernardo, Adrián, Clara, and Margarita!

Cariñosamente, Inyo

Inyo's Ring

BARNA, IRELAND, DECEMBER 1588

The barren trees along the path shrouded themselves in low-hanging clouds when Inyo nudged Merla into a canter, catching up to Brian. The horses' hoofs crunched on the hoarfrost of the empty main road as they rode from Barna and past the sleeping woods. The replacement of the cruel governor had everyone in and around Galway breathing easier; the English weren't afraid of the Spanish fleet landing here anymore, and there were no more patrols on the roads. Inyo inhaled the chilly mist and smiled inwardly, thinking back over the past two months.

During the miraculous reunion in London, Finley's parents hugged him repeatedly and sobbed with gratitude. Grace O'Malley embraced her sons, Ellis and her father held each other in relief, and Tibbot scooped Sarah into his arms. They stayed up late into the night celebrating, then set out on the long journey home the next morning.

Shortly after the Gavilán returned to Ireland, Inyo sailed to Clew Bay with Finley, Grace, Owen, Tibbot, and Sarah. At Rockfleet, the Englishwoman was initially met with suspicion. However, Owen and Grace's high regard for Sarah soon made everyone see her as an ally. Sarah was determined to stay with Tibbot, and there was even talk of a spring wedding. When Tibbot announced his plan, Inyo couldn't help but smile at Finley, noticing her raised eyebrows, her elation. At that moment, when his eyes met hers, a thought formed in Inyo's mind, like a key about to fit into a lock and open a door.

During his week up at Rockfleet, Inyo got to know the Clew Bay clans and helped them with urgent repairs on several vessels. His skills as a ship's carpenter found abundant admiration and praise. Once the work was done, the clans gathered for a splendid feast in the great hall, applauding Grace's successful negotiations with the English queen. The treaty with England had given the O'Malleys and all the people of Clew Bay newfound hope. Inyo and Finley then returned to Barna, where work needed to be done on the Morris and MacDermot farms to prepare for winter.

"We're almost there," Brian interrupted his thoughts, slowing Cormac to a walk. Inyo patted Merla's neck, the leather of the saddle creaking with each of her steps, as they approached the bridge over the Corrib, along with Galway's western gate. They dismounted and led the horses across the bridge, the muffled rush of the ice-fringed river echoing beneath their feet, while Inyo's pulse quickened. There wasn't much time; Finley and Maeve were helping Father Whelan decorate Barna's little church for Christmas, and hopefully they wouldn't notice that he and Brian had left.

They tied up the horses on the main street near a narrow stone building with a wooden door; suspended above its entrance was an ornate metal sign featuring a figure bent over a small anvil. Inyo, grinning at Brian, reached for his leather pouch. On the voyage home from London, Grace had pulled Inyo aside and secretly handed him a handful of coins, part of Sarah and Thomas's gift, she'd told him. At first, he refused, but Grace insisted he take it. He didn't know what to do with the money. Not too long ago, he would have bought safe passage home to Coruña with such an amount. But now, there was no need to flee anymore. Brian had mentioned wanting to visit the goldsmith to find a Christmas present for Maeve, and Inyo indicated he'd planned to come along, an idea of how to spend the money already sprouting in his mind. When he entered the workshop with Brian, he unfolded a piece of parchment that held a sketch.

A short while later, they mounted up again and pressed their heels into the horses' flanks, intent to make it back to Barna before Maeve and Finley would notice their absence.

—

It was the day before Christmas. Finley, Teagan, and Inyo had been working inside, baking sweetmeats and singing songs with Ronin while Brian and Maeve decorated the fireplace with holly. Inyo winked at Finley and beckoned her to follow him outside. They pulled on their boots and headed outside, closing the door quietly behind them. Frost clung in a crystalline coating to the fence and to the blades of grass that crunched under their steps. The sky above was muted; they'd have at least an hour before dusk. Finley shivered and tightened her cloak around her shoulders. Inyo led the way into the woods and reached for her hand, a secret rippling inside of him, silky and smooth. They meandered through the wintry forest and towards the Druid Tree.

The creek was murmuring and lapping at their feet when they hopped across. When they paused between the boulders underneath the branches of the Druid Tree, Inyo pulled Finley into an embrace. Her face was pale from the frigid wind, and she burrowed herself into his chest. She wrapped her arms tightly around him and savored his warm breath in her hair.

"Remember that day in Coruña, *mi peregrina*, when we met at *Libros y cartografía*?" he asked. Finley nodded. "When you left, such sadness fell on me," he continued. "But now—I— *Mi amor*—"

Inyo's hesitation and his intense grip around her waist made Finley suspicious. She tilted her head and narrowed her eyes. "What's going on?" she asked.

He released her, reached for one of her hands, and murmured, "Close your eyes."

Finley obeyed reluctantly, a smile flickering across her face. Inyo tugged off her mitten, placed a small object into the palm of her hand, and curled her fingers around the object.

"Now."

She opened her eyes, hesitating, her fist still closed.

"Go on, look at it," Inyo encouraged her. "It's a gift for you."

"But it isn't Christmas yet!" she protested.

"This gift can't wait any longer. It needs to be yours today."

Finley slowly turned over her hand to reveal a golden ring. She gasped, marveling at its details. The ring featured two symmetrical hands and—centered between them—a heart-shaped scallop shell. "For me?"

Inyo nodded. "A pilgrim's shell. My heart in your hands. And the promise that your heart will always be safe in my hands, too."

A smile spread across Finley's features like a spring sunrise. She placed the ring on her finger, whispered a *te amo*, and melted back into Inyo's embrace.

Their hearts cantered in the rhythm of the gurgling stream, and the ribbons of their breath—hopeful and determined—floated up past the wild tangles of barren branches, into the mist hovering over Galway Bay, and far out over the vast Celtic Sea.

EPILOGUE

Laura's Ring

LA CORUÑA, SPAIN 2023

The lazy breeze stood no chance against the intense summer sun that bathed the alleys and plazas of La Coruña. Laura sighed and wiped a strand of auburn hair out of her face as she left the train station behind and headed towards her grandfather's flat. He'd called her a few weeks ago. "I have something for you, something very special," he'd proclaimed with a surreptitious flair.

Laura followed the familiar shortcut through the park near her old school, across the plaza, and past the sandstone church, catching a brief glimpse of Hercules' Tower in the distance, the lighthouse that harked back to Roman times.

There was Joaquín's house, making Laura smile, wishing she had stayed in touch with him. When she and Joaquín were nine years old, they'd spent a whole summer on the square playing pirates. The massive stone planters were their ships, and she still recalled the exhilaration of their make-believe adventures and sea battles, the earnestness in their voices as they shouted sailing commands and fought off imaginary enemies with wooden swords.

285

Despite Laura's familiarity with every detail of her former neighborhood, the edges of her memories were fading into sepia-toned vignettes, a reminder of how quickly time had flown by.

She arrived at the wrought-iron portal she knew so well and hurried up several flights of stairs to the apartment where her grandpa had lived for decades, her childhood home. Soon, she found herself seated with him, sipping a glass of albariño, surrounded by her grandfather's carving tools, model ships, and tiny canvas sails. Tacked on his walls were a flutter of paper blueprints for his upcoming woodworking projects.

He reached for something on the bench next to him. "All right. The reason I had you come up," he said as his trembling hands opened a small velveteen pouch, retrieving a golden ring. "Here, I want you to have it."

"Abuela's ring," Laura gasped, remembering her grandma's love, her warm, leathery hands, and that ring.

"Go ahead, try it on!" her grandpa urged.

Laura slid the ring on her finger. She wiped the moisture from her eyes while she smiled at the ring and its warm glow. She had always admired the ring's unusual and elegant design, with its two hands holding a scallop shell shaped like a heart. Her grandma had told her the ring was several hundred years old and had often called it "Inyo's ring."

"Do you remember all the stories she told you as a child? About Inyo, one of her ancestors?"

"She said he sailed aboard the Armada and ended up in Ireland. And she talked about pirates, and castles, and the Irish chieftain Grace O'Malley."

Her grandpa chuckled, "Yes, I know. I always wondered where she got all those tales and how many legends were mixed into them." Laura recalled her grandma's special interest in Ireland, sparked by stories about Inyo's ring and the many Irish names in her family tree. "You know," her grandpa said thoughtfully, "she always wanted to visit Ireland."

Laura nodded. Maybe one day it would be she who'd go to Ireland in memory of her abuela, to see Grace O'Malley's lands and castles, to learn more about the Armada and the origins of Inyo's ring.

Her grandpa nodded with a smile, then his eyebrows lifted abruptly as he remembered something. "Oh, and there's one more thing I want you to have. I found it in Abuela's prayer book."

He handed her an envelope. Inside was a folded piece of browned parchment that looked quite old. Laura's hands carefully opened up the brittle page, revealing a poem elegantly handwritten in faded ink. It was signed: *Inyo Fernández*.

You raging winds, I dare you blow.
Push hard against our tight embrace.
The howling gale we fear no more,
As long as love will warm our days.

You savage foe, I dare you fight.
My friend and I our swords have drawn,
And shall defeat the darkest night,
As our love shields us, dusk to dawn.

You wilder waves, I dare you roll.
No roaring ocean, crashing sea,
Shall ever drown us, take their toll,
As long as love our ship will be.

The End

Historical Notes

Although this story is a work of fiction, much of the timeline and many characters were inspired by or based on real historical figures and events.

The 16th century was a time of intense religious conflicts in Europe, but it was also a fascinating and unparalleled period of innovation, technological progress, advances in shipbuilding and navigation, and the spread of the Reformation and Renaissance humanist ideas. Spain was the uncontested powerhouse of Europe and held many overseas colonies. During Elizabeth's reign, England also developed into an ambitious mercantile country with worldwide trade networks and global influence. The arts flourished as well, especially literature and theater.

Grace O'Malley

Gráinne Ní Mháille (anglicized: Grace O'Malley), also known as Connacht's Pirate Queen, was the fearless leader of the seafaring O'Malley clan that defied English rule for four decades. Her life was tumultuous and complicated, as were her political activities and marriages. In the interest of storytelling, I have deliberately emphasized only those parts of Grace's life and time that served as a dramatic backdrop to this novel.

Irish historians might have ignored the O'Malley chieftain, but her meeting with Queen Elizabeth I is documented in official Greenwich Palace records. Grace was approximately the same age as Queen Elizabeth, and both queens left their indelible marks in a world where few women had that opportunity.

Grace O'Malley took over the leadership of the clan after the death of her father. The O'Malleys had dominated Clew Bay and its surroundings for three centuries already, increasing their wealth through regular trade with Spain and France, as well as by piracy and raiding up and down the coast.

Grace married young, and upon the death of her first husband, she inherited his ships and warriors. After divorcing her second husband, she inherited Rockfleet Castle, thereby expanding her realm and power. Her ships sallied out from Rockfleet and Clare Island to confront foreign merchants and fishing fleets, demanding taxes. The O'Malley clan also frequented Galway Bay and charged tolls for safe passage to Galway.

Legends about Grace O'Malley have been passed through generations in story and song. She acquired her famous nickname *Granuaile*, meaning bald Grace, when she was a girl. The story goes that she chopped off her hair to sail, disguised as a man, aboard one of her father's vessels.

Another legend had her fighting off Turkish corsairs the day after she gave birth to her youngest son, Tibbot, aboard one of her ships.

During Queen Elizabeth's reign, the O'Malleys fiercely resisted English control over Connacht and raided English merchants at sea. In 1574, the English attempted an unsuccessful attack on Rockfleet Castle. Then a new governor arrived in Galway and began to reign ruthlessly over Connacht. He killed Grace's oldest son, Owen, imprisoned Tibbot, and took Grace's castles, land, and cattle.

Grace O'Malley saw no other option than to bring her grievances directly to the Crown. She sailed to London in 1593, where she received an audience with Queen Elizabeth at Greenwich Palace. (For purely narrative purposes in *Inyo's Ring*, the meeting between Queen Elizabeth and Grace O'Malley takes place at an earlier date.) Historians believe that Grace must have made a favorable impression and definitely earned the monarch's respect. Elizabeth saw to it that the cruel governor was removed from office, that Tibbot was freed, and that Grace received back her land and her castles. Grace remained an ally with Elizabeth and sided with her during Ireland's Nine Years' War. Grace died of natural causes in 1603, the same year Queen Elizabeth died.

Queen Elizabeth I

Elizabeth was born in 1533 to Anne Boleyn and the Tudor king Henry VIII of England.

Anne Boleyn was beheaded when Elizabeth was less than three years old. Elizabeth was described as serious and highly intelligent from an early age. Elizabeth loved hunting and dancing and was also fluent in at least six languages. During her childhood years at Hatfield House, one of her classmates and close friends was Robin (Robert Dudley, who would later become the Earl of Leicester.)

During the rule of her half-sister, Queen Mary, who attempted to force Protestant England back to Catholicism, Elizabeth was wrongfully suspected of treason and, in 1554, was imprisoned in the Tower along with Robin. She was interrogated and had to refute the evidence against her repeatedly. After her release, she was keenly aware that her survival during dangerous times heavily depended on appearing compliant outwardly and hiding her true religious and political beliefs.

Elizabeth ascended the English throne in 1558, much to the delight of her subjects. King Philip of Spain sought her hand in marriage in 1560, but she refused. This might have marked the beginning of a rift between England and Spain. The years leading up to the Spanish Armada's attempt to overthrow her were marked by increasing tension and religious conflict across

Europe. Elizabeth's reign was long and successful, and she is remembered as a master politician.

Many historians point to the similarities between Grace O'Malley and Queen Elizabeth. Not only were these remarkable women skilled politicians, but they ultimately demonstrated that women could govern and thrive despite the strict patriarchal conventions of the societies they lived in.

The Spanish Armada

King Philip of Spain was enraged by English privateers (including, most famously, Sir Francis Drake) attacking Caribbean ports and the Spanish treasure fleet. Equally frustrating to him was Queen Elizabeth's support of the Protestant Dutch rebels against Catholic Spain – The Netherlands were part of the Spanish Empire at the time. But the final straw for Philip was the 1587 execution of Mary Queen of Scots, Spain's Catholic ally. Queen Elizabeth ordered the execution after it came to light that Mary was plotting against her.

King Philip, who saw it as his life's mission to be the champion of the Catholic Church, desired to overthrow Elizabeth, *the enemy of the true faith,* and restore Catholicism in England. He was promised a monetary reward by the pope for doing so.

The Duke of Medina-Sidonia was placed in charge of the Armada, which consisted of 130 ships and 26,000 men. Priests, along with many spectators—mostly aristocrats with no military experience—were aboard every ship, along with some of the officers' wives. After a storm off Finisterre and extensive repairs in Coruña, the Armada finally set sail in July 1588. During the first English attack near Plymouth, the *Rosario* collided with another ship. Over the following week, more skirmishes took place near Portland and the Isle of Wight, with Spain's ships always forming a defensive crescent while the English (under Howard, Drake, Hawkins, and Frobisher) fired at the flanks from a distance.

The night of the fireship attack near Calais became the turning point of the campaign. Panicked crews cut the ships' anchor cables, causing the Armada to scatter. After the decisive and bloody battle at Gravelines, another harsh enemy took its toll: unfavorable weather. Strong winds pushed the Spanish fleet toward the sand banks of Flanders. When the winds miraculously shifted, the Spanish were hopeful again, only to find themselves chased into the North Sea by strong winds and the English navy. They couldn't return the way they came, so they planned to sail north around Scotland, then out to sea around the west of Ireland, and finally south back to Spain.

Terrible weather while rounding Scotland and hurricane-like storms near Ireland doomed many ships, leading to numerous shipwrecks and thousands of lives lost. Out of the original 130, only 63 vessels made it back to Spain. It is estimated that 17,000 Spaniards died in battle or drowned when their ships sank off the Irish coast. The *San Francisco* safely returned to Spain. The fate of the *Santa Catalina* remains unknown. While many ships simply disappeared, several wrecks are known along the Irish coast. The *Falcon Blanco*, for example, sank in Galway Bay, as did another unknown vessel. The *Girona* was lost near the Giant's Causeway in Northern Ireland. *Lavia, Juliana*, and *Santa Maria de Vision* sank at Streedagh Beach, near Sligo, where over 1,100 Spanish sailors and soldiers lost their lives. Every September, a heartfelt remembrance is held at Streedagh Beach.

The Claddagh Ring

Traditional Irish Claddagh rings feature a crowned heart held between two hands. A few legends exist regarding the origin of the Claddagh ring. The most accepted one involves a man named Richard Joyce, who was captured by Barbary corsairs in the 16th or 17th century. He was sold into slavery, where he learned the goldsmith trade. When he was freed, he returned to Galway, settled in the hamlet of Claddagh, and began crafting the rings that would bear the name of his village.

I remember being told another legend once when I spent time in Limerick. The tale I heard there refers to a Spanish Armada shipwreck off the Irish coast:

Once upon a time, a Spanish Armada shipwreck survivor washed ashore in Ireland. A farm family found him and took him in. He fell in love with the farmer's daughter and asked her father for the girl's hand in marriage. Her father was against their union until the Spaniard gave her his only remaining possession, the golden friendship ring he wore on his finger. It featured two hands holding a crowned heart, indicative of his noble birth.

Acknowledgments

The endeavor to write a book was exhilarating, often all-consuming, and at times downright daunting. I had the splendid fortune to be surrounded by a host of supporters and expert wordsmiths to whom I wish to express my deepest gratitude. Thank you, Claire Baldwin, Sarah Fastelin, Kristyn Miller, Amaryah Orenstein, Roger Marsh, Carly Stevens, Justin Newland, Lindsey Proctor, Rosemary Lawton, Angela and Mikaela Lee, and especially Nate Hoepner. Without you, this ship would not be sailing. Thank you, Jules, Milo, and my entire family on both sides of the Atlantic.

Muchas gracias, Simy Jelaso, María Conroy, Iris Montes de Oca, Olga Rodríguez, y Tania Benedit.

Many people have made a tremendous difference in my life through mentorship, inspiration, and friendship, especially many family members, as well as Heinrich K. Mangold, Billy Renkl, Veronica Kennedy, Joshua Jenkins, Marilyn Coffield, Annie Rose, Gert-Jan van Nispen, Veronique Beaujouan, Inge Henze, and all my SBK pals. Thank you, I owe you more than you'll ever know!

About the Author

Just like Inyo, her protagonist, Nicole N. H. Schwabacher was once aboard a ship out in the Celtic Sea amid a hurricane. Despite this surreal and terrifying experience, the sea still has a hold on her heart.

She leads a nomadic life that has taken her across Asia, Europe, and North America. She has been an educator at museums, various schools, and organizations, and a hiking guide in the American West.

Her favorite pastimes include exploring new cultures, hiking, traveling, and learning about archaeology, science, and history. She is looking forward to visiting more of Grace O'Malley's territory and to sailing again aboard the *San Salvador*, a replica of a 16th-century Spanish galleon.

She lives in northern Arizona with her family and three tabby cats. Inyo's Ring is her first novel.

Thank you for journeying with Finley and Inyo through windswept Ireland and across the sea. If you enjoyed this tale of survival, adventure, and love, I would be deeply grateful if you could share your thoughts in a review on Amazon or Goodreads. Your words help other readers discover this story, and mean more than you might imagine. Thank you!